A SEAL'S TRIUMPH

By Cora Seton

Author's Note

A SEAL's Triumph is the tenth volume in the SEALs of Chance Creek series, set in the fictional town of Chance Creek, Montana. To find out more about Greg, Renata, Boone, Clay, Jericho, Walker and the other inhabitants of Base Camp, look for the rest of the books in the series, including:

A SEAL's Oath

A SEAL's Vow

A SEAL's Pledge

A SEAL's Consent

A SEAL's Purpose

A SEAL's Resolve

A SEAL's Devotion

A SEAL's Desire

A SEAL's Struggle

Visit Cora's website at www.coraseton.com

Find Cora on Facebook at facebook.com/CoraSeton

Sign up for my newsletter HERE.

www.coraseton.com/sign-up-for-my-newsletter

PROLOGUE

One year ago

EVERYTHING WAS GOING wrong—and it was all Boone Rudman's fault.

Avery Lightfoot bent over the stew pot hanging from an iron hook over a crackling fire in a very large, very old-fashioned hearth and listened to her friends talk as they set the table for dinner. She'd been in Montana only a month, but so much had happened in that time, it felt like longer. She scooped the skirts of her Regency era gown out of the way, careful not to spill anything on them, just as much in love with her beautiful outfit as she'd been the first day she came here.

Back then, she and her friends, Nora Ridgeway, Savannah Edwards and Riley Eaton, thought they'd get to spend six uninterrupted months in this beautiful three-story home working at their artistic, musical and literary pursuits. To make sure they didn't stray from Westfield and waste time in town, they'd ditched their normal clothes and stocked their closets with only the things Jane Austen characters would wear. None of them would dare go anywhere dressed like this, which meant they'd make great strides on their projects. It was a wonderful plan, and it would have worked if Boone hadn't come along and spoiled everything.

Even today, when they'd planned to have a nice meal together, he was intruding. Not with his presence—the four of them were alone—but in the way Riley was behaving. She'd been quiet ever since she returned from her last meeting with him, and it was clear something was up.

"Are you ever going to tell us what's wrong?" Nora asked her. Trust Nora to get right to the heart of the matter. She was a serious brunette who'd come here to write her first novel. Riley, whose family had owned this ranch for generations, planned to create enough paintings to have her first show. Her light-brown hair was tucked into a messy bun at the nape of her neck. Savannah, a beautiful blonde whose idea this was in the first place, wanted to brush up on her piano playing in preparation to resume the professional career she gave up after college. Avery had hoped to write a screenplay and prepare to resurrect her acting career.

Their plan had been perfect. Come to Westfield, where Riley had a standing invitation to stay as long as she liked, pool their resources and give themselves a six-month runway from which to launch the rest of their lives.

Unfortunately, it turned out Riley's uncle didn't own this ranch anymore, and the men who lived here now—friends of Riley's from when she was a kid—had other plans for the place. They were here to build a model sustainable community, backed by a billionaire—Martin Fulsom—and they didn't have much respect for the idea of taking six months "off," as they liked to put it.

At least Boone had let them stay on at the manor, and they'd continued to wear their Regency-era clothing, which made Avery proud. As an actress, she'd worn many costumes over the years, but her friends were much more conventional. For them to don their gowns each morning took some determination, especially when two more of Boone's friends, Clay Pickett and Jericho Cook, had arrived—and then six more strangers had appeared a week or so later.

Since then, things had gone as well as could be expected with nine men on the ranch to interrupt their days.

Better, she supposed with a sigh. Riley was smitten with Boone, and Clay and Jericho were pursuing Nora and Savannah hard.

Avery was happy for them all. Really. Despite the little voice in her head that told her once again she'd end up alone while everyone around her paired up comfortably. Someday her prince would come, as the song went.

When was anyone's guess.

Which was fine, she reminded herself. She was supposed to be writing a screenplay, not mooning after some man.

She hadn't had much time to think about either this afternoon, though, because they'd been too busy working on wedding plans for Savannah's cousin,

Andrea, who planned to hold her nuptials here at the manor. They'd managed to salvage only one hour of creative time for themselves out of the whole day. Riley had painted away diligently. Savannah had practiced a sonata. Nora alternately wrote and grumbled; things didn't seem to be going well with her novel. Avery had struggled to settle to anything.

Now she focused on the stew and blinked back the sting of tears. She made herself speak normally when she looked up. "Nora's right, Riley—you've been awfully quiet."

"There is something on my mind," Riley said slowly as she tucked a napkin beside each plate. "You're not going to like it."

"You're leaving?" Avery's mind went straight to the worst possibility, and she stood up, all pretence of stirring the stew forgotten. If Riley left, everyone would go. It would be the end of the experiment, the end of spending time together—a return to a life she hated.

"No. Not that," Riley assured her.

"I can deal with anything else." As long as she didn't lose the friends she depended on so much.

Riley took a deep breath as if she doubted that, and Avery's stomach sank. Whatever was coming must be bad. "After Andrea's wedding, I'm afraid we'll have to put our plans on hold for a while. Fulsom is funding all this." She waved a hand to include the manor and the rest of the ranch. Martin Fulsom, a billionaire known for his environmental causes and his flamboyant self-promotion, was the one who'd purchased the land from

Riley's uncle. "He's given the ranch to Boone and the others to build their community on for now, but he still holds the deed and purse strings, and Boone's let me know they have to do what he says."

"What is he saying?" Nora asked in what Avery thought of as her "teacher voice." Avery figured she must be tough but fair in the classroom, someone students knew they couldn't fool.

"You know Fulsom wants to film a television show about the process of building their sustainable community. Well, he doesn't like that we're wearing Regency clothes when we wander around the place. We have to stop for the duration of filming, which is going to be six months."

"We can't wear our gowns?" Savannah asked.

"No. We'll have to buy some modern things." Riley's hands twisted the fabric of her gown, and it was clear she hated the directive as much as she knew the rest of them would.

"Boone expects us to take part in the show? And he never asked?" Sometimes Boone was arrogant, or at least bossy, but even he had to know they'd never agree to that.

"He'd like us to," Riley nearly whispered. She was obviously miserable, and Avery's heart went out to her, but that didn't change how she felt.

"No," Savannah said. "I'm not going to do that. I know what reality TV is like, and I don't want any part of it."

"Me, neither," Nora said. "Not in a million years."

Avery shook her head, too, desperation growing inside her. What was Boone thinking? Did he think he got to ruin everything, and they'd traipse along after him like happy little puppies? He was stealing Riley, destroying the careful plan they'd made for their futures, making them go back to normal clothes, normal life— and she hated the life she'd left behind. "That's an invasion of privacy. It would ruin Westfield for me," she sputtered. She couldn't say what she wanted to say— that she wished Boone had never come at all.

Riley closed her eyes for a moment, then seemed to steel herself and opened them again. "Then you don't have to do it." She began to lay out the forks and knives, her face white and her eyes bright with unshed tears.

"But you're going to?" Savannah came to her side. "Do you really want to?"

"I plan to."

Avery looked down. She knew Riley cared for Boone and suffered when his interference made the rest of them unhappy.

"There's more you should know, though. About the men," Riley went on.

More? How could there possibly be more? Avery backed away from the fire, wishing she could run out of the kitchen and slam the door behind her. She wished she could go back in time to when they'd first come up with their plan and suggest a different place to settle, one where Boone would never have found them.

"What is it?" Savannah asked.

"The television show is going to be set up like a contest. There are certain benchmarks the men have to meet and they're… unusual."

Avery stifled a groan. Reality television could be brutal. It was all about exposing the participants for the gleeful derision of the viewers. She'd been biting her tongue ever since she found out Boone and the other men were going to be a part of one. She'd pretended to herself it wouldn't affect her or her friends, but she'd known she was wrong.

"Why do I feel like I'm going to hate this?" Nora asked.

"Because you are," Riley said baldly. "You all are. His demands are utterly ridiculous. Boone said he's doing it to make the show controversial enough that the audience will be huge. He's going to spend a bundle advertising it. He wants it to be the most talked about thing on television."

"What are the benchmarks?" Savannah asked.

Avery felt like she was watching their conversation from somewhere far away. She was losing her opportunity to make a better life for herself—they all were.

How could they be so calm?

"It was Fulsom who told them they had to increase their numbers until there are ten men. Now they have to build houses for each of them that use a tenth of the energy an average American house uses. All that energy has to be from renewable sources, and they have to grow or raise all the food they'll need to get through the winter. They all need to marry, too, and have three kids on the way, which means Clay and Jericho need to find wives fast," she added pointedly to Nora and Savannah. "They'll probably want to try for children right away."

Avery couldn't believe what she was hearing. Marriages? Kids? How on earth could Fulsom dictate those kinds of things? She looked around to the others, but they were both staring at Riley.

"How come Boone isn't doing that?" Nora asked finally.

Riley pressed her lips together, and there was a long, uncomfortable pause. Avery knew she needed to put something together here, a leap her mind couldn't make.

Refused to make.

Nora's and Savannah's horrified expressions told her they already had.

Nora was shaking, her hands on her hips. "*Is* he doing that? Riley, what have you done?"

"I'm… I'm going to marry him," Riley confirmed, and Avery felt like she'd been punched in the gut. Marry him? If Riley married Boone, this whole thing was over. "June first will be my wedding day," Riley went on. "You have to understand; Boone's an old friend. We know each other, and we have chemistry. It's not like we just met."

"But if he's using you…" Avery didn't recognize her own voice. It was high and shrill, encompassing all her shock. Why would Riley agree to such a thing just to appease a billionaire with a God complex?

"He's not!" Riley straightened. "If anything, I'm using him. If Boone and his friends fail, Fulsom will take back Westfield and give it to a developer who will carve up the ranch. My ranch! It'll be gone forever. I can't let that happen."

Riley was marrying Boone to save her ranch? To get it back? Was that what she meant? Avery knew how much Riley loved the place and how devastated she'd been to find she wouldn't inherit it like she'd thought.

But marriage—

"I can't believe you didn't tell us," Savannah said.

"I figured you'd react pretty much like you did," Riley said helplessly. "I understand, though. No hard feelings."

There were definitely hard feelings, Avery realized. Riley wanted them to approve of her plans, and their astonishment and disbelief were cutting her to the quick. She was torn between her desire to comfort her friend and wanting to shake Riley until her sense returned. You couldn't trade your future for a piece of property—

"We'll need to move out, won't we?" Nora said slowly, interrupting Avery's thoughts. She caught Riley's eye and hurried to add, "Not because of Boone, because of Fulsom. If we stay on the ranch, his camera crews will try to pull us into the show."

She was right; Boone would make them puppets in his master plan to seize what should have been Riley's, Avery thought. He'd known from day one what he meant to do, hadn't he? He'd stalked Riley, convinced her she loved him—all so he could win his little show and build his stupid sustainable community. He'd never once thought of their feelings—or Riley's, probably.

She opened her mouth to say that but caught sight of Riley's pleading gaze and was filled with the uncomfortable realization she wasn't being very fair. Riley was an intelligent, independent woman. She wouldn't marry someone she didn't think she could love—would she?

In fact, she probably already loved him. It had been clear for days she was falling for him.

Avery couldn't blame Riley, either. Boone was handsome. An old friend. Shared her love for the ranch and this area of Montana. He was a Navy SEAL, for heaven's sake, made to be worshipped by women. And he was a good guy in his own way, even if he had loosed a tornado in their well-laid-out plans.

"We'll have to look for a rental in town, I guess." She leaned against the counter and crossed her arms over her chest, trying to hold in the pain at the thought of breaking up their group so soon after their arrival here.

"Which means we'll need to look for jobs. Just like I said at the outset," Nora said, her jaw tight.

"It's only temporary," Riley pleaded with them.

"Maybe it's time for me to go back to teaching," Nora went on as if she hadn't heard her. "If there's nothing in Chance Creek, there might be in Billings."

"Maybe I should move back home," Savannah said with a sigh. "My parents have a beautiful piano. Maybe if I took a part-time job they'd support me in trying to play seriously."

Avery's heart sank. If Savannah was talking of leaving Montana altogether, then this was worse than she'd suspected. They'd worked so damn hard to get here. They'd sold everything, taken a huge chance. "No," she burst out, and her frustration increased when Riley winced. "Come on. We've come so far; please don't ruin everything now!"

"We're not trying to ruin anything," Nora said reasonably. "Sometimes things don't work out... Where are you going?"

Avery untied her apron and threw it on the table as she marched right out of the house. Riley wasn't to blame for this, and she couldn't fix it, either. Time to go right to the source. "I'm going to tell Lieutenant Boone Rudman what a colossal ass he is!"

"NOW WE'RE TALKING," Greg Devon said, and Walker Norton looked up to follow his gaze. He'd arrived only a couple of hours ago, and it was still strange to be back in Chance Creek, back on this ranch where he'd spent many summers working during his teens with his best friends, Boone, Clay and Jericho. He'd left home after graduating from high school, first to pursue a degree at Montana State, then to join the Navy and serve with the SEALs. It was Boone who'd come up with the idea to start this sustainable community, and he, Clay and Jericho had already been here for several weeks, joined recently by six other men who'd served with the SEALs. It had been strange to arrive in Chance Creek to find the ranch already populated with so many men. Stranger still to know that good old Riley Eaton, who was sixteen the last time he'd seen her, had settled up at the manor with several of her friends.

Right after he'd arrived, Boone had introduced him to all the men who'd come to join their community, but Walker hadn't seen the women yet. Clay had made it clear he was interested in one of them—Nora—and Jericho fairly bristled when anyone mentioned Savannah. Both were content to settle down and marry soon, perfectly happy with the whole situation.

Walker couldn't understand that, even though it was hard to point fingers when he had joined Boone, too, knowing full well what Martin Fulsom's rules for them were. He still didn't know what had made him say yes to this travesty of a project when it was clear it was doomed to fail, but then he'd always had a hard time saying no when Boone, Clay and Jericho had agreed to an adventure. They'd gotten him into plenty of trouble when they were kids. His grandmother, Sue, who'd raised him, used to tell him to give them a wide berth.

"If you went right home to Grandma Diane's after school, you'd keep yourself out of a lot of trouble," she always said, but she was the one who'd made him go to school in Chance Creek rather than on the reservation, where she was principal, so what did she expect?

Grandma Diane's was a silent household, torture for a boy like him. Boone and the others had befriended him right away when he'd started at their school, and their boisterousness held his loneliness at bay.

He would have fit in better at the reservation school than in town, but Sue worried people would accuse her of favoritism toward him. That meant he ping-ponged back and forth, in town during the week, on the reservation for weekends, not truly belonging in either place. Boone, Clay and Jericho were his lifeline, so when they came up with a plan, and he was able to join them, he made sure he did, no matter how much trouble he'd catch for it later.

"You're between two worlds," Grandma Diane used to say with a quiet sigh, but that wasn't quite it. He knew Diane did her best, but she'd never been comfortable with the fact her daughter had hooked up—there was no other word for it—with a man from the nearby Crow reservation, given birth and then taken off to live a life that was increasingly chaotic until finally dying at thirty-four from an aneurysm in Tennessee.

Walker wasn't sure what had made his mother so restless. Maybe it was a reaction to her parents' carefully scripted life of work, church and community service. Diane and Paul tried to love Walker but kept him at arm's length. Sue had explained it once. "Diane can't get over the loss of her daughter. She's afraid to love you for fear you'll break her heart, too." Grandpa Paul was simply too busy to have time for anyone. He worked at the feed store full time when Walker was a kid, was a deacon at their church, volunteered with several local service organizations and served on the board of trustees at the Chance Creek library. He passed away when Walker was fourteen. Walker's paternal grandfather, Gerald Norton, a kind man with a big heart and plenty of time for his grandson, passed away the following year. His grandmothers got him through the rest of high school.

Between Diane's formal wariness and Sue's stiff pride, he was never coddled, but he was always loved, and Walker figured he'd done well enough.

Still, that feeling that he never quite fit in all the way—anywhere—sat deep in him.

He'd thought he'd come to terms with it until the day Fulsom offered to fund Boone's community if, and only if, they all agreed to marry within twelve months. He should have said no. Wanted to say no. Should have moved on and let his friends do what worked for them. For one thing, he'd have to be crazy to marry given what he believed was coming at them all. For another, he'd made a promise—a dumb promise—and needed to find an honorable way out of it before he could make any plans that involved a woman.

He'd opened his mouth to tell Boone—and Fulsom—just that. Instead, he'd heard himself say yes—like he had a thousand times when he was a kid.

And he'd regretted it ever since.

Now he was bound by two promises he couldn't escape. A man lived by his word, that's what his father had told him. A promise was a promise.

He was in big trouble.

Someone whistled, long and low, and pulled him from his thoughts.

A woman he'd never seen before strode down the path from the manor toward them, followed at a distance by Riley and two other women he didn't know.

Their old-fashioned dresses rippled around them as they walked. Boone had told him about the Regency gowns, but seeing them in person was something. The woman in the lead was coming fast, the rest hurrying to catch up with her. Boone straightened.

"She's hot," someone said.

"She's pissed, you mean," Angus McBride said. One of the new recruits to Base Camp, he loved to lay a Scottish accent on thick, although Walker had noticed he could drop it anytime he wanted. "I think we're in trouble, lads."

"Goddamn you, Boone Rudman," the petite redhead yelled as she marched right in among them, "you are a stupid, lowlife, pond-scum-sucking, dirty old goddamn ass, and I hate you!" She gave Boone a shove that actually knocked him off balance, mostly because he was too surprised to react in time. Despite himself, Walker stifled a smile. He thought he heard someone else laugh.

When was the last time Boone had been pushed around by anyone?

"Avery—"

Avery wasn't done. "You've ruined everything, you shitfucking butthead—you and your stupid band of merry frogmen. I hope you rot in hell!"

"Avery—"

The woman could swear like a sailor, but Walker thought she belonged in a Renaissance painting, all curvy and lovely and full of life. He wondered what Boone had done to piss her off so badly. His friend tended to boss people around.

"I've waited years for the chance to live with my friends and quit my asinine job so I could actually do something I loved, and now you want to steal it all away from me?"

"I'm not stealing—"

"Nora's going to Billings to get a teaching job. Savannah's going to California so she can have peace and quiet to practice her piano!"

A silence stretched out as Boone took this in, and if his expression was anything to go by, he knew he was in trouble. "You told them," he said to Riley over Avery's head.

Riley nodded, and Walker's heart twinged with remembered guilt. The last time he'd seen her look this anguished was when Boone had passed her over for another, older girl when she was sixteen. At the time, Walker hadn't been very sympathetic. He'd still thought of her as a kid.

He figured he knew why Avery was so mad now, though. Boone mentioned he'd explained to Riley about Fulsom's rules. Riley must have told her friends.

And they were furious. The blonde and brunette standing behind Riley hadn't uttered a word, but if looks could kill, he and every other man on site would be ready for burial.

"That's right; Riley told us," Avery said to Boone. "Not you—you didn't have the balls to do it. And you—" Avery turned on Clay. "You've had the gall to pretend you like Nora? Like hell! You want to use her to spawn your demon seed. And you—" She pointed an accusing finger at Jericho. "You thought you could sweet-talk Savannah all the way to the altar? Hanging's too good for you!"

Jericho froze like a deer caught in headlights. Clay opened his mouth to protest.

"But mostly it's you." Avery turned back to Boone. "You just… suck! I hope Riley finds a better man to marry. Someone like…" She scanned the crowd, caught sight of Walker for the first time and locked her green-eyed gaze with his.

A zing of electricity traced through his veins, bringing Walker on high alert in a way he hadn't been since the last time he'd come under fire on a mission. It was that same slowing of time, the awareness of his heart beating hard, his breath coming fast—and as the moment stretched out, he knew he'd met someone who'd change his life.

His grandmother talked about these moments sometimes. Pay-attention moments, she called them and had drummed it into his head since he was little that the body knew things the mind couldn't grasp, and it was his job to listen to it.

What did this reaction mean? That Avery was beautiful? Warm? Vibrant?

Everything he wasn't?

No—it was more than that. She was *important*.

"Okay, folks," Boone said placatingly, "let's all take it easy."

They'd gone far beyond easy. Avery's presence here

was going to make his life way too complicated, Walker realized. His throat had gone dry with the understanding that everything had changed. A moment ago, he'd been reluctantly on board with this plan, picturing himself as a bystander who'd do as much as possible to help his friends.

Now his role had changed, and he was as much in the thick of it as anyone else here.

He'd just met a woman he instinctively knew he could love. A woman he could spend eternity with.

Even if eternity was what none of them had.

He had to act fast, he decided. He needed to change the trajectory of this confrontation right now, or the surprisingly wonderful future he'd just glimpsed could speed right by him, like a comet burning past a planet, in and out of its orbit, heading out to the depths of space.

"She's right," he said loudly, and he could tell he'd surprised Boone almost as much as he'd surprised himself. "You have ruined things."

"Hey!" Boone protested.

"These women had a plan; you messed it up."

"It's not that simple."

"It's simple." He faced down his friend.

He had everyone's attention, and he'd definitely riled Boone. This was his project, after all—these were his men—

Walker raised an eyebrow, a subtle reminder that he'd always outranked Boone in the military and had the right to speak now; they all did. Boone bit back whatever he was about to say.

Walker let a moment pass, so everyone could take a breath, and by the time he continued, they were all listening intently. He ignored them, focusing on Avery as if she was the only one there.

She was the only one who mattered to him right now. She still gazed at him, transfixed, and to his surprise, Walker thought he saw interest there.

Interest in him as a man.

Heat suffused him, desire so strong he almost reached out to her then and there, but he held back.

Could a woman like her want him?

He wanted her.

Every vein thrumming with awareness, Walker took in the sweet curve of her cheek, the arch of her eyebrow and the way her body filled out her old-fashioned dress. He hadn't known how much he'd been longing for female company. Had convinced himself he didn't need any of that.

He was a fool.

Now he needed to make her stick around long enough to see if she could feel something for him. Had the interest he'd glimpsed been real or the fantasy of a man who'd gone too long without?

He wasn't sure.

What should he say to her?

He thought about explaining how everything had come about. Maybe if she knew they'd accepted Fulsom's strange terms because they couldn't see any other way to get this project off the ground, she wouldn't judge them so harshly.

He rejected that plan. Like Sue always said, why use ten words when one will suffice?

"Here's the thing," he told Avery. "Sometimes there's compromise. Sometimes there's sacrifice." Would she understand what he was trying to say? He knew a lot about sacrifice and had been raised to withstand every kind of disappointment, but Avery was light and sunshine, a butterfly to his sturdy oak. He hated to ask her to give up anything.

"And you want us to sacrifice," she said flatly.

Maybe she wasn't as much a stranger to adversity as he'd thought. Was he losing her by being so blunt?

He didn't want to lose her.

He nodded. "We want you to sacrifice." Compromise wasn't possible in this situation, not with Fulsom calling the shots. He wondered what he'd do if she refused—or if she took her friends and left. Now that he knew there was an Avery in the world, he wanted to keep her here as long as possible.

"You know how unfair that is?" Her pretty face tilted up toward him, but she didn't back down an inch.

"I know." *It's worth it*, he wanted to add. *What we could be together is worth it.* He couldn't do that, though. Not with so many people watching them.

His fingers itched to reach out and take her hand, to establish a connection and keep it. He wished he was a bolder man when it came to women, but Sue would be appalled if he behaved that way.

Avery deserved the chance to make up her mind if

she wanted to be touched by him. She seemed as caught up in him as he was in her, but that didn't make it fair, either. Did she wonder what it would be like to be alone together? His thoughts were running away with him, imagining talking to her, kissing her—

Riley broke the spell when she moved to stand beside Avery. "This is why I didn't want my friends involved," she said to Boone. She took Avery's arm. "Come on, let's go."

Walker almost reached out to stop them. Racked his mind for something else to say that would keep Avery here with him longer.

In the end, he kept quiet. Either Avery would be as curious about him as he was about her—or she wouldn't.

He kept hold of her gaze, though. Refused to look away. Hoped she could tell he wanted far more than this moment with her.

She flushed a little under his scrutiny. Looked him up and down again.

Stay, he willed at her. *Give us a chance.*

She hesitated, but in the end she turned and faced Boone. "You don't deserve Riley" was her final salvo. She let her friend drag her away, the fight gone out of her. She didn't look back, but he thought she wanted to.

She was tough—but fragile, too. He had to remember that. To take care—

A thought struck him, one painful enough to take his breath away.

He was going to hurt her, he realized. He wouldn't

mean to, but it was almost inevitable, given his circumstances.

Almost.

There was just a sliver of a chance he could pull this off without doing so.

Determination filled him, and Walker swore he'd do everything in his power to prevent Avery from ever learning he'd been promised to another woman when he fell for her. He'd do what it took to hunt down Elizabeth Blaine and free himself from her once and for all.

"Now what do we do?" Jericho asked, his gaze on Savannah's retreating back.

Boone lifted his hands in defeat and walked away.

Looking after him, Clay shrugged. "We're screwed," he said.

Walker wasn't ready to accept that. "We're screwed only if we let ourselves be." He regretted his words when they turned to him. Hadn't he been filled with doubts about this project only minutes ago? Who was he to rally them?

He watched Avery toil up the hill with the other women and knew he'd always be able to pinpoint her in a crowd from here on in.

He was a man who'd fallen hard for a woman at first sight. A man who wanted the chance at a future with her.

"We'll do everything it takes to convince them to give us a chance," he said, his will rising to meet this new challenge. "Everything."

CHAPTER ONE

Present day

"WALKER, SOMETHING'S WRONG!"

At the sound of Avery's voice, Walker sprang into motion before he was fully awake, out of his sleeping bag, into jeans and boots and halfway across the floor before it dawned on him that she was fully dressed and calling him from outside the open bunkhouse door. Had she already started her morning chores?

He was losing his touch.

Walker was still untangling his dreams from reality as he followed her outside. She darted ahead of him, the forest green of her work gown contrasting with the wide, white apron she wore over it. After nearly a year spent with a ranch full of women in Regency garb, he still had to smile to see Avery pick up her long skirts and run toward the closest pasture, but his smile was short lived. She was heading for the bison.

Was something wrong with them?

They'd already been let out once this year by someone trying to sabotage their chances to win Westfield Ranch. Were the bison gone again? Would they need to wake everyone and call all their friends in town to help round them up?

No. There they were, a herd of prehistoric-looking animals in the gloom of an early April morning, their shapes mingling with tendrils of fog.

"It's Ruth. Something's wrong with her," Avery tossed back over her shoulder, still running. She stopped only when she reached the fence.

Walker prided himself on a keen eye, but Avery had him stumped with the way she could discern one bison from another in the herd. The animal she was pointing to stood some twenty yards from the fence, motionless while her herd-mates cropped the pasture around her.

"What's wrong with her?" Walker caught up with Avery, as edgy with the desire to get close to her as he always was when she was around, especially these last weeks when she'd held herself so aloof.

He'd messed up—big time. Accused her of stealing a family heirloom, a traditional Crow fan used in ceremonial dances that had been handed down for generations and given to him by his father. He'd thought he had proof. Clem Bailey, one of *Base Camp*'s directors, had showed them footage of her committing the crime.

He still wasn't sure why he'd believed the man.

"She's just standing there. She won't eat. She isn't moving, except she's—I don't know. She's shaking now and then, and she's making these strange sounds."

As Walker watched, a ripple ran over Ruth's shaggy body, and she emitted a kind of painful lowing sound that must have been what sent Avery running to find him. He didn't blame her; it was like nothing she would have heard from the beasts before. He'd heard it plenty of times, though. There was a bison herd on the Crow reservation, and he'd grown up taking note of all their behaviors.

"She's calving."

Avery's mouth opened, and she turned to him, her face pale in the gray light of dawn. "Calving? Isn't it too early? Her baby isn't due to come for another two weeks."

He smiled at her belief in the punctuality of nature. He knew Avery had been studying about all the animals she helped care for on the ranch. She'd named every one of them, and heartache was bound to follow, given this was a working ranch, not some petting zoo. Avery had hidden depths, though, and a strength that kept her going even when life dealt her setbacks.

Even when he broke her heart.

She'd come to him for help just now, he reminded himself. When she feared for an animal, it was him she'd run to find. She just as easily could have pounded on Boone and Riley's tiny house door or one of the others. Her instinct had been to seek him out.

Maybe he could still fix what he'd nearly ruined.

He didn't know what he'd do if he couldn't.

"We have to help her," Avery insisted.

"We can't. All we can do is be patient. Nature works

on its own timetable. Think of Nora. She was due more than two weeks ago." Walker moved nearer to Avery. Maybe it was unfair; he knew his presence had an affect on her. When he came within a certain distance, Avery couldn't seem to bridge it the rest of the way. Even now she was reaching her hand toward him. He took it softly in his before she could remember they were supposed to be fighting.

"You're right." Avery made a face. Poor Nora was so uncomfortable it was hard to watch. If she didn't go into labor naturally in the next couple of days, she'd have to be induced.

Heartened by her willingness to talk, Walker gave Avery's hand a light squeeze. She'd spurned all the gifts he'd given her these past few weeks, making it clear how inadequate they were to make up for the betrayal of his accusation, but yesterday he gave her the fan that had started all the trouble between them, and since then she'd been wary and thoughtful. He hoped she understood he'd never doubt her again.

He wished he could take her into his arms right now. The past year had been a type of agony he'd never known before in his life. Avery so close—and so untouchable at times he thought he was already in hell.

He didn't want to let her go, but he couldn't pursue a relationship with her until Elizabeth finally came home, and Elizabeth kept cancelling at the last minute.

He wasn't even the only one hounding her to come and sort things out. His grandmother, Sue, had been emailing her since the moment his feet touched Chance

Creek soil.

"It's time," she kept proclaiming. "It's finally time!"

Time to break that old promise, Walker thought darkly. Time for Elizabeth to finally tell the truth about what she'd said all those years ago. She'd promised to arrive tomorrow, and this time she said she wouldn't call off her trip.

Sue would be disappointed when she heard what Elizabeth had to say, but she'd have to see that marrying Avery was the only way he could fulfil the promise he'd made to his friends at Base Camp. Sue believed in keeping your word, after all, and he had just over forty days to marry someone in order to secure the ranch.

"She's in pain." Avery cut into his thoughts, leaning forward as if she might climb through the fence and soothe Ruth herself.

"She's getting ready to give birth. It's uncomfortable, but she's okay. Ruth will know exactly what to do when it's time."

Avery fidgeted in distress, and Walker's heart went out to her. She felt whatever those around her felt, whether human or beast. Avery wore her heart on her sleeve, and her emotions were as intense as the summer squalls that drifted across the Montana plains.

"What if something goes wrong?"

"It won't," he assured her, sending steadiness through his hand into hers, willing her to accept nature's rhythms the way he did.

She looked up, seemed to notice he was holding her hand and lifted hers as if to pull away. Walker stilled, breathing only when she lowered it again.

"Avery." He didn't know how to say everything that was in his heart. How sorry he was for doubting her, how painful it was to know he'd hurt her. "I wish I'd never—"

"But you did."

She wouldn't look at him.

"I always—"

She half turned away, and he thought she'd pull free from him. Leave altogether.

Instead, she surged closer to the fence. "What's happening?" she cried.

Walker held on to her tightly. A herd of bison was a wild force that could be unleashed by any sudden movement. If Avery darted through the fence, her green dress flapping, she'd likely set off a stampede and do more to interfere with this birth than anything else.

"Just watch," he told her.

A ripple passed over Ruth's flanks, and another and another. She was close to her time.

"Get ready," he whispered.

Another ripple.

Ruth gave a low, painful sound, and something poked out of her—a small nose. She gave another lowing sound, and a fierce ripple passed through her flanks.

"Oh!" Avery went up on tiptoe. "Walker!"

Ruth lowed again, her muscles working in waves to expel the baby from her womb. A small, shaggy head emerged along with a tangle of hooves.

"It's a breech birth!" Avery cried.

"It's exactly what it should be," Walker assured her. "Ruth's got this."

Avery was clinging to his hand, twisting and turning in a shared agony with the mother.

"Now," he said, and another ripple of Ruth's muscles expelled the calf all the way. The tiny bison landed on the ground ungraciously, accompanied by Avery's cry.

"Is it all right?"

"It's fine." He had to put an arm around Avery's shoulders to restrain her as Ruth turned in a slow circle, nudged her baby with her nose and gave it a good lick. "See, she's cleaning it up, exactly the way she's supposed to. Ruth's a good mom."

"Of course she is!"

Avery's fierce shift from terror to indignation made him bite back another smile. "Of course she is," he affirmed. "She's a natural." Just like Avery would be if she ever had children.

Avery leaned into him as her relief overtook her and buried her face against his chest. "You always fix things." Her words were muffled, but he understood her perfectly and circled his arms around her. He'd learned this, too; she needed to let out her feelings when they got too much for her, and happiness, worry and anger came out as tears as often as sadness did.

"I didn't do anything," he pointed out. "Ruth's the one you should be praising."

"She's amazing." After another moment, Avery

emerged enough to watch the bison groom her calf, wiping her cheeks. "But you fix things just by being here."

He stilled again, love and pain welling within him in equal measures. He wanted to be here for Avery—always. If Elizabeth would come home and sort things out, he could be.

"One more day." He didn't realize he'd said it out loud until Avery shifted to look up at him.

"One more day until what?"

He hated the wariness in her eyes. He couldn't blame her for it—he'd let her down before.

Could he tell her what he planned? He'd kept his secrets for so long their corners should have worn down, but he felt each one as sharp and ragged as when they were new. He was tired of having to hold back from her, and he was beginning to wonder if that had been a mistake from the start.

Why not say something true?

"One more day until I can be to you what I want to be."

Her brow furrowed. "I don't understand."

"I'm going to ask you to marry me," he clarified. He couldn't pretend any more that he didn't want Avery. Needed to let her know exactly what she meant to him. Elizabeth hadn't come home yet despite promising to several times. There was no guarantee this time would be different, except this time, he promised himself, *he* would be different. If she didn't show tomorrow, he'd tell Sue himself about Elizabeth's lie. "Give me one more day."

Her lips parted, and Walker would have given anything to kiss her right then, but he was a man of his word, and he'd promised—

"Just one," he told Avery.

After a long moment, she nodded.

He held her as the sun rose and the baby calf struggled to its feet.

AVERY SUCKED IN a breath when the calf pushed up on its two front legs as if determined to stand. When its mother's vigorous washing knocked it over again, it scrambled to regain its balance.

Could the baby bison see her? Avery wasn't sure. All she knew was she'd never forget this—coming face to face with such beauty, such newness on the day that Walker had finally let her know what was in his heart. The newborn took an uncertain step, and its mother licked him. The tightness in Avery's chest intensified. She'd just witnessed a miracle.

It was as if the universe was giving her a tiny gift, something to make up for all the loneliness she'd felt in her life. The promise that a new phase was about to begin.

The phase in which Walker wanted her to be his wife.

She was aware of every rise and fall of Walker's chest as she leaned against him. The circle of his arms created a kind of safety she'd come to crave. She'd fallen for this man the moment she'd seen him, and he'd monopolized her thoughts ever since. When he'd believed Clem's ruse, she'd been furious—heartbroken, really—but ever since he'd placed his fan in her hands yesterday, her anger had bled away.

That fan represented Walker's heritage. More than that—his family. She knew he'd lost both father and mother young, his grandfather, too. That fan was a physical testament to all the generations of his past, and aside from his grandmother, he had no other links to them. When it had gone missing, he must have been frantic.

Now he'd given it to her, which meant he must really love her, despite his lapse in judgement. Clem had aired footage of her stealing it, and Walker had believed his eyes. Could she really blame him for that? After all, she was the one who'd been filming a series called *Stealing from SEALs*.

It was costing her to hold on to her anger and resentment, anyway. The last few weeks had been the worst in years, and it wasn't like she hadn't made her share of mistakes in life. Maybe it was time to let her anger go and get back to loving him. Just thinking about it made her heart lift. If Walker loved her, wanted to marry her, that meant they would be the ones to bring the competition for Base Camp to a close. They would win the ranch for all their friends and live here with them forever. Maybe have a baby. So many of the other women at Base Camp were pregnant, and she wanted that, too—so much.

Ruth raised her head suddenly, and Avery experienced that strange transcendence that happens when an animal looks at you—*sees* you—is thinking about you even as you're thinking about it.

She wondered what Ruth saw. A short redhead in a green gown, watching this precious moment in her life?

Ruth grunted at her, a reassuring sound, and Avery let out a shaky breath.

"I love you, too," she told Ruth as tears spilled down her cheeks again—tears of relief that all her waiting would soon be over. Like the bison had carried her calf, she'd carried the burden of her love for Walker for months, growing ever more uncomfortable with it. She was ready to give birth, too, to a lifetime commitment to this man she'd wanted for so long. "I will always love you—you and your baby," she promised, since she couldn't say those words yet to Walker. Not until she was sure of his intentions. "I'll take care of you."

The little bison looked up and bleated. It had wonderful little hooves. Expressive eyes.

Avery was entranced, and she stilled as a soft, warm breeze lifted the wisps of hair at her temples. Suddenly, she grew aware of how quiet it was out here, how startlingly beautiful.

This was exactly where she was meant to be, she realized. On this ranch, with these animals, in Walker's arms. Here was the life she'd wanted for so long.

One more day.

The bison bleated again, and Avery's heart filled with joy. "Walker—" Before she could tell him how much this meant to her, voices intruded on the peace of the morning. Walker stiffened and pulled away. She missed him immediately.

"I told you something important was happening!" William Sykes bellowed. A thickset blond man in his forties, laden with equipment, he was out of breath from hurrying toward them. Avery sighed and faced the camera crew that must have recently arrived from town.

"I'm sorry!" That was Jess Sims, one of the younger crew members. Usually so quiet you didn't notice her, it was obvious William had been giving her a hard time this morning.

"Sorry doesn't get the footage this show depends on. Morning, Walker. Morning, Avery."

Walker grunted something. Avery nodded. William wasn't usually this grumpy, and she wondered what was wrong.

"No coffee," Craig Demaris, another crew member, filled her in as he pointed a video camera her way. "What kind of motel runs out of coffee?"

"We could have stopped at the doughnut shop," Jess said. She wore what Avery thought of as the crew uniform: cargo pants, T-shirt, boots and a long-suffering expression that said Craig had been chiding her since they left the motel. Her dirty blond hair was in a twist on top of her head, her soft features ruddy with embarrassment.

"Yes, we could have—if you weren't late," William said. "What'd we miss?" he asked Walker. "You two looked awfully cozy."

"You missed the birth of the first bison calf." Avery hurried to deflect him, not wanting her love life—such as it was—with Walker dissected by this cranky group. "Come and see."

"I'd better get to the other chores." Walker met her gaze and held it a moment before turning away, and Avery's chest warmed with the promise there.

One more day.

He was going to ask her to marry him.

"What were you two talking about before we arrived?" William asked suspiciously. "Walker was holding you. Did he propose?"

She shook her head. "We were talking about bison. Isn't Champ adorable?"

"Champ?" Craig asked, moving closer.

"That's the calf's name. His mother is Ruth. She's a prodigy among bison." Avery kept talking until she'd deflected the crew's attention. After months working alongside Walker to care for the herd, she could talk about bison all day long.

She wished Walker hadn't left, though, and that the crew hadn't arrived when they did. Walker had wanted to kiss her. Wanted more than that, if she wasn't mistaken. There'd been that tension between them since the day they'd met, an instant attraction that took her breath away on a daily basis.

She couldn't wait to have the right to run her hands all over his body. She dreamed about being with him almost every night. Walker was—

Everything.

She knew they made a comical couple, him so tall and broad and her so... well... short. She knew they'd fit together perfectly, though, when they got the chance. Every molecule of her yearned to be close to him, and she was sure he felt the same way, even if he'd held himself back all this time.

Would he really propose, though?

They all knew he'd been promised to someone; the question was who? And where had she been all this time? Did she still want him? What would it take to dissolve whatever relationship was holding him back?

And how would he resolve the problem in one day's time?

A cold prickle of premonition tripped down her spine. If something was going to be different tomorrow, that meant something had to happen to make it different.

What could that be?

Avery thought it over. Angus and Win would marry tonight, which meant tomorrow would be the beginning of Walker's forty days to marry before his deadline was up. Was he simply waiting for his "turn"?

That didn't seem right. He'd been promised, which meant he needed to break a promise, and Avery couldn't see Walker ever doing that. He was a man who valued honor above all else.

She, on the other hand, valued love, she thought, watching the tiny bison calf wobble through its first tentative steps. Love was more important than anything else. It healed wounds, held families together—held the universe together, if you asked.

Could it hold her and Walker together, too?

She wasn't sure. Could one day really resolve a problem that had existed for a year? Could her happiness be so close?

She'd learned long ago not to rely on things going her way. What made her think this time would be different?

She watched Ruth care for her baby and decided this time would be different because she and Walker were meant for each other and meant for this place, too, both of them glorying in the natural setting they found themselves in, the friends they spent their days with and the activities that filled their hours. Only Walker's old promise kept them apart.

"You know a lot about bison," Jess said when the crew members had gotten all the footage of Champ they wanted. "And you're lucky to have someone like Walker." She followed Avery to the chicken house as the rest of the crew headed for the bunkhouse.

"I don't have him yet."

"Don't you think you'll have him soon? He's got to marry next," Jess pointed out as Avery unlatched the door to the chicken coop and the birds flocked around her.

Jess dutifully filmed the interaction, but they both knew there was plenty of footage of Avery doing her chores and this would never appear on television.

"I'm not one to count my chickens before they hatch," Avery said wryly.

"Ha, ha." Jess lowered the camera. "Do you think Boone would find me a husband if I asked him? I wouldn't mind sticking around when the show is over."

Avery nearly laughed. It had been months since she'd allowed herself to think of anything that might happen when the show was over. "You want a tiny house and a husband of your own?"

"Maybe." Jess shrugged. "You all seem happy."

"Boone has talked about expanding Base Camp when the year is done." She'd never really pictured it, though. "If you want to stay, you should definitely tell him."

Jess put her camera down. "Can I feed them?" she asked, and Avery stepped back to let her handle the chore.

"You're a natural," Avery said. "I hope Boone finds you a good husband."

"From your mouth to his ears," Jess said.

"YOU READY?" WALKER asked Angus.

"More than ready," Angus said. He was due to marry Win Lisle in less than an hour, and Walker and the rest of the men had joined him in one of the large guest rooms at the manor, where the ceremony would take place. They were all wearing the Revolutionary War uniforms they customarily donned for Base Camp weddings, and Alice Reed was present to make sure any unraveled hems were stitched up and loose buttons sewn back on. Angus looked ready to burst with happiness, and Walker relaxed a little. His friend deserved to marry the woman he loved after all he'd been through. Walker could only hope one day soon things would go as well for him.

When Boone burst into the room holding up a single straw in his hand, however, he stifled a groan. He should have guessed the man wouldn't buck tradition. At every Base Camp wedding, they drew straws to see who would marry next.

"You know what time it is!" Boone crossed the room to present the single straw to him.

There was nothing for it. All Walker could do was pluck it from Boone's hand and hold it up for all to see. It was short, of course. He was the only one of the original ten Base Camp men left unmarried.

"Think you can pull it off?" Boone asked. Walker noticed everyone was waiting to hear his answer.

"I'll get it done," he assured them. He felt freer since his decision this morning and had been kicking himself about not taking action sooner. He supposed he couldn't blame Elizabeth for not coming home before now. The confrontation they needed to have with Sue wasn't something you looked forward to. It wasn't the kind of thing you did over the phone, either, and he was surprised Elizabeth hadn't taken the bull by the horns and done it years ago.

Maybe she'd hoped he'd do it for her.

Not a chance. Walker suppressed a smile. Elizabeth was the one who'd gotten them into this mess; it was only fair she get them out of it.

"It's time," Boone said to Angus. "You ready?"

"Hell, yeah," Angus said. "Let's go."

A half hour later, in the manor's ballroom, Walker knew he should be focused on Angus and Win, but he couldn't stop watching Avery, who was hanging on every word of the ceremony.

One more day, he promised himself. One more day, and he could finally propose. His heart beat hard at the thought, but he was determined that in thirty-six hours, Avery would wear his ring on her finger and they'd be preparing their own wedding.

Walker took a deep breath when Angus kissed Win and the preacher declared them man and wife. One step closer to his own happy ending.

He sprang into action after the new husband and wife walked back up the aisle, helping the other men to clear the folding chairs to the sides of the ballroom and set up tables among them, leaving a large area in the center of the room for dancing. Food was set out at one end on long buffet tables. Nearby, there were drinks to be had. At the other end, a local band played the first notes of a waltz as camera crews captured the action. Everything was going according to plan, Walker told himself with satisfaction. And tomorrow his life would change forever—just as soon as Elizabeth got here.

"It's all down to you now." Boone clapped Walker on the shoulder and handed him a bottle of beer. "You got things straightened out with your grandmother?"

"Working on it." He wasn't surprised when Boone sighed.

"Strange your intended wife hasn't turned up in all

this time."

"She's been busy."

"Guess you're lucky you never drew the short straw until now."

Walker nearly smiled—but didn't. Avoiding the short straw was easier than one might think. A time or two, he'd gotten a jump on the job before Boone got around to it, which made it easy to perform the sleight of hand that left him with one of the long ones. When Boone took charge of the operation, Walker had noticed he gripped the straws together in his fist but flicked the bottom of the longer ones with his pinkie finger over and over. If he watched carefully, he could see each of the long ones vibrate in turn as Boone flicked them. The short one remained still.

No one else had noticed, which made it easy for him to draw a long one. Luck had played its part, of course, but not as much as everyone else thought.

"Guess it was meant to be" was all he said to Boone.

"You're not planning to become a bigamist, right?" Boone asked as both watched Avery tilt back her head and laugh at something Riley said.

"Nope."

"Then I'm assuming you're going to make Avery a happy woman."

"That's the plan," Walker conceded.

"The sooner it's June, the happier I'll be," Boone said. "I promised Riley we'd secure Westfield forever, and it would kill me to break that promise."

"I'll get it done," Walker assured him, knowing Boone wanted to hear him say it. One more day, he told himself again silently, letting the music, the conversations and the laughter settle over him as he took another drink of his beer. "Talk to you later," he told Boone and pushed through the crowd to get to the person he really wanted to be with.

"Good wedding," he said when he met her at the drinks table, wanting to keep things light tonight.

"It was a beautiful wedding," Avery agreed.

"They seem happy." He nodded at Win and Angus dancing together, gazing at each other like there was no one else in the world.

"They do."

Walker searched for his grandmother in the crowd. As soon as Elizabeth told her the truth about their promise and he was free of it, he'd be free to dance with Avery like that.

"About the fan," Avery said, turning to him. "We really need to talk about it."

Walker scanned the room again and stiffened.

"I appreciate the gesture," Avery went on, "but…" She trailed off to follow his gaze, since he was no longer listening to her.

Walker couldn't help it, because he'd found Sue. She'd just entered the ballroom from the front hall, dressed in a neat navy-blue skirt and blazer with a pale-blue blouse buttoned up to the top. Her straight black hair was done in one long braid down her back, glints of silver running through it like decorative thread.

She wasn't alone. Beside her walked another, taller woman, with the straight, dark hair of his people, high cheekbones, a full, curved mouth and sharp eyes that missed nothing, just as he remembered them. A woman Walker hadn't seen in years.

Elizabeth Blaine.

His promised bride.

And now Avery had caught sight of her, too.

"WHO'S THAT WITH Sue?" Avery asked, but her stomach tightened, and she had an awful feeling she didn't want to know the answer to her question. Sue wouldn't have brought any old last-minute guest to Win and Angus's wedding.

That was the woman Walker was supposed to marry—it had to be. The reason he'd asked her to give him one more day.

Avery had known something had to happen before he proposed to her tomorrow, but she'd never expected this.

Walker looked surprised, too.

Maybe he'd forgotten his would-be bride was so beautiful.

Tall, regal, with straight dark hair that framed expressive dark eyes, her heritage clear in her features, her pride evident in her bearing, the newcomer was everything Avery wasn't, and she fought a sudden urge to take Walker's hand and remind him of what he'd said that morning—that he wanted to be with her—because surely one look at the woman with Sue would make him forget everything else.

In vain she reminded herself of Walker's intensity as he'd promised to propose to her. The way he'd looked at her like he wanted to kiss her, hold her—do so much more.

Because now he was looking at the newcomer, and she was a woman made for him. A match in every way. She was as beautiful as he was handsome, had as much presence as he did, shared his heritage—and Sue's affection, evidently. Walker's grandmother oozed satisfaction.

No... triumph. That was the word for it.

Now Avery understood why Sue had never approved of her for Walker.

"Stay here," he commanded and took off across the room before she could say a word, shouldering his way through tight knots of people in his hurry to greet his guests.

Without thinking, Avery followed as swiftly as she could, the long skirts of her Regency gown hampering her. She was desperate to know what was going on. Had to hear what Walker would say to the newcomer. She trusted him—when he'd said he wanted to marry her, she knew he'd meant it.

He wasn't the kind of man to lie.

But how could she compare to this woman?

"Who's that with Sue?" Riley intercepted her halfway across the ballroom. Avery kept going, but Riley fell in behind her, holding a hand over her barely-rounded belly as if to protect her unborn child.

"She's the one. The woman Walker's promised to," Avery hissed over her shoulder. He hadn't said as much, but who else could she be?

"Are you sure?" Riley lifted her head to get a better look. "Wouldn't Walker have told you she was coming?"

"I don't know." Her heart beat hard, and she was finding it difficult to breathe. She couldn't say why she was panicking, except she'd thought she'd found a happily-ever-after once before. Thought she'd been on her way to the altar.

She'd been wrong.

Riley linked arms with her, and they pressed forward. "He doesn't seem happy about her being here."

Avery craned her head to look again, her heart lifting with hope. Walker had reached the two women, but he was talking only to his grandmother, ignoring the beauty by her side, who was surveying him with a stony expression.

Riley was right, Walker looked angry rather than pleased to see her. She was being ridiculous. If Walker said he was going to marry her, he meant it. There was no way he'd play with her affections. Not Walker.

As she watched, he finally turned to the newcomer, and Avery's stomach lurched again as some strong emotion flashed between them. Maybe not love, but—

Understanding. A deep kind of knowing that only years of proximity and connection could bring.

Avery stopped. Riley hovered near her. "What's wrong? Don't you want to find out what they're saying?"

Avery wasn't sure she dared. She'd felt beautiful earlier taking part in Angus and Win's wedding ceremony, sneaking glances across the aisle at Walker, who had stood up with the groom. Walker had looked so handsome in the Revolutionary War uniform the men always wore to Base Camp weddings.

He still did, but Avery felt frowsy in comparison to the cool beauty who stood by his side. Her deep-blue gown made Avery's Regency dress seem silly. Her straight, dark hair fell in a perfect curtain, not a strand out of place, while Avery's had gone frizzy in the unusual heat.

And that look they'd exchanged—

Avery didn't know Walker half as well as this woman obviously did.

"Come on. Let's get to the bottom of this." Riley tugged Avery forward determinedly until they could hear what Walker and the women were saying. Avery's hands were clammy, and she wiped them on her skirts, then wished she hadn't.

"Aren't you even going to say hello?"

That was Sue upbraiding her grandson for his lack of manners. Avery watched as Walker turned to face the newcomer again. "Elizabeth."

"Walker." Elizabeth looked him up and down, a trace of amusement touching her lips. "You're looking very… revolutionary."

Avery's shoulder's straightened. No one got to make fun of Walker—or of Base Camp's traditions.

Walker hesitated, and Avery knew Elizabeth had flummoxed him. He probably hadn't intended to meet up with his... intended... dressed this way.

"We're supposed to meet tomorrow," he said, confirming her suspicions.

Elizabeth shrugged delicately. "I got in early."

Between them, Sue lifted her chin. "Now the promise will be fulfilled. The healing will begin for our families. Elizabeth, your grandmother would be so pleased you're here."

Elizabeth smiled, and Avery's heart sank all over again. She was lovely, but was it her imagination, or did that smile contain a trace of bitterness?

What was really happening here?

"Sue." Walker waved a hand as if pushing his grandmother's words away, but Elizabeth moved closer to him and raised her voice.

"She's right, Walker, time to fulfill that promise." The gaze she leveled at him was full of steel, even as the camera crew, who'd raced to film the action as soon as Sue appeared with Elizabeth by her side, pushed closer to record her words. "When are you going to make me your wife?"

Avery's heart stopped. Beside her, Riley gasped.

Even Sue looked uncomfortable at Elizabeth's direct question.

Walker's expression hardened. "Why are you really here?"

Elizabeth met his glare with one of her own. "You made a promise."

"But—"

Elizabeth's gaze swept past him and landed on Avery, who flinched as if she'd been cut. "You said you'd marry me. Did you lie?"

Walker refused to turn. "Why?" he asked again. Simple and direct, the way he always was, Avery thought. Cut right to the heart of the matter and bypass all the rest.

Fury pinched Elizabeth's face. "Do I need a reason?"

"Yes."

For one fleeting moment, Avery saw something like fear cross Elizabeth's features. Then her expression hardened again.

"You owe me. You know you do."

Walker searched her face, opened his mouth to reply, then seemed to notice Sue standing next to Elizabeth. Both women watched him, their features set as stone.

Avery's throat went dry. What did Walker owe this woman?

"So are you going to marry me or not?" Elizabeth hissed.

He couldn't seem to find an answer to that.

Avery didn't think she'd ever find an answer to anything again.

CHAPTER TWO

ELIZABETH HAD CHANGED. Where she'd once been a bright go-getter, now she seemed hard as flint—cynical beyond her years. There were lines around her eyes Walker hadn't expected, as if life had served her a harsh hand. Her shoulders were set. Her mouth drawn.

What had happened to her since he'd last seen her?

"Well?" Elizabeth demanded.

Sue frowned. "Of course he'll marry you. He pledged to do so."

Elizabeth shook her head. "I've been watching this show of his." She gestured to the camera crew pressed around them. "He hasn't been taking his pledge seriously at all. You know that as well as I do, Sue. He's been running around with *her*."

Walker turned to find Avery behind him, her eyes wide with pain, her face drawn into a mask of confusion. His chest burned with frustration. This was exactly what he'd hoped to avoid by meeting Elizabeth tomorrow at Sue's place. He wanted his confrontation with her over and done with before Avery ever knew about it. Now she'd heard every word Sue and Elizabeth had said.

"Avery—" He reached for her.

She shook her head just like Elizabeth had a moment ago and turned to leave. Sue grabbed his sleeve before he could pursue her. "Let her go. This is Crow business. She has no part in it."

"This isn't *Crow* business," he ground out, aching to follow Avery and tell her everything. It wasn't a clan matter—it was a family one. And Avery was as good as family.

Better, he thought as he faced Sue and Elizabeth again. Where had his family been when he really needed them? His mother dead. Father dead. His grandmother present, but so caught up in her private sorrow—

"It's *our* business," Sue said, "and we'll handle it ourselves—when we have the privacy to do so. This isn't the place or the time. Your grandmother would be ashamed of you," she told Elizabeth. "I brought you to say hello and to enjoy the wedding. We're guests here."

Elizabeth didn't blush, but Walker thought the rebuke hit home nonetheless. Her shoulders lowered and her frown deepened as she cast a glance over her shoulder at the door through which she'd entered just moments before. "Normally, I'd prefer to do this privately as much as you," she agreed, her voice as loud as ever, and for a fleeting second Walker wondered if Fulsom had put her up to this, before realizing how improbable that was. His chest tightened as Elizabeth pointed a dramatic finger at him, really playing it up for the cameras still focused on them. "He's the one who's taken this all public, going on this show and agreeing to marry at a certain time. He forced my hand."

Walker couldn't remember Elizabeth ever being so determined to be in the limelight. Sue looked as surprised as he was, but all she said to Walker was, "Tomorrow. Come to dinner as we planned. We'll sort out your future then. In the meantime, remember who you are and what you owe your family."

In other words, forget about marrying Avery. That's why she'd brought Elizabeth here tonight, he realized. Sue knew now that Angus was wed, it would be his turn to marry in forty days. Had she been afraid he'd get carried away by the romance of the occasion and propose to Avery tonight?

He wished he had.

Walker burned to tell his grandmother exactly what he thought of her, but he'd been raised to respect his elders, and he didn't want to ruin Angus and Win's big night by creating a scene.

"Tomorrow," he ground out. He'd put an end to this farce if Elizabeth wouldn't. He should have done it a long time ago.

"Tomorrow," Elizabeth echoed. "Don't think you're going to get out of it," she added in a lower tone, but not so low the camera crew couldn't pick it up on the boom mike. "I can make your life miserable." She cut a meaningful glance at Sue and walked away.

"Yeah, Walker," one of the cameramen echoed. "Don't think you're going to get out of doing this all on camera, either. If you're going to your grandma's house tomorrow, so are we."

Perfect, Walker thought. That was all he needed.

"I NEED TO leave. Tonight. Right now." Avery couldn't stop the tears rolling down her cheeks. After everything that had happened this year—after all the days spent in Walker's company, longing for his touch—pining for evidence that he loved her as much as she loved him—it had all come to nothing. Worse than nothing. He'd known all along this beautiful woman was waiting in the wings to marry him.

"Avery, slow down." Riley had followed Avery up the stairs to one of the manor's guest rooms, where Avery paced back and forth, too distraught to sit.

"I can't compete with her. Did you see her? She's gorgeous. She's probably brilliant. Sue loves her—"

"But Walker doesn't. He loves you."

"Does he? Because he's known me for nearly a year, and obviously he's done nothing to break off his relationship with her! He had plenty of chances just now to tell her he's marrying me, and he didn't." She hated how her voice was rising. How trapped and betrayed and devastated she felt. He'd told her he was going to propose tomorrow, and she'd believed him.

Didn't she ever learn from her mistakes?

"Of course he loves you. Didn't you hear how angry he was? He doesn't want this Elizabeth person. He just didn't want to make a scene."

"But you said it yourself before—Sue is a formidable woman. What she wants, she gets."

"Walker won't marry a woman he doesn't love—"

"Yes, he will. If he thinks it's the honorable thing to do! He always listens to Sue," Avery burst out.

"Not always. At least, he didn't when I knew him as a kid. There's more to this than we know," Riley said reasonably. "You're upset and rightly so, but don't fly off the handle. Give it time. Besides, you can't leave Base Camp. We need you here." She hugged Avery.

"I can't stay if she does." Avery pulled back, even though she appreciated Riley's intentions. She still felt uncomfortable around all her friends—they hadn't believed her when Clem framed her for the theft of Walker's fan. "I just can't."

"Then I'll make sure she doesn't. You stay here. I'll go see what's happening." She sat Avery down on the bed, slipped out of the room and shut the door behind her. As soon as she did, Avery was back on her feet pacing again. She couldn't kid herself; she'd always known this moment would come, ever since Sue had announced to them Walker was promised to someone. All this time she'd managed to keep her hopes in check—until this morning, when Walker had declared his intentions. Then she'd let them run wild.

Here was her punishment, right on time.

All Elizabeth had to do was crook her little finger, and Walker had folded. Maybe it was because Sue was there. Maybe Riley was right, and he didn't want to spoil Win and Angus's wedding.

All Avery knew was that he hadn't stood up for her.

Hadn't said, "I'm marrying Avery."

Hadn't said anything to her at all.

She was so stupid, hitching her cart to a man who wasn't free to be with her. Riley was right; he'd seemed angry at Elizabeth's arrival and stunned when she demanded that he marry her, but he'd known this was coming, and he hadn't stopped it.

A new thought occurred to her, and Avery sat down, the fight going out of her. Had Walker wanted to marry Elizabeth all this time? Had he been afraid Elizabeth might not show up at the last minute?

Maybe she was nothing but a backup bride.

Avery hugged her arms across her stomach, afraid she might be sick. Stayed there until she heard Riley returning.

"Sue and Elizabeth are leaving." Riley said. She sat next to Avery on the bed and took her hand. "They both look mad as hell."

At least that was something.

"Do you think you can pull yourself together and come back to the reception? I'm serious, Avery, you can't leave Base Camp. Not with my baby coming. Not ever. No matter what happens." She patted her belly as if it trumped everything.

Avery let out a gusty breath. At one time it would have, but her friendship with Riley wasn't as strong as it once was. Neither Riley nor any of the others defended her when Clem had accused her of stealing Walker's treasured ceremonial fan. Why should she stay here when everyone she cared about had let her down?

"Avery." Riley's eyebrows knotted. "Avery, you know we're all so sorry we ever doubted you, and we'd do anything to take it back. You know how bad Clem made it look. We shouldn't have been fooled, but we were. I wish I could go back in time and change everything."

None of them could do that. If she could go back in time, she'd erase this whole year—

No.

That wasn't true. It had been the best year of her life even if Walker had strung her along and her friends had been tricked by a conman into blaming her for something she didn't do.

"I love you." Riley held her hand even tighter. "You know I do. You know how much I'd hate being here if you left."

"How can I stay?"

"If anyone leaves, it should be Walker!" Riley cried, and Avery found herself softening—a little.

"Then everyone would have to leave," she said reasonably. The only way for any of them to keep Base Camp was for all ten of the original founding men to marry and stay here—at least until June first.

"You can't quit now," Riley said. "Walker loves you. Nothing can persuade me I'm wrong about that. Give him twenty-four hours to straighten it all out, at least. I can't believe he would marry anyone other than you."

One more day.

Avery sighed, raw with pain. She supposed she could hang around for another twenty-four hours. To leave now meant ruining Angus and Win's wedding, and they didn't deserve that.

Besides, she had no idea where she would go.

As angry as she'd been at Walker and her friends for not believing her, she realized now she'd assumed those rifts would heal over time. She'd wanted to believe in Walker's love—and in the friendship she'd shared with Riley, Savannah and Nora.

She was such a fool. Always looking for things to turn out when she knew darn well she wasn't lucky like that.

For the first time, she contemplated a future without Riley and the others. Without Walker.

What would it be like to be on the outside looking in? To hear about life at Base Camp second-hand?

She couldn't bear to think about it. "I guess you're right," she forced herself to say. She loved it here at Base Camp. Knew in her heart that Riley, Savannah and Nora had been tricked. They still cared about her, and she cared about them.

As for Walker, she was going off half-cocked. She hadn't let him explain.

Didn't want him to.

She didn't think she'd ever forget how it felt when Elizabeth had asked, "Are you going to marry me or not?" and Walker hadn't told her no. It was like someone had torn her in two, pulled out her heart and set it on fire.

This morning, she'd utterly believed he meant to make her his wife.

Now she wasn't sure. Why had he hesitated? Why not just tell Elizabeth no?

To save them all from a scene? Or because seeing Elizabeth again had changed his mind?

Avery closed her eyes in pain.

If he married Elizabeth, he'd break her heart, but it wasn't the first time it had been broken, she reminded herself.

She'd always survived.

Would watching him love someone else be better or worse than leaving Base Camp for good and losing everything?

Avery didn't know.

"Avery—"

"I forgive you." She opened her eyes again and swallowed at the relief on Riley's face.

"Really?"

Avery's heart softened even more. Riley really did love her.

"Of course. You guys thought you saw me take the fan. How could you have known Clem doctored the footage?" she forced herself to say. When it had happened, she'd thought nothing could hurt her the way it did to know all of them believed her capable of such a thing.

Now she knew how much worse things could get.

"We should have known," Riley said. "You'd never do anything to hurt someone else!"

"But I had been stealing things—as a joke." Avery sighed. "That's the messed-up thing, Riley. No matter how much someone else hurts me, I always manage to hurt myself worse." Like the way she'd accepted Walker's assertion that he'd marry her before he'd done what it took to clean up his past.

Riley pulled her into a hug. "We've all made mistakes this year. All we can do is try to move forward."

"I guess." Could she do that if Walker married Elizabeth?

She thought of the way he'd held her hand while Ruth labored this morning. How tender he'd been when she cried with relief and joy after Champ's birth.

Walker understood her better than anyone else. She'd never felt so loved as she did with him. Was she making too much of what had happened tonight? Should she give him the chance to explain?

Once again she heard Elizabeth's voice in her head. "Are you going to marry me or not?"

She didn't need to hear anything from Walker, Avery decided, until he'd answered Elizabeth definitively. Yes or no. It was a simple question.

"It will be so much better if you make an appearance," Riley said. "People will focus on Win and Angus again. Wash your face. Have a drink of water. No one will know you were upset."

Avery doubted that was true. She had always been an open book. Everyone knew she loved Walker—

And now they'd know how miserable she would be if he left her behind.

WALKER LAY ON his bedroll in the bunkhouse the

following morning, staring through the dark at the ceiling, wondering why he'd woken so early with a sense that something wasn't right.

Something besides the obvious.

It wasn't that Elizabeth had arrived in Chance Creek last night and challenged him to marry her, disrupting all his careful plans.

It wasn't that Avery hadn't spoken a word to him since she'd run from the ballroom last night, even though he'd tried to take her aside once the reception was over to explain what had happened.

It was something else. Something he couldn't quite put his finger on until a breeze stirred through the room from one of the windows left open last night.

A warm breeze.

Walker sat up. It was mid-April, and not too long ago, snow lay on the ground outside. April could be mild, but that breeze wasn't chilly at all, and the sun wasn't even up yet.

He noiselessly got out of his sleeping bag, as Avery turned over in hers across the room. Until recently they'd shared the bunkhouse with Byron, one of the cameramen, and his girlfriend, Leslie, who'd come to Base Camp expecting to marry Angus but had shifted her affection to the younger man. That became uncomfortable as soon as Byron and Leslie hooked up, and even though all the single residents of Base Camp were supposed to sleep here, Walker had given them permission to spend their nights temporarily in the shell of the tiny house that was being built for his use when he was married.

He hadn't reckoned with how awkward it would be to sleep alone in the bunkhouse with just Avery when he wasn't allowed to touch her—even more so after Clem pulled his scam. It was torture keeping to his side of the room night after night when he knew Avery wasn't sleeping well, either. As hard as it had been to keep his distance these past weeks, he was grateful now he had.

He couldn't believe the ultimatum Elizabeth had given him last night—or the threat she'd uttered. That she'd make his life miserable.

She was already doing that.

Was Avery awake? Walker couldn't tell.

Last night when the reception was over, she'd gotten ready for bed, disdaining his help with her gown, wrapped herself in her blankets on her pallet on the floor and turned her back to him without a word. The implications were clear; she had nothing to say to him as long as Elizabeth was in the picture.

He couldn't blame her.

Should he wake her up now and explain what was going on? Walker remembered her drawn face and red-rimmed eyes last night. If she was sleeping, he should let her be. Today he'd get his chance to face down Elizabeth and Sue, without an audience—except perhaps a camera crew. Tomorrow he and Avery could start fresh.

As for Elizabeth, what had gotten into her? Walker pulled on his clothes and went outside. Why did she look like she'd fought a war? Why on earth had she come home to marry him? He'd never once considered the possibility she'd hold him to the stupid promise they'd made so many years ago.

Something was wrong. He knew it in his gut. Whatever it was, he'd have to help solve it and send her on her way, before she ruined everything.

As he crossed to the barn, figuring he could feed the chickens and goats and other critters and get those chores done, he remembered what Sue had said last night when she'd called him long after she and Elizabeth left the reception.

"Why would you treat her that way when she's just come home?"

"You know why." He wasn't going to allow Sue to pretend she didn't know he was in love with Avery.

"You made a promise."

"I did," he acknowledged, even now torn between telling her he had no intention of following through and wanting to give Elizabeth the chance to explain why she'd lied in the first place.

"It's time for you to step up. It's your job to give that girl a good life."

His job.

Because of what his father had done.

Would he ever be free of Joe Norton's sins? He remembered little of his father. A tall man—strong. His brooding silences at the dinner table on his rare trips home. His sharp replies when Sue remonstrated him for staying out late instead of spending time with his son.

The way he had of looking into Walker's eyes as if

he couldn't fathom Walker's presence in his life.

His father had joined the Army months after Walker was born and served as if a demon was after him, according to Sue.

Maybe one had been.

Everyone made mistakes, but some mistakes had consequences so devastating it seemed like some independent evil had to be behind it.

Walker stood in the empty barn. Had he been fooling himself all these years? Sue had always spoken of the debt their family owed to Elizabeth's, but the idea of providing Elizabeth protection and sustenance through marrying her was laughable.

At least it had been until last night.

Elizabeth was the most independent woman he knew. She'd made it clear from the time they were children she had no interest in him—not like that. Hell, they were brought up practically as brother and sister. Fought like cats and dogs when they were young. Barely spoke when they got older.

Why was he supposed to shoulder responsibility for the mistakes of a man he barely knew? Or the lie of a teenage girl trying to make her sole remaining relative happy?

Walker shook his head. He couldn't blame his father for the predicament he found himself in. Couldn't blame Elizabeth, either. He'd said he'd marry her. He never should have done that, no matter what the circumstances.

Why the hell would she want to marry him when

there'd never been a spark between them, though?

Something had happened to cause the haunted look in her eyes. Maybe if he figured out what, he could fix it and send her on her way—

Before his forty days were up.

A rumble of a truck and the flash of headlights down the lane caught his attention. Who would be coming so early? Even the camera crews wouldn't arrive for another half hour. He watched as it parked next to one of Base Camp's fancy new electric trucks and a woman got out.

Elizabeth, he realized with a sinking feeling in his gut.

He strode over to intercept her. He didn't even want her on the property. She'd only hurt Avery more, and God knew they'd both done that enough already.

"What are you doing here?"

"Good morning to you, too." Like last night, Elizabeth's expression gave little away. She surveyed the ranch in the early morning gloom, but Walker knew she couldn't see much other than the silhouettes of the bunkhouse and barns against a sky gradually shading from indigo to cerulean. "I have to say, the last thing I ever expected was that you'd land on reality TV."

He grunted. "Didn't expect it either. Here to tell me what's really going on? What happened to having dinner at Sue's and talking things over then?"

She didn't answer at first. She was probably calculating how best to regain the upper hand. They'd always fought for supremacy.

"We have a lot of catching up to do," she allowed. "Forget dinner. I told Sue I'd spend the day with you here, instead. We don't need an audience when we talk."

Like hell they didn't. They needed to tell Sue the truth.

"I've been busy this year—in Siberia," Elizabeth went on.

"So I heard. But what does—?" He broke off at the sound of another engine.

Elizabeth looked over her shoulder and nodded as another vehicle pulled into the lot. "Ah, here they are."

Walker nearly groaned when several crew members got out, bringing their equipment with them. What the hell were they doing here so early?

"Morning, Walker," one called out.

He ignored them. Had Elizabeth told them she was coming? Why would she do that?

She waited until the crew had their equipment, including a circle of bright lights, set up before she went on. "It's my job to study the effects of climate change on wildfires," she said as if this entire situation was perfectly normal. "Right now I'm specifically studying the effect of climate change on fires above the arctic circle."

He shook his head, wanting to tell her to stop bullshitting. "Can't be too many of those."

"You'd be surprised." She spoke clearly for the crew's benefit. "I was certainly surprised last year when I discovered the man who'd promised to marry me had joined a reality television show and never even told me.

Especially since he'd agreed to wed within forty days from the time he drew the short straw. What if I hadn't been able to cut my fieldwork short? What then? Would you have lost the game and ruined Base Camp for everyone?"

He opened his mouth to say he had, too, informed her—through Sue. Had been practically begging her for months to come home and sort things out.

"Oh, that's right." She beat him to the punch. "You had a backup bride, didn't you? Avery."

"Avery isn't a backup bride." He caught two of the crew exchanging smiles. Elizabeth really knew how to keep them happy, didn't she?

She lifted an eyebrow. "Which makes you an oath-breaker, doesn't it? Aren't you afraid the ghosts of the past are going to hunt you down and find you?"

Hell. Walker rode out the shiver that traced down his spine, determined Elizabeth not see she was getting to him. He didn't know what he'd expected, but it wasn't this full-frontal attack. He prided himself on not being superstitious, but plenty of things had happened in his life, both here in Montana and overseas during his missions, that he couldn't explain. Growing up on the reservation you knew damn well the past could affect the present.

He wanted to say he wasn't responsible for what his father had done, but they were all responsible for each other, weren't they? The debts of the parents were passed down to their children—the evidence of that was all around them in the way the world was warming up, the way the poorest nations were paying for the sins of the richest.

"You don't want me." He cursed the upbringing that wouldn't let him destroy her on national television, despite the fact she seemed ready to destroy him.

She laughed. "Is that what this is about? You don't want to trade Avery's idolizing worship for my knowledge of exactly who you are? Should I spell out the past to her? Tell her *everything*?" She emphasized those last words, sending him another message, and he realized this was the reason for the whole stunt. She wanted him to know she wouldn't hold back from saying things in front of the cameras. From airing their families' dirty laundry in front of millions of viewers. He could live with that.

Could Sue?

Walker swallowed. Sue had dealt with so much already.

"Come on, Elizabeth. Avery doesn't idolize me." Elizabeth was pissing him off. She didn't get to come here and cut Avery down. He didn't like the way she was threatening him, either. Threatening Sue, actually. Walker knew Avery—she was compassionate enough to forgive anything. It was Sue who'd be devastated by what Elizabeth might say.

"But she *idealizes* you, doesn't she? Avery idealizes everyone."

So Elizabeth had watched the show. Was she jealous of Avery? Walker couldn't make that fit with the girl he'd grown up with.

"You want to give up your career and come live here—at Base Camp?" he returned. None of this made sense.

"Why not? You're fighting climate change, too, in your way. Lord knows there are wildfires in Montana."

True enough, but who would pay her to study them here?

"Why come so early this morning?"

She shrugged out of the light jacket she was wearing and tossed it through the open window of her truck onto the front seat. "Warm today, isn't it?"

He didn't answer that.

"I'm here to help with your chores," she said in answer to his previous question. "That's what a good wife does, right?"

Now she was goading him.

"Why do you want to be my wife, Elizabeth?" He wasn't going anywhere until he had an answer.

Elizabeth surveyed him, then looked past his shoulder to the crew fanned around them. Grinned suddenly in a way that took him totally aback, so that when she crossed the space between them, went up on tiptoe, cupped his chin in one slim hand and kissed him on the cheek, he didn't react until she was gone again, heading for the pastures.

"Because I've been lying my whole life, Walker." She raised her voice so it would be clear to the viewers when this exchange was included in the next episode. "I've been in love with you since I knew what love was. Now let's see those famous bison of yours."

Walker stayed where he was, stunned. The crew dithered around him, unsure which of them to follow and film.

In love with him?

Like hell.

His attention was caught by the flash of more headlights. A truck he didn't recognize swept into the turnout where the others had parked, caught them all in its beams, paused, reversed with a squeal of tires and high-tailed it out of there. Elizabeth, already some yards away, stopped to look, too, and stayed where she was long past when the vehicle had disappeared again, as if bracing herself for its return.

"Do you know who that was?" he challenged her.

She shook her head quickly. "No idea. Do people do that? Try to get a look at this place? Fans of the show or whatever?"

"It hasn't happened before." Not since Deader Than Ever had picketed them and their fans had thronged the place.

She shrugged. "I'm going to see those bison."

He watched her stride away, thoughts churning in his mind. She was lying. She'd never loved him.

She needed something else from him. Publicity, maybe? Did she want to advance her career by being on TV? Or did she harbor a grudge for the wrong his father had done to her parents? Had she come to wreak some twisted vengeance of her own?

He turned to stalk back to the bunkhouse.

And came face to face with Avery.

HAPPY FACE!

Avery could hear her acting coach's voice as clearly as if she was eight years old again, standing in the mirrored studio at Ms. Samuelson's acting academy.

I don't care if your dog died. When you step onstage, you play your part. You think Broadway stars sulk in their changing rooms if they have a hard day? They're professionals. They show up. They leave themselves at the door. They never let the company down!

Ms. Samuelson's directives had served her well many times during her life when she couldn't afford to let anyone see her true feelings, but Avery had never needed to call on them as much as she did right now. Funny how everyone always told her she wore her heart on her sleeve.

They didn't know her heart. Not really.

And Walker wasn't going to know it now.

Elizabeth hadn't come here on a whim. She loved him.

Had loved him all her life.

"Avery."

She put up a hand to stop Walker from advancing. If he touched her after Elizabeth had kissed him, it would cheapen everything they'd had so far. Maybe that was unfair. Maybe Walker wasn't to blame for Elizabeth's actions.

But he hadn't stopped her.

"I'm going to make this right," he said.

"How?"

He set his jaw and shook his head. "Trust me."

Trust him? Did he have any idea what he was asking of her?

He held out his hand. "Let's do our chores."

Avery let out a sound that was half laugh, half gasp of disbelief. Chores? With him—and Elizabeth? She'd heard what the other woman said. Elizabeth was here to be his wife, starting today.

"Are you sending her home?" she managed to ask, proud of the way her voice remained steady.

Walker hesitated, and Avery knew she'd lost him.

Elizabeth had some kind of hold over him. A promise. And the one thing Avery knew was how highly Walker valued his honor. It was why he hadn't led her on. "When I'm free," he told her once when he'd leaned in to kiss her, then drawn back before their mouths touched. At the time, she'd thought he was as frustrated by the waiting as she was.

But maybe she'd been reading too much into all that.

"I'll sort it out. I promise."

She didn't want to hear about promises. "I… can't do this." She turned on her heel and headed to the bunkhouse, bracing for him to come after her. Praying he would, even if the cameras followed him.

He didn't.

Avery checked over her shoulder despite telling herself not to, but the only ones behind her were crew members.

Walker was giving her up without a fight.

She swerved around the bunkhouse and scrubbed

the tears from her face with her sleeve as she stumbled along. How could she have been so fooled by him? She covered her face with her hands as shame heated her cheeks. He'd never made her any promises, had he? Not until yesterday. It was all looks and little courtesies and dry jokes that only they shared. She'd read love into his tenderness with her, desire into the time they'd spent doing chores. It could just as easily have been the kind of attention a bored man gave to the nearest woman when his real love was miles away.

If that were true, though, why would he say he was going to propose to her today?

She dried her cheeks again and marched on as it grew light. What did it matter? Today had arrived, and he hadn't proposed.

The truth was, Elizabeth had something she didn't have. Walker's ties to his grandmother and the Crow clan meant everything to him. His mother had never figured in his life. His grandparents in town had done their best but had little to offer him compared to the rich community he experienced on the reservation. Over time, the Crow side of his family had claimed his heart.

Elizabeth was part of that.

When her phone buzzed, Avery took the call without thinking and winced when she realized it was her mother. She was feeling far too raw to deal with her mom's happy chatter, but it was too late now.

"How's my favorite daughter?" Diana Lightfoot asked.

"I'm your only daughter," Avery said tiredly.

"You're still my favorite! Has Walker proposed yet, or is he waiting a couple of days to build tension?"

"He hasn't proposed," Avery said flatly.

"He will," Diana trilled. "I can't wait for your wedding. It's going to be so romantic, I just know it. You are cute as a bug, and he's so handsome!"

Nothing about this was romantic, but she couldn't say that to her mother. Her parents' story was all rainbows and sunshine, love at first sight and happily ever after. They called each other darling and honey bunch, tucked love notes into lunch bags and between the pages of books each other was reading, held hands when they walked and smiled when they met up again after the shortest separation.

Once she'd thought she'd have a love like that.

"What about your work? Have you convinced Fulsom to back your project?"

"Not likely." Avery nearly snorted. Fulsom had plenty of money to throw behind Renata and Eve's documentary ideas, but when she'd gathered her courage and called him directly to see if he was interested in funding the romantic comedy she was writing, she hadn't made it past his secretary. She'd let the other women know she was done with going along to get along. She'd be focusing on her own work from here on in, no matter how hard it might be to get anywhere with it. Since then, she'd found it hard to focus.

"You've given everything back you stole, right, honey? You know that worried me. I don't want the others to dislike you."

"I gave everything back." Avery counted to ten. God knew she wouldn't do anything to be disliked. Harmony and friendship, love and cuddles, that's what the Lightfoots were all about.

"Everything will work out. It always does. Oh, here comes your father with the biggest bunch of flowers you ever saw! We're heading out for our morning walk. Call you later, honey!"

Avery pocketed the phone with a sigh. Everything might work out for her parents, but they seemed to have cornered all the luck in the family.

Nothing ever worked out for her.

By lunchtime, she was barely holding on to her sanity, wondering what Walker and Elizabeth had been getting up to all this time. When she arrived at the bunkhouse for the meal, she found they'd beaten her there and were sitting on logs near the empty fire pit, balancing their plates on their laps. Elizabeth was watchful. Both of them silent. Avery slipped past them, entered the bunkhouse and got in line for food.

"When's that woman going to leave?" Hope asked her. She and her husband, Curtis, were in line ahead of Avery, and Curtis was already being served by Kai and Addison. Hope was tall and dark-haired, but Curtis was even taller, a big, burly man who worked on the houses with Clay and the rest of the building crew and carved wonderful things out of wood. Their dog, Daisy, waited patiently by the door.

Avery picked up a plate and moved along behind

Hope. "I don't know." She didn't want to talk about it, either.

"Here," Curtis said, handing his wife a full plate and taking the empty one she held.

"Walker's going to get rid of her, right? He wants to marry you."

Avery could only shrug. When Curtis's plate was full, he guided his wife outside. Daisy followed.

"I'll save you a spot," Hope called back at her.

Avery envied the couple their happiness. Curtis was always like that: solicitous of Hope's comfort and safety. Ever since she'd gotten pregnant, he'd grown even more careful around her, ready to guide her past the smallest obstacle in her path. They were always cuddling and kissing.

It was infuriating.

"Hi," she said to Kai and Addison when it was her turn.

"Salad today and Potatoes Montana."

Potatoes Montana was one of Kai's signature dishes, and Avery knew it contained bison meat, something she didn't allow herself to think too deeply about. She carried her plate outside, took a seat near Curtis and Hope and tried not to look at Walker and Elizabeth across the way.

"Hey, have you guys seen this video?" Hope said suddenly, her exclamation cutting through the rest of the conversations. "Looks like *Star News* started a new daily segment about us. It's supposed to showcase the ways in which viewers are changing their lives since watching *Base Camp*. That's what the tagline says, anyway. I get a notification when people talk about *Base Camp* online," she explained, taking in the confused expressions around the room.

"That's interesting." Riley perked up and reached for the phone, but Hope held on to it.

"Wait, *Star News*?" Boone asked. Avery understood his question. *Star News* didn't generally talk about subjects like sustainability—unless it was to downplay the need for it.

"Yes, *Star News*." Hope made a face. "I can only imagine what they have to say. I'll play the clip." She tapped the screen and held up the phone again. Even with the volume all the way up it was hard to hear, and everyone leaned in to try to make it out.

"It's a reporter on the street," Hope said. "She's interviewing people."

"*Base Camp?* It hasn't changed my life any," a man said on-screen. "I'm not interested in some hippie commune."

All around her, Avery heard her companions huff out exasperated breaths. One thing she'd learned this past year was that Navy SEALs don't care to be compared to hippies.

"My life has been changed by *Base Camp*. Now I gas up my Humvee every week and drive extra, just to show them!" another man said. "I don't need anyone telling me I'm ruining the environment."

Avery exchanged an alarmed glance with Savannah. Could their show really make people want to pollute *more?*

"I've started using reusable shopping bags," a woman said brightly. "I think we can all do our part to make this a better world."

"*Base Camp?* Never heard of it," another woman said.

"It's the one where everyone gets married," a younger voice piped up. The woman's daughter, maybe? Avery couldn't make out the images on the little screen.

"I think those people need to get off their asses and see how the real world lives," another voice said. "All I hear about is climate change. What about jobs? What about crime? When we figure them out, then we can figure out this climate thing."

"And there you have it," a cheerful announcer's voice finished the clip. "*Base Camp*. Seems to me it's not changing much of anything."

Hope lowered her phone and slipped it into the pocket of her green gown, exchanging a look with her husband.

A babble of voices welled up around Avery, none of them happy.

"They cherry-picked those comments," Clay said angrily.

"They weren't interviewing anyone in California, that's for sure," Savannah said.

"I never watch them anyway," Addison said.

"Why the hell are they running that segment?" Boone said. "Our show doesn't air on their channel." He caught sight of Walker, sitting by Elizabeth. "Why aren't you pissed?" he demanded.

"Told you ages ago. People don't change," Walker said. Beside him, Elizabeth nodded grimly.

"Walker's right," she said. "People don't want to hear about climate change. And other people don't want them to be told. It's against their interests."

"People change all the time," Curtis said to Walker. "If they didn't, there wouldn't be any progress at all in the world, and there's plenty of progress."

"There's plenty of money ready to stop it, too," Elizabeth countered. "You can't just be passionate; you have to be smart. This isn't a fight you can win in one television season. It might not be a fight you can win at all."

Her cynical statement left a stunned silence in its wake. After a moment, Walker got to his feet. Avery found herself holding her breath. Surely he couldn't believe that. Surely he'd say something—

But he didn't say a word. Instead he walked carefully to the bunkhouse with his dishes and came out again a moment later, empty-handed, to walk toward the barns.

"Guess lunchtime is over," Elizabeth said dryly and followed suit.

Avery ducked her head to avoid everyone's curious looks and moved her food around her plate with her fork until people turned to their neighbors and continued the conversation in smaller groups.

"That's a pretty nihilistic outlook Elizabeth has." Savannah leaned close to Avery. "I can't see Walker being attracted to a woman who thinks that way. It's not like him at all."

"It's exactly like him," Jericho countered. "You've seen Walker only around Avery." He cut off and cleared his throat. "I mean… he's always been pessimistic as hell. He didn't join Base Camp thinking we'd change the world, you know. He just needed something to do until it all crashes and burns."

"Nothing's going to crash and burn. Jericho, don't say that! That's awful!" Savannah took Jacob from his arms and held her baby close, kissing his cheek as if to protect him from such a future. "Everything is going to be fine," she crooned to him.

"I'm just saying what Walker thinks." Jericho shrugged.

"I think he's wrong," Hope said. "Maybe one show isn't going to change the world, but people will do the right thing when they realize how bad it all could get if they don't."

"Scientists have known about global warming for over a hundred years," Jericho pointed out. "The general public has known since the '70s. Nobody's done anything so far. What makes you think they're going to start now?"

Savannah stared at her husband. "They have to." She looked down at her son again pointedly.

Jericho swore beneath his breath. "I'm sorry. Of course we'll figure it out. Don't mind me, I'm just on edge because we're in the final stretch of this show, that's all."

Avery looked around her. Took in Boone and Riley

talking together. Clay and Nora leaning together on a log, Clay's father, Dell, close by. All the other couples talking over their meals.

She loved these people. Loved this life—and this world.

Elizabeth couldn't be right. They had to be able to fix things. As she watched Elizabeth head off after Walker, Avery wished she would keep on going and never come back.

"Oh!" Nora, sitting on a log nearby, suddenly leaned forward, her plate slipping from her hand.

"Nora?" Clay crouched next to her. "What is it?"

"Contraction," she said through gritted teeth, grabbing hold of his hand. She squeezed her eyes shut.

"Breathe, honey. Remember to breathe," Clay told her.

"I'll get her bag." Riley leaped to her feet and ran for Nora and Clay's house.

"I'll call the hospital and tell them we're coming," Boone said.

Avery looked for Walker, wanting to share the excitement of the moment with him—

And remembered he was gone.

"I REMEMBER, YOU know," Elizabeth said that night as they were getting ready for bed. Walker had no idea where Avery had gotten to. He wondered if Avery would simply refuse to sleep in the bunkhouse with Elizabeth here.

He'd phoned Sue from the hospital to make sure

she wasn't expecting them at dinnertime.

"No need for dinner when you're already living together" was all she'd said. "Elizabeth's got her bags with her. She'll stay with you from now on."

Trust the two of them to think Elizabeth was welcome here without so much as an invitation.

He'd given up, joining the others in the waiting room until Clay came to give them the good news.

After waiting two weeks past her due date, Constance Lizette Pickett had been in a big hurry to see the world, and she was born barely an hour after they'd checked into the hospital. Mother and baby were resting there now and would be discharged tomorrow.

"What do you remember?" he asked Elizabeth tiredly, wishing her back wherever it was she'd come from. Siberia would do just fine.

"The night we graduated. I remember what you said."

Walker wasn't following. Graduation? He was a kid back then. He remembered that night, though, now that she'd brought it up. The reservation school held its ceremony the same night as Chance Creek High. Elizabeth and Netta had stopped by to wish him well, and when the two grandmothers had gone into the kitchen to discuss plans for a party the next day, he'd found himself alone with Elizabeth, who'd told him of her big ideas to change the world. Neither of them had mentioned the promise they'd made half a year before, because neither of them cared a fig about it. Netta was fading and needed to lean on someone's arm when she walked. Her sister was coming to live with her in a week or so to help her until the end. Elizabeth had broached putting off going to college, but Netta insisted she keep to her plans.

"What did I say?" Elizabeth was persistent, and if she had some point to make, she'd make it.

"You said people don't change and never would. You said no amount of recycling would clean up the mess we've made. No amount of government rules would stop pollution. No amount of education would trim down people's buying habits. You told me I should quit trying before I started."

Hell. "I was right, wasn't I?" He wasn't ready to admit to Elizabeth he'd changed his mind. There'd been so much news about environmental degradation that year. The Amazon rainforest was disappearing; species were going extinct. But kids he knew from school were excited about the expansion of fracking in northeastern Montana and North Dakota. Talking about the money they could earn. Calling him an idiot for wasting his time at college.

"You said the world was doomed."

Walker stilled. Elizabeth dropped the bedding she'd been fussing with and came to stand in front of him. "You said you'd never marry and you certainly wouldn't have kids. You planned to walk away from all this when you turned thirty, move north into the wilderness and watch the rest of the world burn."

She had him there; that's exactly what he'd said. Thirty had seemed ancient back then. Now it was in his taillights.

"So what happened to change your mind? Did you see something during your Navy SEAL years that proved you wrong?"

Walker snorted. "Just the opposite," he admitted. "That's what got Boone, Clay and Jericho excited to build Base Camp in the first place. Everywhere we went we saw climate change in action. Not signs that it was coming; signs that it was already here causing problems all over the world."

"And yet you're going to marry me in thirty-nine days."

He swallowed the first words that came to mind: hell no. He couldn't say them until he knew what was going on. Not if she would hurt Sue in retaliation.

When she understood he wasn't going to answer her, she laughed derisively. "You were going to marry Avery, which is even worse. She believes in love and family, Walker. She wants children. Wants a future."

He wanted that, too, now.

"So what changed?" she demanded again.

He'd met Avery. He didn't want to say that to Elizabeth, though. She'd find a way to cheapen it. He didn't want to hear Avery's name in her mouth ever again.

When the bunkhouse door burst open, he was relieved.

Jericho rushed in.

"Get out here," he called to Walker, already back-pedaling. "Intruder. Someone's on the ranch."

Immediately on alert, he snapped, "Lock the door

behind me," and hurried after Jericho. Outside, men had gathered and Boone was issuing orders.

"Clay, Angus, check around the tiny houses. Tell all the women to lock their doors. Greg, Kai, is anyone up at the manor? Check it out."

"What happened?" Walker asked. "Where's Avery?"

"I saw someone near the barn but lost them," Harris said. "He was armed. Heading this way, but he might have already made it past us—lit out for the creek or something."

"Avery's with Savannah," Jericho added. "She was going to spend the night there since I'm on guard duty."

"Jericho and Walker, you check out Pittance Creek."

It was over an hour before they reassembled, and by then Walker thought half of them were wondering if Harris had been seeing things. Walker doubted that. Harris was ever-vigilant and had the best eyesight of anyone he knew. If he said a stranger was on the ranch, then one definitely was.

They collected the women, gathered in the bunk-house, where Elizabeth waited stoically for them. "Was someone there?" she demanded as soon as Walker appeared.

He shook his head.

"Someone *was* there," Harris asserted. "I saw him skulking in the shadows near the barn. Would have missed him entirely if the chickens hadn't been making a racket."

"You think it's about Hansen Oil again?" Hope asked Anders.

"We already handled that," Anders said.

"I'm going to make a stink about this to Fulsom," Boone said quietly. "If he has anything to do with it, it's crossing a line. Meanwhile, we need to operate as if this threat is going to remain imminent and unrelenting. No one goes anywhere alone. Anyone not on patrol sleeps in the bunkhouse. We get our chores done in groups. Everyone armed. Got it?"

They all nodded.

"Right, everyone move in here for the rest of the night."

There was a lot of grumbling, but they all got to work, the couples tramping out into the night to their tiny houses to collect their things.

"You know anything about this?" Walker said to Elizabeth when they were alone again.

"Why would I know anything about it?" she shot back.

"Because first you came and then he did."

She held his gaze defiantly. "Seems to me your lot attracts trouble well enough on your own without having to accuse me." She got back to making up her bed, and by the time the others began to trail in with their gear, she was already under the covers, pretending to be asleep.

"YOU CAN'T KEEP wearing clothes like that," Leslie said the following morning when Elizabeth emerged from the bathroom dressed in jeans and a blue cotton shirt. "All the women of Base Camp wear Regency gowns.

You'll have to get some from Alice at Two Willows."
She lifted her skirts and turned in a circle so Elizabeth
could see what she meant.

"I don't think so," Elizabeth said scathingly, and
Avery winced, but Leslie wasn't fazed.

"It's tradition. You wouldn't want to break tradition.
That's one of the things that makes Base Camp special—" She broke off when Elizabeth walked right past
her out the door.

Walker heaved a sigh and followed her.

Leslie turned to Avery. "I guess some people think
they're better than the rest of us. The joke's on her,
though. It's always more fun to join in than keep on the
outside of things. Don't you think?"

Avery didn't think anything was going to be much
fun while Elizabeth was around. She finished getting
ready for the day and went outside, too.

"Ugh, *Star News* is at it again," Hope was saying as
Avery joined the others grouped around the empty fire
pit on logs. The day had dawned clear and hot, and she
thought everyone was out of sorts. She'd barely slept
the night before, all their bodies crammed into the
bunkhouse close together. She'd been so grateful to
Savannah for inviting her to spend the night in her tiny
house—and so frustrated to be forced back into the
bunkhouse with Walker, Elizabeth and everyone else.

Hope held up her phone so everyone could hear the
Star News announcer.

"Tell me who on earth would voluntarily live in one
of those tiny houses Clay Pickett and his father build?" a

blonde was saying on screen. "They're not tiny, they're infinitesimal. Can you imagine how you'd feel about your spouse after a week in there? I bet those couples fight morning, noon and night, but you never see that on the show, do you? Face it, the whole thing is fake."

"I agree, Marla," a man said. "And that's the problem with television today. You can't believe anything. That settlement isn't run on green energy; it couldn't be. Everyone knows how inefficient solar and wind power is. Do they want us to believe the sun shines twenty-four hours a day in Montana—even in the winter?"

"What is he talking about?" Jericho sputtered. "Hasn't he ever heard of batteries?"

"It's all fake," the man went on. "Every last bit of it. Remember when Clay's wife, Nora, was being stalked? Fake! Her pregnancy is probably fake, too."

"It's a travesty, Paul," Marla agreed. "You can't believe anything you hear, and you certainly can't believe anything you see. Climate change isn't even happening, and if it is, it's a completely normal process. Why can't these *Base Camp* folks admit that?"

Avery was glad Nora wasn't home yet and Clay was with her at the hospital waiting for her discharge.

"And don't even get me started on Harris and his forge," Marla said. "A forge, folks. In the twenty-first century. Yeah, making iron implements the old-fashioned way is going to save us all."

"I never said it would save anyone," Harris sputtered. "It's an art form. A way of slowing down and appreciating life."

"Don't listen to them," Samantha told him, touching his arm.

"As for Samantha, sheesh," Paul said on screen. "I guess you can't expect much from a groupie who drove the bus for Deader Than Ever for over a decade." Both hosts cackled. "What do you think she's growing in those greenhouses, eh, Marla? A little something they can all smoke? No wonder they're clueless."

Samantha grabbed the phone from Hope's hand and stopped the playback.

"We don't need to listen to that," she said.

"We need to know what lies they're telling people about us so we can make sure we counter them," Hope said. She turned to the nearest crew members. "You have to make sure you get footage that shows they're lying."

"Anyone who believes those lies is a fool!" Samantha said.

"What if they don't know any different?" Win spoke up. "What if they're not watching *Base Camp*, so what *Star News* broadcasts is all they know about us? In that case, it won't matter what we do on the show. Why isn't Fulsom doing something about this?"

"Are you kidding?" Renata spoke up. "He must love this. He probably planted the idea in some *Star News* lackey's head. Controversy, remember? He loves controversy."

"Well, I'm not letting this slide anymore," Hope said. "We have to counter their accusations on our website. Put up information of our own that clearly outlines our position. I'll take that on."

Avery couldn't listen to any more of it. She took her plate inside the bunkhouse, dropped it off in the kitchen and was just leaving again when Boone cornered her.

"Can we talk?"

"Do we have to?" She wanted to find some chore to do that would leave her so busy she didn't notice Elizabeth trailing after Walker like a sixth grader after her first boyfriend.

"We have to," Boone said.

"Fine." She followed him a little apart from the others, trailed by a camera crew, of course.

"There's no good way to say this, so I'll just say it," he started. "I don't know what's going to happen with Walker and Elizabeth. I know he loves you," he added, heading off her protests, "but Walker is a man of honor, and there's something about this promise he made he obviously doesn't think he can just walk away from. Fulsom has got a rule: no one on set who's not in the process of working toward being married. I got a call from him this morning, checking up on things. He made it clear; I've got to find you a backup husband."

Avery stared at him. Was he serious? "You've got to be kidding. I've been here from day one."

"I wish I was, but I'm not. You don't have to like the backup, you certainly don't have to marry him, but you have to be filmed spending enough time with him to keep Fulsom happy. Got it? I'll have him here in a day or two."

Avery heaved a sigh. "Fine. Get me a backup husband. Get me twenty."

"Avery," Boone called after her as she walked away. "I'm rooting for you two, you know that, right?"

She didn't bother to answer. Boone caught up to her, and when she turned to tell him off, Harris and Samantha were there, too.

"We travel in groups from now on," Boone reminded her. "Someone was on the property."

"Oh, come on." Avery bit off the rest of what she wanted to say. Harris had seen someone near the barn last night, and Boone was right to put safety first. She longed for the day when life could feel normal again, though.

Whenever that might be.

"I just want to check on the bison," she said.

"Then we'll check on the bison together."

Avery kept going, feeling like a fool trailed by her entourage, and when she reached the bison pasture and saw Elizabeth standing at the fence cooing to Champ, she nearly growled in frustration and would have retreated if Elizabeth hadn't beckoned her forward. They all crowded around her.

"Where's Walker?" Avery asked, but she spotted him talking to Jericho closer to the barn. He'd spotted them, too, and she realized he was keeping an eye on Elizabeth.

"You're not supposed to be alone," Boone told her.

"I'm not." Elizabeth pointed to the two men nearby. "I'm just seeing how the bison calf is doing. God, it's cute."

"It is," Avery admitted. She didn't like this new, human side to Elizabeth. Elizabeth was supposed to be all bad, so she could hate her. Boone and the others moved to talk to Walker and Jericho.

"You've done a lot of work this past year," Elizabeth mused when they were gone. "All those tiny houses. The wind turbines. Everything."

"It's what we're here for."

"Thought you were here to save the world."

"It's the same thing." She didn't want to be sparring with this flint-sharp woman who'd known Walker far longer than she had.

"It's not the same at all, you know." Elizabeth's gaze flicked over her. "You're sending the wrong message altogether."

"How so?" Avery was losing her temper. It was one thing to try to take Walker away—any sane woman would want a piece of him. It was another to talk down their efforts here.

"It's not individuals who are the problem; it's industry. It's government. We're one or two court battles, one or two pieces of legislation away from total disaster. You want to save the world, you need to start educating people on how to lobby the government. That's what big businesses are doing. They're spending millions making sure lawmakers don't regulate them the way they need to. They're fielding candidates for office. Every American could put a wind turbine in their front yard, and they'd still find a way to pump out enough carbon to heat up the earth and fry us all."

"You sound like Walker when he doesn't know I'm listening," Avery said. He was far more cynical when he thought she wasn't around.

Elizabeth rolled her eyes. "Walker sounds like you these days," she corrected her, "all light and hope and unicorns. In a few generations global warming could decimate bison herds like this. Everything we care about could be gone."

"Which is why we have to keep doing whatever we can!"

Elizabeth sighed. "That's what I keep telling myself, but sometimes I wonder—why not forget it? Why not just take a round-the-world cruise, see it all before it disappears? I don't have kids. What do I care what the world looks like in fifty years—or a hundred?"

"If you feel that way, why marry Walker?" Avery asked her.

The look Elizabeth gave her twisted something low in Avery's gut. Determination and desperation were at war there, and for a moment Avery almost pitied her. When Elizabeth turned on her heel and walked away to join the others without answering, all her pity evaporated, and anger simmered in its place. Elizabeth didn't deserve Walker. She certainly didn't love him.

Avery wasn't going to give him up without a fight.

CHAPTER THREE

A WEEK LATER, Walker ducked into the stables after a quick trip to the bunkhouse to grab a drink, and found Elizabeth on her phone, her back to the door. Greg and Hope were sorting through tack at the far end, out of earshot. Avery was hard at work mucking out a stall at the far end of the row.

He edged closer silently, wondering who Elizabeth was talking to.

"I'm being careful," he heard her say. "There are ten Navy SEALs here and cameras on me at all times." He must have made a sound because she turned, spotted him and frowned. "It's under control." She ended the call and faced him.

He waited until she'd pocketed her phone and picked up a pitchfork. "You're with the EPA, right?" He hoped she'd think he hadn't heard anything. She hadn't sounded like she was talking to a boss or coworker. More like someone who cared enough about her to worry about her safety. Had she told him or her about the intruder?

She headed for the nearest stall. "That's right."

"Shouldn't you be working, then?" He stepped in front of her, opened the door and sent Lucifer into the corral outside the stable. Elizabeth began mucking out the stall as soon as the horse left.

"I'm on leave."

Leave was temporary. Did that mean she didn't actually intend to marry him? Or that she'd put her job on hold until the show was over? He figured a direct question wouldn't get him any answers. Elizabeth seemed determined to keep him off-balance.

"You're researching wildfires and air quality?" He pulled that last fact out of his memory. Something Sue had told him once when he hadn't asked about Elizabeth. She was always feeding him tidbits of information despite his lack of curiosity. "Elizabeth is moving up in the ranks. She got a promotion." He'd barely bothered to listen.

"That's right."

"There've been some fires around here the last few years." The cold winters they'd had didn't seem to stop them.

"It'll be worse this year."

His head snapped up at that. "You think?" The way temperatures had shot up in the past days had left him worried about what the summer would bring, but Elizabeth was the expert.

She nodded.

"That's what the government is saying?"

She rolled her eyes. "That's what I'm saying. I can't

predict the weather any better than anyone else, Walker, but I've worked fires for years. I've got a feeling."

Walker was a big believer in feelings. They both grew up here and knew Montana in all its moods.

Elizabeth got back to work without answering the real question he wanted to ask. Why had she come here? The girl he grew up with wouldn't throw over work she loved for an old promise she never believed in.

It wasn't like Elizabeth had been pining for him, either, no matter what she claimed now. She'd never shown him an ounce of respect, let alone desire when they were young. As for him, she wasn't his type. Even if he'd never met Avery and he wanted a partner, he wouldn't choose a wife so aloof from him. Sue was aloof like that. His father had been, as well.

He wanted something different.

Hell, he hadn't wanted anything at all—not for years. Not knowing the way the world was going. Now he did, and it was going to be taken away from him.

"Why are you here?"

Elizabeth sighed and leaned on her pitchfork. "I made a promise—" She cut off and started again. "We made a promise to someone special, Walker. To the one person who was always there for me. I intend to keep it. Don't you understand that?"

Another gut punch. Walker grabbed a rake. Elizabeth knew all his buttons. Knew calling on Netta's memory would strip him of all his ammunition against her, since he wanted to honor Sue as much as she wanted to honor Netta. They were all caught in a spider's web of duty, and Elizabeth was tugging on a crucial strand. She had the power to cut through the ties that bound them or to snare him tight.

She was choosing to snare him.

"Netta wanted us to be together," Elizabeth said primly. A corner of her mouth quirked. "Don't forget I'm madly in love with you."

She didn't sound madly in love, and Netta had been terrified of the thought of leaving an eighteen-year-old Elizabeth alone in the world, that's all. Now Elizabeth was a grown woman. She didn't need anyone to take care of her.

"Why do you think I'll go through with it?"

Elizabeth blew out a breath. "Because you promised Netta—and Sue. And you don't break promises. Especially one that gives you the chance to make up for what your father did."

After that, Elizabeth didn't speak at all.

She didn't have to. Bringing up his father was a punch below the belt that left him feeling helpless. Despite what Sue thought, he'd always felt Netta and Elizabeth had forgiven Joe. What if he was wrong? Did Elizabeth hate his father? Would she hold him accountable for Joe's sins?

He fought the urge to throw the rake to the ground, push past Elizabeth and get the hell out of here, take one of the trucks and drive.

He could abandon it somewhere up north. Go deep into the woods.

Disappear.

Down the row, he heard Avery talking to Hope, and he swallowed down the frustration burning in his throat. He caught Elizabeth watching him, her expression almost pitying.

He set the pitchfork aside as carefully as he could. "Need some air," he growled and moved for the stable door again, cursing the necessity to stay close to the others. He stood outside it, took a few deep breaths and got himself under control.

The morning seemed endless, and when their chores were done, Walker led the way to the bison pasture like he and Avery always did to check on the herd. It wouldn't be the same with Elizabeth and Hope trailing them, but he hoped a little time with the herd would put things in perspective.

Avery walked ahead, eager to see Champ cavort around its mother. Walker wished he could speak to her alone, but Elizabeth stuck close.

"That's a healthy calf," she said as they approached the fence.

"He really is beautiful," Avery said. When Champ got too rambunctious and nearly tripped over its own feet, a fleeting smile quirked her lips. "Aren't you?" she called out to the animal. "Aren't you beautiful?" She stepped along the pasture fence, getting closer to it. Hope followed her. Walker noticed she'd taken on an almost protective role, placing herself between Avery and Elizabeth whenever she could.

"That girl feels things too much," Elizabeth muttered.

Avery was crooning to the calf now, trying to entice it closer.

"Maybe she feels the right amount," he countered in an equally low tone. "Maybe we should all feel so strongly."

Elizabeth studied him. "I think—"

"Walker! Avery!" a familiar voice trilled from some distance behind them.

"Expecting someone?" Elizabeth turned and her eyebrows shot up. Walker knew why. That was Maud Russell's voice, and Maud Russell could be a shock to anyone's system. He braced himself as the stout older woman and her husband hurried their way, waving and calling out.

"Oh, my God, they're even worse in person," Elizabeth said.

"They're good people." Walker didn't want to think about Elizabeth watching the show enough to know who Maud and James Russell were. They'd appeared on a number of episodes but were by no means on every week.

Had Elizabeth watched *Base Camp* front to back, studying each episode to determine just how far his relationship with Avery was progressing? Had she balanced her need to finish her work in Siberia with knowing she had to get back to Montana before he married someone else?

The idea of it made his skin crawl.

"How can they live like that?" Elizabeth asked.

He knew what she meant. While the women of Base

Camp wore their gowns to signify their dedication to their various creative pursuits—and as part of running a Regency-inspired bed-and-breakfast—the Russells had simply decided they preferred the Regency to the current age and went about life as if they were living in it.

James and Maud Russell attended every Jane Austen re-enactment they could. They lived in a true manor-size house, with kitchen staff, and drove everywhere they possibly could in a carriage. Their outsized personalities took over any social situation, and they loved to throw parties and include the inhabitants of Base Camp.

Their arrival freed him of having to answer Elizabeth's question. As far as he could tell, the Russells were experts at creating the reality in which they wanted to live.

He wished he was.

Avery left her post at the pasture fence and came forward to give them both hugs. "Maud, James, good to see you." Was it Walker's imagination, or did she cling to Maud a little longer than usual?

"We're hosting a small get-together tonight," Maud said without preamble and beamed at them, as if assured they'd be as thrilled to receive the news as she was to pass it on. "I do hope you'll join us. And I see you have a guest with you. Please, by all means, join us tonight," she told Elizabeth. "I'm Maud Russell, and this is my husband, James."

"This is Elizabeth Blaine, a friend of my family," Walker supplied. "She grew up on the reservation, like I did."

"Wonderful! You will come, won't you?"

"I don't think so," Elizabeth said shortly. "I'm not much of a partygoer." She could barely hide her distaste at the Russells' elaborate costumes, and Walker had the urge to nudge her to remind her of her manners. "I'll be at the bunkhouse," she told Walker and strode off before he could tell her they were supposed to stay with their groups. He relaxed when he saw Boone and his crew meet up with her not far away. Boone turned, waved at Walker and moved on with her at the center of his work party.

"Well," Maud said, looking after her. "One doesn't like to see such diffidence in a young lady. She'll wind up a spinster with an attitude like that."

Avery covered up a choked exhalation with a cough. Caught Walker's eye, flushed and turned away. Maud patted her on the back solicitously. "Do you have something in your throat, dear?"

"I'm… fine."

"Never mind, my love," James said to his wife. "We'll still have plenty of company without her. But you make sure your friend knows she's always welcome," he added to Walker. "Some people don't like invitations that take them unawares, you know. She may come to a different opinion of the matter later."

"That's true," Maud said cheerfully, giving Avery a final pat. "I'll tell Mrs. Wood to set an extra place at the table just in case! See you tonight!" She took her husband's arm, and they hustled off toward the bunkhouse.

"If Elizabeth is going to marry you, she should be nice to your friends," Avery said tartly when they were gone and Hope had moved back to the fence to watch Champ gambol about.

"She's not going to marry me," Walker said.

"Really?" A flash of hope crossed Avery's face, but she caught herself and schooled it into an indifferent nod. "Someone should tell her that." She turned on her heel and went to the pasture fence. When he made to follow her, she held up a hand. "You've got a fiancée. Go spend time with her."

"I don't have a fiancée."

"Then what do you have?"

"I've got a family problem I have to sort out." He swallowed the frustration building inside him. This was all his fault; Avery was the victim here, and she didn't deserve to be the recipient of his anger. He couldn't explain more than thirty years of history to her in a moment. Didn't want to explore his family's dirty laundry with a camera crew filming all of it. Sue would hate that. It had been bad enough the first time around.

He could show Avery how he felt about her, though. He moved closer. Took her hand gently and drew her in against him. "You know I want you."

"No, I don't."

Avery stood rigidly in his arms, but Walker was patient. He knew she felt as strongly for him as he did for her. They worked together, always had. She was fighting it, but he could see it was a losing battle, and when she finally relaxed against him, he circled his arms around her, needing her even closer. Avery's curves sparked a hunger in him he knew could never be satisfied. He'd need a lifetime with her.

"No." Avery pushed him away, and he let go, surprised at her vehemence. "You don't get to make me feel like this when you've got another woman waiting for you in the bunkhouse."

"A woman I don't want."

"A woman you haven't sent away," Avery countered.

"Because I can't. Because—"

She waited for his explanation, but how could Walker explain generations of pain and obligation? She didn't grow up on the reservation. Didn't know how important promises could be when your people had once been hunted and hounded and forced into settlements that bore no resemblance to their previous way of life. Off the reservation, a man's word meant little these days. You could always explain your behavior based on extenuating circumstances. Change your mind? Let down a friend? Renege on an obligation? Who cared? There was enough money, people, possessions, distractions to solve any little crisis your behavior might cause.

On the reservation, things were different. Everything was finite, everything counted—and a broken promise could lay waste to networks and alliances that held the whole nation together.

He'd spent a lifetime keeping his family's secrets.

Spilling them now felt like—

Walking on his father's grave.

"I'll get it sorted out," he said.

"You could sort it out today if you wanted to. Right now. Find Elizabeth. Tell her you don't want her. Send her on her way."

"It's not that simple." His family owed Elizabeth's family a debt that couldn't be repaid. If he broke his word, it would kill Sue. She was depending on him to redeem his father, to set right the wrongs he'd committed. Sue might not be demonstrative, but she'd loved her son. Sometimes Walker thought it was a miracle she remained alive with his father gone. Especially after Netta passed away.

Her determination to set things right was part of what drove her. All that would be undone if he broke the promise he'd made to Elizabeth. He needed to give her time to admit she didn't want him. "Be patient. Elizabeth won't marry me. You'll see."

"She won't marry *you*?" Avery echoed. "But you'll marry her if need be?"

"I don't want to."

"This is ridiculous. Walker, talk to her. Tell her what you want."

The one thing he couldn't do—not without pushing Sue to the brink. He reached for Avery again, but she nimbly evaded him, backpedaling out of reach.

"She'll make you leave, you know. Elizabeth," she added when he didn't respond. "I looked her up, and her work takes her around the world for months—

years—at a time. She'll take you away from Base Camp. Is that what you want?"

She didn't give him time to answer.

Walker watched her walk away, her back straight, her head high. He knew Avery well enough to know she'd be fighting against tears by now. She hated any tension in the social fabric, especially between them.

Like Elizabeth said, she felt things too strongly.

Hope rushed past him in pursuit. "Walker, we're supposed to stay together!"

He heaved a sigh and followed them.

"AVERY, THERE YOU are! I was just coming to look for you!"

Avery sighed when Boone came bounding up, wishing more than anything she could escape to the manor, let herself into one of the guest rooms, lock the door behind her and be alone for a while.

She couldn't keep going on this path, waiting to find out what Walker planned to do instead of making up her own mind about her future. She needed time to harden her heart if Elizabeth was going to make off with him in the end.

She'd never seen him so stymied by a situation, and that left her deeply unsettled. Normally when a problem came up, Walker surveyed his options and acted decisively. She'd never seen him second-guess himself until Elizabeth came.

For some reason, he'd assumed Elizabeth wouldn't want him and was surprised when she'd showed up and said she did. He didn't seem to think he could call off the relationship but felt Elizabeth had that right. Why?

"What do you need?" she asked Boone, still tangled in her thoughts. Had Walker expected Elizabeth to come home, tell Sue no and let him off the hook?

She couldn't square that with the take-charge man she knew.

"I'm taking Avery to join my crew," he called back to Walker and the others.

"We'll make sure you get there okay." Walker and the others followed them to the back of the bunkhouse and stood watch while they walked.

"Is that really necessary?" she asked Boone, gesturing to them.

Boone didn't bother to answer that. "Come and see what we're doing." As they drew near the greenhouses, she was surprised to see them empty. They kept going, and soon she saw a small group gathered where the ground began to slope upward. Several men were pounding in stakes, and beyond them a series of rectangles were laid out along the rising ground. Renata was directing a film crew to capture the activities. Jericho, Savannah, Clay and his father, Dell Picket, Angus, Win, Byron and Leslie were looking at plans.

"We'll put in a geothermal system, of course," Clay was saying when she drew near, speaking loudly for the sake of the film crew. "And the design for these homes will be slightly different from the first set we built."

"We'll add more wind turbines to our grid," Jericho added happily. "And the homes will have solar, of course. There are some great new panels that integrate right into the roofing materials…"

They were talking about expanding Base Camp, Avery realized. Bringing in new people to grow the sustainable community once the show was over and they'd won. Everything would change around here. No film crews. More newcomers.

She hadn't let herself think about that yet.

"We'll need more greenhouses, too," Boone called out as they approached the others. "I've got some new ideas for those."

"Aren't you putting the horse cart the horse?" Renata asked. Even though she had married Greg Devon and was officially part of the cast of *Base Camp* now, she still helped to direct the show, and today she was acting as interviewer. "After all, Walker's not married yet."

"He will be," Angus said confidently. "He's got two women after him now." He caught sight of Avery behind Boone and coughed. "I mean—sorry, Avery. That wasn't a very good joke."

She hoped her cheeks weren't burning, but she refused to turn and run away, knowing all this would end up in the next episode. Besides, everyone would probably follow her.

"Come on, take a look." Boone steered her to the rectangles marked on the hillside. "A whole new neighborhood. Look at the views from here. We're taking all we've learned from building the previous houses and making these even better. Clay, show Avery the plans for one of your new houses."

As the crew filming them turned to focus on her, a thought occurred to Avery. Boone had come to find her specifically; he hadn't asked Walker or Elizabeth to come along—or even Hope.

Because Walker and Hope had tiny homes already, and Boone thought Elizabeth would soon share Walker's?

"Why are you showing this to me?" she demanded.

Did Boone even care who Walker married? Probably not as long as he was able to stay at Base Camp, she decided. Boone would do anything to keep Riley happy, which meant he'd do anything to accomplish the goals set out by Fulsom.

Including accepting Elizabeth as Walker's wife.

She looked around at the ring of faces watching her. They would all do that, if it came to it.

"Why?" she asked again. She wasn't going to let Boone off the hook.

"Because—" Boone stopped.

"Because Walker is going to marry Elizabeth?" she prompted. "And you're going to shunt me out here in the suburbs away from everyone else? Is that your plan?"

She couldn't believe Boone had the guts to try to spin it as a good thing.

"I'm not shunting you anywhere. I'm trying to tell you you're still part of Base Camp no matter what Walker does."

Still part of Base Camp? Had that ever been in question?

Fury flooded her. She'd come to Westfield the same day he had.

"These new houses are roomier, for one thing," Boone went on. "We've figured out a way to make them more efficient so we can up the footprint, and we've got an improved system for piping water to them, and—" He caught sight of her face, ran both hands over his short hair, then held them to the sky. "Look, I don't want this either, but Walker's ties to the reservation..." He shrugged. "I don't understand how it all works. It's like Sue has something over him."

"If he wants to marry Elizabeth, he can." She crossed her arms over her chest, struggling to contain the pain threatening to overtake her. She'd be damned if she was going to live in the new settlement away from all her friends, no matter what he said.

It's just a few hundred yards away, she told herself sternly, but she knew it wouldn't be the same. She'd be lumped in with the newcomers, and Elizabeth would take her place as a founding member of Base Camp. How was it fair that Riley, Savannah and Nora, who'd come here with her, were getting everything they wanted while she was being pushed aside? What had she ever done to deserve being treated like this?

"He wants you," Boone said bluntly. "But want comes second to honor with Walker. You know that."

His understanding surprised her. "What does Elizabeth have on him?"

"Wish I knew, but I don't. There are some parts of his life he keeps zipped up."

She took a ragged breath. "So you can't help."

"Not with that."

"Hang on," Renata interjected. She held up a finger, and everyone paused while she pulled out her phone and took a call. Avery exchanged a puzzled glance with Boone. Renata never stopped filming, especially in the middle of getting footage that would definitely land on the show. When she hung up, she was smiling. "I'm so glad you're here, Avery. It's perfect timing."

"For what?" Avery didn't think she could take much more today.

"You asked Boone for a backup husband a while back, didn't you?"

Avery groaned. "And then Fulsom said I have to have one whether I want to or not. Boone Rudman, tell me you didn't put out an ad for a husband for me."

"You knew I had to," he said defensively, "but I haven't started going through responses yet. I was letting them pile up."

"Well, I have," Renata said. "I found you the perfect backup husband. His name is Gabe Reller, and his cab just pulled into the parking lot. Let's go. We'll meet him at the bunkhouse."

Disbelief flooded Avery. "You got me a backup husband? You can't be serious," she hissed at Renata. "You're supposed to be a friend."

"I am a friend. Fulsom will kick you off the show if you don't have one. Wouldn't you rather I pick him out than Boone?"

"I suppose so."

"I'm good at picking out backups," Boone put in.

Renata ignored him. There was nothing for it but to follow everyone else to the parking area. What kind of man had Renata picked out for her? Who would want the job?

"Gabe is a scientist. Something to do with climate change, which is what caught my eye. Seems really nice. Maybe you'll like him." Renata marched on, everyone else trailing her.

Avery stalked past her toward the bunkhouse, burning for the chance to tell this interloper where he could get off.

When she arrived there, however, Elizabeth was already squaring off with the stranger, a muscular blond man wearing what looked to Avery like high-end hiking gear. She had one hand on her hip, the other wagging in the man's face, but when she caught sight of Avery, she cut off mid-sentence. Both of them watched her approach, Elizabeth warily, the man with a speculative look in his eyes.

"You the guy who thinks he's hot shit enough to be my backup husband?" Avery asked him.

To her surprise, Elizabeth laughed. The man scowled.

"I'm—"

"Gabe Reller. I know. What I don't know is why you're barging in here where you're not wanted." She crossed her arms, hoping to look intimidating.

"That's exactly what I asked him," Elizabeth said crisply.

"That's rich. You barged in where you're not wanted, too," Jess called out from behind her camera.

"Pipe down!" Renata barked at her.

"Sorry!"

Gabe smiled ruefully. "Barging in where I'm not wanted seems to be my specialty," he admitted. "I'm here because I'm dying to check out Base Camp for myself and see if I can help in some way. A friend turned me on to the show, and I've been watching it avidly ever since."

Elizabeth snorted. "Don't trust him, Avery. Anyone can tell he's one of those guys who thinks everything's about him. Believe me, I know his type—I work with men like him all the time."

Avery glanced at the crew ringing them. They were loving this.

"What makes you think you can help?" she asked Gabe.

"Don't encourage him," Elizabeth said.

What was her problem? Renata had said he was a climate scientist. Had they crossed paths before? "Do you know him or something?" Avery demanded.

"I know his type," she snapped. "Do-gooders who don't believe in mixing politics with science."

"Maybe that's because mixing the two can be dangerous," he countered.

Was there such thing as rival wildfire scientists? Avery wasn't sure, but Gabe and Elizabeth were glaring at each other like lifelong enemies.

"Aren't you happy Gabe is here?" Avery asked Elizabeth. "You came to steal Walker from me. You should be glad I have a backup husband."

"Exactly what I was telling her before you came," Gabe said smugly.

Elizabeth blinked. "You know what? You're right. I don't care what you do. Invite him to stay. Marry him if you want to."

"Maybe I will." Avery looked over Gabe frankly. Anyone who could rile up Elizabeth was okay in her books. "I could do worse, I guess."

"Thanks a lot," Gabe said dryly.

"Whatever." Elizabeth stepped into the bunkhouse and shut the door behind her.

"You sure got on her bad side fast," Avery said.

"Guess it's a good thing I'm not here to marry her. Now what do we do?" he added. "Like I said, I watch *Base Camp*. I know you want to marry Walker Norton, and I understand you probably aren't too pleased to see me, but will you at least show me around before you kick me out?"

She supposed she could do that. She liked Gabe's forthrightness. They could use some of that around here. "We have to travel in groups," she informed him. "Someone was sneaking around the place last night." She turned to Boone. "Should we give Gabe a tour?"

"What's going on out here?" Walker came out of the bunkhouse, and Avery wondered if Elizabeth had said something about Gabe's arrival. Maybe Walker needed a reminder why it would be worth the discomfort of standing up to Sue in order to save their relationship.

"This is my backup husband, Gabe Reller," she told him. "I'm about to give him a tour of the place." She took Gabe's arm. "What would you like to see first?"

JEALOUSY RIPPED THROUGH Walker when Avery took Gabe's arm. He wanted to knock Gabe aside. Tell him to get the hell off the property—away from his woman.

But Avery wasn't his woman, and it was all his fault.

He forced himself to keep quiet as they walked away. Felt for the door handle behind him and stumbled back inside.

"Did you get a load of Romeo and Juliet out there?" Elizabeth asked. She was holding a cup of tea, gazing out a back window, through which Walker could see Avery, Gabe and the others heading for the greenhouses.

"Yeah," he made himself say, wincing at the roughness of his voice. "You must be happy. Your competition is distracted."

"I always thought she'd marry you in the end," Elizabeth said absently.

"What?" Walker straightened with surprise.

Elizabeth came to herself and turned sharply away from the window, nearly spilling her tea.

"You thought she'd marry *me*?" he pressed. "But you said—"

"I was making a joke." She took a sip from her mug and swore. "That's hot." She waved away his next question. "I'm here to marry you, you know that. Stop trying to find ways to wiggle out of it."

"You're the one who—" Walker didn't bother to finish his statement. "Tell me this, then. Who are you always talking to on your phone?" He needed something to focus his anger on. Might as well be her.

"Work."

"I thought you were on leave."

"They can't seem to do without me."

"And when you're married? What then? Are you going to take off again? Leave me holding the bag?"

She sighed. "Walker, give me a break. I'm doing the best I can."

Walker went to the window, but Avery and the others were out of sight. Could she really marry another man? Live on the same ranch as him and Elizabeth?

That would be hell.

"I can't do this."

He didn't realize he'd said the words out loud until Elizabeth set down her tea on the nearest flat surface and marched right over to him.

"You will do this." She jabbed a finger in his chest. "You will do this because you owe me. Because your family owes mine. Because my parents are gone, and you owe me every goddamn thing you can."

She left him stunned, slamming the bunkhouse door behind her. Alone in the sudden silence, Walker felt all chance for happiness in this lifetime slip away.

She was right; he owed her everything.

Which meant he was going to lose it all.

"I THINK IT'S a great location," Gabe was saying enthusiastically about the new settlement when a group of men Avery didn't recognize tromped over the crest of the hillside, their arms full of wooden stakes and white ribbon. She was already regretting her moment of false enthusiasm for giving Gabe a tour. For one thing, she didn't want to encourage Renata, Boone or anyone else to interfere in her life. For another, she didn't want to push Walker into Elizabeth's arms.

Did he understand her feelings were hurt, or did he think she was callous enough she could transfer her affections to someone else? She had every right to be angry and upset, she told herself, but she couldn't help but worry she'd cut off her nose to spite her face.

"What on earth? Who are those guys?" Boone pointed at a group of strangers a few hundred yards ahead of them. He hurried in their direction, the rest of their little group trailing behind.

"Are those surveyors?" Avery asked, taking in the equipment they were carrying.

"They could be," Gabe said.

"Do you think Montague sent them?" Savannah asked.

"Probably." Jericho scowled. "Out to make more trouble."

Boone had reached them already and was deep in conversation, gesticulating as he spoke. "...don't have any right to be working here. We haven't lost yet!" he was saying as they approached.

"Fulsom gave us permission," a man said. "Montague needs us to survey the property so he can start making plans. It's already May—building season is passing by, and when he takes over this land, he needs to be ready to break ground." Several of the men were already at work hammering stakes into the ground and running ribbon between them.

"What are you outlining?" Jericho demanded. "An airplane terminal?"

The foreman guffawed. "It's a house! Airplane terminal," he repeated as if that was the funniest thing he'd ever heard.

"That's a big house," Savannah said. "Almost as big as my parents'," she added in an undertone to Avery.

"What else would you expect from Montague? He builds only the best," the foreman boasted.

"I thought he was going to build an amusement park," Boone said.

The man waved that away. "He thought about it. Figured this was easier—and more profitable."

"I don't want to listen to this," Savannah said. "Avery? Come on, let's go somewhere else. Fulsom is just yanking our chains."

"That's what I think, too," Jericho told her. "You ladies head out. Angus, Byron, mind going with them? Take Gabe here to see the rest of the place. Boone and I will sort this out."

Avery was only too happy to walk toward the manor, but Gabe's presence was a clear reminder of how off-track her life had gotten. Her thoughts returned to Walker. What was he doing now? More to the point, what was he thinking about?

Elizabeth was with him, while she was wasting time with a man she couldn't care less about.

"Do you really think Montague will build three hundred houses that big out here if you lose?" Gabe asked. "Who's going to buy them?" They walked past the tiny houses that had already been built and picked up the trail that led to the manor.

"We're not going to lose. Like Savannah said, he's trying to intimidate us. It's a bluff," Avery asserted. She refused to think about the possibility she could be wrong.

Color flared in Savannah's cheeks. "Fulsom is going for drama again," she said indignantly. "He plays with us like we're a bunch of pawns, and I, for one, am sick of it. You should run away while you can, Gabe."

"Sorry. Can't do that."

"Those jerks up there are only half of what's making me so mad." Savannah shifted Jacob in her arms, bouncing him gently to settle him down as she walked. "That stupid *Star News* had Jericho and me in their sights this time. You should have heard their laundry list of all the pitfalls of green energy. They made us look subhuman for even considering it. They blasted us for our electric trucks. Had ten ranchers on the show, and each of them doubled over in laughter when they heard about them. 'Electric trucks?'" she parroted. "'What kind of fool drives an electric truck?' I'll tell you who: any fool who gives a damn about the world he lives in!"

"They're trying to make us so upset we make a mistake and lose," Avery said.

"They're trying to ruin everything we've worked so hard to build!"

"At least they didn't attack *you*," Avery said soothingly. She bent close to give Jacob a little kiss. A familiar longing kicked up inside her, but she refused to pay it any attention.

Savannah snorted. "Yes, they did! Apparently, I'm the weak little fool who married a man who destroyed my career and stopped me from rising to the top of my profession. And what if they're right? What if I could have been the best?" Savannah blinked back tears, shifting Jacob again. "Was I stupid to throw my chance away?"

Avery ached for her friend. She knew what a hard decision it had been for Savannah to walk away from her career, just when she was ready to work to resume it.

"What did make you decide against it?" she asked. Savannah had tried out to be mentored by a famous pianist she'd always admired but had decided it wasn't the path she wanted to take.

"I didn't want to be playing *for* people, I wanted to be playing *with* people, like I do here," Savannah said without hesitation. "I didn't want to perform. I wanted to be part of what was going on, like when I play and you all dance or when we have singalongs. I wanted that immediate connection, not to be on some pedestal. But…"

"But what?"

"Sometimes I wish I was challenged more. I play fun, pretty pieces for you all, but I don't play sonatas, you know?"

"Sounds to me like that's a goal to keep in mind going forward. The reality show is almost over, Savannah." She gestured at the crew filming them as they walked. "A month from now we're all going to have more time to do what we love. Remember what Boone said—we should be taking more time for what we love now. Jacob looks sleepy. Could you put him down for a nap at the manor and practice a little?"

"Can I hold him?" Gabe asked.

Savannah seemed as startled as Avery was by his question. He'd been so quiet walking behind them she'd almost forgotten he was there. Angus and Byron were several paces behind them, having a conversation of their own.

"Uh… okay. I guess." Savannah didn't immediately hand over Jacob, though.

"I won't drop him," Gabe assured her. "I've got five nieces and nephews, and I babysit all the time."

"Where are you from, anyway?" Savannah transferred her son to Gabe's arms but hovered nearby just in case.

"I'm based in Washington, DC. Work for the government. Do a lot of traveling." Gabe cradled Jacob carefully. "Look at you," he murmured to the sleepy baby, "so brand new to the world. Makes it all worth fighting for, doesn't it?"

Savannah exchanged a look with Avery and raised

an eyebrow.

Avery bit back a sigh. Sure, Gabe was a nice guy. He was enthusiastic. Good with kids.

But he wasn't Walker.

"I guess I could practice for a while if I can get Jacob down for a nap," Savannah said. "But don't forget we're going to Maud and James's house for a party tonight."

Avery had forgotten about it.

"Party?" Gabe perked up.

She was glad someone was looking forward to it. Normally she loved Maud and James's get-togethers. The food was always wonderful, the dancing fun.

Tonight she figured it would be interminable.

"THIS IS ALL your fault, you know," Clay said when he cornered Walker by the window overlooking the Russells' expansive front yard later that evening.

Walker didn't answer him, knowing Clay wouldn't need any encouragement to go right ahead. He wasn't the first one who'd felt the need to put a word in his ear since Gabe arrived.

"You should have proposed to Avery the minute you drew the short straw. Everyone knows she's the one you want. Why are you hurting her—and yourself—by dragging all this out? Tell Elizabeth you're over her and move on."

Elizabeth was talking to Maud Russell, who was giving her advice about finding a good tailor so she could "outfit herself according to the customs of the region," as Maud put it, gesturing to the Regency-era gowns she and all the other women present wore. Elizabeth, wearing a perfectly nice modern skirt and blouse, was having trouble keeping her disdain out of her responses.

"You were taking a chance before, but now Avery's got a backup husband. Are you really going to let him steal her away?"

Walker didn't need anyone to remind him about Gabe. Even now Avery was chatting away happily with him. He'd heard about Gabe's run-in with Elizabeth when he first arrived, but he and Avery already seemed thick as thieves.

He wondered what Gabe had said that had made Elizabeth so mad. He hadn't asked her, and she hadn't said a word to him about any of it, remaining stiff and silent the rest of the day until it was time to go to the Russells' house. Then, even though she'd told Maud she wasn't coming, she'd made a big deal of claiming her seat next to him in one of the carriages the Russells had sent around to pick them up. Walker wasn't sure who that performance was aimed at. If it was Avery, she was far too busy hanging on Gabe's every word to notice.

What did she and Gabe have in common?

He didn't realize he'd asked the question out loud until he caught Clay shrugging.

"I don't know. She showed him all over Base Camp this afternoon. Answered every question he asked. The crew loved every minute of it. I think she even took him wading in Pittance Creek."

"Had to be cold" was all Walker could say.

"Made great footage, according to Byron," Clay said. "I haven't seen Avery this happy in ages," he added thoughtfully, then seemed to remember who he was talking to. "Sorry. I think Nora wants me." He hurried off.

"Lord, that woman can talk." Elizabeth rejoined him as Maud bustled away to the kitchen. Tracing his gaze, she groaned. "Guess Avery's not so devoted to you after all, huh? She sure took to Gabe in a hurry."

"Sounds like you and he had a bit of a scrap this afternoon."

Elizabeth frowned. "He showed up unannounced. I was taking care of it until Boone interfered."

"You thought it was your place to take care of it?"

She took her time answering. "This is my home now, remember? I'm going to be your wife. We'll live happily ever after in our tiny house." She tossed her long hair over her shoulder, practically daring him to deny it.

"You handed in your resignation to your job, then?" he retaliated.

She blinked. "Why would I—?" She stopped. Laughed. "Okay, you caught me. I haven't resigned yet."

"Why not? If you're so set on staying and marrying me?"

He thought he had her at a loss for words, but a smile slipped over her face, and she held up a hand and wiggled her fingers at him. "Put a ring on it, sweetie, and I'll make the call. I might be old-fashioned, but I'm not stupid."

Walker cursed the cameramen who were getting all of this. He had no doubt that exchange would show up on the next episode of *Base Camp*. "You'll get your ring when I'm sure of your motives, because I don't buy for one minute that you actually—"

"Be right back. All this punch is going straight through me." She handed him the crystal glass she'd been sipping from and made for the bathroom, leaving him gaping after her. He snapped his mouth shut. Set down the glass on a nearby end table. Spotted Avery alone on the other side of the room near the refreshments table and started for her, wondering where Gabe had gotten to.

He knew it wasn't fair of him to interfere if she'd made a connection with the other man.

But he couldn't stay away from her a moment longer.

"WHERE'S YOUR NEW lady-love?" Leslie's voice carried across the room. Avery, helping herself to a glass of punch, turned to see she and Byron had cornered Walker.

Maud, coming back from the kitchen, was drawn like a moth to a flame to their conversation. The woman loved gossip, although Avery didn't think she had a mean bone in her body. Avery busied herself with her punch glass, hoping no one realized she was listening in, too.

"Well? Where's Elizabeth?" Leslie pressed Walker. "Elizabeth is the woman Walker's promised to," she told Maud. "Anyone who watches *Base Camp* has heard of her."

"Ah! An arranged marriage?" Maud tittered, ignoring the reference to television the way she and her husband ignored references to all modern conveniences. "How unusual in the new world. How romantic." She must have noticed Avery nearby. "How inconvenient, I mean," she added.

"Walker's like a lot of men," Leslie said airily. "Men like to have everything all at once, you know. They're horrible at choosing. They want this girl and that girl and the other one, and even when you tell them the law says they can marry only one, they seem to think maybe it doesn't apply to them. I knew a girl who married a man in Palm Springs and then found out he was married to sixteen other women—all of them in Palm Springs! Her children had sixty-five half siblings! How do you get away with that? It's a man thing. Men are sneaky! Except my man."

"I should imagine the poor fellow was quite exhausted," Maud interjected. "How did he keep them all straight? What if two wives chose the same name for their children?" She bent closer to Leslie as if to whisper, but her voice was as loud as ever. "How did he keep all those women satisfied?"

Avery needed fresh air. She was sure Gabe would find her when he got back from his foray to find a bathroom, and anyway, there were plenty of other people to entertain him while she was gone.

Outside, on the Russells' front porch, she sifted

through her whirling thoughts. Showing Gabe around Base Camp had distracted her for a few hours this afternoon. He was an intelligent man with more of a sense of humor than she'd first suspected when she'd come upon him arguing with Elizabeth. She didn't know how he'd pissed off Elizabeth so much in such a short period of time when he seemed to be perfectly capable of being a charming companion.

They'd walked all over Base Camp enjoying the fine weather, Avery pointing out every landmark and Gabe comparing them to the way they appeared in the show. As they went, she'd been able to introduce him to most of the cast and crew members, too. He seemed pleased as punch to know them all.

He was a nice guy.

But he'd never touch her heart the way Walker did.

When the door opened behind her, Avery wanted to tell whoever it was to go away.

"We've got only a minute," Walker said, coming to stand beside her. "Avery, you've got to know this is killing me." He gathered her hands in his and turned her to face him.

"Then do something about it."

"I'm trying. I need time."

"That's what you always say."

The anguish in his eyes twisted her heart. "I—"

The door opened again. "Walker? You out here?" Elizabeth called sharply.

"Avery?"

That was Gabe. He pushed past Elizabeth onto the

porch.

Walker let go of her hands as they approached.

"Everyone's wondering where you got to," Elizabeth announced. "Come back inside."

"There's going to be dancing," Gabe said, crooking an arm Avery's way. Wordlessly, she linked her elbow through his. "Dancing is fun, right?"

"I guess."

It would be if she was going to dance with Walker.

But that didn't seem likely anytime soon.

CHAPTER FOUR

"SEE? ALL'S WELL that ends well," Sue said several days later. Walker, Elizabeth, Avery and Hope had just returned from chores to find her sitting on a log section at the fire pit. The others had gone inside to clean up. Elizabeth was nodding at Sue, and Avery was studiously ignoring her.

Walker came to join her, but he wished he didn't have to. There were hours to go before bedtime, but he was already looking forward to when he could turn in for the night. As long as he could sleep.

Everyone was still bedding down together in the bunkhouse, although there had been talk of groups of four or six peeling off into several tiny houses close by. Quarters were much too close, and everyone was cranky and bleary-eyed, their disrupted sleep patterns throwing them off. He figured all the pregnant women had to be suffering, but this was a good group, and people tried to keep their spirits up.

Sue gestured to the big bunkhouse window, through which it was possible to see that Avery and Gabe had taken seats on opposite sides of the little table there that held a scale model of the ranch, carved by Greg.

"She's moved on. Found her soul mate. Which is as it should be because Elizabeth is your destiny."

Destiny?

Elizabeth was visible from here, too. She'd just come back outside and was standing some distance away with her phone to her ear like always, talking, talking, talking to her coworkers in Washington at the job she claimed she would put behind her when they were formally engaged.

Over the past few days, Walker had noticed that wherever Elizabeth stood, her back was to the rest of them, whereas Avery was always in the center of things, always reaching out to someone else, always getting involved, helping out, looking for a way to belong. He knew she'd been shocked when Renata dumped a backup husband on her, but Avery had been nothing but kind to Gabe, who even Walker had to admit wasn't a bad guy.

"You think she's here to stay?" he asked his grandmother, nodding at Elizabeth.

Sue hesitated long enough to tell him she, too, worried about that. "I think she knows where her duty lies."

"And you think it lies on the reservation?"

"Where else? There's plenty of work to do there even if neither of you seem to notice it." Sue pinched her lips together. "There has to be a wedding in a few weeks. Your rules, not mine," she pointed out. "I've heard no plans. No one's consulted me about the guest list. That's why I'm here. These things must be done right."

"Oh, for heaven's sake," Elizabeth exclaimed into the phone loudly enough for both of them to hear. Walker could have seconded the sentiment. "That's not good enough!" She took a few steps away from them and lowered her voice, and they couldn't make out any more of her words.

"Seems to me she plans to head right back to Washington." He ignored Sue's prior statement. He didn't want to marry Elizabeth. Hated watching Avery through the window as she tilted back her head and laughed in the company of another man.

She and Gabe bent over the table again. Were they moving elements around the map? Coming up with ideas for the community? He wanted to be at that table, alone with Avery, making plans.

"I'll talk to Elizabeth." Sue's disapproval was clear.

"Find out who she's on the phone with all the time. Something's up she's not telling either one of us, and if she runs off at the last minute—"

Sue snorted. "You have your backup bride." She shot a severe look Avery's way, and Walker followed it to find Avery looking off into the distance and Gabe focused on—

Elizabeth.

Sue must have seen that, too. "Oh, no," Sue said, shaking her head at him, even though Gabe wasn't looking at her. "That man better get his head on straight. If he thinks—"

A scream, long, high and loud, echoed across the little valley from the direction of the manor on the top of the hill, raising the hairs on the back of Walker's neck. He started running before he made up his mind to it, racing down the incline from the bunkhouse and then up again, following the track to the back of the three-story mansion.

"Someone was here!" Addison yanked the door open and called out when she spotted him. "Someone was looking in the window—just a minute ago. Nora saw him, and she almost fainted."

Clay sprinted past Walker into the house. More men were coming behind him. Knowing Addison and Nora were safe now, Walker veered across the backyard, avoided the clothesline and slowed as he approached the forest. They'd caught an intruder here once before, a man who was hunting Win. Was someone lurking in these woods?

"Spread out." Boone caught up to him. "Let's do this methodically."

They did so, falling in line and walking forward through the trees at an equal pace, inspecting the underbrush and looking for any indication someone had been there. They gave it their best, but the intruder had gotten too much of a head start, and an hour later, they had to admit defeat.

Returning to the manor, they found most of the women gathered in the kitchen around a large table. Avery was setting out cups of freshly brewed tea; she must have seen them coming. Nora, cradling her baby in her arms, was pale and drawn. Clay sat as close to her as he could. Angus was pacing the room.

"Did either of you get a good look at the guy?" Boone asked Nora and Addison.

Nora shook her head. "Just a glimpse." Her voice was low and rough, and Walker could only imagine what she was feeling. Months ago, her stalker had followed her here from Baltimore and nearly killed her in the little old schoolhouse across Pittance Creek. Before his attack, he'd snuck around Base Camp, playing mind tricks on her, making his existence known without providing her the proof she needed to get the rest of them to take her seriously. "Mid-thirties, maybe. Tall and blond." She shrugged. "That's all. He was looking in right there." She pointed to a large window that had been opened wide to let in what little breeze there was. "Then he was gone." There'd only been a screen between the women and the intruder.

They were lucky nothing worse had happened.

Elizabeth sat at the far end of the table, bent over her nearly empty tea cup, running a thumb over its surface, lost in thought. Always on the fringes, Walker thought. Always disconnected from what was going on.

She must have felt his gaze because she straightened, looked his way and shrugged almost defensively.

"Did anyone else see anything?" he asked, still watching her.

This time her eyes widened. "I didn't see a thing," she said. "I was down at the bunkhouse with you, remember?"

"It was a general question." When he realized everyone else was looking at them, he added, "Someone's testing our defenses again. Why were you women up here? We're supposed to stick together, remember?"

"We were sticking together." Addison came to Nora's defense.

"I was upstairs with Hope and Win," Angus spoke up. "We were all inside the house with the doors locked. I didn't think it was a problem to spread out, but I should have kept everyone together."

"Why were you up here at all?" Boone asked.

"We came to make sure nothing was going to spoil in the refrigerator and see if we'd forgotten anything," Addison said. "We figured we'd be in and out of here in fifteen minutes."

"We've got to be more careful," Boone decreed. "We've got only a few weeks to go, and a lot is at stake. We don't know how many enemies we have—people who want to see us fail. It's not just Montague. Lots of folks have a vested interest in everything staying exactly how it is. We've got to be smart. We can let chores go if they put us in too much danger. That includes checking on the manor."

"We might as well close up the manor for the duration, then," Riley said. "We don't have any guests coming between now and the end of the show, anyway."

The rest of the women were quiet. Walker figured it was because many of them used the manor as a place to get away from everyone or spread out if they had a project to do.

"Riley's right," Savannah said tiredly. "Let's do a thorough walk-through tomorrow, all of us together, then close things up."

There were murmurs of assent all around.

"What do we do about Montague?" Clay spoke up suddenly. He was wired, Walker saw. Angry that his wife had been made to be afraid. Worried about the intruder. He was a man who liked to do things, not talk about them or sit around waiting.

"There's nothing we can do," Boone said.

"He sent his men to stake out mansions on our property. He'll be back, I'm sure."

"Let him." Boone raised his voice. "I said it once and I'll say it again: we've got a few weeks to go. We're going to be attacked from all sides. We can't let any of it get to us, and we can't make mistakes. That means we can't go after Montague or anyone else. Just ignore him. That'll make him angrier than anything else we can do anyway." He looked around the room. "Let's clear out of here and get back to work—together."

As they all tramped down the hill, Walker found himself walking with Harris and Samantha. Elizabeth had been one of the first people out of the house, but then she'd stopped and waited until some of the others caught up. Now she was in the middle of a small knot of people. Was she worried about the intruder? He'd never thought of Elizabeth as the jumpy sort.

"You're not going to marry her, are you?" Samantha asked in a low voice, nodding at her.

"Sam," Harris warned.

"What leverage does she have on you? And why does she want to marry you anyhow? I've never once seen her look at you unless she was pissed off."

She was right, Walker thought. He knew one thing for sure: Elizabeth didn't love him, didn't care about him. Hardly noticed he was there.

"I've got to marry someone," he pointed out. "We've got only a few weeks to go." He imitated Boone's serious voice, hoping Samantha wouldn't press the matter.

She smiled. "That's true. You're going to make us or break us."

"I don't care what leverage Elizabeth has," Harris said. "You've got to marry the woman you love, Walker—like I did. To hell with the consequences."

Walker nodded and plodded on, wishing it was that simple.

Or was he the one making it overly complicated?

"WHEN WILL THE rest of the bison calves be born?" Gabe asked several mornings later.

"Any day now," Walker told him.

It had been awkward when Elizabeth had started joining their group for chores, Avery thought, but now that Gabe was along for the ride, it was downright uncomfortable. He remained cheerful and helpful, and she couldn't fault his behavior, but Boone had decreed everyone in a work group had to keep in sight of each other at all times, which meant wherever she went,

Walker, Elizabeth, Hope and Gabe went, too.

Gone were the quiet predawn hours she used to love. Gabe was a talker, and Elizabeth was cranky in the morning. The two of them inevitably argued at some point, Gabe remaining stubbornly cheerful all the while, Elizabeth more and more irate.

Walker didn't say a thing unless asked a direct question or it became necessary to step between Elizabeth and Gabe. More than once he'd exchanged an exasperated look with her behind their backs, but she found it hard to share any private moment with him, knowing he might soon marry someone else.

"Wouldn't be surprised if a few calves came overnight," Walker went on, surprising Avery. It was the most he'd said in days.

"Shouldn't we be here to help?" Gabe asked.

This time it was Walker and Elizabeth who shared a look, and Avery's heart squeezed hard. It wasn't a romantic one, she told herself. Walker had told her there was a herd on the reservation. He and Elizabeth had grown up with bison around; that was all that look was about.

It still stung. Elizabeth knew Walker better than she did and seemed to feel she had the right to him. It wasn't fair when she obviously didn't care about him at all.

"Bison don't need any help," Avery said to spare Gabe the embarrassment of one of Elizabeth's scathing replies. "They're pretty good at welcoming the next generation on their own."

"Breakfast," Walker said and led the way to the bunkhouse.

Avery joined Riley, Savannah, Nora and Clay for the meal, relieved to get away from the others. She felt Walker's gaze on her but kept her back to him. He was the one who needed to sort out his life. He knew where to find her when he did.

Clay held baby Connie in his arms so Nora could eat. Avery was happy to see her friend was blooming; she'd been afraid Nora might struggle after her scare at the manor the other day. Nora had rallied, however. Clay kept close to her and Connie, and the new parents were so joyful about their baby they were a pleasure to behold.

Eve had her phone in her hand, reminding Avery of when they'd all promised each other not to be consumed by social media, back at the beginning of their time on the ranch. As couples had married, the old practice of sharing a cell phone had slid away. After all, the men had never agreed to that rule, and the women who'd arrived later in the year never surrendered theirs at all. Pretty much everyone had a phone now.

"Oh, for heaven's sake!" Eve said. A lively brunette who had come to Base Camp to expose Hansen Oil's wrongdoing and stayed to marry Anders, Eve went on, "I wish those *Star News* people would just leave us alone. Listen to what they said about us last night!"

She held up her phone, and a female announcer's voice cut through the hubbub of the bunkhouse as people lined up to get their food.

"*Star News* has discovered that the entire carbon savings of a year of Base Camp's operations were offset by more than a million times by Anders Hanson's father's energy company. The senior Hanson has pledged to switch his operation to green energy, but so far we see no progress on that account. The hypocrisy is stunning." The woman turned to her co-anchor. "These *Base Camp* people want to have their cake and eat it, too."

"That's not remotely true!" Anders burst out. "As soon as the show is over, I'll be working 24/7 on the transition with my dad. He's already conducting a survey of his operations so we have the information we need to get it done."

"That's the whole point, right?" Eve asked. "That their story isn't true? They're trying to make fools out of us—and out of our audience, too. Trying to make people feel bad for supporting us."

"They want us riled up. We should ignore them," Walker said.

"Easy for you to say; no one's attacked your family," Anders pointed out.

"Figure my time's coming."

Avery knew what Walker meant; it was obvious *Star News* was working its way through the cast of *Base Camp*. What would they hit him on? The fact that the Crow were exploiting their own fossil fuel resources on the reservation? Maybe.

"I'm doing my best to keep up with their lies," Hope said. "Every time they have a segment, I'm refuting it point for point on the show's website."

"Are you feeding them this stuff?" Eve asked Renata.

Renata blinked. "Did you forget I'm a part of this community now?"

"What about you?" Eve turned on Byron. "Or one of the other crew members?"

"Nothing *Star News* has talked about is new material," Avery pointed out. "They're just lobbing mud at us to see what sticks with their viewership. They'll take whatever does, turn it into a slogan and repeat it over and over again. You'll see." She shrugged at the surprised expressions around her. "Come on, you have to watch the channel only a half-dozen times to know their methodology. Every story gets a catchphrase— something that's easy to remember and easy to repeat. They say that catchphrase repeatedly for a few days, and pretty soon anyone who watches is saying it, too. Today's catchphrase is: Those *Base Camp* people want to have their cake and eat it, too. I'll bet it's already a social media hashtag."

"Maybe we should do a segment about that on our next show," Chris said from behind his camera.

"It'll be too late," Anders said. "By then the damage will be done. My dad made a mistake. He should have turned his company around sooner, but at least now he's on the right road. And millions of people are going to attack him for it?"

"We have millions of viewers, too," Eve told him. "And Chris can show them how *Star News* is manipulating people. That would be even better than just putting information on the website, although I think we should keep doing that. Chris, if we pull together a fact sheet about our intentions and a time line for when Hansen Oil is going to pursue them, can you add it to the story?"

"Sure can," Chris said.

"But what makes you think *Star News* viewers and our viewers even overlap?" Addison spoke up. "I mean, aren't you going to be preaching to the choir if you talk about this stuff on *Base Camp*? Our viewers already know Hansen Oil is transitioning to Hansen Energy. They saw it all unfold on the show. And our viewers probably don't get their news from Star Television."

"There must be some crossover," Hope said.

"Some," Addison repeated. "But not much."

"So some is all we can expect," Curtis said, ruffling Daisy's ears. The dog sat at his feet. "But family members and friends probably talk to each other about what they watch."

"Do they?" Hope asked. "Seems to me like people stick to their own side. Half the country is watching one type of news. The other is getting a completely different story. It's like we're not even living in the same world anymore. Every time I update the website, I wonder if I'm wasting my time. Do *Star News* fans ever come to read it? Probably not."

Chris guffawed. When everyone turned to him, he shook his head. "Sorry, but that's an understatement. When I was a kid, we had three channels to choose from. The national news came on at six o'clock. Everyone tuned in to watch it, and when it was over, it was over. And get this—" He paused for effect. "If someone got a big story wrong, they lost their job!"

They all contemplated that.

After lunch, Avery brought her dishes to the bunkhouse kitchen as usual. Gabe and Elizabeth were there ahead of her.

"You're supposed to scrape your plates into the compost bucket," Gabe was saying when she entered the room. "How long have you been here? Have you been leaving your plates and bowls like that for other people to take care of?"

"I've got other things on my mind than compost."

"Oh, right, sorry. You're too busy saving the world to scrape your plate. Let the rest of us underlings take care of the details."

"Can't you give me a break?"

"Can't you—" Gabe realized Avery was there and bit back whatever he meant to say. "Avery. Here, let me deal with your dishes."

"You don't have to do that."

Elizabeth laughed flatly. "Let him. There's nothing he likes better than to *help*."

"Seems like a good quality," Avery retorted. "Why does that make you so mad?"

"Sometimes people want to do things their way."

"Sometimes people want to do things a stupid way. Sometimes people make other people wonder what it is they really want," Gabe said. "Because if it's walking right into a trap—" He set the dishes down on the counter with a clatter and walked out of the kitchen.

"Everyone's so damn jumpy," Elizabeth said after a long moment. "It's that intruder. He's getting to all of us."

"Some more than others," Avery observed. What was that all about? She knew Elizabeth and Gabe rubbed each other wrong, but Gabe was really upset. And what did he mean about a trap? Was he talking about the danger here at Base Camp or something to do with their work? Several times in the last few days she'd caught the two of them discussing climate change. She was pretty sure they both believed in it, and both were working on ways to mitigate its effects. She had yet to discover the point of contention between them.

"You know how researchers are." Elizabeth waved the problem away and left the room, her dirty dishes untouched on the counter. Avery sighed and got to work scraping them. Later that night she was still wondering about what she'd seen when she should have been asleep. In the interest of everyone getting some real rest, Boone had finally broken the twenty-four people into groups of six or so, spreading three of the groups into the nearest tiny houses, the rest of them remaining in the bunkhouse.

Byron and Leslie were tangled up like puppies together in one corner of the room. The rest of them were spread out. Still, Avery found the room stifling. She never got to be alone these days, and while she'd always thought of herself as a social being, now she'd give anything for a few hours by herself.

Even a minute or two would suffice.

She lay listening to the rustling and breathing of the other people in the room, long past when they drifted off to sleep. When she was sure she was the only one awake, she gave up, slipped out of her bedroll and tiptoed to the kitchen. She knew she shouldn't open the side door, but she thought she would lose her mind if she couldn't get a breath of fresh air. She carefully unlocked it and cracked it open just enough to slip outside, keeping her hand on the knob as if that would save her from any danger.

The stars winked overhead, soothing her a little, reminding her that despite her petty worries, the universe was a big place and all was well.

She nearly shrieked when she heard a soft noise behind her. She whirled around, sending the door flying wide open, and let out her breath when she saw it was only Walker crossing the kitchen toward her.

"Shouldn't be out there," he said.

"I know. I wasn't going anywhere. Just wanted a minute alone."

"A minute was all it took and Nora was gone."

Did he still blame himself for that? Walker had been with Nora at the grocery store in town when her stalker snatched her. Sue had distracted him, coming at him because she was furious—

Furious that Walker was falling for *her*, Avery reminded herself. So in a way, Nora's kidnapping was her fault, too.

"I'll go back to bed now."

"Wait."

Avery held her breath when he touched her arm. Waited for him to marshal his thoughts.

"I was seventeen when I promised to marry Elizabeth," he began. "I never thought she'd follow through with it. Never thought she'd want to. Thought I was safe saying it."

Avery's thoughts spun as she tried to process what she was hearing. The last thing she'd anticipated when she'd come outside was that Walker would follow her—or that he'd finally confess his life story. "Safe? What do you mean?"

She sensed his frustration. Walker wasn't one for explanations or for talking in general, for that matter. It was hard to get him going, especially when the topic was himself. In the long hours they'd spent together doing chores this past year, he'd opened up only a few times.

"Elizabeth's grandmother, Netta Blaine, was Sue's best friend—always," he finally said. "There was trouble between our families, but it never touched them."

Trouble. What kind of trouble? That word could encompass so much—and so little.

"Netta meant everything to Sue. She'd lost everyone else. My grandfather. My father. Netta was all she had left."

"Except you," Avery pointed out. He talked so little about his family. She had no idea what had happened to his parents except that they were dead.

He nodded. "I was a kid."

"What happened to Netta?" It seemed the safest

question and a good place to start untangling this knot. It felt intimate standing in the darkness so close to Walker. She wished she could touch him and let him know how much she appreciated him talking to her like this.

"She was diagnosed with cancer—too late. She hadn't spoken up about the pain she'd felt for months. Never liked to complain. Thought it was age, she said. I think she knew she had something she couldn't fight," Walker added. "Sue was so angry with her for not getting treated sooner, that she'd waited too long. She was beside herself. She still felt guilty—" Walker stopped and started over. "She wanted to make up for something that had happened years before. Wanted Netta to die happy. We all did."

"She told you to propose to Elizabeth?" He still wasn't explaining any of the mysteries, and that bothered Avery. Didn't he trust her after all this time?

Walker shook his head. "It was Elizabeth's idea. She just… said it one day when we were all sitting around at Sue's house and Netta was feeling bad. She announced we were engaged. Said we were going to buy a ring when we could. That we hadn't said anything because we wanted to graduate and go to college first. That was a priority to Netta and Sue, so she knew they wouldn't question it. You could have knocked me over with a feather." He spread his hands as if to encompass the surprise he'd felt back then. "I knew immediately what she was doing, though. She wanted to make Netta happy, and why not? Netta wasn't going to be alive by the time we made it through college. She barely made it to our high school graduation. Once she was gone, it would be over and done with. Just words."

"What happened?"

"Sue kept saying them—then and even after Netta was gone. Told everyone we were engaged. Said we'd marry as soon as we graduated from college. Said how happy Netta would be in heaven to see it. Went on and on and on. The whole reservation knew about it and was waiting for the date to be set."

"Oh, Walker." Sue had played the one card they couldn't beat: trying to force a marriage she must have known on some level wasn't going to happen.

"I got the hell out of there. So did Elizabeth. We went to different colleges. Never talked to each other. She never even came home during that time—told Sue she was too busy. Then she signed up for grad school." He rubbed a hand against the back of his neck. "She must have talked to Sue then, because Sue told me I'd have to wait another couple of years for her, acting as if she was worried the delay might break my heart. I was happy as hell to kick the problem down the road. Hell, I could hardly talk to Sue at that point without her bringing it up. I was in the Navy already, and I wasn't waiting for anyone. I made sure to be overseas as much as I could. Elizabeth took a job in DC. Travelled all over the world. So did I. Kept thinking Sue would drop it eventually."

"Why didn't you just confront her?"

"Have you met my grandmother?"

WALKER RELAXED A little when Avery laughed softly. He didn't know what changed his mind about explaining the past to her, but now that he'd started, his relief was overwhelming. At the beginning of the year he'd thought it would be a simple thing to dissolve his ties to Elizabeth and tidy things away before Avery even knew there was a complication. He should have anticipated Sue would keep fighting for the future she wanted.

"You had to know you'd face Sue someday," Avery said, echoing his thoughts. He could just make out the curve of her cheek in the starlight, the glint of her eyes.

Walker nodded. "I figured it was Elizabeth's place to do that. I thought she'd tell Sue she didn't want me. What could Sue say to that?"

Avery pulled back. "That's kind of the coward's way out, don't you think?"

Walker stilled, the burn of shame every bit as raw as he'd feared it would be when he contemplated talking about this with her. When he spoke again, his voice was rough. "I was pretending to myself I was holding up my side of the bargain. That Elizabeth was the one who'd started the lie, and she could end it, and I wouldn't be the worse for it. I didn't want to let Sue down." It was stupid. So much energy expended when they all could have been past it years ago.

But other damage had been done between their families long before that. Old hurts that made a little thing turn into something far bigger.

"You love your grandmother," Avery said softly.

He did, but it seemed a poor excuse for his behavior. "I love you."

As the silence stretched out between them, he wondered if she'd heard. If he'd made a mistake and she didn't share his feelings anymore. If she was too ashamed of the way he'd behaved—

"Don't… say that if you're going to marry someone else." The pain in her voice hit him like a slap, and another wave of shame threatened to engulf him.

"I don't want to marry someone else. I've been… stupid. Too proud to admit I lied all those years ago. So sure I could save face by keeping quiet." His motives were more selfish than anything Elizabeth or Sue had done. "I told myself Elizabeth would break things off. I wouldn't have to go back on my word. I wouldn't have to admit to Sue I lied to her."

Avery watched him wordlessly. As much as he wished she'd take the pressure off him by offering some kind of advice, or hope, or something, he couldn't blame her. This was his doing. His problem to solve.

"I'm going to talk to both of them tomorrow. I'm going to tell Sue the truth and tell Elizabeth I'm not going along with this anymore. I just need one more day to make this right."

Still Avery watched him. Was he too late? Had his actions betrayed her so badly she couldn't forgive him?

"Avery," he pleaded, taking both her hands in his and drawing her closer. He didn't know what else to say so he stopped talking altogether. Lifting a hand to cup her cheek, he bent and kissed her, groaning at the sweet taste of her mouth under his. This was what he wanted—what he'd always wanted from the moment he met her.

When she pulled back, he had to stop himself from wrapping his arms around her. He didn't want to let her go.

Avery touched her mouth with her fingertips, and in the starlight her eyes shone with tears.

"Tell me tomorrow, after you've broken things off with Elizabeth. Kiss me then."

She didn't trust him. The knowledge pierced him like a knife laced with poison. He'd tried to hold his honor above everything.

And all the while he'd been trampling it.

ONE MORE DAY.

She'd heard that before, Avery thought as she slipped back inside the bunkhouse kitchen, Walker a silent presence behind her. Walker had asked for one more day the morning of Win and Angus's wedding and then Elizabeth showed up and ruined everything.

Now he was promising to put Elizabeth aside and break his word to Sue, but he needed one more day—again.

Anything could happen in a day.

When he'd kissed her, she'd wanted to throw caution to the wind, wrap her arms around his neck and cling to him, but she'd had enough of getting her hopes up, only to have them dashed. Sue thought he would marry Elizabeth. Elizabeth thought that, too. Time for things to be done the right way around.

Walker softly closed the door behind them and locked it, and when he touched her hand in the darkness of the kitchen, all Avery's resolutions nearly failed her. She stumbled as he came up behind her and put his arms around her, pulling her back to rest against his big frame.

They stood like that a moment, Avery's heart pounding, aching to turn in his arms and pick up right where they'd left off, but Walker sighed, bent and kissed the top of her head, then released her.

Her steps were unsteady as she crossed the room, tiptoed through the door to the main room of the bunkhouse and made her way carefully to her bed. Leslie and Byron were still a tangled shape in the corner, and she was sure they were fast asleep, but Elizabeth and Gabe—

Was it her imagination, or were they both awake?

The warm feeling Walker's embrace brought forth gave way to a cold shiver of worry, and she braced herself for one or both to sit up and chew them out.

Neither one moved, however.

Walker's fingertips brushed her as he passed on the way to his bedroll. Avery followed his example, slipping into the covers on her thin mat on the bunkhouse floor. She lay there listening. Neither Elizabeth nor Gabe had the long, easy breaths of someone sleeping. She was sure they were listening just as hard.

What had gone on in here while she and Walker talked outside? Had Elizabeth and Gabe been talking, too? Comparing notes?

Making a plan to stop them from being together?

She would never sleep now, Avery thought as she rolled onto her left side, pulling a blanket with her. Between Walker's explanation for what he'd done, his kiss and that embrace, she had more to think about than she could process.

But the next time she opened her eyes, sunlight was streaming in through the windows and everyone was already up.

CHAPTER FIVE

"**A**REN'T THEY SWEET?" Avery asked when she followed Walker out of the bunkhouse, her breakfast in her hand. Elizabeth had been at the head of the line and was already sitting on one of the farthest logs, cell phone in her free hand. Gabe had taken a seat not far from her. He was picking at his food, gazing off into the distance, lost in thought.

Walker followed Avery's gaze and realized she wasn't talking about either of them. She gestured to where Nora and Clay sat close together near the fire pit, their plates balanced on the wide log, Connie in Nora's arms, Clay bent close to both of them.

Something hard and tight around his heart melted a little. He nodded, his body coming to life as he pictured Avery with his child in her arms. It had become a favorite fantasy of his. Having a baby with her would be as sweet as anything.

How far he'd come from his determination to end up alone, a witness to the apocalypse. He was as in love with life now as he'd once been obsessed with the idea it would all soon come to an end. He took a deep breath, hoping the future he wanted would come one step closer today. He'd already called Sue and asked her to stop by as soon as possible. After a long pause, she'd assured him she'd be here right away.

Did she think he and Elizabeth were ready to announce their engagement? If so, she was in for an unhappy surprise. He wasn't afraid to confront her anymore, however. Now that he'd decided to tell Sue the truth, he couldn't believe how long he'd lived with a lie. Why had he kept punting the problem into the future? Who had it been kind to? Certainly not to Netta's memory. Netta was a proud, upright woman who'd never lied in her life.

"Sue's coming after breakfast." He led the way to another log no one was sitting on yet.

"You're going to tell her?"

Walker nodded, taking a bite of the omelet Kai had served him.

"Does Elizabeth know?"

He shook his head. "I'll tell them both at the same time. Last thing I need is Elizabeth making a fuss or taking off before we can sort things out. She was supposed to come home months ago—never thought I'd have to wait this long to deal with this."

"Is that why you didn't tell me before about her?"

The shame that washed over him was nowhere near as bitter as what he'd felt last night, and Walker knew he should have faced it years ago. "That's right. Thought I could sort it out before you even knew. Meant for

Elizabeth to whisk in, tell Sue she wanted no part of marrying me and take off again. Figured I'd tell you after the fact. Done deal and all that."

"Why didn't you just tell me at the start?"

He thought about that, not wanting to blow her off with a shallow answer. "Guess I'm used to playing it close to my vest. Don't talk about the family secrets and all that."

She lowered her voice. "If we're going to be family, we can't have secrets."

She had him there. He knew he needed to apologize. Would probably need to do it a few more times before all was said and done. Avery was the opposite of him when it came to that. She'd answer any question. Tell you her life story if you wanted to hear it. He loved to listen to her chat about growing up, her parents, her college days with Riley, Nora and Savannah—the works. She was so different from the other women he'd known. Netta and Sue had been best friends and liked to sit on a front porch and talk things over but not in the way Avery did. They spoke in low, measured tones, chuckling sometimes over a bit of shared history, sighing over the loved ones they'd lost. Growing up, his home had always been quiet. He'd been loved, but no one in his family could be called boisterous.

"I don't want to keep secrets from you," he said honestly.

"We—"

"Avery? You here?"

A half-dozen heads turned when Boone called out,

approaching from the parking area.

"Who's that man with Boone?" he heard Savannah ask.

"I don't know," Nora said.

Avery stood up slowly and shaded her eyes against the bright morning sun.

Boone spotted her and waved. "Hey, another back-up husband showed up. I don't know where they're all coming from! Renata—this more of your work?"

"Came here all on my own," the man following him announced. He was tall, lanky and dark-haired in jeans and a Western-style shirt. He had a strong jaw and the kind of blue eyes people took notice of. "And I'm no backup husband, either. Avery here is my wife. Got the paperwork to prove it."

OH, HELL NO, Avery thought.

What on earth was Brody Campbell doing here? And who was that following him from the direction of the parking lot? She squinted against the sun's glare and groaned.

Sue had arrived.

Perfect.

"What's all this?" Sue demanded as she strode up among them, immediately commanding everyone's attention despite her diminutive stature.

Bile rose in Avery's throat as she took in the implication of Brody's words.

Married?

His wife?

No. It couldn't be. It—

"I'm Brody Campbell," the newcomer said cheerfully, sticking out a hand that Sue ignored. "Nice to meet you." When it was clear Sue wouldn't shake, he tipped his hat, instead. Avery remembered that hat. Remembered how intrigued she'd been to meet a real cowboy when she was eighteen.

She bit back another groan. There were no real cowboys in Vegas. What had she been thinking? She covered her eyes, peeked out between her fingers.

He was still there.

"What do you mean you're Avery's husband? I'm the one who's supposed to marry her." Gabe pushed to the front of the crowd that had gathered. Avery wished she could crawl under a rock, but it wasn't Gabe she was worried about. She turned her head and peeked at Walker.

And wished she hadn't.

"Sorry, kid, I'm not into sharing." Brody spotted her. "There's my girl! Come on, Avery, give me a big ol' smooch. Been missing my baby."

Avery dropped her hands. "Ugh—I am not your baby. And we're not married. What are you even doing here?" Renata had to be behind this. Or Fulsom. Or Montague. Someone was messing with her, because the one thing she knew, she was not married to this man.

At least, she hoped like hell she wasn't.

"You know this guy?" Gabe asked.

"Know me? Of course she knows me. We're husband and wife. Where's our tiny house?" Brody made a show of looking around. "Or do you want to marry all over again, sweetheart, so you can have that big white dress you said you wanted? Not that I minded what you were wearing the first time—it was awful cute."

Were her cheeks scarlet? They felt like they were. "We're not married," she said again.

They couldn't be.

"Check it out." He shoved the papers he was holding into Boone's hands. "Neutral observer," he told Avery. "He'll tell you the truth of the matter."

Avery held her breath while Boone looked over the pages, not daring to look Walker's way again. Where had that paperwork come from? What was Brody playing at?

"Looks legit," Boone said finally. "Avery, that's your signature, isn't it?"

She stepped forward reluctantly and took a look. "I... guess." It sure looked like hers. Memories she'd long repressed began to bubble up in her mind. Memories she hated.

"Baby, you'd had a few on our wedding night, but you weren't that drunk," Brody said loudly. "You signed the paperwork fair and square, just like I did. I'm still wearing my ring. What the hell did you do with yours?"

He flashed a wedding band. Avery shut her eyes against the unwelcome reminder, and more images appeared in her mind. Meeting Brody at a country and western bar where she wasn't carded at the door, even though she was still dressed in her prom gown. Dancing and drinking for hours. His ridiculous proposal. Her assent. The cheap rings they'd bought at the chapel where they'd pretended to be wed. She'd thrown hers away when she'd woken up in a two-star motel the next morning blocks from the strip—

Alone.

"That paperwork can't be real," she said loudly. She wasn't going to take this from a jerk who'd hit on a girl far too young for him. "It was a joke. The whole thing was a joke. We were blitzed. It was a silly thing to do. That's all."

She didn't know why her voice sounded so shrill. Why her friends looked so shocked. They all believed her, didn't they?

"No joke, honey," Brody proclaimed. "It was as real as my love for you, which means you and I can take up right where we left off." He flashed her a smile she was sure had melted her heart the first time she'd met him. Now she felt nauseous.

"Take up where we left off—after a decade?"

"Okay, calm down, everyone," Boone said. "Let's go to the bunkhouse and sort this out. We'll call Fulsom. He'll be able to put someone on it and determine whether you two are actually married."

"We're not," Avery said again. Why wouldn't anyone listen to her?

Boone turned toward the bunkhouse. Brody shrugged and followed him, trailed by Gabe, who was still complaining.

All Avery could do was follow suit.

Behind her, Sue said, "Guess it's a good thing you're marrying Elizabeth after all."

Avery didn't wait to hear Walker's answer.

"I'M NOT GOING to talk to you until you put down that ax," Boone said several hours later.

Walker didn't remember how he got to the wood lot, or when he'd stopped to fetch the ax and head out that way, but his shoulders and biceps ached from the activity, so he must have been here for some time.

He had no desire to hear what Boone had to say, but he knew the man too well to think that continuing to chop wood would deter him. Boone would shout his news if he had to. Walker didn't think he could take that.

Anger, fierce and hot, still burned through his veins the same as it had the moment Brody showed up and pronounced Avery his wife. He expected a woman Avery's age would have a past. Assumed she'd had partners. So had he.

The thought of that two-bit fake cowboy being intimate with Avery in a way he'd never gotten to made him want to bash a fist in the man's face, though. Nothing against the guy personally. Everything against Fate for arranging things in such a thoroughly idiotic way.

How the hell had Avery ended up with him?

No. He didn't want to know any of it. Wanted Brody gone from Base Camp. The memory of him erased from his mind.

Was this how Avery had felt when Elizabeth showed up?

The thought made him sick.

He hadn't realized he'd lowered the ax until Boone came and took it from him. He carried it several yards away and leaned it up against a tree. Now that Walker's strokes weren't ringing out, the woods around them were quiet until a bird chirped timidly somewhere close by.

"They're married," Boone confirmed.

The knot around Walker's heart tightened.

"It's going to take time to get the marriage annulled. Too much time, because Brody won't cooperate."

Icy cold fear replaced the heat of his anger in his veins. Avery was married to Brody.

To Brody.

To that wise-ass punk of a fake cowboy. And there wasn't enough time to annul the wedding?

"So the question is are you going to lose your shit, or are you going to keep it together and marry Elizabeth?"

Every muscle in his body was tight, tensed for action. Walker forced himself to unclench his hands. None of this was Boone's fault. Not really. He was simply trying to remind him of the greater good.

"How could she not know she was married?" Walker couldn't even bring himself to think about Elizabeth right now.

"Like she said, she thought it was a joke. Fake, I guess. I don't know what happened. What I do know is she's miserable, you're miserable—everyone's miserable, and we still have a goddamn ranch to win." Boone began to pace. "I wish I'd never come up with the stupid idea. It's been twelve months of hell and for what? What have we even accomplished?"

He didn't have time for Boone's angst. That's what you got when you thought you could change people: disappointment. No one changed. Nothing changed.

You never got what you wanted.

The cancer got you. Or a car crash. Or you put a gun to your head, pulled the trigger and did the job yourself.

"You need to come back to where the rest of us are and see this shitshow through. There's a crazy man stalking us, remember? No one gets to be alone anymore. We've got twenty-five more days of this crap, and we're going to survive it if it kills us!"

Boone's raised voice penetrated Walker's bad memories. His friend was losing his cool, something Walker hadn't seen too many times before. Twenty-five more days. Boone was right. No matter what came at him next, he'd survive it.

That's what his time with the SEALs had taught him—humans could survive almost any trauma. It was what came next that really hurt.

With a sigh, he fetched the ax and started for the bunkhouse.

"I'm sorry," Boone said as they walked. "I never should have asked you to be part of all of this. It wasn't fair."

"I could have said no."

"You joined only because you didn't want to disappoint us."

"You're wrong about that. I joined because I wanted to be with my friends."

Boone stumbled. "Don't think I've ever heard you call us that," he said a minute later.

Walker turned to him sharply. "Course I have."

"No you haven't." Boone walked on. "You've never admitted you're one of us. Every time Riley called us the Four Horsemen of the Apocalypse I always thought, 'It's the three horsemen and the guy who's hanging around waiting to see if what happens next will be worth his while.' Never thought you were all in on us, you know?"

Walker was stunned. All in on them? Was Boone shitting him? "Never knew if I was really welcome."

Boone stopped and faced him. "Never knew you were welcome? Hell, Walker, nothing got going until you arrived. You know that."

Did he? Walker didn't think so. In fact, he thought Boone had it all wrong.

"You three came as a unit," he said. "Met you all at once. You were already thick as thieves. Had known each other since birth, practically. I was the latecomer."

"The latecomer? We met in kindergarten!"

Boone had to know what he meant. "Spent half my time on the reservation."

"Don't I know it," Boone said resentfully. "Drove us crazy wondering what you got up to there. We were positive we were missing out, and you hardly ever invited us over!"

How could he invite his three boisterous friends to Sue's quiet, orderly house?

"You came to the powwows," Walker pointed out.

"As guests. We didn't get to dance or any of it. We had to sit on the sidelines and watch while you had all the fun."

Walker chuckled suddenly, a vision of his friends in traditional regalia sprouting in his mind.

"What?" Boone demanded.

"Never knew you felt left out."

"Never knew you did, either."

They contemplated each other.

"Hell, what the fuck, Walker?" Boone laughed. "We're really sorting this out nearly thirty years into being friends?"

"Guess so."

They thought about that.

"Really didn't think you'd agree to join us here, you know. You surprised the hell out of me."

"I'm here." Walker turned serious. "Mean to stay, too."

Boone shook his head. Turned to look at the mountains far in the distance. "I depend on you," he said roughly. "The others are my friends. You're my rock. I'll never forget that you trusted me enough to join me in this thing. And I'll never forgive myself for causing you so much pain."

Walker cocked his head. Shrugged. "You meant well."

Boone stiffened, then laughed again. "Damning

words, my friend."

Walker chuckled along with him, glad his joke had landed right. "You did your best." He patted Boone's shoulder.

"Jesus, Walker, give a guy a break!"

"At least you tried."

They were both laughing when they made it to the bunkhouse, and if their laughter had a tinge of something darker underlying it, who could blame them?

"There he is," Leslie exclaimed when they arrived. "It's funny how men always take off when there's a problem to sort out and then they try to make you think they're the problem-solvers. Since when does chopping wood solve any problems, except for heating a house in the winter, which is a good thing, but it's nowhere near winter, and even though I believe in thinking ahead, I don't really think you were thinking at all, or if you were, you weren't thinking very effectively because an effective bout of thinking would have led to a plan, and I haven't heard you mention a plan at all, Walker."

"How could he mention a plan when he just got here and you've been talking the whole time?" Boone pointed out. "Where did Brody and Avery get to?"

Byron scowled and stepped between him and Leslie. "You don't need to speak like that to my—"

"They're in the kitchen with Kai and Addison. Kai's making Brody chop vegetables," Savannah said. "He put Avery to work on dessert."

"Good plan," Boone said.

"I've been thinking of a whole bunch of plans,"

Leslie went on, undeterred. "We could kidnap Brody and dump him in the wilderness somewhere with a bunch of supplies so he's safe until the show is over, or we could take him to the nearest port and pay a captain to take him out to sea, or we could lock him in the root cellar, or we could just send him outside on his own a lot and see if that intruder comes back—"

"Oh, my God." Savannah covered her ears with her hands. "I didn't even hear that last one."

But the camera crew was making sure to get all of it.

"It'll work out somehow." Byron spoke right over Leslie. "Just when you think it can't, love finds a way. Don't give up, Walker."

"Don't give up on Base Camp," Clay said. "Just do what you have to do for now. We'll sort out this mess when the show is over and we've won the ranch for good."

"Avery isn't going to stay with that guy," Byron argued. "Brody is an opportunist. Anyone can see that. Where the hell has he been for the last decade if they're really married?"

"They're married," Boone told him.

"Still, funny that he shows up now, right? When Avery is on a television show."

"Maybe he didn't want her to commit a crime by marrying Walker when she's already hitched," Riley said.

"Or maybe he wants something else," Byron said.

For the first time, hope edged into Walker's heart. Byron was right—maybe Brody wanted something else.

And maybe he'd be willing to give up Avery to get

it.

"THEY'RE GOING AFTER a bunch of us today," Addison said when Avery met up with several of the women during a morning break five days later. She was avoiding Brody—and Walker and Boone and just about every other man on the place out of her irritation with all of them. "*Star News* is really having a field day with Base Camp, aren't they?"

"I wish they'd just shut up," Savannah said with un-characteristic savagery. "I have a baby, and I would like to enjoy one week of his little life without some disaster happening, especially fake disasters. Could those people lie any more than they do about us?"

Avery understood her frustration. They had twenty days to go until *Base Camp* was over, and the film crews were falling over themselves trying to document every last minute of their time here. Brody was following her everywhere. Elizabeth had attached herself like a limpet to Walker, and Gabe, cast off from his role as backup husband, had attached himself to Elizabeth. Walker was as growly as a bear, and Avery had had no chance to explain to him any of the circumstances of her stupid marriage to Brody. His expression was so stony every time he was near her, she wasn't sure she'd dare to.

She had gotten on the phone to Fulsom herself and explained as best she could that she couldn't even remember if she'd slept with Brody, and if she hadn't, surely the marriage couldn't be real. She'd tried to keep the conversation under wraps, but the camera crew following her around had crept in closer and closer until it was like being in a scrum.

Addison turned up the sound on her phone, despite the others' groans.

"We need to know what they're saying about us so we can counter it."

"Angus and Win," the female announcer was saying. "I mean, come on—Win's family could buy a ranch like Base Camp five times over. So who cares if they win it or not? They can reproduce their community some-where else if they lose."

"Her family is pretty shady, though, Marla. I hear Win hasn't talked to her parents in months, and can you blame her? What kind of sick parents arrange for their own daughter's kidnapping, not once but twice? Angus ought to be on his guard. The apple doesn't fall far from the tree, you know. When they have children of their own, I'd sleep with one eye open if I was him." The male announcer chuckled. "Who knows what she'll get up to with them."

"Is he implying I'll keep up the family tradition and start kidnapping my own kids?" Win cried.

"For a bunch of do-gooders, they sure are a barrel of rotten apples, Paul," Marla agreed. "Take Leslie and Byron. They're not even supposed to be on the show! Byron's a cameraman. Leslie's one of the 'backup brides' we keep hearing about who never actually marry anyone."

"She's going to marry Byron," Paul pointed out.

"Maybe. They're sure taking their time about it. I

wouldn't be surprised if it's just a hoax the directors cooked up to keep the rest of those backup brides from continuing to picket the show. Bet you the minute the show is over, Byron kicks her to the curb and finds someone more suitable."

"More suitable?" Leslie echoed. "There's no one more suitable for Byron than me, and I'd like to see that Marla woman try to find someone better. She could search everywhere, in all fifty states and the territories— even Puerto Rico! Did you know that people in Puerto Rico are US citizens, but they can't vote for president because Puerto Rico is a territory, but if they move to any of the fifty states, which they can at any time, of course, because they're US citizens, they can vote for president because they are in a state, which doesn't make any sense to me. Either you're a citizen or you're not, and citizens should be able to vote no matter where they are, and what about those people in Washington, DC? It's a district, not a state. Does anyone actually live in Washington, DC, or do they all have homes some-where else like representatives and senators and just go to Washington when the government is in session? But what about all the houses and stores and restaurants there. Someone has to keep them all running, and they can't just stop and empty out anytime Congress isn't in session, and anyway the president lives there, and he or she has to be able to vote, right? So—"

Savannah grabbed the phone from Addison's hands and tapped at it until the broadcast stopped.

"I am so done with *Star News*!" she proclaimed.

"And you're perfect for Byron, Leslie," she added.

"And people in Washington, DC, do get to vote for president," Nora said. "The district gets as many electoral votes as the least populous state does. They don't have any representatives or senators, though, so they're not represented in Congress."

"And it's not just Puerto Ricans who don't get to vote when they live in Puerto Rico," Win piped up. "No US citizen living in Puerto Rico gets to vote in a federal election, even if they were born in Texas or Montana or anywhere else."

"Which is really strange because when a US citizen lives in a foreign country, they absolutely get to vote in US federal elections," Addison said. "Unless the last place they lived before moving abroad was Puerto Rico, I guess."

"I've got to go see what Brody's up to." The political discussion was making Avery's head spin, and she was desperate to escape it, even if she had no real intent to actually track down the man. No sooner had she said the words than she spotted him heading her way, breaking off from another work group making for the bunkhouse.

"Damn that Boone," he called out before he even reached her. "He keeps giving me the worst chores on the place, and what does he mean by assigning me to a different work group than the one you're in?"

"I don't know," she said innocently. Bless Boone, he was doing his best to make this easier for her.

"If you think you're going to scare me off with a

little hard work, you're wrong."

"We all work hard around here, but this kind of place isn't for everyone. You could admit our marriage is fake and help get it annulled. Then you could be on your way."

Leslie's recommendation to wave him like a red flag in front of their intruder came to mind, and she had to admit she was tempted. There'd been another sighting a couple of nights ago. Nearly all the men patrolled through the dark hours, which meant everyone was losing sleep. Avery wondered if Montague was behind it, trying to slowly drive them mad playing whackamole with a man who refused to be caught.

"I don't want to be on my way. I came here to be with you. Looks like you ladies are having a much better time than I've been having. What's going on here? Why all the cameras?" He raised a hand to settle his hat on his head at a different angle.

"Just talking about *Star News*. They keep trying to make us look bad," Riley said.

"Well, you know what I always say—all publicity is good publicity!"

Savannah let out an exasperated sigh. "What is it you do again? Because you're not very good at ranch chores, obviously."

Brody puffed out his chest. "I'm a country singer. I'll play you a tune tonight. See if you like what I've got. You won't be disappointed."

"I wouldn't be disappointed if you fell off a cliff," Savannah muttered.

Avery bit back a laugh, but the ache in her heart didn't dissipate. If she couldn't convince Brody to agree to an annulment, all hope of happiness was lost.

"I'm looking forward to hearing you play," a woman's voice said. Avery looked around for its source with everyone else and found Jess red-faced under the sudden scrutiny of so many people. One of the other crew members trained his camera on her.

"Thanks, Jess. Glad to have a fan," Brody said happily and settled his hat on his head again.

"How the hell does he know her name already?" Riley asked.

"I know all the crew members' names," Brody said proudly. "I've personally introduced myself to each and every one of them. It pays to be polite, my mama always said."

"Hmm," Riley said.

Hmm, indeed, Avery thought. Brody was a country singer. She'd met him in the parking lot of a club on the Vegas Strip a decade ago. He'd gotten her in with the band, she'd danced for hours while they played and he'd come to see her after the show. They'd found a bar that stayed open even later. She'd been so drunk.

Which of them had come up with the idea to tie the knot?

Why on earth had Brody gone through with it?

The details of that night were fuzzy, but she'd never forget waking up the next morning—

And realizing she'd been dumped again.

CHAPTER SIX

WALKER WASN'T SURE how he made it through these days. It was like his body was on autopilot, his hands and feet doing his chores and moving him around the ranch even though his mind was thoroughly frozen. He couldn't wrap his thoughts around the fact that Elizabeth was still here, and Avery was married, and her husband—her *husband*—was walking around Base Camp happy as a clam despite being universally hated. Boone assigned him chore after chore, and Brody did them badly, whistling tunes all the while. He loved the presence of the camera crews, talked and joked with them constantly despite all their pleas for him to act like they weren't there.

Whenever he approached Avery, her withering looks and snippy answers rolled right off his back. "Just making sure you know I love you," he'd say and get back to work again, careful to arrange himself in the best angle as far as the cameras were concerned.

He liked to roll up his sleeves and show his mus-cles—what he had of them. He made a big deal out of every job and talked endlessly of gigs he'd played and musicians he'd accompanied. At the moment he was perched on a log near the fire pit strumming his guitar, talking a mile a minute to a small group of crew members who had gathered around him, including Jess, who'd become his number-one fan.

"How the hell did Avery fall for him?" Clay asked from where he was seated at another log near Walker. Dinner was delayed tonight, and they were all waiting around, stomachs growling, for Kai to ring the bell and feed them. "God, he's annoying!"

"I don't think she fell for him for very long." Nora sat beside her husband, Connie in her arms. "Sounds like they spent a single night together."

"That's not a marriage."

"Unfortunately, it's not the length of time they spent together; it's the paperwork that matters," Nora said.

"And Brody's refusal to agree to an annulment," Renata said, as if someone had asked. "I looked into it. Those two could get it done in a matter of days if both agreed to it, but he won't agree, no matter what Avery tells him."

Nora perked up at that. So did Walker. "How many days?" Nora asked.

"Four," Renata said.

Four days? Walker straightened. Then there was time. He could see everyone else had the same thought.

"I bet he'd sign if we left him alone with Walker for an hour or two," Nora said darkly.

"Then Walker would be behind bars," Renata pointed out, "and he wouldn't be able to marry anyone. We need to convince Brody it's in his best interest—without roughing him up."

"Why does he want to stay married to Avery anyway?" Clay asked. "I haven't seen him touch her once."

"Avery would kill him if he touched her," Addison said.

"He hasn't even tried."

Clay was right; Brody spent far more time hamming it up for the cameras than he did trying to reconcile with Avery. If he was married to her—

No. Walker couldn't let himself even think about it.

Nora was staring at him. "Come to think of it, why does Elizabeth want to marry *you*? She never touches you, that I've seen. Hardly even acknowledges your existence."

The group turned to look Elizabeth's way. Once again she was standing on the outskirts of the log circle—on her phone.

"What do you mean they changed the hearing date? Are you kidding me? After all that work?" he heard her say.

Work. Again.

"I thought she was quitting her job," Nora said.

"Not yet," Walker said.

Elizabeth paced up and down. "How long did they postpone it for? A couple of days?" She stopped dead. "What?" She raked a hand through her long dark hair. "No, that doesn't work. You can't let them push it back that far." A pause. "Because it doesn't work! I'm not kidding, Erin. You've got to get them to move it up." Another pause. "I don't know—talk to someone on the committee!"

Walker spotted Gabe standing a dozen feet away. He'd been sitting on his own, bent over his phone and tapping away at it, sending messages to someone. Now his phone was out of sight, his hands were shoved deep in his pockets and he was staring at Elizabeth.

"He's sure got the hots for her," Nora said.

Walker was beginning to think she was right. At first, he'd thought Gabe latched on to Elizabeth as one outsider desperate for the company of another. There was true concern in his expression, however.

"I can't wait that long," Elizabeth was saying. "I—" She turned. Caught them all looking. "Jesus, I've got to go. I don't know how you make them change it. Just do it!"

She ended the call, shoved the phone in her pocket and faced them. "So eavesdropping is just normal now, huh?"

"Something's got you in a dither," Nora drawled. "Is there anything we can do to help?"

Walker didn't think he'd ever seen Elizabeth look so flummoxed.

"It's just… it's just a problem with my job."

"The job you're quitting?"

"The job where I still care about my coworkers and the effort they're putting in to make this a better world," Elizabeth retorted. "Surely you all understand about that."

"We understand about wanting to change the world," Addison put in calmly. "But we also want to win this ranch, and you're spending way more time talking to that coworker than you are talking to Walker."

"You ever tried talking to Walker?" Elizabeth stalked off to the bunkhouse before any of them could answer.

"She's got a point," Clay said.

"She does," Nora agreed.

"What's going on?" Avery asked, coming out of the bunkhouse with a cup of tea a moment later. "I heard yelling."

Her presence focused Walker's mind on what was important. "Your marriage can be annulled in four days."

"Only if Brody agrees, and he'll never do that. Don't think I haven't tried to convince him."

"You all are giving up way too easily," Eve spoke up for the first time. Walker had noticed her sitting nearby but hadn't known if she was following the conversation. "We need to find footage of Avery's and Brody's lives from the time of their so-called marriage up to the present. We need to prove they've lived separately all that time, never mingled their money, never lived together, never even spoken to each other in all these years."

"Then what?"

"Then we put it on the show. If Fulsom won't help us get a rushed annulment, maybe someone else will step up. We can put pressure on the Vegas chapel that married them, make it clear what an opportunist Brody is being by refusing to sign the paperwork. We can tell fans to send him hate mail. I don't know!"

"It's a good start," Renata said slowly. "Avery, pull together all the evidence you can find that you weren't with him all this time. Statements from boyfriends, friends and family, photos from that time period, emails that reflect your single status, rental records for the apartments where you lived. Eve and I will find evidence about Brody's life. We'll stay up all night if we need to, right, Eve?"

"I'll help, too," Greg spoke up. "We did this once before, remember. We can do it again."

"Sure, I can do that," Avery said. "I don't know if it'll work, though. He's pretty stuck on the idea of staying."

"I have another idea," Eve said. She lowered her voice, casting a look over her shoulder to make sure Brody wasn't in earshot. "Brody's getting awfully close with Jess these days. I think you should ignore him, Avery. Don't even go near him. He'll make a play for Jess sooner or later. That type of guy can't stand not to have an adoring woman on his arm."

"Who'll get that footage?" Greg asked.

"I will," Eve said confidently. "Just leave it to me."

"What do you think?" Renata asked Walker.

"Do whatever it takes," he said. "Let me know how I can help."

IF ELIZABETH HAD been consumed with her phone before, now she clung to it like a Jack Russell terrier who'd caught a rat. She tapped at it all day long. Took calls at all hours. Grew as snappish as a wolf guarding its kill when anyone came close.

"You planning that wedding?" Sue asked Walker one morning, calling him from her school.

"I'm not doing anything but keeping my distance," he told her honestly. "Elizabeth's like a wolverine who's been poked with a fishing rod. You want a wedding, you plan it!"

Sue hung up on him.

Everyone else at Base Camp was busier than ever, and he should be busy, too, but instead all he could do was wait. Wait for Avery to amass footage of her life. Wait for Renata and Greg to research Brody's and wait for Eve to catch Brody in the act—if there ever was an act between him and Jess.

Boone had ordered Avery to the manor, on Renata's recommendation, telling everyone Avery was giving the building a top-to-bottom clean, a ridiculous notion since the women had just done that and closed it up.

Since no one could be alone, Boone had assigned Angus, Win, Hope and Curtis to join her. Walker found his way there whenever he could until Boone intercepted him one morning before breakfast.

"You're supposed to be spending time with Elizabeth."

"Don't want to."

"There's no guarantee Renata's plan is going to

work. You need to marry someone in two weeks. If Elizabeth takes off—"

"What makes you think she'll take off?"

"She doesn't look like a woman who plans to stay," Boone pointed out. "In fact—" His attention was captured by something behind Walker, and Walker turned to see Jericho running their way.

"It's Montague. He's sent his men here again. They're staking out more mansions."

"Not again," Boone exclaimed.

He marched off to confront them, and Walker followed, knowing his friend was near the breaking point.

"Don't mind us," Montague's foreman said cheerfully when the three of them reached him. "Just bringing our beautiful housing development to life." He unfurled a sheaf of plans. "Want to see?"

An army of men swarmed around the sloping ground, groups of four staking out the corners of homes all over the place. They'd come with premeasured ribbon this time, he realized. Four men to a group. Each held a stake and marched as far as he could go until the ribbon went taut. Then they pounded the stakes into the ground. An entire neighborhood of rectangular houses was springing up before them, an awful vision of what was to come.

"If you're trying to intimidate us, it isn't going to work," Boone said.

"I'm trying to show you the light, friend. Tiny houses are over. People want space and lots of it. They want to spread out. Face it, we all hate our families; why not get as far as possible from each other if we have to live together?"

"Because it's a waste of resources!"

Did people hate their families? Walker hoped not.

The foreman stepped closer to Boone. "Who cares? Dude, you're so busy playing your little games you haven't even noticed you already lost! Climate change is happening. Global warming is happening. The seas are going to rise, the storms are going to come, everything's going to go extinct. Who... fucking... cares? If we're all going down, why not do it in style? Why not make a few freaking dollars before the apocalypse?"

Boone stared at him a long moment, then shoved him with both hands—hard. While the man stumbled backward, Boone charged past him, straight for the corner stake of the closest mansion marked out nearby. He yanked the stake out of the ground and kept going, the ribbon attached to it fluttering in his wake. He yanked another stake out and another and another until the men caught on to what was happening and went after him.

Walker raced to stop them, bellowing for Clay and Jericho, knowing anyone who heard his voice would come running.

They did, half of them veering off to help him prevent Montague's men from interfering with Boone's rampage through the staked-out mansions and half of them starting to rip out stakes on their own.

Soon the camera crew had caught up and started filming the melee. Walker, Jericho, Kai and a couple of others were doing their best not to let the fight devolve into an all-out brawl as the rest of them laid waste to the work Montague's men had done so far.

"Tell Montague next time he'd better come here himself, and when he does, he'd better be ready to face me!" Boone called.

Walker caught Boone's arm before he lost all control, and the foreman and his crew retreated the way they'd come, muttering among themselves.

"Feel a little better, Chief?" Clay asked when they were gone.

Boone snorted, then covered his face with his hands. "Hell, I've really put my foot in it now, haven't I?"

"Not sure Montague can let that challenge go," Jericho said. "Not if he doesn't want to be a laughingstock around here."

"In other words, I took a bad situation and made it worse." Boone dropped his arms and looked to Walker. "What do you think?"

"I think we'd better expect more trouble before this is all over."

AVERY WISHED SHE'D been there to see Boone's rampage, as the incident was named in the days following the event, but she was pleased at how much footage and documentation she'd been able to amass and hand over to Renata and Greg. Having hours at the manor away from Brody made it easy to get the work done.

She trusted Renata to do a good job with it but

wished she'd been allowed to stitch the footage together for this episode herself. Instead, she'd get to see it for the first time with everyone else, including Brody, when their preview started in a few minutes.

How would he take it? Last night, as usual, he'd made a big show of bedding down near her, but he hadn't made a pass at her yet, thank goodness. She thought Eve was right and he was forming an attachment to Jess, a sweet, young thing who really deserved better in Avery's opinion. Brody had never slipped in her presence and betrayed himself, though.

"Ready for this?" Riley dropped down in the seat beside her. The episode would air nationwide tonight, but like usual they got to see it ahead of time. Boone was huddled with some of the other men by the bunkhouse door, assigning watch duty shifts for the next week. Everyone else was finding seats and chatting.

"I think so. Just wish I knew if it would do any good."

"Where's Elizabeth?"

Avery looked around. "There." She had just emerged from the bathroom and was making her way toward the chairs, studiously avoiding looking at Walker.

"Have you noticed she seems... I don't know... *desperate* lately?" Riley asked.

Desperate. That was a good word for the look in Elizabeth's eyes. Or hunted, Avery thought. That was an even better word. "Something's going on. I think it has to do with her job. Remember how she was yelling at someone on the phone the other day?"

"Something got postponed, right?"

"That's right. Wish I knew what it was." Maybe she'd understand the woman and her motivations better. If Elizabeth made any pretence of being attracted to Walker, Avery would understand perfectly why she was fighting for him, but Elizabeth never did. Unless one of the crew questioned directly about her intention to marry him, at which point she declared her undying love for him in no uncertain terms.

At the front of the room, Renata and Greg set up the laptop and screen and queued up the episode. Sometimes Avery didn't know if it was better or worse that they got to see it before it went live on television.

As the familiar intro music began to play, Avery clasped her hands in her lap, her fingernails biting into her palms. Walker sat down not far away but didn't look at her. The episode began with its usual montage of activities around Base Camp, Kai and Addison in the kitchen sweaty from cooking on a hot spring day, Walker and Avery near the bison pasture—that footage must have been captured before Elizabeth or Gabe or Brody came—Jericho and Savannah sitting in front of their tiny house, Jacob asleep in Jericho's arms.

A recap of the events of the last few weeks came next, even though some of this footage had been shown on previous episodes. Win and Angus's wedding and Elizabeth's surprise arrival, caught in excruciating detail. Avery lived her anguish all over again as Elizabeth asked Walker on-screen when he meant to marry her. There was footage of Nora and Clay heading to the hospital. Everyone greeting baby Connie after she was born.

There was an interlude that included the birth of one of the bison—a birth that had happened several days after that first magical one that Walker and Avery had witnessed alone—and then there was Gabe's arrival.

Next the footage changed to highlight Montague's crew staking out mansions near where they planned to build the next set of tiny houses. Booing and hissing rose from the assembled crowd before the show flipped back to Gabe following Avery around and Elizabeth sticking close to Walker. The contrast between Gabe's willingness to help with chores and Elizabeth's obsession with her phone was played up to comic effect.

"What about Brody?" Avery hissed to Riley.

Riley shrugged, but there he was on screen, arriving with his guitar case and cowboy hat.

"There's a handsome devil," Brody called out. There was a polite titter, but only Jess laughed.

In the show, Brody strummed on his guitar and sang a song by the fire pit, footage Avery was sure he loved because it showed him at his best, but before any of them could settle in to enjoy—or endure—the song, the scene changed to show a much younger Brody playing with a band at some club. A date flashed on-screen, one perilously close to when she'd met him at eighteen. He was lankier back then with a hat so pristine and new it nearly glowed. A montage flipped by of his life: his tours with his little known band. Photos of his apartments, family reunions he'd attended. "I hope he settles down one of these days," a woman labelled "Brody's

Mom" said into a camera. "But my son dates a new girl every week." A date flashed up on the screen. Five years ago—well into his supposed marriage to Avery.

The footage changed to start including clips from Avery's life. She'd kept a video diary for years, and it had been easy to coordinate footage with dates. On-screen, images of Brody at shows, Brody kissing other women, Brody on vacation and more flashed up with pertinent dates, alternating with entries from Avery's video diary, showing her in other locations, at other occasions, with other men in other homes and with her own family.

The message was clear: she and Brody were never in the same place at the same time, even within days of their marriage. They never talked to each other, never called each other—Avery's phone records flashed on-screen—were never photographed or caught on camera together despite both of them spending considerable time being filmed. The episode ended with Renata interviewing Avery.

"Tell me about your marriage to Brody," she asked.

"I danced with him at a club, went to some chapel, went to some motel and fell asleep. When I woke up, he was gone. All in all, I spent less than six hours with the man. I've never heard from him since until he showed up here. Is that what you call a marriage?"

The footage switched again. Here was Brody playing a song at the fire pit, Jess watching avidly from a few feet away. Brody going for a walk with Jess. Brody eating dinner with Jess. Brody leaning in close to talk to Jess. Leading her behind the bunkhouse.

Brody and Jess locked in an embrace.

Someone whistled.

"Well, hell," Brody said when the episode ended and quiet descended on the room. "Guess you got me." He took off his hat, looked at it and settled it on his head again. "Look a little foolish now."

Someone gave a sob, and Jess, who'd been in the back of the room with the rest of the crew, rushed out of the bunkhouse.

Avery held her breath as Brody watched Jess's flight.

"I did marry Avery," he said, turning in his seat to face the rest of them. "Hell, she was cute and sad and lonely, and I thought, why not?"

"What did you think in the morning?" Avery stood up. "When you woke up early and skedaddled?"

A camera crew was capturing all this, and she wanted to get his words on the record.

"I thought, hell, I'm not ready to be married! And you're right; I made a run for it."

"But you kept the paperwork," Riley pointed out. "You must have known you were doing something wrong."

"Always keep the paperwork. That's what my mom says," Brody said. "Doesn't matter how you do it—just shove it in a file somewhere and keep it. Never know when it will come in handy."

Riley laughed, then covered her mouth. "Sorry," she mumbled, "but that's such a mom thing to say."

"When I saw you on *Base Camp*, I told myself, 'This is it; this is why I had to keep the paperwork,'" Brody went on.

"Because in your heart you still loved her?" Leslie asked.

Brody made a face. "Because it was my ticket onto television. You know how long I've been trying to make it big? It's not easy out there. Now the whole world is going to hear me play and sing."

Avery lifted a hand to her forehead. Fame? That's what this was about?

Of course it was.

"So you'll agree to an annulment?" Riley said. "You'll sign the paperwork right now?"

"As soon as that episode airs tonight and the world gets a gander at my singing, I'll sign whatever you want," he said. "I didn't come here to be the bad guy. That's not my brand."

Avery let out her breath in a whoosh of relief. Savannah leaped up from her seat beside her. "I knew it would all work out," she cried and hugged her.

Avery turned to Walker. There was still time to get that annulment.

She could marry him—

"Don't even think about it!" Elizabeth stood up, too, and blocked her.

"If you and Brody aren't going to be married much longer, guess that means I'm back on deck, then!" Gabe jumped into her path, as well.

Avery couldn't stand it anymore.

Any of it.

She fled out the bunkhouse door, the same way Jess had.

CHAPTER SEVEN

"**D**AMN IT, GO after her!" Boone yelled. "No one goes anywhere alone!"

"Someone needs to find Jess, too," Chris barked, shoving other crew members toward the door.

Walker was already in motion. He caught Avery right outside the door. "Rules," he said, taking her hand.

She tried to fling it off. "To hell with the rules. I'm going for a walk!"

"Then we're all going for a walk," Jericho said, spilling out of the bunkhouse behind him. "Come on. We told Elizabeth and Gabe to stay put with the others. Chris and Byron will catch up with Jess." He slapped Walker on the shoulder, and when Clay and Angus appeared, the men fanned out around Avery, who stopped in her tracks and growled with frustration before striding on.

Walker kept pace with her.

As he'd expected, she headed for the pasture where the bison herd cropped grass, several calves frolicking among the older animals. If he didn't know Avery well, he would think her thoroughly engrossed with their antics, but he knew her better than that. Her shoulders were straight and high, her hands clasped tightly behind her back. Avery was struggling to hold her emotions in check. Fair enough; he was, too.

When Brody agreed to sign the paperwork asking for an annulment, Walker's chest had flooded with heat. Elizabeth's challenge hadn't changed that. Nor did Gabe's attempt at humor.

"He's going to sign those papers, right?" Avery asked.

"That's what he said." Brody had gotten exactly what he wanted, exposure on national television, and Walker had no doubt he'd capitalize on it.

All he cared about was Avery, however. He leaned in close, still holding her hand.

"Say it," he said. "Say you'll marry me."

"You haven't talked to Sue. You haven't even talked to Elizabeth. She hasn't agreed to free you from your promise."

"You're killing me," he said.

She faced him. "We still have to do this right. Brody has to sign the paperwork. You have to tell Elizabeth you're not marrying her. You have to call Sue."

"I will," he said. "I just want to know your answer."

"You know my answer. You've always known it."

Walker cupped her chin with his hands, bent down and kissed her. With the herd rustling and lowing behind the pasture fence, he savored the feeling of Avery, the aliveness of her. They had met right here on a hundred mornings in all kinds of weather, drawn together by their love for the bison, the big open sky and each other. He'd never been able to make his feelings clear to her, and he was damned if he was going to wait another moment now.

She met him with a sigh, her mouth soft under his. He traced her jaw with his thumb and tangled his other hand in her hair, needing to feel all the different textures of her. A cool breeze played over them, and she shivered in his arms. Walker held her even closer. He never wanted to let her go, never wanted to live another day without her by his side.

When they parted again, she sighed. "Is it really going to work out this time?"

"It damn well better." He couldn't stand much more of this. Walker wanted all of Avery—forever.

Now.

"I'm going to call Sue. I'll tell her to come here before school tomorrow so we can have it out. By lunchtime it'll all be over."

"I'm afraid to even hope."

He stopped himself from crushing her to him. He didn't want to hurt her, but he wanted to prove he wouldn't let anything get between them again. She was his everything. His whole world.

Avery pressed her hands against his chest and lightly pushed away. He let her go reluctantly.

"We have to go back," she said. "We need to strike while the iron is hot and get Brody's signature on that document."

He bent toward her one last time, speaking softly, aware of the cameras on them. "Later," he said into her hair. "By the creek. When everyone else is asleep." She nodded, and his heart lifted. If she would agree to that, then she was agreeing to be with him, to spend a life with him. He knew Avery. The one went with the other.

"When everyone else is asleep," she agreed.

Back at the bunkhouse, they found Brody already signing documents on Boone's old wooden desk, a host of witnesses gathered around, ready to sign, too. Renata was on the phone to Fulsom, explaining the situation. "I'll send you photos of them right now," she said, "and I'll get the original documents off in the mail in the morning. I'm faxing them straight to a law firm in Vegas, too, which guarantees an annulment within four days."

Elizabeth met them at the door, her eyes blazing, Gabe not far behind her. "We have to talk about this," she said.

Walker squared off with her, drawing himself up to his full height. "We'll talk about it in the morning, when Sue is here. I'm going to do this only once," he said. When she seemed about to protest, he repeated, "In the morning."

Her shoulders sagged. She searched his face. "Fine. In the morning." But she didn't look happy.

MANY HOURS LATER, Avery turned onto her shoulder, tense and listening for movement in the bunkhouse. It had taken forever for the groups sleeping in the tiny houses to say their good-nights and leave. First, Brody had decided he needed to recap his performance on the show, pulling out his guitar and playing and singing, segueing from one tune to the next until Jericho finally took the instrument away from him. Everyone else stayed to chat, speculating on what would happen next. Jess, who'd been persuaded no one was mad at her, hung around close to Brody until he deigned to notice her, and soon they were huddled over cups of tea, whispering like schoolchildren. He left with the crew when they finally departed, loudly proclaiming how happy he was he could finally get a decent night's sleep at the motel in town.

Elizabeth kept to herself, her jaw set and her gaze tracking Walker wherever he went. Several times, Avery thought she would confront him again, but she didn't. Gabe stayed close to her, murmuring in her ear now and then, as if he was asking her if there was anything he could do.

Avery couldn't decipher what he thought about it all. Despite his joke about being back on deck, he didn't speak to her the rest of the evening, although he shot her curious looks now and then.

She was relieved when everyone retired for the evening, but when it was just the six of them in the bunkhouse, Leslie started in on her.

"Now you're free to marry whoever you want, and Gabe wants to marry you, but you want to marry Walker, but Elizabeth wants to marry him, too, so it's all just as much a muddle as it was before, if you ask me. I

wonder if any of you has considered pol-y-am-or-y."
She said each syllable slowly, and Avery had the feeling
Leslie had come across the concept recently.

"No. We haven't," Walker growled at her.

Leslie tossed her hair. "Maybe you're too much of a
stick in the mud for your own good," she said tartly.

"Okay, Leslie. Time for bed," Byron whisked her
off to their corner of the bunkhouse.

For one moment, Avery thought Elizabeth might be
amused, but a second later, her face smoothed out again
and she was as serious as ever. They got ready silently,
except for the continuous whispers coming from Byron
and Leslie, and Walker turned out the lights when
everyone had climbed into their bedrolls.

Two hours later, Avery would swear every person in
the room was still awake.

Elizabeth kept sighing. Gabe tossed and turned as if
bedbugs were making a meal of him. Leslie and Byron
were still whispering. And Walker—

When she turned his way, she caught the glint of his
eyes. He was awake and watching her.

Longing, deep and primal, made her ache to be
down at Pittance Creek in his arms. She'd fantasized
about just such an occasion too many times to count
lying here at night, but tonight it was far worse, because
tonight she knew if she could get to the banks of the
creek, she could be with Walker for real.

She bit back the groan that fought to escape her
throat. To be with Walker—to feel him moving inside
her—

She rolled onto her other side. What was he thinking?

Was he imagining making love to her? Imagining stroking her skin, exploring her body? Heat washed through her at the thought. How would he go about it? What position would he choose the first time they were together?

What would he feel like under her hands?

Elizabeth sighed again. Gabe turned in his bedding. Leslie whispered on and on to Byron, then giggled, a sound like the scrape of nails across a blackboard.

Avery started counting but gave up when she reached 546 and still no one had fallen asleep. She turned to face Walker again. Saw him staring back. Longed to cross the distance between them and slide right into his bedroll no matter who was awake to see them.

She began to count again. Slowly. All the while imagining what she would do to Walker when they were—

When she opened her eyes again, the morning sun shone in the windows. Everyone was finally sleeping. Except Walker—

Who was still watching her.

His tender, regretful smile made up for everything.

Almost.

HAD HE EVER spent a more agonizing night?

Once, in Yemen, he thought, when they'd tried to rescue four aid workers and several dozen schoolchildren caught in a bombed-out school between rival sides during its civil war. It had been his turn on the satellite phone to keep up the spirits of the workers while Boone, Clay and Jericho took turns sleeping and working out a new plan to save them.

They'd talked to those aid workers for days and nights on end in four-hour shifts. Walker had been paired with Andrew Chin, a religious man from Dallas, Texas, who'd been a veterinarian for thirty years before shifting to NGO work.

They'd spoken of death that night, of what constituted a life well lived, what could be done to save the children, not just in Yemen but in perilous circumstances around the world—and what Andrew had learned during his veterinary practice.

"A dignity comes to animals at the end that many humans lack," Andrew had said. "Animals accept their fate. Not all people do."

Walker thought Andrew had been one of the ones who did. He'd been calm that night, willing to discuss hope and resignation. "I have no regrets," he'd said near dawn.

Through the long hours of the past night, Walker tried to be resigned, even after Leslie, Byron, Elizabeth and Gabe finally dropped off one by one, and he realized it was too late to slip off to the creek—Avery had fallen asleep, too.

It had been a bad idea, anyway, with a stalker out there. He'd let his desire override his common sense.

Now he was beyond tired into a realm where he could concentrate on only a single thing at a time, and that one thing was Avery.

He made a call before breakfast. Sue sighed when she answered.

"Another meeting," he said without preamble. "Get over here."

"I've got work. I have to go in early."

Walker counted to ten. He'd told Avery it would all be settled by lunchtime.

"When you're done, then." He knew better than to push. She had a mulish tone in her voice today he knew too well. When Sue dug in on an issue, it was rare to be able to dig her out.

"I watched the show last night," she said.

"Then you know what I mean to say." He hung up. Sue would come, and she'd be ready for a fight.

He went to find Avery. Relayed his conversation to her, then did the same thing with Elizabeth. The two women's reactions were remarkably similar. A disgusted shake of the head. A sigh of frustration.

"Fine," Avery said.

"Whatever." Elizabeth turned her back to him.

Brody arrived at Base Camp with the crew, ate breakfast and presented himself to Walker and Avery when it was over. "I'm up for chores," he said brightly.

"What are you even still doing here?" Elizabeth put her hands on her hips. The strain they were all feeling showed in her face.

"What do you mean?" Brody asked.

"Your marriage is getting annulled. You have no other purpose on the show but to bother Avery."

Elizabeth ticked off her points on her fingers.

"I have a purpose," Brody sputtered. "I play guitar. I entertain you guys."

"You can't mean to stay."

"What about you?" he returned. "What's your purpose? I'm not marrying Avery, which means Walker is going to."

Elizabeth's mouth dropped open, but she couldn't seem to think of an answer. "No one wants you here," she finally spit out and strode away.

"I want you here," Jess said from behind the camera.

"Thanks, darling." Brody blew her a kiss.

"Why *is* Elizabeth still here?" Avery asked Walker as they fell behind and let the others get ahead of them. "Besides waiting for your confrontation with Sue. She's got to know what's coming next. Why doesn't she give up and leave?"

"She's stubborn," Walker told her, but Avery made a good point. Elizabeth was too smart to fight a lost cause. Which meant she still thought she could win. Unease prickled down his spine. "Don't worry, Sue will be here before the end of the day." He wasn't clear if he was reassuring Avery or himself.

"Can't wait."

WOULD THIS DAY ever end? After a night of too little sleep, all the endless May sunshine and heat were getting to Avery. When a bead of sweat rolled down her collarbone and between her breasts, she stood up from where she'd been mucking out the chickens' pen and wiped a sleeve of her gown over her face.

She was thankful when the bell rang out signalling lunchtime, and she hurried back to the bunkhouse with the others in her work group, dying for a tall glass of water. She found Curtis and Hope standing near the kitchen door talking to Kai and Addison, who looked like they'd stepped out of the hot kitchen to get a breath of fresh air before starting to serve the meal. Daisy nosed around the edge of the bunkhouse nearby.

"What's going on?" Avery asked.

"*Star News*. What else?" Hope said angrily.

"Who have they got in their sights this time?"

"Me. Curtis. Apparently, Curtis's woodworking is second rate. Can you believe that? He does beautiful work!"

"I'm no master," Curtis started, but Hope wasn't having it.

"Yes, you are. Stop being modest, and don't let those idiots plant thoughts in your head. Your work is fabulous. I'm honored to live in a house you built." She turned back to Avery. "Meanwhile, my bison research is really a front for my crusade against the cattle industry, paid for by radical leftist vegans, if you want to know the truth. Never mind the fact bison aren't vegetables!"

"They're just trying to make you mad," Avery told her.

"It's working!"

"Shh!" Addison hissed, bent close to the little screen. "Now they're after Kai and me!"

They listened to the show playing on Curtis's phone.

"Have you seen his so-called 'cooking show'?" the female announcer asked. "There's no cooking, Paul! It's just playing around with solar ovens and a lot of talk about using windmills to make your dinner."

"What the hell is she talking about?" Kai sputtered. "I've never talked about windmills."

"You know that's what they call wind turbines," Avery said. They'd been through this all before. The announcers loved to play dumb, to get the terminology wrong—to pretend they were living in the 1950s. Avery wondered how their audience could stand it.

"She's skipped about ten steps between the wind turbines helping to power our energy grid and the recipes I make on the show, which do involve cooking by the way, most of the time in regular ovens."

"We know," Addison said soothingly.

"As for his wife, Addison?" Paul said. "What kind of a name is Addison, anyway? Sounds foreign to me."

"Sounds like a woman trying to be a man," Marla said.

"She always said 'yes,' remember? No matter what you asked her, she always said yes. You think she still does that? Must make her husband awfully happy!"

"Eww," Addison said. "That gross man is talking about us having sex!"

"And how you say yes to me no matter what." Kai leered at her, and she smacked him away.

"Stop it! I'll never be able to be with you again if you keep that up!"

"Kai! Curtis! Come on—there's someone down at the creek!" Harris yelled, racing past them.

"Get inside," Curtis barked at Avery and the other women. "Lock the doors!" He and Kai pounded after Harris, Daisy loping alongside them, all the men disappearing with them around a bend in the track that led to Pittance Creek.

"Inside," Renata snapped from the bunkhouse door. "Everyone inside—doors locked!"

Avery hated the feeling of being herded inside like a bunch of useless cattle, but Renata was right; they were sitting ducks out here. They peered out the windows, talking quietly among themselves. Avery wondered what they'd do if a stranger appeared outside, with the men all gone.

In the end, it didn't come to that. Soon the men trooped back again, Montague walking sheepishly among them.

"I don't know why you're making such a fuss!" he cried when they reached the bunkhouse. "I was just doing recon. Getting to know my property."

"Someone's been skulking around *our* ranch at all hours—someone we think is armed. We're patrolling night and day," Jericho told him.

"And we're armed, too," Curtis growled. "Want to get killed?" Daisy sat alertly beside him.

Montague paled. "You wouldn't shoot someone, would you?"

Curtis just looked at him. Daisy did, too.

Avery lost her temper. She was sick of being afraid

all the time. "Ten Navy SEALs," she spelled out for Montague. "That's the whole basis for the show, remember?"

"I… was just checking things out," he repeated feebly.

"Down at Pittance Creek? Why? Are you planning to build creekside mansions now?" Nora snapped at him.

"Creekside mansions." Montague straightened and smiled, rolling the phrase around his tongue. "Now that's a good idea. Has a real ring to it, don't you think?"

"Get. Out. Of. Here," Curtis said.

"My car's that way." Montague pointed the way they'd come. "I parked at the old schoolhouse across the creek."

"You'll have to take the long way around, then. You aren't setting foot on this ranch again today."

Montague looked like he'd argue, but then he sighed gustily. "Fine, I'll take the long way." He walked on to the lane that led to the main road. He soon had his phone out, and Avery figured he was calling a cab.

"You think he's the one who's been sneaking around?" Eve asked.

"Definitely not," Boone said. "We've had more than one sighting, remember, and it wasn't Montague. Back to work, everyone. And stick together."

CHAPTER EIGHT

B Y THE TIME Sue arrived just before dinner, Walker was beginning to feel the fatigue like a crust of rime covering his normal good sense.

Elizabeth had shadowed him like a ghost all day, followed by Gabe, who seemed to have stopped talking in the last twenty-four hours. Avery came and went, her joy at being free of Brody unmistakeable. If he hadn't had such a gloomy entourage, he would have pulled her into his arms and kissed her several dozen times already, but Elizabeth looked ready to scratch out Avery's eyes whenever she got too close.

Sue called ahead to let him know she was on her way, so he and Elizabeth met her at the parking area. Walker had asked Avery to stay behind, knowing Sue wouldn't like any interference in what she thought of as family business. Gabe wasn't in sight, either. Elizabeth must have told him to back off.

"I'm here," Sue announced when she got out of her car.

"You're here," he confirmed.

"So make your important announcement." She stood with arms crossed, daring him.

"I'm not marrying Elizabeth. I don't love her. I never have. I never wanted to marry her in the first place. Elizabeth made up the whole story of our being engaged."

Sue turned to Elizabeth, whose eyes glittered with frustration and anger.

"Is this true? You made it up?"

"I—Fine, it's true," Elizabeth admitted, surprising Walker. "I did make it up. Netta was dying. I wanted to see her happy. Is that so wrong?"

"So you lied. Both of you. Because you thought a ghost wouldn't care whether you followed through on your promises."

Elizabeth shook her head. "Honestly, Sue, how about taking responsibility for your part in all of this!"

Sue blinked. Walker didn't think anyone had spoken to her like that in years.

"My responsibility?" she asked slowly. Walker knew that tone of voice. If Elizabeth was smart, she'd back down now.

"We were teenagers when I said we were engaged. Far too young to know our minds, anyway," Elizabeth said. "If Grandma hadn't been sick and we'd come and asked you for permission to marry right then, the two of you would have been up in arms! I can just hear what she would have said. 'Not until you've finished school. We don't want to hear another word,'" she mimicked in a very Netta-sounding voice. "So what's your rationale for holding us to that promise now?"

"Because you need looking out for! Because it made Netta happier than I'd seen her in years. She worried about you being alone in the world after she was gone. It kept her up nights!"

"Are you sure that wasn't the pain keeping her up?" Elizabeth countered. "Come on, Sue. You know if Netta was standing here today she wouldn't try to force Walker and me to marry."

Sue threw her hands in the air. "If you don't want to marry him, why are you even here? I'm doing all this for you!"

Walker had been wondering that himself. He'd assumed Elizabeth would fight him every step of the way, given how she'd acted all day.

"Look," Elizabeth said. "It wasn't supposed to be like this."

"You can say that again." Walker couldn't help himself. "You were supposed to come home months ago and tell Sue what you said tonight. None of this would have happened. You would have been here and gone before Avery or anyone else even knew you existed. You know how badly you've hurt the woman I love?"

"How badly *I've* hurt her?" Elizabeth raised an eyebrow. "I think you've got that turned around. You're the one who made her wait months with no explanation. You could have told her all of it right from the start."

"Why didn't you come sooner?" Sue demanded before he could protest. "Why string us all along when you knew you'd break your word in the end?" She was holding it together better than Walker had expected, but then she'd watched last night's episode. She'd known this was coming.

"Because I'm fighting for something bigger than all of us—and I need your help!" She had their attention now. "I didn't get here sooner because I've spent the last year touring arctic areas to study the effect of climate change on wildfires above the arctic circle."

"And?" Sue asked pertly.

"And the situation is getting worse year by year. I've been studying tundra fires. You've never seen anything like it. They don't burn on top of the tundra—they burn underground, sometimes for years. There's no way to put them out," she went on. "You can't reach them with traditional firefighting equipment, so they just smolder away, sending tons of carbon into the air that used to be sequestered in the ground, and that carbon adds to global warming, and global warming sends higher temperatures and storms into the arctic, and those storms spark more fires."

"You're working to stop the fires?" Sue asked. She looked confused. Walker knew he was. What did arctic fires have to do with him?

"I'm working to stop carbon emissions. Seeing those fires in person brought it home like nothing else. We're in trouble—big trouble. And no one's stopping it." Elizabeth took a breath. "Look, there are so many things we need to do to halt global warming, but the first and most important is to keep as much carbon in the ground as humanly possible. That's a concept that's easy enough to explain to anyone. Or it should be, anyway."

"Keep the carbon in the ground. By stopping the fires," Sue repeated.

"By stopping the expansion of oil fields," Elizabeth corrected her. "We need to cut our use of oil and gas, not increase it. We need to shut down oil fields, not open new ones, but that's exactly what we're doing."

Walker struggled to follow her explanation. She was trying to keep carbon in the ground. Trying to limit the tundra fires. Trying to stop global warming altogether—by shutting down oil fields.

Or stopping new ones from opening?

"What I saw changed me." Elizabeth tried again. "It made it impossible for me not to do something—something important."

Walker remembered the phone call when she'd been pacing and yelling about a postponed hearing. She'd been so distraught. He was missing something here, some link that put it all together.

The hearing.

She'd been angry because a hearing was postponed.

"The Renning field in Alaska," he said. It had been on the news a lot lately that Congress was debating whether to allow drilling there. "Isn't there a hearing or something coming up about that?"

Elizabeth nodded. "That's right, and I'm a key witness testifying at that hearing. It's my job to spell it all out. How more drilling leads to more oil consumption, which leads to more emissions, which leads to more climate change, which leads to more fires, which leads to more carbon emissions—"

"Which leads to disaster in the end," Walker finished for her.

"We're heading for a world of heat and storms. More disease, fewer resources, more war, more famine—"

Walker knew exactly where it would lead: a world into which no sane person would bring a child.

And he wanted children—with Avery.

"So why come to Base Camp?" She still hadn't explained that.

"I never meant it to be like this," she said again. "I did mean to come last spring and tell Sue that I lied. Let you off the hook. But then talk about opening the Renning field started. And I… I found out some things. I had to pursue that."

"Why didn't you break off things when you finally did come home?" Walker pressed her.

"I've had… death threats," she explained. "Credible ones. The government offered protection, but honestly, I wasn't sure I could trust that offer."

"Death threats?" Sue breathed.

"And you came here?"

"Ten Navy SEALs," she explained. "What better security crew could a girl ask for?" She tried for a smile, but it fell short, and Walker suddenly realized how terrified she really was. He thought back over her time here. The way she'd stuck to him like a burr on a shaggy dog's coat. Everything started to make sense.

"Why pretend you wanted to marry Walker?" Sue demanded. Walker knew she was finding it hard to get past the affront to her beloved Netta.

"Because I've watched all the *Base Camp* episodes, and I know what happens when people appear on the show. Fulsom makes them marry someone, or he kicks them off. I figured it was only temporary—only until the hearing."

"When's that?" Walker asked.

"Yesterday," she said ruefully. "Or it was supposed to be. I was going to tell you everything right before I got on the plane to Washington."

Walker thought back again to that phone conversation, the one where she'd been furious about a change of dates. "You thought you'd be gone by now."

"Leaving you plenty of time to marry Avery after I left. I never meant to screw things up for you, Walker," she went on. "I can tell you and Avery are meant for each other, and I'm happy for you. But I need more time."

Sue's eyebrows met in the middle over the bridge of her nose. "Why?"

"When is the new date for the hearing?" Walker asked.

"May twenty-fifth. I'm on at four thirty in the afternoon. I'll leave first thing in the morning to catch my plane. You'll still have plenty of time to marry Avery after I go. Look, when we're done here, you can tell her everything I've told you, but you can't tell anyone else.

Everyone else has to think our wedding is still on—for real."

"No one thinks your wedding is on," Sue said. "I've read the forums," she answered Walker's surprised look. "You two don't care a fig about each other. Everyone's sure it's a ploy to get ratings up. And now that Avery's marriage to that… cowboy… was annulled, they know you'll dump Elizabeth and marry her."

"We'll have to change their minds, then, and that's mostly on me, I guess," Elizabeth said. "I mean it, though. No one but Avery can know. I still need you to keep me safe. I need you to remember what's at stake. Things are bad now, Walker, but if more oil fields are opened, I don't think there's hope for any of us. It's too much carbon. Too much warming. We're already at a tipping point. We can't recover from that."

Walker knew what she meant. They were pushing the world past its limits already. "Boone and the other men have to know. Everyone does. That man Harris saw—he's here for you, isn't he?"

She nodded. "I think so."

"He's dangerous. We need to protect you."

"I'll keep sticking close to you," she countered. "If you tell everyone else, there's no way Fulsom won't find out. He'll kick me off or interfere in some way. I've watched the show—I know he will. It's only a few more days. Then I'll be out of your life. I promise."

Conflicting duties warred within him. She was right; there were too many people at Base Camp for secrets to last long, and Fulsom used every opportunity to mess with them. He weighed his options, not happy with any of them.

"Avery needs to plan our wedding," he pointed out. He knew she loved pageantry and parties, and she'd once confessed that she'd been planning her wedding day since grade school. It wasn't fair that she was the loser in all of this.

"She can plan *our* wedding," Elizabeth said. "And then take it over when I'm gone. It's only five more days, Walker." When he hesitated, she added, "Please. I wouldn't ask if everything wasn't riding on this. Literally everything. I'll play along and give her cover so she can set up things the way she wants them. I'll keep a low profile. Make it impossible for someone to get to me."

Could he do this? Help Elizabeth, appease Sue and keep Avery happy, as well?

While keeping his friends in the dark?

"You should come to the reservation," Sue said. "We should be the ones to keep you safe."

"No." Elizabeth shook her head. "I won't bring this kind of trouble there. That's the last thing our people need."

"But it's fine for us here at Base Camp?" Walker said.

"Only because of the cameras. Think about it. No one can get to me while I'm being filmed, and I'm always being filmed. By the time the crew goes home, I'm tucked away in the bunkhouse, safe for the night."

It sounded almost reasonable when she put it that way, but it wasn't reasonable.

"You're leaving on the twenty-fifth?" Walker hedged.

"I promise," she assured him.

"Okay," he said reluctantly. "I'll tell Avery what's happening. She'll keep your secret." He didn't like it, though. Didn't like any of this.

"What about me?" Sue said. "What about the promise you made to your grandmother?"

Elizabeth softened. She took Sue's hands. "I have nothing but gratitude and honor for you both," she said. "The two of you taught me what's important in this world, and you taught me to fight for what I believe in. I believe in this. I'm sorry Walker and I don't love each other the way you'd like us to, but we don't. We never have. You know that."

She held Sue's gaze until Sue was the one to look away first.

"I hope you'll give me your blessing," Elizabeth said softly. "It would mean the world to me."

"I hope you give Avery and me your blessing, too," Walker said.

Sue shook her head. "We dreamed about your wedding day, Netta and I. We hoped for our families to heal together. My child and Netta's looking out for each other all their lives."

"We'll look out for each other," Walker assured her. "We know how precious friendship is."

"That's right. Whenever this troublesome grandson of yours gets in a fix, I'll be there to bail him out, don't worry," Elizabeth said.

Sue wasn't placated. "My son, Walker's father, wronged your family," she said. "I'd hoped a wedding would heal that."

Elizabeth closed her eyes. "Nothing any of us does will bring back my parents—or your son. Joe paid a price he didn't deserve to pay for my parents' deaths. The slate is clean, Sue. It's time for us all to move on."

AVERY'S HEART SANK when Elizabeth came with Walker to talk to her after their meeting with Sue. Even when they explained what was going on, she didn't feel much better.

"Five more days?" she asked. "That means I'll have to do everything in a rush at the very end to prepare for our wedding. There'll be only five days after you're gone to get everything together."

She wanted everyone to know how happy she was—right now. She'd spent a lifetime dreaming of the joy of planning each and every detail of the splendid day she joined her life to someone else's. She wanted to revel in it for as long as possible. Ten days were barely enough. Five were a joke.

"You can still get started on planning your wedding. You'll just have to pretend you're planning mine," Elizabeth told her.

"No one will buy that I'm planning your wedding to Walker," Avery pointed out.

"Sure they will. You're such a pushover. We'll pretend I bullied you into it."

Avery looked to Walker for support, but he

shrugged. "You're definitely too nice for your own good."

"I'll have you know I steal from SEALs," she said, thoroughly affronted. She wasn't... *nice*.

"Before you know it, I'll be gone, and Walker will sweep you off your feet and down the aisle," Elizabeth promised. "You'll have five wonderful days of preliminaries and a beautiful wedding."

"But I'll have to watch you two be all lovey-dovey until then." They'd explained Elizabeth's fear that Fulsom would make her leave the show, and Avery had to admit the man was capable of kicking her off. That didn't make it any easier to swallow.

"I'm not going to be lovey-dovey," Elizabeth said. "People would really wonder what was up if I started acting that way. Anyway, it's just for a little while. Then you'll do the big reveal that you and Walker planned to marry all along, and everyone will be shocked and happy, and your wedding will be all people talk about!"

"I guess that will end the show with a bang." She sent a sideways glance Walker's way. "You promise you're actually going to marry me after all this?"

"I promise. Just give me a few more days."

A trickle of unease threaded through Avery's veins, although she tried to shrug it off. *A few more days. Just one more day.* He'd said that before, and he hadn't come through.

This time he would, she told herself. He had to.

They'd all lose Base Camp if he didn't.

HE'D ASKED TOO much of her already, Walker thought as he watched Avery take it in. How could he ask her to trust him when he'd betrayed that trust several times already?

Avery had been so happy when she'd thought he was free to marry her. She'd waited so patiently for so long, then he'd dashed her hopes again, agreeing to help Elizabeth when he should be putting her first and foremost.

"What happens after the hearing?" Avery asked.

"There'll be a vote on whether to allow the drilling. It's scheduled for May thirtieth—probably right when you'll be walking down the aisle. Private interests are pushing hard on legislators to get it done. I'm pretty sure they're the ones who got the hearing postponed so it'd be a one-two punch. They don't want people to have much time to digest the information our side is bringing and look into it more before they hold the vote."

"If you're trying to influence legislation, why aren't you using the show to do that?" Avery asked.

Elizabeth cocked her head. "What do you mean?"

"State your case so our audience, which is huge, by the way," Avery pointed out, "can make up its own mind. Teach them how to call their senators and lobby for the result you want. I thought you were all about lobbying, remember?" That's what Elizabeth had told her when she'd first arrived.

"Is that possible?" Elizabeth asked. "I mean, would I be allowed to do that?"

"Have you not watched this show?" Avery asked her. "People get away with a lot!"

"Wouldn't that make people suspicious, though?"

"Maybe," Avery conceded, "but maybe not. We're all passionate about something. If I were you, I'd set it up so someone asks you questions about your job, and you can innocently answer with all the information you want people to know. Renata would be the one to work with on that front."

"That's genius," Elizabeth said.

"That's generous," Walker corrected her. It was just like Avery to take the side of a woman who had been her enemy just minutes ago.

"It's important," Avery said. "That's why we're here, right? To save the world?"

"Something like that." Elizabeth hugged Avery impulsively, then pulled back, blinking hard. "Sorry. I don't usually act like that."

"Don't be sorry. That's the first nice thing you've done since you've gotten here."

"I'm not always a bitch, I promise," Elizabeth said.

"Only when you're fighting for everyone's future. That's fine." Avery waved it off. "Do I really get to plan my wedding?"

"Of course. But we can't be friends—not until after this is all over."

"Deal. Enemies." Avery held out her hand. Elizabeth took it, and they shook.

"Enemies," Elizabeth agreed.

"And then—get this—she marries him! The guy she didn't recognize for half a year even though she worked with him every single day!" the *Star News* announcer, Marla, said. She turned to her co host. "The question is, Paul, why did Greg marry Renata? Is he used to being ignored? Did his parents keep mistaking him for a coat rack when he was a kid?"

"Maybe they had anger issues," Paul said. "Heaven knows Renata Ludlow does. All that ordering people around. Playing with their lives. How do we know she didn't force Greg to propose to her? Maybe she's blackmailing him because she knows some deep, dark secret. She's a master manipulator."

"That's true, Paul. She could be blackmailing him. All of America—the whole world—could be watching a hostage situation play out on live TV. And the radical left is probably celebrating it!"

"Turn that off!" Greg roared, startling Avery, who found that her mouth was hanging open as she watched the show while gathering her things to prepare for a visit to Two Willows. *Star News* had said a lot of poisonous things about *Base Camp*, but comparing Greg and Renata's marriage to a hostage situation took the cake.

It was a rainy afternoon, and while some groups were still managing to do chores, others had come back to the bunkhouse to wait for the shower to end.

"Ready?" Elizabeth asked her. "The Russells are here. I'm glad they sent a closed carriage this time."

"Their barouche has a hood you can put up," Avery

told her, "but you're right, a closed carriage is better in this downpour."

"I'm not sure why we aren't simply taking a truck."

"Because if James Russell was forced to spend a whole day inside without exercising his horses, he'd fall into a depression and never recover again, as Maud told me when she called earlier."

Nothing Elizabeth could say about their transportation could ruin Avery's good mood, even if they were supposed to be enemies. She was going to try on wedding dresses today. Everyone thought it was Elizabeth who Alice would be fitting for the gowns, and more than one of her friends asked why she was accompanying her on such an errand, but Avery brushed them off, saying she needed to order a few new things of her own and added a couple of veiled references to keeping your enemies close.

Elizabeth had been touchy today. Avery understood she was nervous about the hearing tomorrow, but her mood improved during the carriage ride over. No one could remain gloomy in a carriage, and by the time they'd arrived, Jericho and Curtis in tow to be their bodyguards, she was almost chatty. The rain was tapering off, and the sun threatening to come out. It might turn out to be a nice day, after all.

"Where's Daisy?" Avery asked Curtis.

"With Samantha."

Avery nodded and allowed him to help her down from the carriage. Curtis helped Elizabeth down, too.

"I always thought I'd get a plain gown," she announced for all to hear, "but now I'm thinking something really showstopping. A dress that belongs in a fairy tale."

Avery appreciated the bone Elizabeth was throwing her. Now she could get Alice to design her exactly the kind of gown she wanted. Even though everyone thought that gown was for Elizabeth, they wouldn't be suspicious if they saw it.

"Whatever." Avery made a show of pushing past her grumpily to meet Alice, knowing she had to keep up the pretence until she was upstairs in the studio situated above the bays of the old carriage house. Jericho and Curtis would remain outside, standing guard.

Alice's studio was as bright and cheerful as ever, especially with the sun breaking through the clouds. Avery shrugged out of the jacket she was wearing and shook the skirts of her gown. They were a little damp, but not bad.

Elizabeth stepped into the large, open room behind her and stopped. Avery knew just how she felt. Alice's creations hung on clothing racks everywhere you looked. Large tables filled the center of the room, some of them empty, waiting to be used to cut fabric or pin patterns. Others held sewing machines of all sorts and kinds. At the far end was an array of mirrors and a changing room.

Elizabeth moved toward the first rack of costumes as if drawn by them and was soon leafing through them, taking some off the rack to look at more closely.

"These are… amazing," she said.

"I have some Regency gowns ready for you if you'd like to try them on." Alice gestured at the far end of the room. "They're in the changing room."

"Oh, it's Avery who's getting the wedding dress. I thought you knew," Elizabeth said.

"Yes, but you're living at Base Camp. You should have some gowns. I'd hoped you'd surprise me and come sooner, you know."

Elizabeth raised an eyebrow. "How would that be a surprise? You couldn't have known I wouldn't."

Alice shrugged. "I knew."

"Go try them on," Avery urged. "Yell if you need help with the underthings."

"I'm here only a few more days."

"Shift first, then corset," Alice instructed. "I'll be over in one minute to show you how."

Avery thought Elizabeth would protest, but in the end she drifted down the room and pulled the curtain shut on the changing room.

Alice turned to her. "Let's look at material first. I picked out an array of possibilities for you. And here are some preliminary designs." Alice placed a pile of material swatches and sketches in front of her. "I'll help Elizabeth and come back to see what you like best."

Avery barely heard her leave, she was already so entranced by the drawings and the wonderful materials Alice had left. A few minutes later, she heard the door open and close again but didn't look up until a young woman sat down next to her.

"I like that one." It was Josephine Reed, Jo for

short. She was the youngest of Alice's four sisters, and as usual, she was holding a black-and-white puppy. Jo bred McNabs, placing them in homes only if she determined the owners were worthy. She and Avery had talked about bison before, although Avery had found Jo's older sister Lena had more to say about the critters. The Reeds ran a cattle operation, and while Lena was curious about Base Camp's experiment with bison, she was a die-hard cattlewoman, and Avery didn't think that would change.

"I like it, too." It was a very traditional-style Regency gown with cap sleeves, a fitted bodice and an interesting train.

"Did I hear someone talking about a wedding?" Another Reed sister came through the door, the oldest—Cass. She was a pretty blonde, who Avery thought of as the mother hen of the family. Cass was always in her kitchen, waving through the windows when anyone arrived to talk to Alice or visit one of the others, keeping Two Willows running despite all the chaos around her.

Things were a little chaotic despite Cass's best efforts, Avery thought. The five sisters were all in their twenties, all unmarried, and their boyfriends were… well… questionable, in Avery's opinion. How such wonderful women could choose so badly when it came to their partners, she didn't know. She supposed it wasn't any of her business, though.

"You heard something," Avery told her, "but you have no idea who the bride is and isn't."

"Really? That sounds intriguing."

Avery knew the Reed sisters could keep a secret. Riley, who'd met them occasionally over the summers she'd spent in Chance Creek growing up, had told her a little about them. How their father hardly ever came home when they were little, working his way up through the ranks of the military until he became a general. Then he stopped coming home at all after their mother died when they were still fairly young.

"They were basically raised by wolves" was the way Riley put it. "They never went to school. Hardly ever came to town. I've never, ever seen all five of them together in one place except at Two Willows. It's like their ranch is enchanted, and they can't bear to leave it."

Avery thought the whole situation was romantic— except for those boyfriends, whom she'd met now and then on her trips here to see Alice. Maybe someday a bunch of princes would come along and set them free.

Cass didn't seem to need saving, however. She bent over Alice's designs happily, debating them with Jo until Alice returned.

"We like this one best." She pointed to the fanciest of the bunch. "I'm not sure which one Avery likes, though."

"She's playing it close to the vest," Jo agreed.

"Off you two go. The bride has to choose for herself," Alice told them. "I'll bring Avery and Elizabeth over for tea before it's time for them to leave."

Cass and Jo left good-naturedly, and Alice took a seat beside Avery. "Which one do you like?"

"This one. It's simple, but it's stunning, and I can't take my eyes off it." Avery pointed to a design that showed a plain gown gathered just below the bustline and swooped over the model's curves, with a gossamer overgown that trailed behind it.

"That's the perfect one," Alice exclaimed. "These are the fabrics I would use for it. In fact, let me show you. I couldn't help myself." She moved swiftly to the other side of the room and came back lugging a dressmaker's form.

Avery laughed. "You already made the dress?"

"Just a mock-up, but… well… yes." Alice blushed, looking prettier than ever. "I knew it had to be this one."

The gown was satin, the overlay sheer with the most delicate embroidery around the hemline. Avery knew she'd be the image of grace and purity in it. Maybe she was far from pure in life, but somehow the gown embodied who she wanted to be—regal and joyful, something bright and beautiful in the world.

"It will look fabulous on you," Alice said. "Let me finish up with Elizabeth and then you can try it on. I made it to fit your measurements."

She moved off again toward the fitting room, and Avery circled the mannequin, entranced by the wedding dress Alice had created for her. When she looked up again, she sucked in a surprised breath. Elizabeth was standing close by, her sensible clothes replaced by a deep wine-red Regency gown.

"Oh, you're stunning!"

She could only wish for Elizabeth's tall figure, high cheekbones and the glorious fall of her long, dark hair. "If Walker saw you in that, he'd ditch me in a minute."

Elizabeth shook her head. "Walker has eyes only for you. I wonder what—" She bit off the end of her sentence and just smiled. Avery's curiosity grew. Was there someone else Elizabeth wanted to impress?

Interesting.

"Your turn," Alice told Avery and ushered her to the fitting room. She helped Avery change into the fabulous gown, then led her to the mirrors.

Tears pricked at Avery's eyes when she took in her reflection. She was no tall, dark beauty, but the draped fabric accentuated her curves, while the delicate overlay took the design to a higher level. With her auburn hair tumbling over bare shoulders, the fitted bodice emphasizing the curve of her breasts and the long skirts trailing behind her, she'd never felt prettier.

"Walker is going to lose his mind," Elizabeth told her when she saw her. "Avery, that's wonderful."

"Thank you," Avery said happily. "You're right," she told Alice. "It's perfect."

When they left the studio some time later, she reminded herself that Elizabeth was the one who'd supposedly tried on wedding gowns and tried to erase the beatific smile from her face. Jericho and Curtis were suitably impressed with Elizabeth's new wine-red gown, which she was still wearing.

"Can we check out that hedge maze?" Jericho asked when they were done oohing and aahing over Elizabeth's new clothes.

"Of course," Alice said.

"I'll take them." A woman stood up from where she'd been weeding rows of carrots nearby. Sadie Reed. Her kitchen garden was enormous, and Avery knew she ran a vegetable stand through the summer months along with brewing herbal remedies in her greenhouses.

"I'll help Cass with the tea," Alice said. She squeezed Avery's hand before she left. "Sometimes your dreams come true even if your dreams don't come true," she said kindly and was gone before Avery could ask her what she meant by that.

She followed the others to the hedge maze, Alice's words tickling at her like the buzz of a fly in a bedroom at night. She'd heard rumors of the woman's fey qualities, as Riley called them. Had Alice seen a glimpse of her future?

Were her dreams not going to come true?

Avery shook off her fears and hurried to catch up to the others. Alice wouldn't have spent an hour helping her choose her wedding dress if she didn't think she was going to marry Walker.

She forgot all about the strange incident as they paced the dark, green passages of the maze, the evergreen shrubs that formed the walls stretching high above their heads.

"How do you keep it trimmed?" Elizabeth asked.

"It isn't easy," Sadie told them. A young, sprightly woman, her love for all growing things was evident. She ran her hand along the hedge as they walked. If Avery didn't know better, she'd have thought Sadie was communing with it.

When they finally reached the center, Elizabeth gasped. "How did that get here?"

A huge, upright slab of stone stood at the center of the maze like a monolith stolen from Stonehenge and shipped across the ocean. Jericho and Curtis immediately went to inspect it.

"No one knows," Sadie said with a shrug. "One of our ancestors must have put it here, but there's no record of it, and the stone itself comes from hundreds of miles away."

Elizabeth walked around it in a circle, disappearing behind its broad back and reappearing on the other side. "It's remarkable."

Jericho and Curtis were arguing. "… faster than you," Jericho was saying.

"No way. You couldn't find your way out of a paper bag," Curtis said.

"Wanna bet?"

"Yeah."

"Can you ladies do without us for a minute?" Jericho said. "We won't go far."

"We're perfectly fine," Sadie told them.

They watched the men position themselves at the opening of the nearest passage. In a sudden burst, they raced off. Sadie shook her head. "They're in for it now," she said. Turning back to Elizabeth, she added, "The stone will answer any question you have."

Elizabeth laughed. "Answer it? How?"

Sadie shrugged again. "Try it and see. Just touch it and ask what you want to know."

Elizabeth contemplated the tall stone, shrugged. "Oh, why not?" She stepped forward and put her hands on its surface. "Will I... win?"

A breeze picked up, lifted tendrils of Elizabeth's hair and brushed Avery's cheek.

"Well?" Elizabeth asked the stone. "Where's my answer?"

"It takes time," Sadie told her.

Elizabeth dropped her hands and brushed them off on her gown before she seemed to realize what she was doing. She sighed. "I don't have time."

The wind gusted through the clearing again, and a scrap of newspaper floated along with it, lifting and twirling until it almost hit Elizabeth in the face.

With a little cry of surprise, she snatched it out of the air and crumpled it in her hand.

"No!" Sadie jumped to rescue it. She smoothed it out again. "Look."

Avery came close to peer at the faded newspaper. "Climate Change is Unstoppable, Experts Say," read the headline. Elizabeth expelled a breath.

"Unstoppable? That's my answer?" She turned back to the stone. "There's no hope at all?"

"Wait, look at the subheading," Sadie said, pointing.

"But with Effort We Can Mitigate Its Effect," Avery read out loud slowly. "With effort—like what you're doing testifying to Congress."

"You're testifying to Congress?" Sadie looked impressed.

"No one can know that," Avery told her. She was doing a lousy job keeping secrets today.

"I won't say a word."

The men thundered into the clearing, both of them clearly confused by how they'd gotten there.

"I told you that last turn was wrong," Jericho said.

"We're supposed to be guarding the women," Curtis bluffed. "I brought us back here on purpose."

"Avery? You want to try asking a question?" Sadie asked.

Avery remembered Alice's strange prophesy earlier and shook her head.

"Another time."

CHAPTER NINE

"**Y**OU'RE MAKING A huge mistake," Angus said. "You're killing Avery, and you're going to wish you were dead, too, if you go through with this wedding."

One more day, Walker promised himself. In less than twenty-four hours, he'd bring Elizabeth to the airport, and he could stop evading confrontations like this. He wanted to tell Angus he was right, but he couldn't. Renata had let it slip last night how closely Fulsom was monitoring everything that went on at Base Camp right now.

"He knows this show has to end strong," she'd put it. "I think he wants to throw us another curve ball or two before it's over."

Exposing Elizabeth as a fake and booting her off the ranch would rank right up there, Walker knew. Even twenty-four hours without protection could be time enough for someone to find her and make sure she never got the chance to testify.

"Some promises have to be kept no matter what,"

he said.

"I don't buy that, and I don't think you do, either."

"I do. Sometimes." Walker held his gaze. "I know what I'm doing, Angus," he added, hoping the man would drop it.

"I sure as hell hope so." Angus stalked off.

Walker hoped he could regain his friends' respect when this was all over. Elizabeth and Avery were doing their part by barely speaking to each other, except for the times when Elizabeth ordered Avery to attend to a certain part of her wedding preparations.

More than once he'd heard the other women speculating on why Avery was letting her get away with it, but Avery went along with the charade, grudgingly carrying out orders he knew she was secretly loving.

"We need to stage an intervention," he heard Savannah say once. "All this helpfulness toward the person who's stealing her happiness. It's sick!"

Whenever they could, he and Avery stole moments together in the barn, the stables—wherever they were away from other eyes. It was difficult when they were supposed to stay with their work groups, but they still managed it. A quick kiss here, an embrace there—

All of it adding to his continuing frustration.

One more day.

He got to his morning chores with a vengeance, scowling whenever one of the others was near, relaxing when they weren't. It was hard to hide his optimistic mood, and he had to counsel himself to frown a little on his way to the bunkhouse at midday after the bell rang for the meal.

When he met up with Elizabeth, who'd been standing a little apart, speaking on her phone as usual, his frown turned to genuine concern. Her arms were crossed over her chest, her lips pinched together in an angry line. Her hair, usually tied back so neatly in a braid when she worked, was coming down as if she'd raked her fingers through it more than once.

"What's wrong?"

"They moved it again." Her words were barely audible. "The Senate. They pushed back the hearing. Now it's the same day as the vote—the last day before one of their state work sessions. In other words, they're going to cram it all into one day with no extensions, because all the senators will have plans to travel home that night. What are they up to, Walker? They're going to sabotage this somehow! They're not even going to give me a chance to be heard!"

He'd never heard her so distraught before, and it unnerved him. "The day of the vote? What day is that?"

She shook her head and covered her face with her hands. "That's the worst of it. May thirtieth." Her voice was muffled, but he heard her loud and clear.

The air whistled out of his lungs. "May thirtieth?" His wedding day?

She dropped her hands. "We can still do this," she urged him. "I know it's awful, but we can still pull it off. I'll leave early that morning, and you can still have your wedding day."

"And keep the truth secret until then? That'll kill

Avery."

"We have to! Walker, where else can I go?"

"Why does it have to be you?" he demanded, losing his cool. "Other people must be able to present the same information you can."

"I'm… better suited to presenting the information. I've seen what's happening, not just on our continent but in Siberia, too."

He stared at her a long moment before shaking his head slowly. That didn't add up. "There's something else, isn't there? Something you haven't told me."

She closed her eyes.

"Elizabeth."

"There's more," she confirmed. "It's an open secret that if this bill passes, Lawrence Energy will win the contract to extract the oil there. I've got footage from Lawrence's other operations. Whistleblower stuff. No one knows. No one can know."

"Someone knows if they're trying to kill you."

She swallowed. Nodded. "They already killed the whistleblower. That's why I haven't been home before this—I was in the thick of it. Securing the information, the proof they've never operated within the rules and won't this time, either."

"Jesus, Elizabeth. That's the mess you brought to my door?"

"That's the mess they're taking to the world! Don't you get it? They don't care what they're doing. They don't care what will happen in thirty years. They're willing to kill people to keep on polluting and sending more and more carbon into the air, as long as they get their money."

Walker ran both hands through his hair. "Avery deserves a real wedding!"

"She'll get a real wedding," Elizabeth promised. "It will all be set to go. I'll disappear the morning of the thirtieth. Once I'm on that plane, I'm not your concern anymore. You and Avery will have your day."

A commotion near the bunkhouse caught his attention. "Now what?"

Elizabeth hurried after him as he went to investigate and found Montague and several of his men clustered around Boone.

"No way. Absolutely not. What are you thinking?" Boone looked up as Walker approached. "They say Fulsom told them they can disassemble the wind turbines."

Walker turned on Montague. Got right in his face. "Get. The. Hell. Out. Of. Here." He pronounced each word in turn, slowly and distinctly.

Montague took a step back, his smug smirk slipping away fast. "I'll have Fulsom call you," he said. "He'll sort this out. We need to get cracking—the building season's slipping away." He turned and strode off, his men trailing him. "Be back tomorrow," he called over his shoulder.

Walker found Boone considering him, an eyebrow raised. "What's eating you?"

"Everything," Walker said.

"HONEY, YOUR DAD and I are worried about you," Avery's mother said when Avery accepted her call after lunch. "Why are you planning someone else's wedding to Walker instead of your own?"

Now that the show was down to the wire, the crew was posting daily updates to the website, and today's featured footage was of Elizabeth surveying the manor's ballroom to see where her reception would take place. Avery had been present, offering suggestions for how to arrange it all. It had been like a game pretending to help Elizabeth decide things about her wedding when really she was planning her own.

Now everything had changed. Walker and Elizabeth had sat her down and explained the delay to the Senate hearing. Avery had listened with growing horror as she realized she was barely going to get a wedding day at all. No one could know that she was marrying Walker until Elizabeth boarded her flight.

Which meant no planning sessions with her friends. No rehearsal dinner. None of the little traditions that made a wedding special. She had to arrange everything in secret. No one else could know until hours before she walked down the aisle.

She kept her voice even. "Because we all pitch in to help."

There was an uncharacteristic silence on the other end of the line.

"But you're supposed to marry Walker, honey."

"I know." She hated everything about the situation. Was holding back tears even now. She'd always thought she'd savor every aspect of planning her wedding.

"I... don't understand."

Welcome to the club, Avery thought. "Elizabeth and Walker have known each other a long time. He can't let her down."

"But he loves you."

"Yes." She wasn't going to lie about that.

"Are you marrying him or not?"

Avery couldn't answer that. If she said yes, her mother would tell everyone she knew. If she said no, she'd be lying to her mother.

"Avery Lightfoot, stop playing games!"

Avery pulled the phone away from her face. Her mother hadn't yelled at her in years.

"We don't play around with love in this family," her mother went on. "We don't lie to each other, either."

"I don't want to lie to you." She really didn't. "So I can't answer that question. You'll have to be patient— and ready for anything. Can you understand that?"

"Of course I can, but I'll point out that you lied once already. You were married, and you never said a word. We had to find out about that Brody fellow by watching the show. I can't believe you never told us about him. We could have helped you get it annulled, sweetheart. Why would you keep that from us?'

So they'd seen the latest episode. She supposed it was a miracle her mother hadn't confronted her sooner.

"How on earth could I tell you how badly I'd screwed up? You and Dad are the king and queen of romance. You never got dumped. You never screwed up everything and had to limp home in disgrace. I didn't even allow myself to think about Brody after it was over. I hoped none of it was real. I wanted to forget the whole thing even happened."

"Life doesn't work that way."

"I know."

"This is all our fault," her mother said. "We thought we could create a world for you where love reigned supreme. We wanted to give you the best example of marriage we could."

"You did."

"But we went overboard, didn't we, if you think we've never made any mistakes. Sweetheart, your father and I have made tons of them. Everyone does. Nothing you can do would disappoint us. It's okay if you don't get married. You know that, right?"

Avery opened her mouth to say she was getting married.

Realized she couldn't.

"You're a strong, wonderful, amazing woman, and if Walker marries someone else, it's his loss. You'll be okay. Call us up, and we'll come get you."

"Mom!"

"Honey, if he'd proposed, you would have told me, so we know things aren't going well. Do what you have to, but we're always here for you. You know that, right?"

"Of course." She wanted to explain everything, but she couldn't, and she knew if she said anything else, she'd start stumbling over her words. One thing her mother said kept playing over in her mind.

If Walker had proposed, she would have called her.

But Walker hadn't ever proposed, had he?

Not really.

Not in all this time.

Her mother sighed. "Keep us posted, honey. We'll be ready for anything."

"Thank you." Avery hung up, her head spinning.

Why hadn't Walker proposed?

Why didn't she have a ring—if not to wear yet, then at least to look at when she was all alone?

She tried to shake off her doubts. She was going to marry Walker on May thirtieth, and that was all that mattered. Which meant she had to get Kai and Addison on board for preparing the food for the reception.

She ducked into the kitchen to find them cleaning up after the noon meal.

"Let Elizabeth plan her own wedding," Addison said when Avery explained her errand. "Let her grab something at the grocery store. Cold cuts and cheese platters or whatever. It's not like we're going to celebrate her and Walker getting married. I can't believe she asked you to handle this."

"Elizabeth would like a full sit-down dinner." Avery named the number of guests. Everyone at Base Camp plus her parents. She would have liked to invite other people, but there was no way to do that now that she couldn't tell anyone about the wedding until the day itself.

"Elizabeth can go screw herself," Kai said. "I'm not

cooking for those two."

"But—" She closed her mouth. She wasn't allowed to tell them the truth. Walker had reiterated the need for secrecy this morning.

"Avery, let me give you a little advice," Addison told her kindly. "You can't let people push you around. You care about Walker, and you want him to have a nice wedding, even if it's not to you. I get it, even though I could never carry off that kind of altruism myself, but martyring yourself like that isn't going to do anyone any good. Least of all you. Sue will take care of Walker and Elizabeth's wedding. They can have it on the reservation, which I'm sure is where Sue would prefer to hold it anyhow. It's not your place to be involved in this travesty."

Avery left the bunkhouse kitchen before she spilled the beans or worse, cried with frustration, and returned to the main room, where everyone else was finishing their meals and milling about talking. She understood the need to protect Elizabeth and keep Fulsom from kicking her off the show, but her own happiness kept getting snatched out from under her, just when she thought it was secure.

A group of women had gathered in one corner of the room, chatting. Through the large front window, Avery spotted Maud Russell coming their way. A shriek made her jump, and she turned to find Leslie had just spilled a cup of tea down her gown and was fussing and fretting over it, trying to blot the liquid with napkins the other women were handing her. Avery took advantage of the distraction to slip outside the bunkhouse and head off Maud.

"Where's James?" she asked.

"With the carriage. We just stopped by to say hello." She frowned. "Just in time by the looks of things. Is there something I can do to help, my dear? You look distraught."

"I… I'd love a ride in your carriage right away," Avery confessed, needing to get away from Base Camp and all the secrets and frustrations, even for a short time.

"That will make James very happy!" Maud exclaimed. "Come on."

Avery hurried along with her, hoping no gunmen were lurking about in the broad daylight, happy to escape the ranch before anyone noticed her. "I'm with the Russells," she texted to Riley so no one would worry. "Perfectly safe."

She figured it was only a matter of time before some of the men hopped in a truck and came after them to guard her, so as soon as the carriage was underway, she wasted no time in telling her problems to Maud. She'd learned over the time she'd known Maud that the woman might seem like a flighty Regency-era matron, but the reality was she was smart as a whip. She was playing a part, and as an actress herself, Avery understood that. It was a part Maud had chosen to act out 24/7, but a part all the same.

"I need a wedding. A real wedding. But it's got to be a secret; no one else but me can know about it until the day."

"A secret wedding. How intriguing!" Maud leaned forward. "Tell me all about it."

Avery did, explaining Elizabeth's predicament and the need to hide her in plain sight at Base Camp. She explained Fulsom's rules, too, and the reason for all their secrecy. She even filled in Maud on her parents' inability to keep a secret and her fear they wouldn't make it to her wedding—and her inability to invite anyone else she might want to be there.

"I don't know what to do. I love Walker, and I would marry him in a chicken coop if I really had to, but I've dreamed of my wedding day my whole life, and if it's at all possible, I want the whole nine yards: flowers, music, dancing…"

"And that's exactly what you shall have, my dear," Maud said comfortably. "I'll tell you what. James and I shall throw a party in your honor."

"We're never happier than when we're throwing a party," James tossed back over his shoulder from where he sat guiding the horses.

"We won't tell anyone else at Base Camp about it, but rest assured we will be prepared for them all to attend once Elizabeth flies to Washington. It shall be a very wonderful, very secret, very *formal* party, and we'll invite everyone you know," Maud went on. "Including your parents. And if there happens to be a wedding when they all show up, including your Base Camp friends, who won't have anything better to do, well, I doubt any of them will mind!"

Avery beamed. "I knew you'd have an answer. You're so good to us." She threw her arms around Maud and hugged her.

"Other girls dream of being Cinderella," Maud said happily, "but personally I always wanted to be the fairy godmother."

"Uh oh, we have company," James said.

Avery looked over her shoulder. Just as she thought, a Base Camp truck was following close behind.

The scolding she was sure to get was worth it, she decided.

"What color scheme were you thinking of, dear?" Maud asked. "Don't worry; those cranky men can wait. You and I are going to plan every last detail."

"ADDISON IS RIGHT, Sue would have liked the wedding to take place on the reservation," Elizabeth said when Avery told her and Walker everything that had happened, including her disastrous attempt to get Kai and Addison to cater the affair.

"Do you mind if I let it slip that's what's happening?" Avery said. "That your wedding is going to be a small affair on the Crow reservation, and I'm done helping you? That will explain why I've suddenly stopped preparing for the wedding here."

"Sue doesn't like lies," Walker said.

"Don't tell them anything," Elizabeth advised. "If they ask why you've stopped planning my wedding, just say, 'Ask Sue.' No more, no less. None of them will dare ask her anything, and she'll be none the wiser."

She was right, Walker had to admit, and it was good to hear Avery laugh. They all looked around to make sure no one else in their work party had heard them.

"So the wedding is sorted," Elizabeth said. "I wish everything else was, too."

"That's the next item on my agenda," Avery assured her. "Maud's handling my wedding, so now I can handle your publicity problem."

"Publicity problem?"

"Like we talked about, you need to educate the public. Get everyone to call their senators to get them to vote against allowing drilling in the Renning field."

"We've worked with all the usual groups to get the word out."

"You need to go where the kids are."

"Kids?"

"Yes, the kids. Teenagers and twentysomethings are far more aware of how climate change is going to affect their future than anyone else. All those old geezers in the legislature? They don't care because they'll be dead before things get bad."

"Avery!"

"It's true. Every time we say Greenland's ice will be gone by 2100, everyone over forty shrugs. They're not going to live that long, so why give up any creature comforts now? The teens and twentysomethings, on the other hand, might still be here. They've been hearing about the problem since they were in diapers. They're not asking *if* climate change is going to affect them; they're asking how bad it's going to be. How will it affect their jobs, their health, their ability to get married and have kids? Will there be enough water when they're older? Enough food? Will all the fish be gone? What about animals and birds?"

Elizabeth nodded. "What's your idea?" Walker could tell Elizabeth had a whole new level of respect for Avery.

"We're going to tell those kids the most effective way to get their message to Congress," Avery said. "And they'll do it."

Elizabeth turned to Walker. "What do you think?"

"Give her everything she needs." Avery had a way of connecting to young people and a savvy style of video production he was sure would strike a chord with them.

"I'm sure Renata and Eve will help when they see what I'm doing," Avery said confidently. "They'll go after the older voters."

"I hope this works," Elizabeth said.

"Walker? Avery?"

They turned when Hope came in.

"It's your turn," she said, holding up her phone. "*Star News* just announced before the commercial break they had things to tell their audience about you."

"Are you watching that stupid station all day, every day?" Avery asked her.

"I can't stop," Hope admitted. "It's like watching a train wreck, gruesome and disturbing and something you can't turn away from. Every time I think they've said the craziest thing they can think of, they say something else, and it's even crazier. It's like those old tabloid magazines on steroids."

"Those old tabloid magazines still exist, you know," Elizabeth told her.

"Do they? It's been so long since I've been to a supermarket I don't even know anymore. Anyway, I update the website with our side of the story each time they do a segment, so I have to watch."

"Let's talk about Walker Norton," the blonde TV host said as the commercials ended on Hope's phone. "The enigmatic Indian."

"Enigmatic Indian?" Elizabeth repeated. "Are these people from the nineteenth century?"

"I believe they're called Native Americans these days, Marla," the male host said on the screen.

"Have you ever noticed how picky everyone is about what they're called now, Paul?"

"I have. Lot of fuss about nothing if you ask me."

"They have to be from the nineteenth century," Avery said. "That's the only explanation for how ignorant they are."

The man held up a sheaf of papers. "Walker Norton and his purported fiancée, Elizabeth Blaine, are from the Crow reservation in southeast Montana," he intoned.

"They've got such normal names," Marla pointed out.

"You're right; I expected something more... I don't know... Indian-sounding." Paul's face creased in earnest confusion.

Avery put a hand to her forehead. "I can't watch this."

But she stayed exactly where she was.

"You don't expect people like Walker and Elizabeth to be interested in sustainable living, do you?" Paul went on conversationally.

"What the hell should *people like us* be interested in?" Elizabeth asked Walker.

"Really?" Marla said on the screen. "I mean, one could say the Indians—Native Americans, sorry." She made a face. "Are the first sustainable people. It's not like they were driving cars around before we got here."

"Right. They didn't have roads or running water or—"

Walker quietly took the phone from Hope's hand and turned it off.

All four of them stared at each other.

"What do we do with that?" Hope said. "What do we do with that level of stupidity? A whole network trying to make us look down on or even hate each other—pretending to be national news?"

"We stop pretending the world makes sense," Avery said. "We stop being surprised and start getting to work fixing things ourselves. And we look around for other people who are ready to help."

"We need the kids?" Elizabeth prompted.

"We need the kids."

"WE NEED AN extra pair of hands. I'd like Avery's help, if you don't mind," Avery heard Clay say two days later.

"We're supposed to keep to our cohorts," Hope said. She was helping Avery with the chickens, Walker was tending to the goats and Elizabeth was slopping the pigs, all within eyesight of one another. Avery had been online a lot in the last forty-eight hours, putting out videos and memes on all her social media channels and encouraging her followers to do the same.

"She'll be in the building cohort for the rest of the morning, and we'll deliver her back to you at lunch," Clay said.

Avery straightened. She'd been trying to pet a black-and-white speckled hen she'd named Nora months ago, but the hen wasn't having it. "I don't mind lending the building cohort a hand this morning." She figured Clay wouldn't have come asking if he didn't need her. Behind him was Curtis, Clay's father, Dell, Harris and the real Nora, carrying baby Connie. Daisy brought up the rear. They were taking the rules about traveling as a pack seriously.

"I'll finish up here," Hope assured her.

"What are we building today?" she asked Clay as they headed for the cluster of tiny houses arrayed on the slope outside the bunkhouse. She bit her lip when he led her to the one that was designated for Walker. She hadn't let herself think about the possibility of sharing it with him for a long time, even after she'd learned the truth about him and Elizabeth.

Now the prospect of a future with Walker hit her squarely in the chest. She'd spent some nights in this house when it was unfinished and already felt an affinity for it, but she hadn't entered it in weeks.

Clay ushered her inside, and she sighed happily. It was as beautiful as all the others, the floor-to-ceiling, south-facing windows letting in the glorious June sunshine. The kitchen was as tidy and inviting as a fairy-tale cottage.

She noticed the other builders had remained outside, and she wondered if they were all standing guard or if some of them were working on a different project. She peeked out a window and was relieved to see Nora sitting comfortably on a bench someone had placed nearby.

"I wanted your opinion about a few things, as a close friend of Walker's," Clay said.

She shot him an uncertain look. Clay didn't know how things stood; he thought Walker was marrying Elizabeth. Surely he saw how inappropriate it was to ask her anything that had to do with him.

"I wanted your opinion," Clay repeated slowly. "About what *you'd* like to see in Walker's tiny house. Just a few details."

She tried to decipher his expression. What was he really trying to say?

Clay huffed in exasperation and lowered his voice. "Look, Avery, I don't know what's going on, and any minute a film crew is going to burst through that door." A hubbub outside proved his prediction true. Were the others trying to distract the crew and give them a few minutes? "But I know Walker, and he's not marrying anyone but you. So tell me what you want in this house.

Quickly."

Should she pretend she didn't know what Clay was talking about? Avery decided against it.

"I love Curtis's woodwork," she said. "I know Walker likes anything that reminds him of the natural world. Clean lines. Nature needs no ornament, that kind of thing. Oh, and I want a shelf right here. Big enough to display the fan you all thought I stole from him."

Clay made a face. "Sorry about that," he mumbled. "We can do that. Do you want the outside edge left raw? That can be striking."

"That sounds great."

"What about you? Anything special you want?"

"I just want a home," she said simply. "A forever home. A place to raise my kids. A place that feels safe and cozy and like a big hug."

"A big hug." Clay nodded. "Something natural and clean. We're on it."

A camera crew burst in, and Avery decided it was time to call on her acting skills. "You're asking me?" she said loudly, allowing her voice to slide up an octave in mock fury. "Walker's marrying someone else, and you want me to help you decorate his house? Clay Pickett, you can go… screw yourself!"

She flounced through the knot of crew members and slipped out the door, knowing Clay would be amused by her theatrics.

"Should we take you back to the chickens?" Curtis asked as he and the other builders fell in with her.

"I'd rather hang out with you," she whispered.

"Demand to show me your plans for the new tiny houses you're going to build when the show is over."

Curtis brightened. "Definitely." He led her over to sit by Nora. "You have to see the plans. We're showing them to everyone. Getting all the input we can." He ducked closer for a moment. "You sure you don't mind?" he whispered back as the camera crew scrambled to surround them. "I know it's a touchy subject."

She didn't mind a bit—now that she knew she wouldn't have to live in one.

CHAPTER TEN

"**O**H, MY GOODNESS," Elizabeth said a couple of mornings later as people got ready for their jobs after breakfast. "She did it. Avery came through for us. She got everyone talking about the vote on the drilling legislation."

Walker held out a hand, and Elizabeth gave him her phone. He scrolled through a social media feed and saw what she meant. Video after video addressed the topic in different ways. There was a short video featuring a teenage girl in tears reading a long list of species that were being driven to extinction by climate change. A more professional video from a twentysomething student talking about oil spills in pristine environments. An ad for a luxury hotel. A post from someone they both knew on the reservation. An ad for an airline. Walker looked questioningly at her.

"Ignore those. I travel for my job a lot," she told him. "They've got me pegged as a rich adventurer. Look at this one."

She scrolled down a little and showed him a ten-second video whose background footage featured oil derricks and a skull and crossbones. A young man flashed on the screen. "Are… you… trying… to… kill… us… all?" he screamed in a thrasher-band snarl.

"Huh," Walker said.

"Whoops, not that one," Elizabeth said. She adjusted something on-screen, scrolled a little. "Look."

These posts were far more polished, narrated by political commentators.

"It's all over the internet this morning, Barry," one of them said. "It's a groundswell that came out of nowhere. All the kids are talking about it."

"About what, Neil?" the other man said.

"Drilling in the arctic. The opening of the Renning field. They're saying it's the final straw—the straw that's going to break the camel's back, if you will. The doomsday clock hitting midnight. If Lawrence Energy gets its way, all bets are off for the human race."

"We've heard that language before, Neil," the pundit said. "Seems kind of overblown."

"We've never seen pushback like this. Not everywhere at once. Not targeted at a single company whose project is the basis for a single piece of legislation. I've been calling senators, and this burst of activity is changing minds, Barry. Yesterday, I would have said this legislation was going to pass, hands down. Now I'm not so sure. And word is, there's some damning testimony due to be aired at the upcoming hearing."

"I'll be interested to see what happens next."

Elizabeth took back the phone. "Avery is smart.

You all don't take her seriously enough."

"I take her very seriously."

"Those guys are right, you know," she added, studying him. "We might be getting close to having the support we need. We'll keep the heat on, but it's looking better than I ever dreamed possible going into my presentation."

"Glad to hear it."

"Walker?" Renata called, appearing in the bunkhouse door. "Get over here. Outside."

"Now what?" he grumbled to Elizabeth, but he got up and followed the director outside where Avery, Gabe, Hope and Anders were hanging out with Brody and Jess not far off.

"Brody, this concerns you, too. I've got something to show you." She held up an envelope. "Your marriage to Avery is formally annulled. Congratulations, you two. You are free."

"Really?" Avery snatched the documents from Renata's hands, read them and looked up, eyes shining as she met Walker's gaze. "It's true—" She faltered, clearly remembering too late she was supposed to still be miserable. She flung the papers at Brody. "Doesn't matter, does it, though?" she said and walked away.

Walker's heart ached for her, appreciating her acting skills but knowing how much it cost her not to be able to celebrate her happiness openly. He promised himself then and there he'd find a way to toast the future with her later.

"That's right," Elizabeth said firmly, taking his arm.

"Doesn't matter now that you're with the person you were always meant to marry."

Gabe rolled his eyes but went to follow Avery. Renata studied them, but she was distracted when Brody, reading the paperwork for himself, whooped.

"I'm a free man. And I'm a star on a national television show. What could beat that?"

"You could find the woman you were always meant to marry, too," Jess called from behind a camera.

For a moment, Brody hesitated, clearly taken aback, but then he rallied. "That's true. That's very true. That could happen. Come on, darling, let's see if Kai's got something we can celebrate with."

Elizabeth leaned in close and brushed her mouth near Walker's ear. "Leave it to me. I'll get you some time alone with Avery."

Walker nodded, but he didn't hold out much hope.

"I'VE GOT TO hand it to Elizabeth. She's a mastermind getting us this ride alone together," Avery told Walker the following morning. She was back in James Russell's carriage, snuggled happily against Walker's side, enjoying the May sunshine and the fresh smell of the morning, not a camera crew in sight.

"Let us off here," Walker called up to James.

The older man looked down from his seat, where he was directing the horses. "Here?"

"What are you doing?" Avery asked him. She looked around. They weren't anywhere near Two Willows, and there was nothing but pastures here.

"That's right. Pick us up again at eleven thirty?"

James raised his eyebrows, and Avery wondered if he'd object, but the man nodded a moment later. "I'll take the horses for a good, long drive and pick you up again on my way home from Two Willows."

"You don't mind finishing our errand for us? We're just picking up some more gowns from Alice Reed."

"Don't mind at all," James said happily. "It's a beautiful day for a walk in the countryside. Don't blame you a bit for wanting to get out and stretch your legs."

"Exactly," Walker said.

"I can't believe we might actually get away with this," Avery whispered as Walker helped her down from the carriage, shouldering a day pack he'd brought along. There were no cameramen with them. Not only had Elizabeth ordered them on this errand to pick up her wedding gown, but also she'd created a scene with Gabe at the same time James had arrived to pick them up. They'd been able to sneak off without anyone noticing.

"We'll get away with it," Walker assured her. "I told you we could count on James—and Elizabeth."

Walker shouldered the pack he'd prepared for the situation. "Walk on," James said to his horses when they were free of the carriage. He tipped his hat to them as the carriage rolled away.

"What now?" Avery asked.

"Just an innocent, little walk."

She grinned. Her intentions for this precious time alone with him were hardly innocent, but they needed to clear the air before they could do anything else.

Walker crooked his arm, and she took it as they set off across a meadow. She had no idea where they were going, but Walker had grown up in these parts, and she trusted him.

Maybe now she could finally get a few things off her chest she'd been wanting to say for a while.

"I need to explain something," she said.

Walker waited patiently, guiding her over the rough ground.

"It's about Brody. Why I married him and why I never told you about him before he showed up." She took a moment to gather her thoughts. "The thing is, I was supposed to be married to someone else that year."

She could feel his surprise in the way his grip tightened a fraction on her arm. She could almost feel him willing himself to be calm as his fingers relaxed again, but there was a wariness about him now.

"You have to understand I always wanted to get married. My parents—well, I hope you'll meet them soon. They have the best relationship of anyone I've ever met. Thirty years in, they're still madly in love. I used to open the refrigerator in the morning and find little love notes they left each other attached to the margarine. They stuck those notes everywhere. On the bathroom mirrors, the dashboards of each other's cars. They went on date nights every week, held hands wherever they went. They don't just love each other; they like each other tremendously. I want that, too."

She matched his pace and tried to think how to explain it all. She'd been in such a fervor of romance back then. Probably understandable in a teen but embarrassing now none the less. Her stomach twisted with the memory of it.

"Prom was supposed to be the best night of my life. I'd made sure everything was perfect. I looked amazing." She laughed, but it came out flat. "Honestly, it's true—my dress was the most gorgeous thing I've ever owned in my life."

It was a deceptively simple gown that accentuated her curves and made her look taller than her five-foot-one stature. Her auburn hair had been professionally done that afternoon. Her makeup applied by a cosmetician her mother, Diana, had scheduled to come to their home. The photographer documenting the occasion had snapped away all the while, as if she were a famous actress preparing to walk the red carpet.

The busy day might have flustered another eighteen-year-old, but Avery took it all in stride. After all, she'd been acting on and off in local productions since she was five. She'd had her hair and makeup done dozens of times. Had dressed up in all sorts of costumes—some beautiful, some decidedly not. Just because she'd never had a major part yet didn't mean she wasn't professional.

"That night was going to be the most important night of my life," she told Walker. "I had planned everything so I'd sweep into adulthood in the kind of fairy-tale romance my parents had. My dad proposed to my mom on their prom night. They married before they left for college together that fall and hit every major milestone together, from college graduation, their first real jobs, first house—and having me. Their love for each other just kept growing. I figured the love Daniel and I had for each other would be like that, too."

She shook her head. "I was so damn young, Walker. I thought I could make it happen by force of will, and Daniel went along with it. Prom was huge at our school. First we gathered with all the other students to show off our fancy clothes and get our photos taken. Then we joined five other couples for dinner at the best restaurant in town, all of us riding in a stretch limousine. Then we went to the hotel where the formal part of the evening was held. I was so excited. I thought our slow dances were good practice for our wedding waltz in a few months."

She hadn't allowed herself to think about that night for a long time, and her throat thickened with the pain of it.

"I'd already started planning our wedding, even though we weren't engaged yet. I researched everything from venues to catering and more. It was going to be simple but lovely and happen in mid-August, so we'd have enough time for a tiny honeymoon before heading off to school. I was going to study acting, and Daniel was going to do pre-med. Once we graduated from college, we'd travel to California so he could be doctor to the stars, and I would be—well, one of those stars."

"What happened?" Walker asked softly when she didn't say any more.

"The dance was fine, even though Daniel was a little

strange. Kind of distant, you know? Nervous. I thought he was twisted up about the proposal. I'd told him just how it happened for my parents. How they'd danced all night and then my father proposed…" She remembered the excitement blossoming in her stomach as the hours ticked by. "It was supposed to be a night to remember. A proposal. A ring—"

Except it hadn't worked that way at all.

"By the time the dance was over, I knew something was wrong. We went upstairs to the room we'd gotten, and Daniel went to the bathroom. Stayed there a really long time."

Walker's fingers tightened on her arm again, in sympathy this time.

"When he came out, he was wearing street clothes. He said he couldn't go through with it. His voice was rough. Higher than usual. He looked like he'd been… crying." That part shamed her more than the rest of it. "He said he didn't love me. Didn't want to marry me. Sure as hell didn't want to go to med school." Her voice cracked. "I was so desperate to salvage something, I told him it was fine with me if he wanted to change his major." A tear slipped down her cheek, and Avery fought to hold back the rest of them. "He laughed at me." She put a hand to her chest remembering how bad that had hurt. "He said, 'I don't want to change my major. I want to change everything. Didn't you hear me? I don't love you. I've never loved you. You're nice, don't get me wrong, but there's got to be more than nice.'"

Walker stopped in the middle of the meadow and took both her hands.

Avery hung her head. "He said he was leaving," she whispered. "I thought he meant he was leaving the hotel. Turned out he'd packed up his car. He'd parked it outside earlier that day. He said he was leaving town and wouldn't be back for months. He said, 'Find someone else for your forever. I don't want it.' That's who I was, Walker—the kind of girl someone like Daniel had to run like hell from."

Walker pulled her into his arms, and Avery breathed in the familiar scent of him. His comforting strength.

"I didn't know what to do. My parents had planned a party for the next day to announce our engagement. They'd invited everybody. How was I going to face them?"

Her words were muffled against his chest, but she had to tell him all of it. "The only good thing was that I'd parked my car at the hotel earlier, too. We were supposed to take it to the party the next morning. I managed to slip out of the hotel with no one seeing me, found my car, got in and started driving—still in my stupid prom dress. I drove all night. Drove all the next day. Just kept going. My parents were frantic. Everyone was frantic. I got a million texts and calls, but I didn't answer my phone. I got to Vegas the next night, found a dive bar, still in that dress. Brody thought it was awesome—the girl who ditched prom to come see him play." She buried her face against Walker's shirt. "He was the one who got me in even though I was clearly underage. He spotted me in the parking lot—they got there the same time I did. Told the bouncer I was with the band. I got really drunk. Danced a whole bunch. When their set was over, Brody and I kept going. I must have told him what happened." She let out a long sigh. "He said I should marry him instead, and I said yes. It was obvious to me no one else would ever want me. I was so hurt and so sad—and so damn drunk."

"So you married him."

"I guess. I don't really remember much." She had a shadowy sense of a chapel. An officiant. Brody sliding a cheap ring they'd gotten somewhere onto her finger.

Saying the vow she thought she'd say to Daniel.

"I woke up the next morning and didn't know where I was. I was still in my prom dress. Brody was gone. I thought I'd dreamed the whole thing, but there were too many details. I don't think we even slept together." Shame suffused her. "I think we fumbled around a little." God, it was so tawdry, she couldn't stand to think about it. "I think we both fell asleep."

"He wasn't there when you woke up?"

She shook her head. "Like he said, he took one look at me in the daylight, freaked out and split. He left nothing behind. I figured the wedding couldn't be real." She pushed away from him, and Walker let her go. Avery dried her eyes. "I hoped it wasn't real. Years went by, and I never heard from him again. I let myself forget the whole thing."

She let the whole grim affair sink in. "I... lost myself that day. I thought Daniel stole my pride, my self-worth. I thought Brody took whatever was left afterward. That wasn't true, though, was it?" A sob escaped her. "They didn't take anything; I gave all my self-worth away. And I've been giving it away ever since. I don't know why I keep doing that."

"You'll stop now," Walker said calmly. Avery felt as if he'd absorbed some of her pain and was using his strength and level-headedness to diffuse it, so it wouldn't overwhelm her.

She let out a shaky breath. "You're right. Now that I've seen the pattern, it's so obvious, I won't be able to do it anymore. I won't let myself."

"I've got something I need to say to you, too."

Avery braced herself.

Could she take any more pain?

"THERE'S A REASON I promised to marry Elizabeth." Walker wondered how it was that people managed to tie themselves into knots given the least bit of string. He ached to go back in time, meet eighteen-year-old Avery and take her to the prom himself. He wished he could spare her every hardship.

Life wasn't like that, though.

"You told me that reason," Avery reminded him.

"I told you about Netta and Sue, but I never told you the rest of it. Why I felt I had to go along with what Elizabeth said that day. The reason behind the reason."

Avery waited, wanting to give him the same attention he'd just given her.

"Before I was born, my father, Joe, was best friends

with Netta's son, Worth. Dad and Worth did everything together, and when Worth got a girlfriend, my dad did, too. Sounds like he did it mostly to keep up and be able to double date. They were barely eighteen when Worth and Tricia had a baby. I don't know, maybe Dad knocked up my mom on purpose." Walker shrugged. "I think he didn't want to be left behind. Worth was the kind of guy who lit up a room when he walked into it. No matter who he met on the reservation, he had something to say to them. That's what I was told," he amended. "Never met him myself."

Avery wanted to reach out to Walker, but she knew instinctively he needed space to be able to go on.

"An oil company came to the area looking to start a project. Outside the reservation but inside traditional Crow territory. It was a setup for trouble, and they knew it, so they came knocking, offering jobs, money, if we endorsed it."

"How did that go over?" Avery asked.

He shrugged. "Some people were for it, some against, just like you'd expect. My dad and Worth were against it. My family has always put the health of our land and the waterways over profit, but you have to understand money can be hard to come by in Crow territory. Lots of temptation there."

"What happened?"

"There was a protest. Worth and Dad went to it. So did Worth's girlfriend, Tricia, but Dad and Mom had split up already a few weeks earlier, and he was feeling it. Worth's girlfriend didn't mind him hanging around usually, from the sound of things, but she didn't want Dad tagging along that day. The protest was off the reservation. She and Worth left the baby behind. Netta once told me those two were talking about getting married around that time. She was all for it, of course, and she took the baby for the day, wanting to give them some time to themselves. Anyway, I think Worth and Tricia believed in the cause, but I get the feeling it was supposed to be a bit of a getaway for them, too. Only problem was Worth didn't have a car. Dad did. So he drove them. You've got to remember, they were all still kids, really, even if Tricia and Worth had a kid themselves."

A pit was forming in Avery's stomach. She already knew this wasn't a story with a happy ending.

"There must have been an argument at the protest," Walker went on, his gaze far off on the horizon. "Or maybe Tricia made it clear she didn't want Dad around. I don't know. They separated. Planned to meet up the next morning to drive home. Worth and Tricia got a motel room, spent the night. There was proof of that afterward. They checked out the next morning, went to the rendezvous point, I guess."

"But your dad didn't pick them up? Did he go home early?" Avery guessed.

Walker shook his head. "He was late. Dad found a girl. She took him home. Spent the night with her. Overslept. By the time he made it back to where they were supposed to meet up, Worth was furious. He'd been calling friends, trying to find out where Dad was.

Those people Worth called said later they'd never heard him so angry."

Avery waited.

"Guess Dad was angry, too. People saw them at a gas station, filling up the car. Worth and Tricia in the back seat. Dad pumping gas. He got into it with some local guy who'd stopped to fill up, too. The guy had seen Dad at the protest. He wanted the project to go through. Nearly came to blows, but other people intervened. They testified that Dad was really furious—both of them were. He got back in his car. Took off. The other guy followed them." He swallowed, and Avery felt his pain in her own body, an ache in her throat, emptiness in her heart. "They were playing chicken on the highway until the other guy hit them and ran them right off the road. He kept going. By the time help came, it was too late; Worth and Tricia were gone."

Avery couldn't imagine how bad the crash must have been for the people in the back seat to have died. "I'm so sorry, Walker."

"When my dad woke up in the hospital and heard what happened, he took off and didn't come home for weeks. Sue said when he did, it was to tell her he'd enlisted with the Army and would never be back again. She said he'd lost thirty pounds, looked like a ghost. Like he was dead already."

Avery covered her mouth with her hand.

"A week after he was gone, my mom came around looking for him. She was from town. A White girl," he spelled out, although Avery already knew that. "Her parents marched her over to the reservation to demand that my dad do the right thing and marry her. Sue was glad Dad was gone then. They weren't doing it to get him to take responsibility for me; they were doing it to punish their daughter." His bitterness was clear. "Later, they were sorry for that. My grandparents did their best by me after they lost Grace."

"Grace was your mom? Is she—?"

"Dead, yeah. But she took off right after I was born. I never knew her. She lived a rough life. Had an aneurysm in her thirties."

Avery let out a breath. He'd never once mentioned a mother. Not once. Now she understood why. Grace had abandoned him. And then his father had died.

"I don't hate my mother, Avery," he added quietly, and maybe it was true, but he hadn't forgiven her either, Avery thought. One thing you could say about Walker: he was loyal to a fault. Grace's deliberate absence from his life must have hurt him to the core.

"So Sue brought you up," Avery said.

"She did. When Mom took off, Sue heard about it. Grandma Diane told me she showed up a couple of days later. 'He belongs with us,' she said. Grandma Diane went along with it."

Avery tried to take it all in. "How can you possibly be as together as you are after all that?"

"Sue," he said simply. "And Netta. And the others. Despite his threat, my father came home now and then on leave until I was seven. His father, my grandpa, lived until I was fifteen. Netta's husband passed a year later.

That gave me four stand-in parents on the reservation through half of my teenage years and Elizabeth as a very annoying sister. And Grandma Diane and Grandpa Paul in town. Grandpa Paul might not have been the friendliest guy, but he was there, always working, always doing good in the world. Diane and Paul really regretted their earlier behavior. They tried to make up for it."

"That's good." But it wasn't enough. Walker deserved so much more.

"When I got to school age, I spent the weekdays with them. Diane passed away only last year."

"How old was Elizabeth when Worth and Tricia died?"

"Four months. Netta and Sue saved both our lives. Made sure we grew up surrounded by love and family. Made sure we knew our heritage and honored our parents, no matter what they did. I have to hand it to Netta for never making Sue feel bad for what my dad did. She was a friend to Sue until the end, and Sue worshipped her."

"All your dad did was be a stupid teenager," Avery pointed out. "I ran off to Vegas and married a stranger when I was his age. If you blame Joe for Worth's and Tricia's deaths, you should hold me accountable for what I did, too."

Walker stared at her. Blinked. For one moment, anguish creased his face before he got control of his emotions again. "He got in that fight. He was driving erratically on the highway. He should have pulled over."

"What if he had? What if that other man pulled

over, too, and pulled out a gun—or came back and ran them over." Avery stepped closer to him. "Walker, sometimes people make mistakes. Big, messy ones, but they're still mistakes." She tried to see it from his point of view. "I understand that's why it was so important to you not to break your promise to Netta that you'd marry Elizabeth. You wanted to right your father's wrongs. Or at least let Elizabeth be the one to break it off. But, Walker, remember that Netta never blamed Sue. She didn't hold on to resentment or anger. She just kept loving everyone."

Walker turned away. Avery put a hand on his back, waiting. She knew better than to think Walker would cry; that wasn't his way, but she felt the tension of his pain in every muscle in his body—and then, some time later, its release.

She didn't know how long they stayed like that, and it didn't matter. She could do this for Walker for eternity. Stand with him. Let him know she was with him.

Wait.

When he turned again, she went willingly in his arms and held him tightly, hoping he could read everything in her heart. This was the man she loved, and she'd take his past along with everything else he could offer her.

"You must miss your father so much. Did he die in combat?"

Walker stiffened. Let go of her and made as if to step back but in the end stayed where he was.

"Killed himself" was all he said.

Avery absorbed the horror of it like a blow, feeling the bile rise in her throat. Walker had been seven when his father died.

Seven.

Couldn't his father have found the strength to stay for him?

She held on to him tightly and thought she could sense everything he couldn't say: that he missed his father, was sorry not to have known Worth and Tricia. Wished Netta was still here, along with his grandfather and her husband. That he'd grown up in a world of ghosts and pain and loss, death taking the people he loved one by one.

Was afraid he'd lose her, too.

"I'm here," she told him. "I'll always be here. You'll never lose me. I promise."

When he lowered his mouth to hers, she went up to meet him willingly. Now she knew this man. Knew he had always wanted her. He hadn't held back because he didn't care; he'd held back because he did. Because he knew if he got too close, he'd lose himself and wouldn't be able to fulfill the debts handed down to him from his father. He must have thought giving in to his desire—and hers—would only make it worse if they were separated again by those obligations, but to Avery's way of thinking they'd lost months of precious time. She wanted all of Walker she could get, and damn the consequences.

She didn't waste another moment trying to put that into words. Instead, she found his mouth. Kissed him, then kissed him again, her hands cupping his jaws, her passion telling him what she couldn't.

No matter what their circumstances, she wanted him. Always had. Always would.

She would never leave.

Walker pulled back, his dark eyes searching hers. "Avery—"

"Yes. Please, Walker." She pulled him close again. Pulled him right down to the ground.

To her relief, Walker didn't argue. He kissed her back with equal hunger, gathering her beneath him, crushing her to him, unleashing the full force of his desire in a way he never had with her before.

Avery trusted him utterly and let herself go, allowing him to take the lead, glorying in the feeling of a man of Walker's size and strength focusing every ounce of his attention on her. She laughed when he fumbled with his backpack while still kissing her, pulling things out of it and flinging them away until he found what he'd wanted, a picnic blanket. He tossed it out beside them, spreading it as best he could, making clear he wasn't going to let go of her if he didn't have to, then rolled her onto it.

When he tugged at the fastenings of her dress, Avery pushed him away, sat up and undid them herself, knowing he was likely to tear the fabric. She made it a game, teasing him as she undressed until he nearly growled.

"I can get that off a lot faster."

"I don't doubt it." But she took pity on him, finished the job, undid her corset and drew her chemise over her head, then faced him on the blanket clad in only her panties. "Your turn."

Walker was a lot faster as he got to his feet and stripped down, and he tossed away his boxer briefs without a second's hesitation.

Avery could only stare in admiration. Walker was handsome with his clothes on.

With them off, he was magnificent, a monument of muscle and bronzed skin.

He offered her his hand. She took it, got to her feet and approached him. When he hooked his thumbs in the tiny waistband of her panties, she nodded. He tugged them down to her feet, and she kicked them away.

This must be what Adam and Eve felt like in the garden of Eden, she thought, standing with Walker in the bright sunshine, not a stitch on. A rise of ground hid them thoroughly from the road here, and she doubted anyone else would come this way. Walker's hands rested on her hips, drawing her inexorably toward him. When their bodies met, she went on tiptoe, needing more of his kisses.

Walker obliged, moving his mouth over hers until she was breathless. His hands explored her body, the swoop of his fingers over her skin leaving her tingling with anticipation.

When he laid her down again, she drew him to her. This was where he was meant to be: between her legs, in her arms.

"I want you," he whispered, his lips brushing her cheek and then her temple.

"I've always wanted you," she answered. Ever since she'd first laid eyes on him, she'd dreamed about this moment. She shifted her hips, wanting to feel his hardness, at the same time wanting this to go on forever.

Avery shifted again until she found what she wanted. She opened to him, urging him with her hands on his back. "Don't make me wait," she told him.

Walker hesitated only a moment, positioned himself—

And pushed inside her.

Now THAT HE'D started, he couldn't hold back.

As Walker moved inside Avery, every stroke lit him up until his body blazed with heat. As she clung to him, moving with his rhythm, he forgot about his past—and hers. This was all that mattered. This was what love felt like, and nothing else could match it.

He'd wasted so much time trying to protect his honor, and now he wished he could have all of it back. He needed a lifetime with the woman in his arms and swore from now on, she'd be the only thing that mattered to him.

He needed to show her how he felt, but he was quickly losing control. Avery was hot, wet, coaxing him with the movement of her hips until he hung on by force of will.

She was soft but insistent. Yielding but strong. Every fiber of his being focused solely on her need, he increased his pace, doubling the sensation, nearly succumbing to it.

Not yet.

"Avery."

She opened her eyes, and he read the hunger there—and the love.

He hoped she knew he loved her, too. Knew how much he craved her. Every touch of her hands, the brush of her breasts against his chest, the pulse of her hips against his, all sent sensation burning straight through him.

"Will you marry me?"

Her gaze filled with love. "Yes."

He crushed her to him, burying his face against her neck, pumping inside her, unable to hold back any longer.

He wanted to spend forever like this, but that wasn't possible. His body wasn't having it.

Avery arched back and gave a cry that swept away the last vestiges of his control. He thrust again and came with a groan half frustration, half blessed relief. As his release swept through him, he bucked against her, her cries sweet in his ears until they both were sated.

Afterward, they lay together in a tangle of limbs under the strong sun, and Walker stroked Avery's hair. She was thinking—

And he was afraid of what she'd say. Would she change her mind?

When she turned to him, he traced a hand down her

shoulder to her back and over her bottom. Every curve of her body entranced him. What he would give to lie here with her forever.

"This is heaven," Avery said, gazing up at the sky.

"This is." He kept his gaze on her. Kissed her again.

"I wish we could stay."

"You mean that?"

"Of course. There's nowhere else I'd rather be than here with you."

"Exactly how I feel." He reached for the backpack. Rummaged through it until his hand closed around a small velvet box. He pulled it out. Opened it. Showed the ring inside to Avery.

The ring he'd bought the first week he'd known her."

"Walker," she breathed.

"I love you. I've always loved you." He took out the ring, slid it on her finger.

"It's perfect." Avery held it where she could see it, tears sparkling in her eyes. "Are you sure?"

"Of course I'm sure. I knew you were going to be my wife the moment I saw you." His mouth found the base of her neck. Traced along her collarbone. For several long minutes he lost himself in her again. He knew time was ticking away, though. They had to be ready for James's return.

"We have to go back."

"Why?" she complained, running a hand over his shoulder. "I want to stay here."

"I know, but this isn't over yet. I might not be marrying Elizabeth, but I still owe her—and I owe Sue, too. We still have to play our parts."

A memory flashed into his mind. His father sitting on the end of his bed at Sue's house, a photograph in his hand.

"You're the only good thing left," Joe had told him. "My son. The question is—why are you even here?"

At the time, Walker had thought he was in trouble—he'd snuck into his father's room when he was supposed to leave Joe alone. His father was always a moody man on his infrequent visits home. Sue was forever telling him to be quiet—to leave his dad alone, let him rest.

Now Walker thought the words had a different meaning. *Why was he there?* In other words, why was he even born? Why had Joe deserved the gift of a son when his mistake had taken the lives of two people he loved?

Walker had thought he'd been born to right his father's wrongs. To play a small part, then stand on the sidelines as everyone else took center stage.

Now he knew he had a different role. He was Avery's leading man. He was meant to share her days. Her happiness and pain. Her triumphs and tragedies.

He wasn't a bit player.

He wasn't relegated to the sidelines.

He had his own life to live.

"We have to go back," he repeated to Avery. "But this is only the start of what we're going to do together."

"I suppose I can't wear this yet." She held up her hand and touched the ring.

He hadn't thought about that.

"I'll wear it like this." She sat up, removed a locket she wore around her neck. Its chain was long enough that the locket slipped under the edge of her bodice. Avery threaded the ring onto the chain, too, and replaced it around her neck.

Walker helped her with the clasp.

"There," she said. "I'll have it on all the time, but no one but us will know."

"Good," he said, but he couldn't wait for the day when he could tell everyone he was marrying Avery.

JAMES RUSSELL PICKED them up right on time. If he noticed a certain disheveled appearance about them, he didn't mention it. He was downright chatty on the drive home, talking to them over his shoulder, paying so little attention to the roads Avery thought it was lucky his horses seemed to know their own way. Before she was ready, they were back at the ranch, being let out in the parking lot near the bunkhouse.

She knew immediately something was wrong when she spotted most of the men gathered together near the fire pit, so when Riley saw them through the bunkhouse window and came to meet them, she had already braced herself.

"Someone tried to kill Elizabeth!" Riley was pale, a hand on her belly as if determined to protect her baby at all costs. "Gabe thought he'd got him, but the guy still got away, and now we're not sure."

"Got him?"

"Shot him," Riley clarified. "Did you know he was carrying?"

She didn't, and by the look on his face, neither did Walker, who strode away to confront the other man.

"It was terrifying," Riley said. "We were outside, gathering for lunch when I heard a sound I couldn't even identify at first. I found myself on the ground. I guess my gut knew what it was before my brain did. Someone was shooting at us, at Elizabeth."

"How do you know she was the target?"

"She was standing a little apart from the rest of us, and the shots were aimed her way. We all dropped to the ground. The men burst into action, but Gabe was there first. He was crouching behind that log." She pointed. "Firing like you wouldn't believe. We heard a shout. The men found blood, but the shooter was already gone on a motorcycle. The gunman must have had it parked in the brush over near the parking area. Boone thinks he probably walked it in from the highway sometime in the night and waited until he could get a good shot."

"That's crazy." The thought of walking past a man lying in wait this morning when she and Walker had gone to meet James's carriage in the parking area sent shivers slipping and sliding down her spine.

"So it's Elizabeth they're after, not us," Riley said. "Why would someone want to kill her?"

Avery couldn't answer that question until she had

Elizabeth's permission. "Let's go inside." Her neck and shoulder blades were prickling like someone had a weapon trained on her even now. Gone was the light and warmth from her time with Walker. She hustled Riley inside, where it had to be safer, and waited until Boone and some of the other men returned, bringing Cab Johnson, the local sheriff, with them. Film crews followed, and soon the room was packed.

Walker was stiff and watchful, and Avery wondered if he blamed himself for not being here when Elizabeth had come under fire. Elizabeth was composed, but her fingers twisted the fabric of her Regency gown.

"I think you've got some explaining to do," Boone told her.

She nodded unhappily. "I know." Avery could see she didn't want to, though. She was still afraid Fulsom would make her leave. Avery wondered if she was regretting coming here altogether.

"Wait," Walker said. "We can't talk in front of the crew."

"You know the rules," Renata said sharply.

"This is a matter of life and death," Walker returned. "Fulsom likes to play with our lives, and I won't let him put Elizabeth in danger."

"She put *us* in danger," Savannah pointed out. "If she knew someone was after her, she should never have come."

"You're right," Elizabeth said loudly before Walker could argue with that. "And all of you should know that I kept Walker in the dark about this until only recently."

"In the dark about what?" Nora asked. "What's going on?"

"I think everyone better start at the beginning," Cab said.

When Walker hesitated, she wondered if he'd cooperate with the sheriff. His loyalties were still to his family—and Elizabeth.

Elizabeth spoke first. "It's okay, Walker. There's no sense trying to hide anything anymore. If I can't stay here, I'll find somewhere else to go." She addressed the others. "In two days, I'm going to testify in front of the Senate about opening the Renning field in Alaska to oil exploration and drilling. I'm testifying against the bill that's on the table to make it possible for that project to go forward. I have a lot of information and personal stories from observing conditions in the arctic—how global warming is running amok there, how the risk of fires above the arctic circle is increasing and how none of us can afford to let so much carbon, sequestered for now in the tundra, escape into our atmosphere. I don't have to tell you all that's enough to make powerful groups want to stop my testimony."

People around the room nodded.

"That's not all," Elizabeth went on. "I have whistle-blower information about the company that stands to be awarded the contract."

"And someone is trying to kill you in order to keep you from presenting it?" Nora asked.

"They are," Elizabeth said simply. "I'm the opposition's prime witness. As soon as I knew that, I realized I needed a safe place to hide, or I might not make it to the hearing. There's a lot of money riding on that project going ahead. I figured Base Camp was one of the safest places I could go."

Boone nodded. "Hiding in plain sight."

"You always had a camera on you while you were here," Clay said.

"And ten Navy SEALs watching out for me," she said.

"You should have told us," Boone said.

Eve was studying Elizabeth. "You didn't because of me, right?" When everyone turned to her in surprise, she added, "Remember? I came here and tried to stay with you so I could expose Hansen Oil, but Fulsom said I wasn't allowed to stay unless I would marry someone."

"That's it exactly," Elizabeth told her.

Avery watched as the others absorbed the information. She wasn't surprised when Riley turned to her. "You knew, didn't you?"

"I found out recently."

"Whose wedding have you been planning, then?"

"Mine," she admitted. She pulled the chain out of her bodice, undid the clasp, took the engagement ring off it and put it on her finger, holding it up for all to see.

Riley let out an exasperated huff. "I can't believe you kept that from us. Well, thank God for that, anyway. I would have had to kill Walker if he married Elizabeth."

"Wait—hold on, let's not get ahead of ourselves," Boone said. "You testify in two days?" he asked Elizabeth.

"That's right."

"And all we have to do is put you on a plane? What then?"

"I'm being met on the other end by a group that will take me straight to Congress. I figure if someone's going to take me out on Capitol Hill, there's not much I can do about it."

"I think I've been following this story so far," Cab drawled, "but who are you?" He pointed at Gabe.

"I'm Elizabeth's fiancé."

"Fiancé?" several people exclaimed at once.

Avery turned to Renata. "You got me Elizabeth's fiancé as a backup husband? How did that happen?"

"I got in touch with Renata as soon as Elizabeth told me her plan and I realized I couldn't stop her," Gabe said. "I thought it was crazy for her to come here. Hell, I still think it's crazy for her to testify at all. I don't want her to be a target." He let out a sigh. "I didn't know what else to do, so I told Renata everything. Begged her to find a way to get me on the show. I still think we should have gone somewhere no one could find her."

"They would have found us wherever we went," Elizabeth said. "That's why I had to come here."

Avery recognized this was an argument they'd had before. It probably was what they'd been talking about the day Gabe had arrived and she'd found them squared off on the bunkhouse steps.

"So you knew everything?" Boone asked Renata.

"Wait, I don't understand this," Savannah said loudly, her voice cutting through everyone else's. She was holding Jacob tightly in her arms. "You came here knowing someone was after you. You deliberately put us in danger. There are seven pregnant women here—not to mention two babies!"

"And there are seven billion people and counting in danger because our planet is heating up past anything we've ever known before," Elizabeth snapped back at her. "Isn't that why you're building a sustainable community? You're letting your lives be filmed in order to light a fire under the viewing public's asses. Well, I'm trying to save the entire human race. Not to mention the animals and birds and fish and trees and every other living thing on this planet. Do you really not understand that we're hurtling toward a cliff, and we've got about a second left—maybe—to swerve in a different direction before we all go over it?"

Savannah stared back, wide-eyed. "But—"

"But nothing!" Elizabeth burst out. "No one's willing to inconvenience themselves the slightest bit to stop it. No one's even paying attention! There are fires and droughts and hurricanes and heat waves and mass migrations and extinctions, and no one even cares! Maybe I should have let that guy shoot me. At least I wouldn't be alive to watch it all happen!"

"Elizabeth." Gabe reached for her. She warded him off, still facing Savannah.

"Don't you get it? We don't have any more chances. We don't have any more time. We're right at the brink, and I don't know if what I plan to do will change a damn thing! Even if I make it to Washington. Even if I give my presentation. I mean, who's going to listen to me? What happens if I fail?"

"Honey—"

Elizabeth stopped Gabe with a raised hand.

"My family has passed down stories from generation to generation. My grandmother's grandmother remembered when there wasn't a single paved street in Montana. Her grandmother's grandmother remembered when there wasn't a single White person in the territory. What kind of stories will my grandchildren's grandchildren have? One in which I'm the person who let it all go to hell?"

"You won't," Gabe told her. "You'll make them see sense."

"What if I don't?" She looked around her, challenging each of them in turn. "What if I don't?"

It was a question they'd all been asking themselves through their year of filming *Base Camp*.

Avery couldn't bear to see Elizabeth's anguish or the way Savannah was cradling Jacob close, tears slipping silently down her cheeks. "We'll keep on fighting," she said when no one else spoke up. "All of us. No matter what happens when you go to Washington. Because there's no end to this fight until there's an end to us all. This is existential. We all live or die— together. Which means no one in this room is going to tell Fulsom what's happening until it's over, right? Right?" She faced off with the crew.

After a long moment, Renata came to stand next to her. "That's right. This is too damn important for anyone to break ranks. By now everyone in this room understands what's riding on Elizabeth's testimony. We've taken a lot of risks, pushed the envelope a lot of times on this show. Anyone who's willing to risk not just Elizabeth's life but the future we all share needs to speak up right now."

No one said a word.

"William, Craig, you with me on this?"

Both of the older cameramen nodded.

"Byron?"

"Of course."

Renata ran through the crew's names one by one until each of them had vowed to keep the secret.

"You realize you're putting us on the wrong side of a billionaire," Craig said.

"I realize that. Want to change your answer?" Renata challenged him.

"No. It's the right thing to do—unfortunately."

Elizabeth dropped her head into her hands. All the fight went out of her, and she allowed Gabe to embrace her. As he murmured into her hair, the rest of them moved away as best they could in the enclosed space to give the couple privacy.

Riley was still pressing her hands to her belly.

"Are you okay?" Avery asked her.

Riley nodded. "She's right, though. What kind of world are we going to give them—our babies?"

"The best one we can," Avery promised her.

CHAPTER ELEVEN

"**E**VERYONE READY?" BOONE asked three days later.

Walker wondered if anyone had slept the previous night. For the last two nights they'd given up the separate sleeping arrangements and moved back into the bunkhouse. They'd given up almost all their other activities, too. Elizabeth never left the bunkhouse. The rest of the women spent almost all their hours indoors. One party of the men worked only the most crucial chores as a group while the rest stood guard.

Renata split the camera crews, too, some keeping to their normal task of getting footage for the show, others manning cameras pointed in different directions from the bunkhouse to capture any approach by an intruder. When the sun went down, they set up the enormous lights they used for nighttime filming in a circle around the bunkhouse pointed outward and kept them on until sunrise, lighting up the exterior until it was bright as day.

Now it was time to get Elizabeth on her plane. They were all going to the airport with her, figuring it was safest to keep together. The most dangerous part of the operation was getting from the bunkhouse to the fleet of trucks they used. The men, bolstered by the deputies Cab Johnson had sent to help them, formed an armed corridor, and Elizabeth and the rest of the women hurried along it, Savannah and Nora with their babies in tow. The men fell in behind them, bringing up the rear until everyone was loaded into five trucks. With a cruiser ahead of them, one behind them and one in the middle, plus several vehicles filled with the camera crews, they made their way, sirens blaring, for the twenty-minute drive to the airport. Walker was one of the drivers. Gabe rode shotgun. Avery, Elizabeth and Hope squeezed onto the bench seat in back.

Walker didn't realize he'd been holding his breath until he let it out after pulling up and parking in front of the terminal. Chance Creek's airport was tiny, which made things simpler. The men spread out, a wary perimeter protecting the women as they hurried Elizabeth inside. Gabe accompanied her, and they all flocked into the building, saying their goodbyes and wishing the couple luck as they made their way to the ticket counter. Cab Johnson met them there.

"I've got deputies stationed throughout the building. I'll take it from here."

Walker turned to Elizabeth. "Are you going to be okay?"

She nodded. "I'm fine. Thank you for everything you've done." She went up on tiptoe and pressed a quick kiss to his cheek. "Really, Walker. Thank you. I know I've caused you a lot of headaches."

"Thank you for being willing to speak for all of us."

She turned to Avery.

"I hope your wedding is wonderful. I'm sorry I've been stealing your thunder all this time. I promise this is the last you'll see of me today." She made a show of turning off her phone and sliding it into her purse. "After I testify, I'm going to head to a hotel and get a good night's sleep!"

Still, no one wanted to leave even after Elizabeth and Gabe had gone through security and disappeared into the waiting area for their flight. When they heard the announcement that their flight was boarding, the rest of them went back outside to watch it take off.

"Nothing more we can do now," Walker said, relieved that everything had gone so smoothly. He wondered where the gunman was now. Had he been injured badly enough he needed to go to a hospital? If so, he hadn't gone to the local one. Maybe he'd already left the state.

"Is there any way her attacker could be on that flight?" Savannah asked, cutting into his thoughts.

Boone shrugged. "Anything is possible, but let's hope not. Cab beefed up the security here; it would be hard to get on the plane armed with any kind of weapon."

Walker knew no one would rest easy until they'd heard that Elizabeth had testified late this afternoon, but this was his wedding day, and Avery deserved for the rest of it to be about her. "She'll be fine," he said loudly.

"She's got Gabe with her and people on the other end to help keep her safe."

"Meanwhile, we've got a wedding to prepare for!" Riley said brightly. "I don't know about the rest of you, but I've been so caught up in worrying about Elizabeth, I haven't had time to think about tonight. Thank goodness Maud and James are arranging everything." Avery had told everyone about Maud taking charge of her wedding.

"Lunch first," Savannah said. "I don't know about anyone else, but I'm starving, and we've got plenty of time. Let's go home and eat, catch up with the chores and rest a little before we head to the Russells' at three. I'll help make sure you've got everything you need, Avery."

"We'll need a truck just to carry all our stuff," Hope joked.

"Two trucks." Avery beamed at them before turning to Walker. He couldn't help himself. He bent down to steal a kiss from her, and she met him halfway.

Riley tsked. "Enough time for that after the wedding! Avery, you ride home with us. We have lots to talk about."

"Let's keep being careful," Boone cautioned them. "Let's walk out to our trucks together. And drive together, too. We can't assume we're out of danger."

Walker reluctantly let go of Avery as her friends flocked around her, joking and laughing now that Elizabeth was safely away. Boone was right: they needed to keep their guard up, but a weight had slid off his shoulders. By the end of the day, this whole long nightmare would be over.

IT WAS FINALLY happening.

Avery blinked back tears as she looked into the full-length standing mirror in one corner of the enormous, beautiful room Maud had assigned to her.

Her wedding gown fit like a dream. In less than an hour, the ceremony would start. Walker and the rest of the men should be on their way from Base Camp now. Jericho, Kai and Angus were already here, taking turns standing guard and getting ready for the event in a room of their own. Her parents were on their way from the airport. In seven and a half hours the show would be over, the contest won, all the cares and worries of the last year gone in a puff of smoke.

She and Walker and all their friends could get down to the business of really living. Building their community. Making their dreams come true.

She couldn't believe they'd almost made it.

"You're shaking," Win told her. "Are you cold?"

"Not at all." Avery laughed. If anything, she was warm. It was the last day of May, but it felt like July. Her cheeks were flushed, and if she didn't watch out, she'd start sweating in her wedding gown.

She fanned her face and backed away from the mirror. "Finish getting ready," she admonished her friends. Everyone had been so helpful to her they had neglected themselves. They all looked pretty in their blush-red bridesmaid gowns, but half of them needed to finish makeup, find jewelry and the like. "I'll be over here not wrinkling my gown." She moved out of the way and left the others to it, pacing slowly around the room, trying to keep the butterflies in her stomach in check.

Were Walker and the others here? Maud and James's house was so well built you couldn't hear a thing once you closed a door.

She went to open the one that led to the hall.

"Don't you dare," Win cried, darting over to stop her. "You can't let Walker see you! We don't need any more bad luck!"

Avery supposed she was right. She wandered across the large room in the other direction, to the sliding glass doors that led to a wooden deck. The day was beautiful, the light softening now that it was late afternoon. The sun wouldn't set until nearly nine thirty tonight, and she expected much of the party would spill out into the Russells' beautiful grounds.

She slid open the screen door and stepped outside gingerly, appreciating the sweet scent on the air from the blooming shrubs that ringed the house. Surely Walker couldn't see her here. If he'd arrived already, he would have joined the other men in their room that faced the front of the house. A light breeze lifted the tendrils of her hair and cooled her cheeks. She leaned on the railing and took a deep breath.

Too bad she couldn't stay right here until it was time to walk down the aisle. She needed to go back inside, though, and help her friends. Check and make sure her hair hadn't slipped.

Get her veil secured to her updo.

As she turned, something caught her eye. One of the strings of fairy lights wrapped around a nearby tree had come undone and was trailing down to the lawn, an almost jarring sight among the Russells' perfectly manicured grounds.

Avery had no doubt once the sun set, the whole place would be a fairy-tale setting for the reception. She couldn't wait to dance with Walker after their sit-down dinner. She had to hand it to the Russells and the way they paid attention to every detail. Who would even come back here behind the house? They'd made sure that no matter where their guests wandered, they'd find something beautiful to see.

She stepped down the stairs carefully and tiptoed across the grass to set the fairy lights to rights. She knew if Riley or Savannah saw her, they'd read her the riot act for putting her gown in jeopardy, but the grass was completely dry, and the tree was only a few steps from the deck.

She bent to pick up the end of the trailing lights, straightened—

A hand clamped over her mouth. An arm hooked around her waist. She was lifted in the air.

Everything went dark.

"FINALLY," BOONE SAID. "I can't believe we're pulling this off."

"This time tomorrow we'll have it made," Jericho said.

"Hell, in about seven hours we'll have it made," Kai said, checking the time on his phone.

"Midnight can't come fast enough," Angus said.

They were putting the final touches on their wedding outfits, the Revolutionary War uniforms they'd worn for every ceremony so far. Walker knew Sue would think it ridiculous, but he didn't mind. Traditions formed in all kinds of ways. This was the last time he'd wear one, most likely. The show was coming to an end.

"You did it." Boone clapped Walker on his shoulder. "Wasn't sure if you'd sort out things with Elizabeth in time, but you got it done."

"Thanks to all of you."

"When does Elizabeth's testimony start?"

"She's the last witness. She thought it would be late afternoon, but sounds like things got started late." Gabe had texted him several hours ago to tell him they'd touched down in Washington. Had texted him an hour later, sounding half-annoyed, half-jubilant that they were finally reaching the capital.

You wouldn't believe the crowds, he'd written. *Protestors everywhere. Avery really got people whipped into a frenzy. The start of the hearing was delayed—some of the senators couldn't get past the protestors. Elizabeth won't go on for a while.*

Good old Avery. She certainly knew how to get the word out.

"You got the rings?" Walker asked.

Boone produced a small box. "Got them."

Walker pulled out his phone to check the time just

as another text pinged. "Gabe again." His fingers tightened around the gadget as he read.

"What is it?"

The other men gathered around.

"There's been a bomb scare at the Senate building. They're clearing everyone out of there."

"Is Elizabeth all right?"

Walker kept reading. "He says they're fine. They're being taken to another building." He exchanged a glance with Boone. If they'd been at the capitol tasked with Elizabeth's safety, they'd both be on high alert. Unexpected events meant a mission could go off the rails. "She could be in danger."

"I'm sure there's a ton of security," Boone said. "All those senators…" He let his thought trail off.

Boone was right. Besides, there was nothing he could do from here. He rubbed the back of his neck, unsure how to proceed. At the very least, he could remind Gabe to be extra vigilant.

He started typing.

"Forty minutes until the ceremony starts," Angus reminded him. "Time to focus. Elizabeth will be fine."

A pounding on the door startled them. More than one man reached for a holster.

"Boone? Walker?" It was Riley. "Avery's gone!"

"…CAN'T BELIEVE YOU fucked things up this bad."

"Can't believe you missed your shot, asshole."

"… hell to pay when…"

"… eyes on the fucking road, Owen, and let me figure this out. The bomb scare will give us more time."

Avery woke up slowly, blinking several times and licking dry lips before she understood where she was. A plaid blanket, much too hot for this weather, covered her. Her hands were tied behind her back. She was lying down on the seat of a car or truck, bouncing and bumping around as it drove.

She remembered the hand clamped over her mouth, the strong arm lifting her.

Who the hell had kidnapped her? How long had they been driving?

Bomb scare?

Fear spread through her. Whoever had grabbed her had tried to kill Elizabeth.

What would they do to her?

She fought to control her breathing as her heart sped up, thumping in her chest. It was still light, she saw as she turned under the blanket. Sunshine was seeping under its folds. She bent her knees, poised to kick the thing off, then paused. Maybe she should stay quiet, listen to her captors. Get a sense of what was happening before she let them know she was awake.

There were two of them, judging by their conversation. Americans. Their voices had no discernable accent, not even a country twang. She wondered what they planned to do with her. By the sound of it, they were wondering the same thing.

"Step on it. We've got to go to ground. They'll be out looking everywhere for us."

"Then what?"

"Then we make the call. Tell Blaine exactly what she's got to do."

Avery held as still as she could, listening, but a moment later, the vehicle swung hard and parked. Two doors opened. Someone whipped the blanket off her, and the barrel of a handgun pressed against her temple. It was a Glock, she recognized. Walker had one of those.

"Don't scream, don't fight, don't do a damn thing to call attention to yourself. You're going to get out of the car and walk inside with me. Don't be stupid," a middle-aged man with the build of a retired boxer told her, his blue eyes searching hers. "You know what this is about. You know we've been trying to silence your friend. You know we failed. Trust me when I say I'm in a very bad position right now, which means you're in a very bad position. Got it?"

She got it. Someone had put a lot of effort into stopping Elizabeth from testifying. Whoever it was wouldn't scruple at her death.

"Come on."

The man pulled her from the car, wrapped the blanket around her and hustled her up the steps of the house. Her updo was spilling apart, and she nearly tripped over the hem of her wedding dress. She struggled to shake the hair out of her eyes and almost yelped in surprise; they were still in Chance Creek, right in town, in fact, across from the Whispering Pines motel. A snatch of music filled the air. That was the Dancing Boot down the block. It was early, but from the sound of things they were gearing up for a good night.

"Inside," the man growled. His friend, Owen—a tall, muscular man with shaggy blond hair—was right behind them, shielding her from sight of anyone on the street. The man holding her seemed to be the brains of the operation. Owen was the muscle.

She just had time to spot a small plaque by the door as the man pushed her past it. The *Cozy Cottage Guest House*. This was a vacation rental.

They hurried her up the stairs and tossed her onto a bed decked out in cheerful yellow, daisy-patterned linens, where she curled up on her side, her wrists aching from the tight ties binding them. Someone had put a lot of effort into this room, she noticed. If she'd chosen the place herself for a vacation, she'd be very pleased with how pristine it was.

"I need a bathroom," she said. Maybe there'd be something in there she could use as a weapon—or to cut the ties that bound her wrists.

"For God's sake," Owen said. She noticed a bandage visible under the stretched-out neckline of his T-shirt—large enough to cover most of his shoulder. Had he been the one taking shots at Elizabeth? The one Gabe hit?

"Take her."

Owen hauled her to the bathroom, cleared the counter of anything useful and shut her in. "Hurry up," he said through the door.

She wished she knew how to concoct a weapon from the deodorant and bar soap near the sink, since that was all that was left, but she really did need to use the facilities, so she took care of that first. It wasn't easy to wipe with her hands tied behind her back, especially in a wedding dress, but she managed it. She flushed the toilet out of habit and then wanted to kick herself as she realized she'd just lost any time she'd bought to be alone. The door swung open again.

She had to give it to the guy; Owen helped her wash her hands before hauling her back into the main room. A true gentleman.

But then he spoiled it by looping another length of rope through her arms and through the spindles of the headboard, tethering her to it.

"Sit down, shut up and watch the television," he told her.

"You're Owen. Who's your friend?" She wanted to establish she wasn't afraid of them, but it was a lie. She was terrified. One of these men had shot at Elizabeth. They'd probably shoot her soon.

Her throat was dry. She was a moment from panicking. Should she start screaming?

She eyed the weapons holstered on both men's hips. No one would save her before she was dead.

"You can call me Mr. Smith," the other man said. "Now keep quiet."

She perched on the bed as best as she could with her wrists tied behind her back, scanning the room, trying to make some sort of plan to escape, but she couldn't see any way to get past them, even if she could get free.

She braced herself for whatever might happen next, but Mr. Smith simply grabbed the wooden desk chair, moved it so he could see through the sliding doors onto the balcony outside and down to the street. Owen stood on the opposite side of the room, bouncing on the balls of his feet. Mr. Smith turned on the TV, found C-SPAN and grunted when he took in a screen that said, "Please stand by."

"At least something's gone right. They've cleared everyone out of there."

"How long do we have?" Owen asked.

Mr. Smith pulled out his phone. Tapped on it. "No word yet on how long they'll be delayed, but they've admitted a bomb threat was called in. The building is being swept."

"What happens when they don't find anything?"

"They start the hearing again." Mr. Smith sent Owen an exasperated look. "But by then, Blaine will be long gone."

"You think she'll skip testifying—just to save this one?" Owen nodded at Avery. "I hope you're right."

Was that what they were counting on?

Avery's heart sank. Nothing would stop Elizabeth from testifying. She'd already put them all in danger to make sure she made it to the hearing.

"She's a bleeding-heart liberal," Mr. Smith said. "She'll cave."

He was dead wrong.

Which meant she was as good as dead, Avery thought. She had to look for any opportunity to get away.

"Call her," Owen urged.

"I'm calling her. Time to put this to bed." Mr. Smith tapped at the phone again. Held it to his ear.

Waited.

"What the fuck?" he finally growled. "She's not picking up!"

"Call her again."

Mr. Smith did so. "Still not picking up," he said a minute later.

"She's got to pick up." Owen paced closer, blocking the television. "This is fucked, man. We are in trouble—"

"Shut the fuck up. Get out of the way." Mr. Smith waved him off. Made the call again. "God damn it, she's not answering. Who doesn't answer their fucking phone?"

Someone who turned it off because she was determined to focus on her testimony, Avery thought.

"Call her friend," Owen said. "That dick for brains who shot at me."

Mr. Smith turned to Avery. "What's his number?"

"Who's number?"

"Gabe Reller. What's his number?"

"I don't know!"

Mr. Smith stood up. Advanced on her. Stuck his handgun against her temple again. "I'm giving you one more chance."

"I never called him. I didn't have to; he was at the ranch with us."

"You don't have his phone number?" The weapon

pressed harder into her skin.

"He might have texted me." Avery shrugged. "The number's probably on my phone."

Mr. Smith reached out as if he meant to pat her down and find it.

Realized she was wearing a wedding gown.

"Where's your fucking phone?"

"At the Russells'." Avery cowered, thinking he was going to hit her, hating herself for letting him see her fear.

"For God's sake, this is a shitshow!" Mr. Smith sat down again. Tried another call on his phone. Threw it down.

"Now what do we do?" Owen advanced again. "Call those Base Camp people. One of them has Reller's number."

"No way. Right now they've got no idea what's happened to her." He pointed his weapon at Avery. "She could have run off on her own, for all they know. Runaway bride. It happens. We can't give them any clues."

She would never run from Walker. She didn't say that, though.

"We've got to get in touch with Blaine somehow."

"We'll keep calling. She'll pick up sooner or later."

"What if she doesn't?"

Mr. Smith picked up the remote again. Found a game. "Shut the fuck up. Let me take care of this."

"What about the hearing?"

With an overblown sigh, Mr. Smith toggled back to

C-SPAN. The same bland screen greeted them. He put the game on again.

Owen threw his hands in the air. "We're fucked."

"We're not fucked!" But Mr. Smith looked grim. "We've got time." He tried his phone again.

"Well?" Owen challenged him.

"No answer."

Avery flexed her wrists behind her back, trying to wriggle out of the ties that bound her. Her arms, wrists and shoulders ached.

"Stop squirming," Mr. Smith barked at her.

She stopped.

She had no idea what to do next.

"CHECK THE TRUCKS. Are our vehicles still here?" Jericho ran outside past Maud and James, who had come to see what all the fuss was about.

"He thinks someone stole one of our trucks?" Win asked.

"No," Walker said slowly, his blood running cold in his veins. He knew what Jericho meant, and it wasn't that. "He thinks Avery took it."

"Avery?"

"There's no way Avery ran off," Savannah asserted, stepping forward. "Why would he think that?"

"She wouldn't run," Riley agreed. "She just went outside to get a breath of fresh air. Someone took her!"

"Buddy up—start the search!" Boone called. The men scattered, Walker following the others heavily. Avery wouldn't leave him. He knew she wouldn't, but even as he pounded out the door and down the front steps, a small part of him wondered if he should be so sure. He'd led her on for months. Put Elizabeth first again and again. Let her impose on their wedding day.

Then there was the whole mess he'd made of blaming her for stealing his fan. Maybe she'd gotten cold feet, decided to drive to Vegas again.

Jericho was back. "All the vehicles are here. Avery didn't take one."

Relief whooshed out of him, followed closely by a wash of cold fear.

If Avery didn't leave on her own—

Someone else took her.

"Angus, Kai, Anders, Greg, search the grounds," Boone called out. "Jericho, call the sheriff. Tell him what happened. Tell him we need help. Walker, I'm coming with you."

Walker ignored him, halfway to a truck already. When Boone slid in beside him, he gunned the engine, reversed and headed down the Russells' drive.

"Which way?" he asked when they reached the street. No one was in sight in either direction.

Toward town or toward the country? Where would he go if he was stealing Avery?

"That way." Boone pointed the opposite direction from town. "They have to know we'll call this in. No way they'd head to town."

Cab Johnson and his deputies would be coming from that direction, anyway, Walker figured. They'd intercept anyone suspicious driving toward Chance

Creek from the Russells' place. He spun the wheel, put his foot on the accelerator and drove.

Ten long minutes later, Boone took a call. "That was Riley," he said when he was done. "They've searched the grounds. Avery's definitely not there. Cab has got all his men out looking. The women are calling all the guests and everyone else we know, getting them to join the search for Avery. They're asking some people to drive around looking for any sign of her. Others are making more phone calls and knocking on doors."

"Good."

Boone's phone buzzed again. "It's Cab." He put it on speakerphone.

Walker's pulse leaped.

"I've got the state police on the case." Cab's voice was staticky but audible. "They're getting their choppers out. We'll have blockades on the surrounding highways pretty soon."

"No sightings?"

"No sightings," Cab confirmed. "Hang in there. Be safe. We'll find her."

The next call came from Savannah. "We've got a room at the community center where we can coordinate with all the volunteers. Maud and James have offered to bring the food and drinks they were going to serve at the wedding for the search parties. They've got Avery's parents with them. It's already becoming a major operation. Everyone's helping us look."

"Tell people to check their outbuildings," Walker

said, eyeing a barn as they drove past. "There's a million hiding places they could go." There was still no one in sight. Had they chosen the wrong direction? Had Avery's captors already pulled off the main road and hidden somewhere?

Or were they still ahead of him?

He accelerated again.

"They'd have to hide their vehicle," Boone pointed out.

"Millions of places to do that," Walker said. "Get everyone to check their own properties as best they can," he told Savannah. "But tell them to be careful!"

"Will do," Savannah said. "We're heading over with the Russells to the community center."

"Okay. Stay safe." Boone cut the call. "We'll find her," he assured Walker. "I swear."

But would they find her in time?

AVERY'S STOMACH GROWLED.

For heaven's sake, she thought. She was in a life-or-death crisis here. What did her stomach want?

Food.

It growled again.

She'd barely eaten today. Should be eating her wedding dinner right about now.

Should be married to Walker.

A sob welled up in her throat, but she forced it down. She wouldn't give these men the satisfaction of knowing how terrified she was—and how angry.

She wanted Walker's ring on her finger. Wanted to

be in his arms. She was supposed to spend her life with him—

Not get shot in the bedroom of a stupid vacation rental.

Mr. Smith was listening to his phone again.

"Well?" Owen demanded.

"Still not picking up."

On the television screen, the hearings were finally getting started. People filed into a large room and took their seats. Avery shifted on the bed.

Her stomach growled again.

"Go get her some food!"

"Are you serious?" Owen crossed his arms.

Mr. Smith pointed to the door, and Owen didn't ask any more questions. He went downstairs and returned with a stale banana-nut muffin that looked like it had been purchased at a gas station mini market.

"Eat." He aimed his gun at her head, set the muffin down on the bed, broke it into pieces and fed it to her a bit at a time with his other hand.

Avery followed his instructions. Might as well keep up her strength. She gratefully took a long drink from the water bottle he held for her, gasping when some of it splashed down her gown.

She'd noticed a smudge or two on it already but had been telling herself Alice could fix it—

If she made it out of here alive.

Another sob welled up. Avery fought to contain it. Where was Walker? Were they trying to find her?

How would they know where to look?

"You talk to the boss yet?" Owen asked Mr. Smith.

"Why would I?"

Owen narrowed his eyes. "We fucked up the plan. He needs to know about it."

Mr. Smith didn't answer.

"Jesus, Blaine's supposed to be dead already. You didn't check in and tell him what's going on?"

"Of course I didn't. I'm buying us some extra time," Mr. Smith snarled at him. "He doesn't need to know we've fucked up if we can fix it."

"What if we don't fix it? Those Lawrence Energy guys aren't going to be happy, which means the boss isn't going to be happy, which means we're fucked."

"We'll get it done. No way her friends let her die." Mr. Smith pointed to Avery.

"We'll get it done if we can ever reach Blaine. When the hell is she on, anyway?"

Avery glanced at the television, where everyone in the Senate room was milling around.

"All right, folks, it's obvious we're going to run very late tonight," a man on the screen said, speaking into a microphone. "I know you all have plans to fly back to your districts for the next few days, and I can't help that. We've got to get this done. We're going to take a two-hour break for dinner. We'll reconvene then and keep going as long as it takes. Rebook your flights if you need to."

No one on-screen looked happy, but Mr. Smith straightened.

"She's bound to answer the phone now. She'll be

looking for dinner reservations." He tried to make the call again.

Elizabeth didn't pick up.

"This is ridiculous," he said.

"Call this one's boyfriend," Owen said, gesturing at Avery. "Tell him to get it done."

"I'm not willing to take that chance yet. We've got two hours before they start the hearings again. If Blaine doesn't answer by then, we'll make that call," he added before Owen could protest.

Owen swore beneath his breath but paced away again.

Avery settled in as best she could, swallowing the grief that kept welling up inside her every time she thought about the wedding she wasn't attending.

An hour later, she was still trying to find a comfortable position. With her hands tied behind her back, she couldn't lean against the headboard. Her legs kept going to sleep, but every time she moved, she found herself face to face with a handgun.

At some point, Owen took her to the bathroom again. Later, he fed her another muffin.

Despite her best efforts, a tear slid down Avery's cheek. Then another. She should be dancing with Walker at her reception. This should be the happiest night of her life.

"That's not going to work," Owen growled at her. "No crocodile tears."

"Leave her alone. She just missed her wedding," Mr. Smith said. "You should have ditched Walker a long time ago, anyway, you know," he added. "A man who makes you wait like that isn't going to be any kind of husband to you. Yeah, I watch the show," he growled when she lifted her gaze to him in surprise.

"Walker's a good man," she said.

"He took his eye off the ball. Didn't put you first," Mr. Smith retorted. He switched from C-SPAN to a news channel. "'Scientists face off with would-be polluters,'" he read off the screen. "Bunch of crybabies."

"When the hell are they getting back from dinner?" Owen complained an eternity later, when Mr. Smith flipped back to C-SPAN just to check. There was nothing to see yet. "Who takes two hours to eat a meal?"

"Politicians," Mr. Smith said scornfully. He found another game, checking C-SPAN now and then. He called Elizabeth continually.

She never answered.

"There they are," Owen exclaimed finally as people began to file into the Senate chamber on-screen a couple of hours later.

Avery straightened. They kept their eyes on the screen but sighed when a man took a seat at the table where all day long witnesses had given testimony.

"State your full name and occupation, please," the man chairing the meeting said.

"My name is Bryce Wollcroft, and I work with the Department of the Interior."

"This is getting us nowhere," Owen said. "If you

don't call Base Camp, I will."

"WE'RE STOPPING VEHICLES leaving Chance Creek," Cab said. "We've got the highways blocked in every direction. Choppers in the air."

"We must have called everyone in town by now," Clay added. "We've checked the motels and bed-and-breakfasts."

"We've got search parties everywhere," Boone said. "Where is she?"

Walker wished to hell he knew. They were standing in front of the community center, where they'd convened to swap information. He and Boone had been almost to Wyoming before they gave up and turned around. They'd been searching for hours, but there was no sign of Avery. He couldn't help wondering if her kidnappers had made it out of town and eluded Cab's blockades before they were set up. If so, she could be anywhere by now.

"What about Silver Falls?" Riley asked. "There are plenty of places up there to hide."

"We're on it," Cab told her. "But you're right; there's a lot of ground to cover."

Walker's phone buzzed, and everyone stilled.

"Walker here."

"You're about to get a message. Watch the video," a man's voice said and hung up. His phone blipped again, and Walker tapped it when the message appeared. A video began to play on the tiny screen. He sucked in a breath when he saw Avery. She was trussed up, her hands tied behind her back, her wedding gown looking the worse for wear. The kidnappers' faces weren't visible, but a man's hand pressed the barrel of a Glock to Avery's temple.

"Hell," Clay breathed.

"Avery!" Riley cried.

An iron band of pain and fury tightened around Walker's heart. He needed to find her. Save her.

"Look for clues. Where are they?" Boone asked.

Walker snapped back to his training. "That's no motel." It wasn't generic enough. He could see a bed's headboard. A side table.

"We need to grab screenshots and post them," Renata said. "Someone's going to recognize that comforter."

She was right, Walker realized. That daisy comforter was unique.

"This is Mr. Smith. Expect a call from me soon. If Elizabeth Blaine testifies, your friend dies. It's up to you to stop her," said the voice on-screen. The Glock pressed harder against Avery's temple, and she shut her eyes. "When I call, you tell me the good news—that you've persuaded Blaine to walk away."

Walker's heart squeezed. There was no way Elizabeth would walk away now. Even if she did, there was no guarantee that man wouldn't shoot Avery anyway. The minute the screen went blank, he got to work, though. "Sent you a few images," he said to Renata.

She got busy with her own phone.

Walker forced himself to take a deep breath. Focus.

"Where are you going?" Boone called after him.

"To find her."

"Where?"

"I don't know!"

"I'm coming with you."

Walker kept going.

"That ought to light a fire under your friends' asses," Mr. Smith said.

When the pressure of the Glock's barrel against her temple lifted, Avery opened her eyes again. Swallowed against the fear that had threatened to close her throat. She knew these men needed to keep her alive for now to motivate Walker and the others, but what would happen when Elizabeth testified?

Because Elizabeth was going to testify—whether or not Walker or anyone else asked her to stop.

Her only hope was for Walker to find her. Surely he'd check the vacation rentals like this one—anywhere an out-of-towner might stay. Didn't places like this have to be licensed? There'd be a list of them somewhere.

Mr. Smith's phone buzzed. He glanced at the screen. Made a sound of impatience and accepted the call.

"Yes?"

Avery could make out a woman's voice on the other end of the line.

Elizabeth?

She didn't think so, especially given the way Mr. Smith was acting. Owen crossed to her and aimed his weapon at her head, lifting a finger to his lips to shush her.

"Yes, it's very nice," Mr. Smith said in a smooth voice. "Yes, we love Chance Creek so far. The weather? It's been lovely. Couldn't ask for better. How is it in Florida?" He listened again. "Your management company is doing a fine job. Everything was ready for us. The keypad worked fine. Yes, we found the extra pillows. Thank you. Thank you very much. Yes, we're off for a walk. Thank you again." He tapped to end the call. "Nosy bitch."

"We're her first customers, remember," Owen drawled as he slid his handgun into its holster. They both chuckled.

Avery swallowed. First customers? This was a new rental?

Did anyone know it was here?

She must have made a noise. Owen was back, his weapon pressed to her temple. "What?"

"What?" she parroted. "What do you mean, what? I've been sitting here for hours. My arms hurt, everything hurts, I'm tired—I'm scared."

"Settle down," Mr. Smith said. He came to stand beside her. Pushed her forward and sliced through the ties around her wrists with a knife he pulled out of his waistband. Tangled a hand in her hair, dragged her off the bed and marched her around the room.

"What are you doing?"

"Letting you stretch your legs."

It wasn't much of an improvement, but there wasn't anything she could do about that. Avery marched along with him back and forth, her head at an awkward angle, his fingers pulling her hair.

Her updo was toast. Her wedding dress wrinkled. Full of crumbs.

She might be dead before the night was over.

Desperation dried her throat and thickened her tongue. She wanted Walker's arms around her. Wanted him to tell her it would all be all right.

She yelped when Mr. Smith tossed her back on the bed.

"Tie her wrists in front of her this time."

Owen did as he was told, but Avery was ready for him and braced against his strength. When he finished tying her hands, there was a little slack. Not much but enough to give her hope. Something to work on. He nudged her over on the bed and sat beside her, weapon at the ready. It was a Glock, too, she noticed. Had he and Mr. Smith bought matching guns?

How sweet.

"Don't even think about doing something stupid," he said.

She was definitely thinking about doing something stupid.

Mr. Smith took out his phone again. Tapped the screen and held it to his ear. "Well?" he demanded.

"Look!" Owen pointed at the television. Avery's breath whooshed out in a rush. She could easily identify the woman who'd just taken her seat in front of the room full of senators.

Elizabeth.

"IS THAT YOUR phone?" Boone asked.

Walker didn't know how long they'd been driving or what he was looking for. He doubted Avery's captors would be hauling her around the streets of Chance Creek at this time of night. He simply didn't know what else to do.

Walker answered the call.

"Well?" a man demanded.

In the background, Walker heard another man say, "Look! That's her—she's testifying!"

Testifying? Did he mean Elizabeth?

If so, they'd run out of time.

A crash of noise made Walker wince, and it took him a second to realize it had happened on the other end of the line. The caller swore a string of curses, and there was the sound of a door opening and a change in audio quality that suggested he'd changed location— maybe stepped outside. A burst of music blared in the distance and then dimmed, as if someone near the caller had opened another door and shut it.

Opened a door. Shut it.

Walker tried to parse the sound in his mind. That music hadn't been close enough to be in the same building as the caller. It was as if the sound had come from down the road. Like someone in the distance had walked into an establishment that was blaring music on the inside.

Where had he heard music like that?

He covered the phone with his hand, juggling it against the steering wheel, trying not to lose control of the truck. "The Dancing Boot. They're near the Boot!" he hissed at Boone.

"Like in the motel? The Evergreen? People already checked there."

"I don't know." He lifted the phone to his ear again. "Hold on. We've got a plan!" He hung up and tossed the phone to Boone.

Let Mr. Smith think he meant a plan to stop Elizabeth.

He'd find out he was wrong soon enough.

ELIZABETH WAS GOOD at her job, Avery had to admit. The presentation she'd prepared showed step by step how opening the Renning field in Alaska to oil drilling and letting the Lawrence Oil project get underway would help push global greenhouse emissions over a cliff in a way that could not be reversed. She didn't get mired in numbers and graphs; instead the images that flashed on the screen behind her showed the cost in photos of current environmental devastation, with overlaid projections of how much worse those natural and humanmade disasters would become in the future if even more drilling was allowed to happen.

With every sentence Elizabeth spoke, however, Avery knew her own time on earth was growing shorter. Her captors seemed mesmerized by the scene on the television screen, pinned to it as if they thought the people at Base Camp had somehow arranged for a band of rogues to burst into the senatorial chamber and carry Elizabeth off midsentence.

Avery worked at the rope that bound her wrists as quietly as she could. She'd opened her mouth to yell at the phone and tell Walker exactly where they were, but Owen must have expected something like that. He'd lunged at her, slapped a hand over her mouth and kicked over the bedside table in the process. Before she could recover, Mr. Smith was out of the bedroom and onto the balcony, where he stayed until he'd completed his phone call. Owen checked the binding on her wrists and trussed up her ankles, swearing all the while.

"We don't have much time left," Elizabeth said on-screen. "The clock is ticking down if we want to save ourselves."

Don't I know it? Avery shut her eyes and sent up a prayer.

She'd already missed her wedding.

She didn't want to die.

CHAPTER TWELVE

"**F**UCK!"

Walker spared a glance at Boone.

"It's Montague—he's at Base Camp, and no one's there to stop him."

Walker stayed focused. A glance at the clock a minute ago had told him they were running out of time in more ways than one. All the delays at the hearing had sent it into the wee hours in Washington, DC, time. It was nearly eleven thirty here in Chance Creek. Elizabeth was wrapping up her testimony. Avery's captors would have to admit defeat and deal with her one way or another. He could only hope that killing her would serve no purpose to them, so they'd simply leave her behind, but he knew he couldn't count on that.

"Looks like he's about to bulldoze everything we've built."

Walker spared another glance his way and saw a live feed of Base Camp playing on Boone's phone. There was the bunkhouse surrounded by the crew's bright lights. There were the nearby tiny houses. Something was moving in front of them.

Something big.

He glanced over again. Bulldozers. Lots of them. "Tell me."

"They're lining up in front of the tiny houses." Boone's voice was rough. "Montague is going to do some kind of synchronized demolition, isn't he? Is Fulsom in on this? I bet he is. I bet he planned this ending all along. Maybe he kidnapped Avery—"

"I don't think so." Someone with a lot of money and the desire for a lot more set this up. Fulsom was a billionaire and a real piece of work sometimes, but Walker thought he genuinely wanted to leave things better when he was gone.

"This is Marla Stone, reporting from Base Camp in Chance Creek, Montana," a familiar voice said on-screen.

"Is that *Star News*?" Walker asked in surprise.

"You got it."

"How the hell did they end up at Base Camp?"

"They're working with Montague—they have to be. He must have lured them out there." Boone swore again.

"They can't start demolishing anything until after midnight."

"Tell that to Montague."

Marla was still talking. "Viewers around the world have watched this group of deluded men and women try to block progress by taking on the clothing of our ancestors and living like prisoners in barely habitable tiny houses."

"For the love of all that's holy," Boone growled.

"Led by Boone Rudman, who has been accused of having a God complex more than once by viewers," the woman went on. "It's his wife, Riley, who I'm really sorry for, though. Did you know this property should have been hers? Stolen out from under her by the ruthless leftist agitator Martin Fulsom, this ranch has been in her family for generations. When Fulsom's henchman, Boone, arrived to kick her out of her home, Riley had no choice but to marry him. It's obvious she's been miserable ever since."

"She's not miserable!" Boone exclaimed. "Is she miserable?" He turned to Walker.

"Now this miscreant of a husband is going to lose her property and her heart. It's the final hour of the last day of their chance to win this ranch and all the buildings on it, and where is everyone? Gallivanting around the countryside from what we've heard. Base Camp's inhabitants have one task left to achieve their goal: get Walker Norton to the altar with the woman of his choice. But there's no wedding happening here. No wedding happening anywhere, as far as we can tell. Which means on the strike of midnight, Montague's bulldozers will start their engines, and Base Camp will be toast."

"Walker," Boone said, and Walker knew exactly what his friend was thinking. They were about to lose their homes, everything they'd built, everything Riley loved—and Boone would do anything for Riley.

But Walker had to think of Avery now. He had to put her first. He never had before, and now it was almost too late.

The blonde announcer gave a shriek, capturing Walker's attention again as Riley appeared on-screen and grabbed the microphone off her lapel.

"What the hell is Riley doing there?" Boone sputtered.

"Walker, Boone," Riley said into the microphone. "We got a head's up about Montague's plans. We're here, but don't worry—no ranch is worth anything compared to the life of my friend. You bring Avery home. We'll stop Montague."

The show cut quickly to a commercial break. Walker spared a glance at Boone as he pulled into the parking lot of the Evergreen Motel.

"We're going to have to go door to door."

"Right. Yeah." Boone was still staring at his screen. He shook his head, lifted the phone and tapped it. "Cab? Boone here. There are bulldozers at Base Camp—" He cut off. Listened. "Okay, thanks, glad you're on it. We think Avery's somewhere near the Dancing Boot. We're going door to door. You sure you searched the motel?" He listened. "Okay, we'll cross the street and start there." He cut the call. "Cab's got men on the way to Base Camp. The rest of them will meet us."

"Let's go."

"WE'RE FINE," OWEN said. "We're going to be fine. No

one's going to listen to all that wishy-washy crap. Those senators know which side their bread is buttered on."

"Shut up," Mr. Smith said. "We're fucked no matter what. We need a plan."

Owen drew his Glock and pointed it at Avery. "I say our plan should be to put a cap in this one. More trouble than she's worth."

Avery drew back against the bedframe and braced herself, but Mr. Smith knocked Owen's hand aside. "Put that away, shut the fuck up and start using your head. She's our ticket to safety. We'll use her to get across the border. Lay low for a while in Mexico."

"Hell, I don't want to go to Mexico."

"I don't really care."

Mr. Smith flipped the channel on the television. During a lull in the proceedings, he'd found the Base Camp live feed on *Star News*. Ever since, he'd been switching back and forth between the two. "What the hell is that?" Avery saw a line of bulldozers lined up in front of the tiny houses on-screen. Mr. Smith laughed. "Gotta hand it to these guys; they know how to put on a show." He turned to Avery. "They tell you ahead of time they were going to do this?"

She shook her head. She wasn't sure she could speak if she tried. Where had all those bulldozers come from?

"This is a surprising turn of events." The announcer seemed to be wrestling with Riley and finally yanked what looked like a tiny clip-on microphone out of her hands. "The women of *Base Camp*, who've been searching for their missing friend, Avery Lightfoot, have just arrived back."

Someone off-camera yelled. Avery thought it was Savannah. Riley whirled to see and then darted out of view.

Marla, the *Star News* announcer, watched her go. "They're linking their arms and standing in front of the tiny houses. They're actually going to try and stop the bulldozers." The camera moved to follow her pointed finger.

"No!" Avery cried. "Riley, get out of there!"

What if the bulldozers didn't stop?

She cried out again when Mr. Smith switched back to C-SPAN. "The presentation's over. They're fucking starting the vote!"

Was that fear in his voice?

A shiver slid down her spine. If the bad guys were afraid, whoever controlled them must be truly dangerous.

Would they really take her to Mexico? What then?

Mr. Smith flipped back to the Base Camp live feed. "What the hell? Look at those women!"

Avery leaned forward. There was Riley, Savannah, Nora, Addison, Hope, Renata, Samantha, Eve, Win and Leslie standing between the bulldozers and the tiny houses. Was that Jess joining them? Sure looked like it. Her stomach cramped with fear.

"They're all going to die!" Owen crowed.

"This is getting good," Mr. Smith said, but he flipped to C-SPAN.

"Aye," said a senator. The speaker read another name, and a man stood up. "Nay," he said.

Mr. Smith flipped to the live feed.

"The bulldozers are moving!" Owen said.

Avery's mouth went dry. He was right; the bulldozers were advancing, eating up the ground between them and the tiny houses—with all her friends in between.

"Run," she called at the screen. *Run! Run!* she willed at them in her head.

"There's not enough of them," Owen said. "Most of those bulldozers can go right around them and get at the other houses."

Mr. Smith flipped back to C-SPAN. "Aye," said a woman. "Nay," said a man.

Flip.

Avery nearly screamed when she saw how close the bulldozers were. Suddenly a roar went up from the screen, and people started flooding into view.

"What the hell?" Owen cried. "Who are those people?"

Avery wasn't sure. Wait—wasn't that Autumn Cruz, who ran a bed-and-breakfast at her ranch in Chance Creek? And wasn't that Marta, the librarian? And if she wasn't mistaken, that was Elle Hall, who used to be a movie star and now ran an equine rehabilitation program over at Crescent Hall.

Women were pouring in from all directions. Chance Creek women. They were swarming the space between the bulldozers and the tiny houses. No—

They were climbing up into the bulldozers.

Pulling out the drivers. Dragging them away.

"Go!" Avery cried. "Go! Go!"

Mr. Smith flipped back to C-SPAN.

"The votes are in," the man on the screen was saying. "The ayes have forty-nine, the nays have fifty-one. Bill 134 has been defeated."

Avery cried out in relief, then fear as Owen spun around to face her, the Glock in his hand again.

"There goes our money," he snarled at his friend.

"Fuck," Mr. Smith growled. "Fuck, fuck, fuck! We've got to go. Tie her up."

"She'll slow us down!" Owen trained his weapon on Avery. "Bye-bye, little girl—"

Avery shut her eyes and ducked.

"I HAVEN'T SEEN anyone," said the man at the door of the seventh house Walker had knocked on. "It's been quiet all night. I heard there was a search for your friend. We checked the house and the garage, just in case. You're welcome to check again."

"Is there anything for rent on this block?" Walker was losing his patience. Anything could have happened to Avery. It had been hours since she'd been taken from the Russells'. She could be hundreds of miles away. She could be—

No, he wouldn't let himself think that.

"I don't think so."

A woman appeared behind the man in a faded bathrobe. "Yes, there is." She shoved her husband aside with her hip. "Right at the end of the block. They made that old blue house into a vacation rental. The outside isn't much to look at, but the inside is done up quite nicely."

Walker's heart pounded. Vacation rental? That was it. It had to be. "Thanks!"

He dashed down the front steps and across the street to where Boone was talking to another home-owner. "I got it!"

"Thanks for your help," Boone called as he raced to join Walker. "Where?"

"End of the block. Brand-new vacation rental. It's got to be where she is."

"We'll find out."

Walker heard sirens wailing in the distance. Cab coming to join them? He didn't want Avery's captors alerted. "Call Cab. Tell him to knock that off!"

Boone stopped to do so. Walker kept going. When he reached the house in question and found the small plaque by the door, he was doubly sure this had to be the place. There was a car in the driveway with rental decals. The lights on the first floor were out, but the second story was blazing with lights in every room.

She must be up there.

Boone joined him again.

"I'm getting in there. Take the back door, in case someone makes a run for it."

Boone nodded.

When he was gone, Walker got to work on the front door. His SEAL training came in handy, but it wasn't difficult. Maybe the homeowner had spruced up the interior, but this keypad lock was as cheap as they came. Once inside, Walker crept toward the stairs, listening intently.

He could hear a television playing upstairs and had a momentary qualm; if he walked in on some poor, unsuspecting couple watching TV in bed, he was going to hate himself.

Still, he had to find out if Avery was there. He stopped at the bottom of the staircase to listen.

Whoever had control of the remote was flicking from channel to channel, the sound changing every few seconds. Walker crept step by step up to the second floor.

"What the hell is that?" a man said.

Walker froze and didn't breathe easy until another man replied, "Gotta hand it to these guys; they know how to put on a show. They tell you ahead of time they're going to do this?"

Was he talking to Avery? What were they watching?

"This is a surprising turn of events." A different voice—from the TV.

Walker knew that voice, but from where?

"The women of *Base Camp*, most of them pregnant, have just arrived back."

Was that *Star News*? It had to be. They were still reporting from Base Camp.

There was a yell, still on the television, but Walker recognized that voice, too. Savannah. What was happening?

"They're linking their arms and standing in front of

the tiny houses," the *Star News* announcer said. "They're actually going to try to stop the bulldozers."

"No!"

Ice sliced through Walker's veins. That was Avery!

"Riley, get out of there!"

What the hell was Riley doing? Trying to block the bulldozers?

Boone needed to know—

But Avery needed him right now.

Avery gave a cry. The sound on the television changed. Walker crept up another step, his Glock in his hands.

"The presentation's over," one of the men he'd heard before said angrily. Was that Mr. Smith? The guy who'd called him? "They're fucking starting the vote!"

The sound on the television switched again. "What the hell? Look at those women! They're all going to die!" the other man said.

"This is getting good," Mr. Smith said. The television sound switched again.

"Aye," a man said. Walker heard a man's name read out. "Nay," another man said. That had to be the Senate taking its vote. How had Elizabeth's presentation gone?

The sound changed.

"The bulldozers are moving!" the second man said.

"Go," Avery called out. Walker's heart squeezed. She was so close—so close—

But he couldn't blow this.

"There's not enough of them," the second man said. "Most of those bulldozers can go right around them and get at the other houses."

The sound changed. "Aye," a woman's voice said. "Nay." That was a man.

The sound changed again.

The cry Avery gave chilled the blood in Walker's veins. What had she seen on the television? Walker held steady. He had to choose the right moment. There were two men in that room, both of them probably armed.

Suddenly a roar went up from the television.

"What the hell?" the second man cried. "Who are those people?"

"Go!" Avery cried. "Go! Go!"

The sound changed again. Walker steeled himself. He had to make his move.

"The votes are in," the man on the television was saying. "The ayes have forty-nine, the nays have fifty-one. Bill 134 has been defeated."

Avery cried out in relief, then shrieked.

What was happening?

"There goes our money," the second man snarled.

"Fuck," the first man growled. "Fuck, fuck, fuck! We've got to go. Tie her up."

"She'll slow us down!" A slight pause. "Bye-bye, little girl—"

Walker launched himself up the stairs and across the hall.

WHEN THE DOOR burst open and something catapulted across the room, Avery screamed again. Owen hit the ground, his Glock knocked from his hands, and the two men grappled on the ground until Walker got the upper hand. He pulled back and punched Owen.

The man went limp.

Mr. Smith, shocked into stillness by Walker's sudden appearance, reached for his gun. Avery, getting over her own surprise, moved without thinking. She tucked her trussed legs underneath herself on the soft mattress, rocked back and launched herself toward him.

The impact knocked the breath from her lungs, and they collapsed in a tangle to the floor. A moment later, the man tossed her aside, but someone else burst through the door—

Boone.

"Don't move!" He trained his weapon on Mr. Smith. "Don't even try it." Boone advanced when Mr. Smith made to pull Avery in front of him as a shield, but Walker got there first. He plucked Avery from the man's hands. A second later, Boone's weapon was in Mr. Smith's face. "Give me one reason," he growled.

"We don't have time for that," Walker said. He still held Avery in his arms. She wished she could fling hers around his neck and bury her face against his chest, but her wrists were tied. "We've got to get back to Base Camp."

Walker deposited Avery on the bed, pulled out a knife and cut through the bindings on her wrists and ankles. Then he cupped her chin and kissed her. Pulled back and met her gaze with his, his eyes telling her everything he didn't have time to say.

He loved her.

He'd nearly lost her.

He'd never let her go again.

"Riley," Avery croaked.

"That's where we're headed next," Walker assured her.

"Stopped the bulldozers," Avery managed. "People came to help."

"You sure?" Boone had gone pale where he stood, his weapon still trained on Mr. Smith.

Avery grabbed the remote. Changed the channel back to *Star News*. Crowds of women were dancing and singing, climbing all over the bulldozers that stood unmoving near the tiny houses.

"Never seen anything like it," Marla was saying on-screen. "You know, these women aren't that bad—"

More men burst into the room, Cab and his deputies.

"It's all right," Boone told him. "Avery's safe."

As Cab took over the situation, Walker drew Avery to the far side of the room. "You okay?" he asked her gently, running his hands over her as if making sure she had no injuries.

"My arms hurt. Wrists and ankles are sore, but I'm okay."

He wiped her cheek with a finger. Avery hadn't realized she was crying.

"I was scared," she admitted as he drew her into an embrace.

He tightened his arms around her until she was wrapped in a comforting fortress and bent down to speak in her ear. "I was terrified."

As the tears ran down her cheeks, Avery breathed in Walker's comforting scent. She never wanted to leave the safety of his arms again. Behind them the television still played, and she heard the voices of her friends mixed with others on-screen. They were safe—and so was Base Camp. Elizabeth had defeated the new drilling plan, and there was hope for the future. Maybe they could save the world, after all.

"Hey," Cab called from across the room. "Weren't you two supposed to get married tonight?"

Avery pulled back with a gasp. Met Walker's shocked gaze. Turned to find a clock on the bedside table.

It was five minutes past midnight.

CHAPTER THIRTEEN

"IT'S NOT THE end," Walker told Avery again when they parked in Base Camp's parking lot a half hour later.

"I know."

"I want to marry you."

"I know." But she didn't stop crying. Her tears had slipped silently down her cheeks since before they'd left Cab Johnson putting the two kidnappers in his cruiser. It had been a long drive back to the ranch.

"We'll find a way to stay together—all of us."

"I know."

Walker's heart squeezed at her grief.

"We'll take Champ with us. I'll steal him if I have to."

"And Ruth. Champ is too young to be separated from his mother." A tremulous smile quirked her lips before her tears overwhelmed her again. "It's just... wherever we go, it won't be the same."

"Don't give up. Not yet."

A murmur of voices told him the crowds he'd seen

on television gathered at Base Camp hadn't thinned yet. If anything, they'd grown. He realized the search parties must have come to join the women who'd saved the tiny houses. It looked like all of Chance Creek was here to greet Avery's safe return.

As they approached the community, the floodlights lit up the bulldozers still strewn around the hillside. Women were perched on them, inside and out. More were milling around, setting up tables of food and drinks, holding babies, wrangling children they'd brought along with them, dressed in pajamas.

The men of Base Camp stood gathered together, speaking in low voices, already planning their next steps, Walker assumed. This was too dynamic a group for there not to be next steps, but like Avery said, it would be hard to leave Base Camp after everything that had happened here.

"Walker! Avery!" Jericho called out, and instantly they were swarmed. Avery submitted to the hugs of her friends. Walker shook Jericho's hand, then Clay's.

"I can't believe we didn't find you sooner," Clay said. "I can't believe that vacation rental wasn't on our list."

"It's okay. It's over," Walker told them.

"It really is," Boone said, running a hand through his short-cropped hair and looking around them. Everyone went quiet, all of them counting their regrets.

"No one can say we didn't try," Clay pronounced roughly. "We gave it everything we had."

"We did the right thing protecting Elizabeth, too,"

Jericho said. "Maybe we lost the ranch, but she persuaded those guys in the Senate. That's something."

Walker was grateful for his friends' support, but he knew everyone was hurting and would continue to do so long after the high of defeating the legislation ebbed away.

"I'll be right back." Avery went up on tiptoe to press a kiss to his cheek. "Just need the washroom."

"Your parents are on the way," Clay told her. "They're with the Russells."

"Thanks."

Walker watched her until she disappeared into the bunkroom, wanting to follow her there and guard the door, finding it hard to believe the threat to their lives was really over.

"We'll figure out something," Greg told him. "With so many of us working together, there has to be a way to recreate what we have here."

Murmurs of assent came from all around.

"We can start fresh. Learn from past mistakes," Kai said.

"Hell, it's Fulsom," Harris said wearily, pointing. "I don't know if I have the patience to listen to that windbag right now."

There were a few chuckles as they shifted to make way for the man to speak to them.

Walker wished the night was over and all was said and done. He was ready to cut his losses and move forward—with Avery.

Wherever they might go next.

IT WAS ALL her fault, Avery decided as she splashed cold water on her face and tried to hide the traces of her fresh tears. If she had never come to Westfield in the first place, Walker probably would have cut a deal with Elizabeth and married her in exchange for protecting her until the hearing. If she hadn't been so restless at the Russells', she wouldn't have been kidnapped. Either way you looked at it, it was her fault they were going to lose everything they'd worked so hard to build.

Had this been Fulsom's plan all along—to make them lose? To make their audience so angry they'd finally fight for the changes they needed to keep carbon emissions low?

If so, Avery thought it would backfire. People were already tired. They were overwhelmed with bad news and too much information. They were struggling to hold their own lives together, let alone try to save the world.

As she slipped out of the bunkhouse into the surrounding crowd, she spotted a new surge of people approaching from the parking area: Fulsom and his entourage. She fought an urge to go right back into the bunkhouse and hide. Instead she made her way to them and quietly joined the group around the billionaire.

"I thought we agreed at least two houses would be damaged," Fulsom was saying to an aide as they walked toward the gathered crowd. "There was supposed to be drama!"

"The pregnant women in danger were the drama, sir," his aide pointed out. "Not to mention the kidnapping."

"She's back, right? Don't need any deaths on my hands."

Anger kindled in Avery's belly. At least two of the tiny houses were supposed to be damaged? So Fulsom knew all about Montague's attempt to bulldoze them early? He knew about her kidnapping, and he'd only just made it here? Had he tried to help find her at all?

"Here she is. Right here! Get those lights over here."

A woman's hand closed around her arm, and Avery looked up to see Marla and the rest of the *Star News* crew focused on her.

"Can I get a statement about the spectacular failure of Base Camp to accomplish anything?" Marla asked.

Avery yanked free of her grip. "What are you doing here? Who gave you permission to film on our land?"

"It's not your land anymore, is it?" Marla persisted. "We're here on the invitation of Martin Fulsom, the colossally reckless billionaire who started this whole thing. I saw him walk past just now. What would you like to say to him?"

Avery turned away. Had Fulsom been feeding stories to *Star News* all this time?

It was another kick in the gut.

By the time she recovered herself and caught up to Walker and the others again, Fulsom was miced up and addressing the crowd. Anger and indignation built inside her with each passing moment. He'd risked their homes—their lives.

"Thank you all for being here tonight. First I want

to welcome everyone to this special place and say a few words about what's happened here. We took on something big when we started *Base Camp*."

"We?" Avery called out in indignation. "What did you do? We're the ones who spent a year building this community."

If her interruption surprised him, Fulsom recovered quickly. "We aimed for the stars, you could say," he boomed. "And if we failed to reach them, at least we tried. Fulsom Industries has been proud to back this noble effort, and we remain proud of our investment—"

Walker surged forward and ripped the microphone off Fulsom's shirt.

"Hey!" Fulsom reached for it, but Walker held him off with one outstretched hand.

"*We* came to Chance Creek to build a better future. To show everyone it could be done. To test out new ideas in technology and food production and the organization of people in communities. We've done everything we set out to do and more, and while we did it, we opened up our lives to scrutiny by the entire world."

"That's more words than I've heard Walker say in twelve months," Savannah hissed. Riley elbowed her into silence, but Avery understood her shock. Walker wasn't one to grandstand like this.

"*We* built a renewable energy system. *He* tried to sabotage it." Walker pointed a finger at Fulsom, who began to protest. "We grew enough food to feed ourselves and more through the winter. He stole it. We built ten tiny houses that were beautiful and functional, each of them different because of the finishing touches of the homeowners. He tried to bulldoze them."

Fulsom kept protesting, but no one was listening to him. Walker had them hooked.

"Here's the thing about the world. There are builders and there are destroyers, givers and takers. We all know that. But there's another class of people, too. The users. The ones who foment chaos between everyone else and then make billions off both sides when strife erupts. The ones who offer something for free but then make billions by selling our most personal data to those who want to influence us. The ones with so much money invested in things staying the same, they won't ever allow conditions to improve for the rest of us. Tonight everyone watching this show needs to ask themselves, am I a builder, am I a destroyer or am I a user?"

Fulsom rubbed his forehead. Waited to see if Walker was done. When Walker didn't go on, Fulsom leaned in to speak in the little microphone.

"I'm a builder! Everyone knows that!"

"Are you?" Walker challenged him. "Really?"

"I built all this!" He waved a hand to include all of Base Camp.

"Did you?" Walker waited him out, and Fulsom began to sputter.

"Without my money—"

"Without the money you earned in your oil empire, you mean?"

Fulsom flushed. Avery knew he'd spent years trying to change his image from oil man to environmentalist and entrepreneur.

"I'm using my money to fund—"

"You're using *our* money, you mean."

Fulsom gaped at him. "Your money? I'm the one who—"

"What? Pulled the oil out of the ground? Out of *our* ground? Ruined *our* air? Polluted *our* water? Changed *our* atmosphere?" Walker held out his hand to include everyone present. "And now you think you have the right to spend the money you earned doing that? To control where it goes? To play with our lives?"

Avery held her breath. There it was—the real reason Walker was speaking up. Fulsom *had* played with their lives—his and hers. All of theirs. Maybe he'd done it for the best of reasons. Maybe he'd done it for the most selfish ones.

It didn't matter.

Because in the end, none of them had to let a stupid billionaire control anything.

And she'd had enough.

Avery marched up to where they stood and took the microphone from Walker. She faced the crowd.

"Our show has come to an end, but here's the moral of the story," she said. "If you want change, you have to bring it. If you want to end pollution, you have to stop polluting. If you want to have a civil society, you have to be civil. If you want to build a community, you have to build it. All of us here at Base Camp can't change the world for you. Billionaires *won't* change it for you. Your government is too hamstrung to change it for you. It's all up to you. All up to each of us. We can encourage each other, reach out to each other, help each other, but at the end of the day, and especially in the middle of the night, in our darkest, loneliest hour, it comes down to us. We are all of us, every single one of us, alone in this fight—together."

As her friends converged around her and Walker pulled her into a rough embrace, Avery dropped the little microphone and let it all go. This was what was important: this moment, these people, this man she loved.

But even as they came together, Fulsom called out, "Wait!"

Avery sighed but turned to listen.

"I… may have let myself get carried away." Without his microphone, Fulsom had lost some of his bluster. "I wanted to be sure everyone watched *Base Camp*, so I did everything I could to make it popular: high stakes, dramatic problems, love and lust and weddings. So many weddings."

A couple of people in the gathered crowd chuckled.

"I wanted a grand finale that would keep people talking even after the show was over, and I wanted everyone to know there's no guarantee we win this thing. We're in the middle of an extinction event. We're destroying the world's forests at an unprecedented rate. We—" He shook his head. "You know this. All of us know all this. And yet it goes on." He raised his hands in supplication. Paced a few steps. "Here's the thing. I'm afraid." He pointed to Walker. "You're right: I've got billions, and even I can't seem to make a difference, so what does that mean? And you're right: more than anyone else—anyone here, anyway—I helped cause this problem. So I need to fix it! But you're right again. That's where I lost sight of the goal. I've..." He paused, as if swallowing a bitter taste in his mouth. "I've got to ask for help. I've got to stop playing God. So what I'm going to do is... what I'm going to do is use my money better. I'm going to fully fund the Fulsom Foundation, expand the board of directors and take on a broader set of goals. I'm going to get more experts involved—and listen to them. Less flash, more substance."

"Sounds like a good start," Walker called out.

"And I'm going to hand over the deed to this ranch to the person who should have had it in the first place. Riley, Westfield is yours. I know you'll know what to do with it."

Riley covered her mouth with her hand, then buried her face in Boone's chest. Avery's eyes filled with tears of joy for her friend.

A cheer went up from the crowd, and more than one Base Camp couple kissed.

"Wait!" a man cried. "Wait, wait, wait!"

Avery nearly groaned when Montague pushed his way through the crowd and stormed up to Fulsom.

"You can't give this land away. It's mine now! I won. They lost."

Fulsom stared at him, and Avery remembered Montague was right. Walker hadn't married her. Midnight was long past. The women of Base Camp and their helpers from town had stopped the bulldozers, but that didn't change anything.

"Well… I… I mean." For once in his life, Martin Fulsom didn't seem to know what to say. "I know I set up the rules, but—"

"But nothing! This ranch is mine. I'm going to build that subdivision. I won fair and square."

"No, you didn't!" Avery cried. "You cheated every step of the way, including bringing those bulldozers here well before midnight, when you didn't have any reason to be here at all!"

"That's right." Fulsom cleared his throat. "You broke the rules."

"Because you told me to." Montague didn't back down. "This is a big pile of baloney. You've been manipulating me all along."

"I'll… I'll give you another ranch." Montague was making a mess of his big moment, and Avery could see Fulsom was determined not to let that happen.

"You're going to reward him for all his bad behavior?" Riley asked. "What's the message in doing that? You'll be encouraging people to do the wrong thing."

Fulsom threw up his hands in frustration. "What do you want me to do?"

"Nothing," Walker said. He stepped forward. "Here's another idea," he said to Montague. "How about you join us?"

"What?" several people cried at once.

"Why would I want to join you?"

"Because you're a developer, and we can help you be a leader in that industry. Trends are changing. You need to adapt to keep up. People need houses that several generations can share. They need houses that work for retirement. They need houses that run on green energy and return power to the system rather than draw it down. They need a new way of coming together in community, sharing resources rather than being isolated. Work with us. We'll help you design a new kind of subdivision. One that works more like a town than an afterthought. Step into the future with us. You're looking for success, right? We know how to get there. Fulsom can give you the land. We can give you the know-how—and our seal of approval. Think of the publicity you'll get."

Montague stared at him. "After everything I've done, you'd let me work with you?"

"It's a hell of a lot better than having to keep fighting you." Walker waved a hand to encompass the crowd. "We might have different ways of going about it, but we're all after the same thing, aren't we? We all want a steady job, a way to pay our bills, a roof over our head, food and safety for our families. We want to belong to something. To feel good about how we spend our time. We aren't all that different. You're a builder. We're builders, too. Why not work together?"

Montague processed this. "You know… I made some plans recently," he said slowly, scratching the back of his head. "Don't know why, really; I don't build little houses. After seeing yours, though, I knew I could do better. And I did."

"We'd love to see those plans," Clay assured him, joining Walker.

Avery held her breath. Montague chewed on his lip. "Guess I could show them to you. Working together could be… interesting."

She let it go.

"That's agreed, then," Fulsom spoke up. "We'll work out the details and make sure the stakeholders get their say, but I'm still returning Westfield to Riley. Can you live with that?" he asked Montague.

"Guess so. If I get a piece of land somewhere of similar value," the man grumbled. When Riley threw her arms around him and gave him a big kiss on his cheek, he pretended not to like it, but it was obvious he did. Soon he was deep in discussion with Clay and Dell about plans and possibilities.

"Okay, folks, it's official," Fulsom said. "Base Camp forever!"

"Base Camp forever!" the crowd cheered.

Someone's fingers twined in Avery's, and she looked up to see Walker next to her. A wave of relief swept over her, then a wave of love. For the first time ever, she knew he was inevitably, utterly hers.

Nothing could stop them from being together now.

He nodded. Turned her to face him and took her other hand, too. "Want to try again next week?" he asked. In the din around them, his eyes held a world of patience and peace—and love.

Avery's heart swelled until she thought it would burst out of her chest.

"Yes."

"Avery!"

Before she could turn to see who was calling her, she was enveloped in a double hug. Her parents clung to her.

"Are you okay?"

"Did they hurt you?"

"I'm fine," she assured them, meeting Walker's gaze. As long as she had him, she'd always be okay.

CHAPTER FOURTEEN

One week later

O KAY, NOW YOU can look."

Walker blinked when Avery uncovered his eyes and straightened, taking in the beautiful wooden shelf now installed in the living area of his tiny house. On it lay the ceremonial fan he'd given Avery just a few weeks ago.

"I thought it needed a place at the heart of our house."

His chest flooded with warmth. She had to know she would always be the heart of the house to him, but he appreciated the gesture more than he could say.

"It's perfect." When she hugged him, he bent to kiss her, wanting her to know what he was feeling.

When they pulled away again, Avery said, "I have to get going. I'll meet you at the altar in a few hours. Let's try to get there this time." She went up on tiptoe for another kiss and held on longer than he expected.

"You okay?" He pulled back and tilted up her chin with a finger. Tears shone in her eyes.

"I'm scared that something is going to happen. I never want to be taken from you again."

"No one ever will," he promised her. "I'll walk you to the manor, then come back here."

"Okay." She gratefully took his hand.

When they stepped outside, however, they found the other women of Base Camp had gathered there.

"We'll walk Avery to the manor," Savannah told him.

"I'll watch to make sure you make it," he assured Avery and passed her over to her friends, but she had already relaxed. It was hard to hold on to any fear in a day as brilliant as this one. The sun in the blue sky above them beamed down. The whole world seemed scrubbed brand new. Mr. Smith and Owen were behind bars awaiting trial—they couldn't hurt them now.

He watched the gaggle of women in their colorful gowns trail up the path to the manor. Maud and James were still helping with the wedding, but they'd decided to hold it here at the ranch this time. None of them wanted to leave it much these days, too enamored with the idea it was theirs now for good.

A half hour later, he was back in his tiny house when a knock on the door announced Sue's arrival.

"Looks good in here," she said, standing stiffly in the living room when he ushered her in. He noticed her gaze resting on the fan. She nodded in approval, and he stifled a smile. He wouldn't tell her it was Avery who'd put it there.

"It's nice to have the house all finished. Glad it's still

here, actually," he admitted. It still stopped his heart when he thought about Montague's bulldozers ready to flatten the home in which he'd meant to share his life with Avery.

"You cleaned up outside, too," she observed, looking out the floor-to-ceiling windows down the slope.

He nodded. They'd done their best to smooth out the gouges in the land from Montague's heavy machinery. By the end of the summer, he was sure the scars from the bulldozers would mostly fill in.

"So now it's all yours."

"All ours," he corrected. Or it would be. Riley was working with a lawyer to create a trust in which to hold Westfield ranch in perpetuity. It was complicated, and he was sure someone would spell out the terms and conditions to them eventually, but the takeaway was that he'd live here at Base Camp forever—they all would.

"You've built something good here."

Walker nodded. He knew Sue wished he'd concentrated his attention on the reservation. "I haven't left, you know. I never did. My heart is always at home." And now that he was in Chance Creek for good, he meant to spend a lot of time in the place where he'd grown up, renew all his old connections and forge new ones. He might have found a different place to live, but the home of his ancestors would always be important.

"Bring some of this energy back to us" was all Sue said, and he knew she understood that he would. They all would. His friends here were ready to share their knowledge with anyone who asked—and he knew Sue would ask. She was already talking about the possibilities of training her students to be ready for a green energy economy. Every time she visited Base Camp, Boone and Jericho cornered her to share ideas about joint projects and school initiatives.

He found himself more drawn to the bison herd than ever, studying them at all times of day until Hope joked that he was going to be competing for her research dollars.

"Just wondering what makes them so peaceful," he told her.

"I wonder about that, too. I think it's the same thing with most animals. They're just themselves, you know what I mean? A bison doesn't try to be anything other than a bison, and he takes life one minute at a time. He gets stirred up when there's a reason to be stirred up and shakes it off when the danger has passed rather than ruminating on it endlessly."

That sounded right to Walker.

"Guess it's time to shake it off and start enjoying the moment," he said.

"Exactly."

"I heard from Elizabeth," Sue broke into his thoughts, dusting off a speck of dust from his blue Revolutionary War uniform jacket. "She and Gabe are planning a wedding for next spring. At the reservation."

He could tell she was pleased. "That's good."

"You should have heard her. Proud as anything. Says Lawrence Energy is being investigated based on the information she presented at the hearing."

"She should be proud. She did a brave thing."

"So did you." Sue lifted her chin, and he knew that was the extent of the praise he'd get from her.

"Cab says those men who grabbed Avery will see jail time—a lot of it."

She nodded her approval.

"I like that Gabe," she added. "He says he'll bring Elizabeth home every few months. Says Montana is good for her."

"He believes in family," Walker guessed.

Sue nodded. "He is a good man."

As soon as Gabe had announced that he was Elizabeth's fiancé, Walker wondered how he'd ever missed it. His love for Elizabeth had been evident in a hundred ways.

"I'm glad they found each other."

Sue stepped back and looked him over approvingly. "Your father should be here. I feel him close by this time of year. He loved summer when he was a boy."

"I wish I'd gotten to know him better."

Sue shut her eyes but didn't allow her emotions to carry her away. "I feel him closeby all the time," she admitted. "I see him in the apple blossoms in the tree out back every spring. He loved to climb that tree. I feel him in the west wind when a storm's blowing in. He used to love the wild wind. I smell him when rain falls—he used to track in the mud and laugh at me when I scolded him. He's everywhere."

That was good to know. "He's everywhere," he repeated, letting his gaze rest on the sloping land outside the tall windows of his home.

"It still hurts," Sue said simply.

It did. Far more than he'd realized. "We don't talk about him enough," he said. "I want to talk about him. I want to hear the stories."

"Yes."

"We should have a memorial," he heard himself say. "Bring our people together to talk about my father's life."

Sue pulled back. "It's been years. We had a memorial."

Had they? He supposed so, but he could barely remember it—a solemn, silent affair that hadn't eased their pain.

"We need another one. A celebration this time of all he was." He waited, knowing Sue would pull no punches if she thought it was a bad idea.

She took a deep breath and let it out. "Yes."

"He was a good man." He held his breath.

"He was a good man." Sue's eyes shone. "My boy was a good man."

"Time to tell his story." As soon as he said it, he knew it was true. No one died on the reservation without it affecting everyone else. The unspoken pain of Joe's passing must still be carried in everyone's hearts, given how firmly it had lodged in theirs. They needed a chance to clear the air, remember the good times along with the bad. Remember all the ways they were still connected despite the pain that had come with their losses.

After a long moment, she nodded. "You're right."

He took her hands in his and squeezed them. "We'll heal the old wounds," he promised her. "We'll build a better future."

She admired him in all his wedding finery. Nodded. "You already are."

"I TOLD YOU to be patient, and your true love would find you," Avery's mother said, joining her in one of the large guest rooms on the second floor of the manor. Her parents had stayed all week, delighted with an extended visit to their daughter's new home.

"Never doubted it for a minute. No daughter of ours could ever be lonely," her father chimed in.

Avery smiled, her heart full of love for her parents even as she acknowledged to herself there was a lot about her they never seemed to see. That was all right. Caught up in their own happiness, they imagined everyone else felt similarly, and bearing witness to such a complete relationship had brought her two pieces of knowledge. One was that she wanted a true, strong love of her own, and two was that she'd always make sure to leave the door of that love open a crack so she could share her attention with everyone else in her life, too.

"I'm so glad you could stay until the wedding. I'm sorry it got postponed."

"We got to spend a week in Chance Creek! And help our daughter get ready for her wedding instead of showing up at the last minute."

"I'm glad it all worked out. It wouldn't have been

the same without you."

"Wouldn't miss it for the world. Our little girl is all grown up. Our little actress is a star."

"Hardly." Avery laughed. "I still haven't done what I set out to do."

"Star in a romantic comedy? You sure about that?" her mother teased her.

"More like a romantic horror show," Avery joked, but she was grateful for all she'd gone through since it had led her to a life with Walker. And she was still working on her screenplay. These days Fulsom seemed more approachable. Maybe she'd try for a conversation with him again.

She'd build an acting career for herself sooner or later.

"This dress is beautiful. It's perfect for you," her mother said, and Avery understood she wanted to turn the conversation to happier topics. That was fine with her. She'd had all the drama she could stand, and for now she wanted nothing other than some smooth sailing with the man she loved.

"I wish you could have seen the original. I really loved it, but it was ruined when I was kidnapped."

"You liked it better than this one?" Her mother frowned in concern.

"Actually... no," Avery admitted with a laugh. "I did love it, but then Alice came and made this one even better. She's really something." The new version of the gown was embroidered to the hilt. Avery wondered if Alice had known all along she'd need a second version and had been working on it behind the scenes ever since she'd made the first one. Avery thought any museum or art gallery would be proud to display this gown after her wedding. It was a masterpiece.

"You're something special, too," her father said. "And as beautiful as ever." He kissed the top of her head.

"Are you ready?" Riley came into the room, followed by the other women of Base Camp. Under Maud's insistence, they'd planned the wedding all over again, making it bigger and better this time. While the ceremony was invitation only, the reception would be open to anyone in town who wanted to come. The women of Base Camp were her bridesmaids.

Alice Reed had spiffed up their gowns, too. There had been trips back and forth to Two Willows at all hours of the day and night during the past week. All the men would stand up with Walker. All the women would stand with her. Her father would do the honors and give her away. Her mother followed Sue everywhere, because *The Mothers*, as she'd designated the two of them, had to stick together. Sue had grown increasingly harassed with each passing day, but Avery thought she was pleased with her mother's attention.

Avery took a final look in the mirror and smiled at her misty-eyed reflection. As heartbroken as she'd been to miss her wedding last week, this one was shaping up to be even better.

"I'm ready," she said as her friends lined up. She followed Riley out of the room.

Her father met her in the hallway. As the music swelled in the ballroom and they heard the hush of hundreds of guests holding their breath, her friends descended the stairs. There were soft murmurs as each one appeared through the hall into the big room beyond.

"You know, before this week, we never worried about your future, Avery," her father said as they walked down the stairs, "not only because we knew such a loving woman couldn't help but be surrounded by other loving people but also because we knew you had everything you needed inside yourself to make the life of your dreams no matter what happened. You are truly inspiring to me." He patted her hand as Avery swallowed hard in a throat that felt tight. Then she stepped through the doors into a room brimming with friends and neighbors, all looking at her with so much joy and hope and love in their faces, she couldn't hold back her tears anymore.

Someone let out a cheer. "Go Avery!" Someone else whooped, then the whole room filled with thunderous applause as she made her way down the aisle.

"You represent hope," her father whispered in her ear. "You represent all that's good and wonderful in this world, even when times are at their darkest."

Avery couldn't take it in. When she reached the altar, with Walker flanked by all the men she'd come to love and respect during her time at Base Camp, her knees felt weak.

"Take care of my girl," her father said to Walker,

placing her hand in his.

"Always," Walker said.

He met her gaze, and her breath nearly left her. He was going to be hers—forever. He lifted her hand to his mouth and kissed it solemnly before turning to face Reverend Halpern. Avery found it harder to shift her attention to the reverend. Her heart was beating hard. She felt light-headed. Walker's strong arm supported her.

"Dearly Beloved," the reverend began. "We are here to celebrate a wedding between two people we hold very dear, and we are also here to celebrate a small triumph of the light over the dark, hope over despair. When you think back on this day in the future, I hope you remember that most of the people in the world are good. Most of us want to heal rather than tear asunder. Most of us do love our fellow man. We have all been through hard times, but the men and women of Base Camp have been tested severely this past year. Today's wedding marks the triumph of their determination to meet all challenges head on—together."

When it came time to speak her vows, Avery made sure to say the words in a clear, strong voice she knew would carry to the back of the audience.

So did Walker.

He put the wedding band on her finger with infinite care, his fingertips brushing her palm before he pulled away. She knew that tonight, finally, they would have all the time they wanted to be together.

For now she was going to enjoy every moment of

making promises to him, every hug and kiss from her friends, every bit of the good food Maud and the other women had arranged and every dance on the ballroom's wonderful dance floor until she couldn't dance any more.

This was her life. This was her moment.

She was happy.

HE'D BEEN SHAKING all day, a fine tremor Walker knew no one else could detect but felt like a live current racing through his veins.

Avery was his. For now and for always.

They'd said their vows. They'd exchanged rings. They'd looked into each other's eyes and shared the love that had kindled a year ago when they'd met for the first time.

No one could take her away from him again. He'd never let them.

As the evening wound down and the band played a slow song, he cradled Avery in his arms and moved her slowly around the ballroom.

"Are you ready to go?"

She nodded. They'd spend their honeymoon in their tiny house. Good enough for him. He hoped Avery wasn't disappointed.

"It's perfect," she said as if reading his mind. "I don't want to have to wait a minute longer to be alone with you."

"It'll take more than a minute to get down there from here," he pointed out.

"Not if you run."

Walker pulled back. Checked to see if she was serious. Tossed her over his shoulder and dashed from the room. A cheer went up from the other men when they saw what was happening. Laughter and applause followed them down the hill, but Walker slowed as they passed the edge of the illumination of the manor's lights. He shifted Avery in his arms so he could see her face. She looped her arms around his neck and gazed at him happily as he carried her to their new home.

"It's all over," he said. "No more cameras or television crews."

"I'll believe that when I see it," she told him. "Anyway, I've gotten used to them."

"No more sabotage by Fulsom."

"I hope not."

"Just life."

"I know."

"I can't wait to get you alone," he growled into her neck. Avery laughed, a sound that brought joy to his heart. This was how he wanted to spend his days, making Avery smile.

She loved to smile, so it shouldn't be that hard.

"Watch your head," he told her as he opened the front door, turned sideways and carefully carried her over the threshold. Inside, he set her gently down. "What do you think?"

"I love it. All of it," Avery said. Of course she'd been in here many times before, but it was different this time. Now it was their home.

"I need to see the loft, though," she added. "I haven't gotten a real good look at that."

Walker chuckled and gladly led her to the ladder. He handed her up it, following slowly until she was over the top and perched on the bed. When he reached the top, he had to smile.

"That's exactly where I want you," he admitted.

"It's exactly where I want to be."

He joined her there, pulling her into a long, soft kiss that grew harder and hungrier over time. When they were both breathless with longing, he shrugged off the uniform jacket and began to undo his shirt. Avery kicked off her shoes, reached around and started to undo the fastenings of her gown before she gave a little groan of frustration. "I don't want to wait," she told him. "I want you right now."

She climbed into his lap, helped him off with his shirt and reached for the waistband of his pants. Their hands tangled together as they opened his fly, and Avery tugged up the skirts of her gown, guiding his hand to the discovery of what she wore underneath—

Nothing.

It was Walker's turn to groan. He grasped her hips, lifted her and hesitated wordlessly.

"Yes," Avery said. "Please, Walker."

As she sank down around him, they both gave a low sound of desire, but soon Walker was moving inside her, Avery holding on. There was no time for finesse, no long, slow lovemaking. This was just to take the edge off.

She felt amazing around him, hot and wet, her body designed to strip him of his defenses. He didn't fight the feelings that overtook him, surrendering to his desire for this woman, eager to show her all the love he had to give to her.

He kept his strokes strong and sure, pleased with the way she moaned in his arms. Avery never held back with him, and her obvious enjoyment stoked his desire even more.

He ran his hands over her, her gown pooled between them. Soon he'd strip it off her, but for now he was content to watch her face as her pleasure built.

She gave a cry, and Walker's pulse leaped. As Avery's fingernails dug into his shoulders, he held on, riding out her release, then let himself go in turn, crushing her against him, letting her know how badly he needed her.

When she slumped against his chest, he held her there, breathing hard, already wanting more.

Avery laughed. "Yes," she said again. "A thousand times yes."

He fell back on their bed, inched up it until they were lying on it properly, then turned Avery over. "I want to see you," he told her.

"Sounds perfect."

She lay still as he carefully undid the fastenings of her beautiful gown and peeled it up and over her head. As she shrugged out of her underthings, he took a good look at the woman he'd just married.

"Beautiful," he breathed.

Avery stretched luxuriantly, and he took the opportunity that afforded him to get better acquainted with her breasts. Every inch of her was marvelous. As he teased and tasted her, he knew he'd never tire of this. Avery was an unending mystery to explore, and he was determined to spend his days unraveling her.

"Happy?" she asked him, moaning with pleasure under his touch.

"Happy," he confirmed.

WALKER'S TOUCH WAS everything she'd hoped it would be. Avery knew when he pushed into her again, he'd please her every time they were together. He filled her like no other man had before, coaxing sensations from her that made it all too easy to lose control.

This time she wanted to savor their lovemaking and enjoyed his caresses, moving with him slowly, softly, until he rose above her, his strong arms framing her, his thighs flexing against hers.

Avery opened to him, content to let him take control. She closed her eyes and sent her awareness through her body as he entered her, becoming pure sensation until his every stroke had her tingling to her fingertips.

Walker was magnificent, and each sweep of her fingers down his muscular back increased the tension building inside her. Could she ever get enough of this?

She didn't think so.

As he increased the pace of his thrusts, her body hummed with pent-up wanting until Avery knew she was close to losing control.

"Avery," he murmured. She opened her eyes to meet his gaze, seeing so much love there, she thought she might get lost in it. With a final thrust he undid her, and she arched back, waves of release rippling through her over and over again until she didn't know if she could go on. Walker bucked against her, his muscles a thing of beauty as they tensed and released. She clung to him, riding the wave of his body, then cried out with a second release of her own.

When she finally came to herself again, Walker had spilled over to rest beside her, one leg still flung over hers. His arms held her against him, and he was pressing kisses to her neck and collarbone.

"How will we ever stop?" she asked him.

He gathered her closer. "I don't know." He was already coming back to life, already caressing her again.

"I love you," she told him. "Always will."

"Love you, too."

"It was all worth it, wasn't it?"

He turned over and pulled her on top of him again, pushing up to his elbow to take one of her nipples into his mouth. "I would do it all over again if it meant getting to be with you," he confirmed.

And then she was lost in him again.

EPILOGUE

One year later

I T'S GOING TO be a busy day," Riley said to Boone as they snuggled together in bed. He liked this time of day best of all, waking well before sunrise naturally from years of habit. Riley woke early, too. Usually their son, Jason Jericho Rudman, JJ for short, was the first one up, but today he was still sleeping. Boone couldn't believe that he was over eight months old already. JJ was alert, interested in everything—and fast. Boone was amazed at how much trouble a baby could get into if you turned your back on him.

He was happiest crawling around the floor of their tiny house and already attempting the ladder to the loft. Curtis had come up with an attachment designed to foil the baby from making it up the rungs. Just in time, too—Boone had caught Jason three feet off the ground the other day before they installed Curtis's safety device.

"I'm not sure if I'm ready for all the people coming today." It was still blissful to wake up most mornings and know the day was his own. No nosy cameramen looking over his shoulder while he planned improvements to the greenhouses or community. No one lurking around when he and Riley stole a moment alone.

"It's for only a few hours," Riley reminded him. "I wonder how many people will show up for the open house?"

"Renata thinks it will be a lot. That's why Fulsom is filming it." Boone had thought the man would disappear from their lives as soon as they'd played out their parts on his television show, but to his surprise he had more contact now with the billionaire than he did when they were being filmed for the weekly show.

"I needed to keep my distance to keep things fair," Fulsom had told him once when he'd spent a weekend at Base Camp after the show ended. "Now I can keep in touch more. Get to know you all better. Base Camp is like a living laboratory. You can tell me what's working and what isn't, and I can put my innovation divisions to work to find solutions and enhancements."

Fulsom was already working to design better mid-range wind turbines big enough to power small communities like theirs but not so big that they require more resources to maintain than a small community might have. Boone hoped he'd take on some other projects as well.

"I'd better look my best, then, especially since there will be cameras around. *Base Camp, One Year Later*," she intoned dramatically. "We wouldn't want to disappoint the viewing public." She edged out of his arms, ready to get up, but Boone pulled her back again.

"One more minute."

"You always say one more minute and then it's an hour."

He smiled, pressing a kiss to her neck. "I can't help that I'm irresistible."

"You really are," she agreed, melting in his arms, but when Jason let out a soft cry from his crib on the main floor, she sighed. They both knew there was no putting off their son. He might start slowly, but those cries would ramp up fast. "Be right back."

In a moment, Riley had slipped from their bed and stepped down the ladder, reappearing some minutes later with a freshly diapered baby in her arms. They'd installed a railing and baby gate across the edge of the loft so Jason could hang out with them up here safely while they got ready for the day. Handing him to Boone, she crawled back under the covers.

"Thought you were getting up." He smiled at her.

"One more minute," she said. "I want to spend some time with my two favorite men." When she was comfortable, she added, "I wonder how Byron will frame this show." It was to be a two-hour special. Film production capabilities had grown rapidly at Base Camp. Renata and Eve had taken the first few documentaries they'd worked on and run with it, and Byron kept working for Fulsom even after the show was over. As the community had expanded, Fulsom had hired him for other one-time shows featuring new members of the community and their experiences, and Boone knew Byron was developing a new television show in partnership with him.

"I suppose he'll compare how things were two years ago when we first arrived to how they are today."

"I can't believe we have sixty people living here now."

"I can't believe we survived the show."

"It's been a year!" Riley reminded him.

"Every day I wake up, look around and think, 'Fulsom can't take Base Camp away,' and I'm just as relieved as I was the day Fulsom gave you the deed."

"I guess I've settled in more than you," Riley said. "This is my home. It was always meant to be, and now here we are. This is the only possible ending I could stand." She bent down to drop a kiss on Jason's little forehead. He was struggling to pull himself up to a standing position, gripping fistfuls of his father's skin, pinching Boone.

Boone detached him and let his son hold on to his fingers instead. "Look at you. Soon enough you'll be riding a horse!"

"He is not riding Behemoth," Riley said automatically. It was a topic they'd covered many times before.

"Not to begin with," Boone agreed. "Maybe something smaller," he told Jason.

Riley leaned her head against his shoulder. "I'm happy," she told him. "I have everything I want."

"Then I'm happy, too."

IT REALLY WAS time to get up, but Riley still hesitated. She loved these quiet times with her husband and baby son. All too soon they'd join the others for chores and breakfast, and their busy day would start, but Boone's words had reminded her of all she had to be grateful for.

Just over two years ago, she'd received word that the adoption she'd counted on wouldn't go through. The grief she'd felt that day had faded, replaced by the wonder and joy of holding her son in her arms. She hadn't just wanted a baby back then; she'd wanted a partner to go through life with. A man to love, who would love her back. A family.

Now she had both.

She wasn't lonely anymore, the way she'd been in those days. All her best friends—old and new—lived with her, worked with her and celebrated their mutual accomplishments with her. Every day there was a new challenge to face together. She couldn't believe how different her life had become.

As she slipped out of bed to get dressed for the day, she wondered how many other people would choose to band together as she and her friends had. It was true Base Camp was growing, but one of the innovations they'd put into place was the concept of micro-communities, groups of ten to fifteen families that lived near each other, turned primarily to each other for mutual aid and voted for a representative among them to meet with other representatives to sort out larger issues that affected them all.

Base Camp could hold only so many people, but Boone was very involved with a group who were drafting resources for others who might want to form similar communities. Riley knew how important it was to him to pass on any help he could to those just starting out. Fulsom was making grants available to those needing to purchase land. She had no doubt in the next few years other groups would replicate what Base Camp had done.

She liked to focus on more local, intimate things. Boone shared the responsibility of watching Jason, of course, and there were always plenty of hands around to help out in a pinch. Everyone had drawn up a roster of child-care hours. With twenty-two of them, including Byron and Leslie, who weren't pregnant yet but were determined to do their share, it was easy to divvy up two-hour shifts. With two people watching the kids at any given time, that meant each of them pulled one shift about every other day, leaving them with plenty of time to get to their other chores.

"I'll be quick in the shower and get coffee on while you take your turn," she told Boone. Downstairs, she hesitated as she passed the large canvas on an easel in one corner of their living room area. Fitting in time to paint wasn't always easy, but she'd amassed enough work to secure her first public showing in town. Her audience would be local. While she was far from gaining fame from her paintings, she'd come a long way from the days when she didn't pick up a brush for months at a time.

She had more to inspire her these days, as well. As she worked in the greenhouses, or explored the ranch with Jason and Boone, ideas percolated in her mind. She found herself tuning her palette to the colors she saw outside, and the energy of the land and workers around her funneled through her onto the canvases she painted.

She checked to be sure she'd laid out the outfit she wanted to wear. These days, they saved their Regency gowns for Sunday dinners, special occasions and when they worked at the bed-and-breakfast. Sometimes she missed the crazy, early days of her time at Base Camp, but it was a relief not to have to do all the hard work in a fancy dress. It made the times they wore them more special. The best of both worlds.

She had everything she wanted, she thought as she stepped in the shower.

And every day brought some new experience to treasure.

"ONE YEAR DOWN, four to go," Dell said.

Clay grabbed a plate off the stack set on the table in the bunkhouse and advanced in line to get his breakfast. Ahead of him, Nora was chatting with Savannah about the day's plans. He switched his daughter to his left arm, hoping he could manage without spilling his food when the time came. Constance was just over thirteen months old now, a sweet brunette with a bow-shaped mouth and the determination to take on the whole world. For now, she was watching the gathered breakfast crowd.

Plotting her next attack.

"That's right." Sometimes Clay burned to be further along in his studies, but he was pleased he and his father had both made it through the first year of their architectural program. They were enrolled in a five-year professional course. He'd thought they might take much longer to accomplish their goals, only attending school part-time, but his family had gotten together and worked out how to make it possible for them to attend full-time.

Nora took his child-care shifts and still worked with the building crew, as did he and his father in their spare time, the two of them getting as much work done as Clay would have if he hadn't been attending school. His mother, Lizette, had taken on more shifts to cover expenses at home, and the rest of Clay's siblings were doing what they could to pitch in with maintenance, shopping and other chores at their parents' house to make things easier while Dell was in school.

Someday both of them would be licensed architects. Meanwhile, they planned to spend the summer working with Nora, Curtis and the rest of the building crew. They had three tiny house projects lined up off Base Camp, along with helping with all the new construction on the ranch itself and consulting with Montague on his latest development.

"Nice to have a day off," Dell said.

Lizette, who'd just joined them, laughed. "You hate days off."

"Not when they aim to be busier than a regular workday."

Clay knew what he meant. Today was Base Camp's first annual open house, during which the public could come and tour the ranch, see the original tiny houses, the gardens and the new groups of homes going up in several areas of the property. They could learn about renewable energy and the way Base Camp's inhabitants were getting things done. A cross between a party and a symposium, it was bound to be an all-hands-on-deck type of day.

In other words, right up Dell's alley, which was why he'd opted to arrive before breakfast.

"I'm sure you'll have fun." Lizette patted Dell's shoulder affectionately. "I've been drafted to lead tours of the manor. Let me take Constance," she added when the little girl began to wiggle. "I'll get my food when you two are settled in."

Clay handed her over gratefully. "Be good for Grandma," he told Constance.

"You're always good for Grandma, aren't you?" Lizette kissed Constance's nose and elicited a giggle.

"You've got a lot to be proud of here," Dell said.

Clay nodded. He was proud. Sometimes he thought back to his time in Yemen, Hendrik Fergusen on the other end of the satellite phone, talking about being content in the middle of a disaster. Like Hendrik, he felt fulfilled. He was doing work he loved, studying to be an architect. He had found mutual respect with his father and grown closer to his mother.

He spent his days with his friends, men and women he trusted to have his back.

And then there was Nora.

He still couldn't believe he'd won her hand in marriage, and he was happy to see that as time went on, the worried frown that had often creased her brow when he met her smoothed. Smiles lit up her face far more often these days, and love shone in her eyes—for Constance and for him.

She'd rallied over the last year, overcoming the trauma of her stalker's attack and healing her wounds, physical and mental. These days she jogged every morning, worked hard with the building crew and spent the remainder of her workday split between home and the Crow reservation, developing textbooks and curriculum with Sue. They'd launched their flagship textbook to quite a bit of praise and were working hard to expand the curriculum. Clay had no doubt someday the two of them would head an educational publishing empire.

"Clay? I said you have a lot to be proud of," his dad repeated.

"Thanks." He gripped Dell's shoulder for a minute, then released him. "So do you."

NORA CHECKED TO make sure Constance was secured in her backpack carrier as she waited with Clay, Dell and Curtis for the open house to begin and the public to arrive. She was one of several people tasked with walking people through a tiny house to give them a better perspective on living quarters at Base Camp and answer their questions. Clay and Dell were manning a booth with pamphlets and information about their construction business, while Curtis would be answering questions about his finish work. Daisy had found herself a patch of shade to rest in.

Nora looked forward to the day and was pleased to find almost no traces of the fear that had dogged her in her early time at Base Camp. As the months passed from Andrew Pennsley's death, she became more secure that her ordeal was truly over. She was safe here at Base Camp, surrounded by friends who loved her rather than teaching colleagues who bore a grudge.

Clay made her feel safe and loved every day. He made time every evening to sit with her under the stars, if the weather was good, or snuggle up on their couch inside if it wasn't, to talk through their days, patient with the petty worries and issues she was sure would bore a man.

In turn, she tried to be patient with his frustrations as he navigated school and work. Sometimes she knew it galled him he was getting to his education this late in the game, especially when his classmates acted their youthful age, but most of the time he was able to see the humor in it and was grateful he'd gotten the chance at all. "At least I'm not my dad's age," he often said.

"Here they come," Dell said.

"Ready?" Clay asked her.

"I'm ready." Nora's heart expanded when he reached over to kiss first her and then Constance, who was bouncing up and down in her backpack with excitement at the people streaming toward them. Constance loved everyone, and Nora had no doubt she'd make friends today. Lizette had promised to take her when she got tired of being carried around.

As the first people arrived at their station, couples young and old clustered around the booth to talk to the men about the construction process, while others came straight to where Nora and the other "tiny house tour guides" were waiting to show them the actual houses. Nora's first customers were three twentysomething women who oohed and aahed over every inch of her home.

"We're looking at a piece of land near Billings," one of them said. "We think we can afford it if we pool our money. Then we'll need to build something."

"We all just graduated," another said. "We don't want to pay rent; we want to try to own something."

"Are all three of you going to live in one tiny house?" Nora loved her friends, but she wasn't sure how that would have worked out.

"We thought we'd build one, move in together to save money, build the next one and so on. They're about the size of the dorm room we shared."

"You'd better check the building code," Nora warned them, and they were off on a conversation that kept going until she turned them over to the men outside. She saw them loading up on brochures and pigeonholing Dell soon after. If they approached the whole project with this kind of enthusiasm, she was sure they'd get it done.

"You're glowing," Lizette said when she stopped by several hours later during a break from working at the manor.

"I love any kind of teaching," Nora admitted. "Even

when it's as open-ended and unstructured as this. I'm an information junkie and love to share everything I learn."

"Clay said someday you'll reopen the one-room schoolhouse across Pittance Creek and teach the Base Camp kids there." Lizette's brows tugged together. "You won't be overwhelmed by bad memories if you do that?"

Nora shook her head. "Sue said she'll help me purge it of any bad energy left over from that day. I trust her to be able to do that. Besides, I think the process of cleaning it up, restoring it, giving it a new coat of paint—and knowing all the children I'll teach there— will erase anything that happened before."

She looked forward to those days, although she was content to enjoy her time with Constance and Sue now. When she began teaching Base Camp's children, she wouldn't have as much time to work on curriculum. She had decided not to worry about that yet. She would make the most of each stage as it happened. She and Clay were talking about trying for another child later this year, to keep their children close in age. They'd be consumed with diapers and strollers and backpack carriers for several years yet. Time enough for everything else later.

"I'm so happy you met Clay here and the two of you decided to stay. All those years he was away with the Navy, I wasn't sure if he'd ever come home." Lizette looked at her husband and son. "It means more to Dell than I can say that Clay is working and going to school with him. My husband is a changed man, content for the first time in his life."

"I'm glad we're here, too. I miss my mom." Nora swallowed hard, emotion overcoming her for a moment. She knew her mother would be proud of everything she'd done and would want her to be among people who loved her. "Having you and Dell here, your kids— and Sue, too—makes me feel like I have a real family again."

Lizette hugged her, wrapping her arms around Constance in her backpack carrier, too. "We love you like one of our own."

"I appreciate that." Nora hugged her back, something she was becoming far more comfortable doing. For years she'd been much too standoffish. It had been a way to keep people at bay who could hurt her by leaving, like her father had when she was young and her mother had when she lost her battle with cancer. Now she didn't have to hold back. The people here gave their love and approval freely, and that love filled her up enough to brave any small chance of rejection elsewhere.

"Here come some more people." Lizette let her go. "I'll take this batch. You take a break."

"My grandsons would like to see a tiny house," a white-haired woman accompanying two teenaged boys said.

"Right this way," Lizette said.

Nora watched them go, then turned to find Clay smiling at her as a cluster of people bent over the pamphlets and house plans spread on the counter of the booth.

"Love you," he mouthed at her.

"Love you, too."

"How is it going in the greenhouses?" Harris asked when Samantha stopped by with a sandwich to tide him through the lunch hour. No one was going to get a lunch break, given how many people were still flowing through Base Camp. Even now he had a ring of expectant onlookers waiting for him to start his demonstration again. As the only blacksmith, he didn't have anyone to fill in for him while he took a break, but Sam had announced to the crowd when she arrived that he was going to take five minutes to eat.

"Busy, busy, busy," she said, going up on tiptoe to brush a kiss across his cheek. "But with Boone and Leslie to help, I was able to get away for a minute."

Harris peeked into the fabric sling she wore. "Evan's asleep?"

"Yes, thank goodness. He was getting pretty fussy for a while, but he's out like a light now." She adjusted the sling. At eight months old, he was getting heavy for her to carry like this, but Harris couldn't take over while he was working the forge. He'd have to do double duty tomorrow to make up for it, he decided happily. He loved spending time with his son, and everyone at Base Camp had decided to take a rest day tomorrow.

"I've got to run. See you later." With another quick kiss, Samantha pushed her way through the throng that had gathered in the last few minutes and headed in the direction of their tiny house.

"Got your sandwich?" Alan Bennison asked, edging his way close in the crowd. He was one of the new inhabitants of Base Camp and had joined them three or so months ago. This wasn't the first time he'd sought out Harris.

Harris held up the remnants of it. "Yep." He finished it off in a couple of bites and moved to take up his tools again.

"Was wondering if I could take a shot at that sometime," Alan continued, gesturing to the forge. An earnest man from Georgia, he usually tended to hang back when there was a crowd.

Harris paused, ready to start the spiel he'd given about his craft a dozen times already. "Sure. Any time."

"I've always been interested in learning the farrier trade," Alan explained. "Just never had the opportunity."

Harris had wondered when the younger man would get up the courage to ask. His curiosity about the forge was unmistakeable. "I'm spending tomorrow with the family, but any other time," he told him. "Would be glad of the company."

"Great." Alan looked over his shoulder. "Better get back to it. I'm on cleanup duty."

"See you later." Harris watched him go. There had been a time in his life when friendships were difficult and he'd thought himself consigned to a solitary, watchful existence, forever on the outside looking in. That lonely feeling was long gone. He belonged here at

Base Camp in a way he'd never felt before. He had roots for the first time in his life. A home of his own, tiny as it was. A wife and child he adored.

No hurricane or anything else could wash that away.

He turned to the crowd. "How many of you have worked with metal before?"

SAMANTHA TOUCHED THE iron door-knocker Harris had made for their tiny house before turning the handle and opening the front door. It was time to put Evan down in his crib and give her back a rest. She had reluctantly kept her home off the tiny house tour, knowing she'd need a break at some point. It was too bad Harris's beautiful iron cabinet and drawer pulls—and the rest of the personal touches he'd added to their home—wouldn't be seen by the crowds thronging Base Camp, but the open house was meant to be a yearly affair, and Harris had a whole display of his work by his forge.

She was greeted at the door by the yip of their new puppy, Emma, a golden retriever Harris had surprised her with just a few weeks ago. "Hush, Emma!" she said. "Evan's sleeping!"

"Not fair that Curtis stole our dog" was all her husband had said as he placed the squirming ball of fluffy fur in her eagerly outstretched hands. He'd been smiling, though. Daisy remained faithful to Curtis but was content with head scratches and belly rubs from any of them.

Emma wagged her tail so hard Sam worried it would

fall off, but the puppy seemed to understand her words and didn't bark again.

After laying Evan in his crib, she picked up Emma, showering kisses on her furry head as she moved silently around her small home on stocking feet, touching the metal handles Harris had forged into flowers and herbs to honor her love of gardening. She loved that his work was so tactile; every time her fingers slipped across the metal she felt connected to her husband. He'd worked hard to tailor their home to suit her, and she'd found a contentment here she hadn't known in years.

She had to admit it was ironic to find herself living in a small space after escaping the Evermobile, the large van she'd driven for her parents' band for years, but she didn't mind. She was in and out of her friends' houses constantly, up at the manor to help with guests, in the bunkhouse for shared meals, meetings and get-togethers.

And besides, she spent most of her day in the extensive greenhouses. They had six of them now, and besides the crops and gardens they'd planted outside and the traditionally potted plants in several of the greenhouses, they'd now filled two with a hydroponic system she hoped would provide plenty of fresh vegetables through the winter. They'd even started a small orchard in the last greenhouse, hoping to extend their growing season and include fruit that usually required a more southern setting to produce.

After pouring herself a tall glass of water, Samantha sat down on the sofa with the puppy and put her feet up, content to rest while her baby did and glad that Byron had followed through with his promise to pop in earlier and give Emma a good long run around Base Camp to tire her out. The puppy flopped down beside her, heaving a happy sigh. Samantha knew just how she felt. There would be plenty to do later.

For now she'd rest and relax.

"CROQUET?" JERICHO COULDN'T hide his surprise, but his cousin, Donovan, just laughed at him.

"They'll have to think of something different for the winter, but for now it's croquet. You should see them going at it; you'd think the Stanley Cup was at stake."

Jericho wasn't sure he could picture his mom and dad playing croquet against Aunt Patty and Uncle Chris, but the important thing was that they were socializing at all. Chris and Patty had been through a stint in a treatment program and had been sober ever since.

"I'm glad they're doing so well," he told Donovan.

"I'm glad we're all happy these days. I hope Jacob and Wade are good friends."

"I'm sure they will be." Donovan, his wife and seventeen-month-old baby had already been to visit them several times, and he, Savannah and Jacob had returned the favor. The baby boys played together as much as any toddlers could be expected to. Jericho hadn't thought it possible he'd ever be part of such a happy family and was grateful to Donovan for how open he'd been about re-establishing ties between the branches of the Cooks.

"You've got more interested people coming," Donovan said, pointing to a knot of visitors making their way toward the wind turbines. "I'll let you go for now but look forward to seeing you tomorrow."

"Me, too."

"Say goodbye to Jacob and Jericho," Donovan told his son.

"Bye!" Wade crowed.

"Bye!" Jacob echoed.

Donovan headed to where his wife, Jackie, was talking to Savannah. He looked forward to the big family gathering his parents were hosting tomorrow. His sister, who'd also joined a twelve-step program, and her family would be there as well as Donovan, Jackie, Wade, Pam and Chris. It would be like old times—except much better. These days, food was the star of the show rather than alcohol, and no children were shunted to the side.

He was grateful for how Savannah had forgiven his parents and sister for their prior behavior and greeted them now without hesitation, embracing family life wholeheartedly. Her parents had softened, too—a bit. He wasn't sure they'd ever fully understand their daughter's choices, but they were doing their best.

Meanwhile, he had his business to focus on. Savannah's meeting with Simon Brashear at her audition in California had opened a world of possibilities for him. Sunset Group had hired him as a consultant in their quest to become carbon neutral, and as soon as Fulsom had gotten wind of it, he'd made his own offer of funding so Jericho could take the business large. Fulsom's money had allowed Jericho to bring a number of other energy consultants onboard, and business was booming. When Anders made the transition to running Hansen Energy next year, he knew his friend would make an offer to bring him on board. They were still discussing the best way to do this, but Jericho knew that with a client the size of Hansen Energy in his pocket, he could write his own ticket and expand in multiple ways.

One step at a time, though, he reminded himself. Today he would introduce a few dozen people to the basic concepts of green energy. Tomorrow he'd spend the day with his wife, baby and extended family. He had purpose and was loved.

What more could a man want?

"BYE," SAVANNAH SAID, helping Jacob wave to his cousin as Donovan and Jackie carried Wade away. With a sigh, she settled Jacob more firmly in her arms, his legs clinging to her waist as she began to walk to where Jericho was chatting with a group of interested people. "I'm taking a break," she said to him as she passed. "Be back in a half hour."

Jericho stopped what he was doing, as he always did, and came to kiss her and Jacob. "Nap time?"

"You got it." She kissed him back, breathing in the familiar scent of her husband. Jericho always laughed at her when she did that, but to her it was the scent of comfort, love and belonging, and she wouldn't give it up.

"See you at dinner."

"You bet." She kept going and ducked into her tiny house with a sigh of relief. As usual, Jacob had other ideas about nap time, especially because he could hear so many voices outside their home, but he fell asleep at last in his crib, and she climbed up to the loft and pulled her electronic keyboard onto her lap. With earbuds in, she could play without waking Jacob and work on the song she'd been writing these past few days. Once she'd rediscovered her love of singing last year, she'd begun to catch herself humming snatches of tunes and bits of melodies and had started to write them down. It had been some time before she reached the point where she was willing to share her efforts with anyone. When Samantha had offered to put her in touch with her parents, who were part of the famous cover band Deader Than Ever, she firmly said no, but one of the new Base Camp recruits, Martina Lovatt, turned out to be a backup singer for several garage bands and was familiar with the process of cutting a demo and even selling music directly online. She had helped Savannah secure studio time locally, and her folk-inspired children's album was making a tiny stream of income.

Savannah was so delighted anyone was listening to her at all, she pocketed her tiny paychecks with more glee than she could have imagined doing if she'd cut a classical piano album, although she wasn't ruling out anything at this point. When she had filled out her current melody and whisper-sung it into her phone to send to Martina to listen to, she lay back on the pillows and let herself daydream about the years to come.

Tomorrow, when they were surrounded by Jericho's family—hers now, too—she would break the news about her new pregnancy, knowing this time Jericho would be overjoyed. When they got home from the Cook family picnic, she'd announce her pregnancy to everyone at Base Camp and knew they'd be just as happy.

She'd never expected what would come about when she first arrived at Westfield two years ago, and she wouldn't change a thing—not even the sad parts, knowing how much she'd learned and grown along the way.

She'd been daring the night she seduced Jericho into making love to her in the Russells' fancy bathroom two years ago, and she meant to be daring for the rest of her life. Her days would be full of music and children. Her nights spent in her husband's arms.

Nothing could be better than that.

"THIS IS IT, folks, the test-kitchen and stage set for my *SEALs Making Meals* show." Kai ushered a group of people into the bunkhouse's new wing. It had been added on last fall to the original building to make cooking for a crowd easier as well as for filming his hit show. As Avery had once predicted, the minute he started airing episodes, streaming services fell all over themselves to option them, and now he could afford the production quality of a traditionally produced show like the one he'd walked away from during his first year here. Byron, who was working his way up in the business quickly, still helped out, taking a producer role as well as directing most of the episodes. Avery liked to be involved, too, as a recurring cohost who didn't know much about cooking but loved to learn. The episodes she appeared in were some of his most popular ones.

"How do you get your ideas for your recipes?" a young woman asked.

"I look at what's available in the garden or greenhouse or my cold storage and work from there. It's fun to take three or four ingredients, put them in a search engine online and see what recipes come up. Once I get some inspiration, I veer off on my own tangents, adding herbs and spices and seeing what I can come up with."

"Are you going to publish another cookbook?" an older man asked.

"Definitely. I'll keep putting them out until no one is interested anymore. My next one takes its inspiration from the kinds of dishes pioneers to Montana would have cooked. They knew a lot about getting by with whatever they had on hand. I've taken their classic recipes and updated them for our tastes and ingredients."

"Sounds great!"

"Are you going to do more episodes where you make your friends cook something for you?"

Kai laughed. Those episodes were popular, too. "You bet. I've got Boone on tap for an upcoming show. I'm going to make him cook a bison lasagna." In those shows, he handed his guest a recipe and gave a running commentary on their cooking skills as they attempted to follow it, allowing guests to call in and give advice, too. Those episodes were messy but a lot of fun.

"Where's your daughter?"

"She should be here any minute. Wait—there she is!"

Addison appeared with a yawning baby girl in her hands. "Can you take Felicity? I'm due at the manor. Some of the other women have been covering for me."

"Absolutely." Kai took the baby to a chorus of "oohs" from his audience and gave Addison a quick kiss. "Knock them dead up there."

"I hope I can secure bookings for all of next year in one fell swoop," she said, nuzzling Felicity one last time before she hurried away again.

Named for Addison's sister, Felicity was a precious little girl with red-gold hair and big eyes. At eight months old, she was one of the Contingent, as they'd named the group of babies that had come one after another last October. She was just beginning to pull herself upright and wobble on her feet before plunking down again and reverting to crawling everywhere. She was small but swift, as Addison always said, and her trilling little laugh elicited a surge of love in him every time he heard it.

She surveyed the gathered group placidly and yawned again.

"Are you having any more kids?" someone asked.

"We're not sure yet. With my show and Addison running the bed-and-breakfast, we're pretty busy."

"Do you still cook for everyone?"

"I'm the designated neighborhood cook, with everyone else taking turns as prep cook, but these days people do their own breakfasts except for Sunday. I do lunch and dinner on weekdays. Aside from Sunday brunch, people are on their own on weekends. We like the variety. I'm also involved with the local food bank program, making sure everyone in Chance Creek has the food they need."

"And you do the weddings."

"I help with weddings, although we also offer packages with a catering company in town," Kai corrected. "So I've got a lot of irons in the fire, so to speak. Now who's ready to try some bison sausage?"

As his audience gathered around, pride filled Kai at how far he'd come. There were so many possibilities for what he could do next, he knew he'd never be bored, and someday Felicity would be old enough to stand at this counter and learn the basics of cooking beside him. Would she join him someday, or would she fall in love with the bed-and-breakfast? Or would she go in some other direction he couldn't even guess at right now?

It wouldn't matter. She could choose anything, and he'd encourage her. Fatherhood had swept away all his fears about not being enough as a parent; his instincts had been right on the mark so far.

He remembered a conversation he'd had with his sister the other day.

"Now that I have my own kids," she'd said, "I can't fathom what Mom was thinking when she abandoned us. She must have been so far gone in her addictions.

These days I'm sadder for her than for us."

"I know what you mean." He'd been holding Felicity and had settled her carefully in his arms. Nothing could persuade him to take a chance on her health and safety, but he knew enough of the world these days not to get too bogged down in judgments. "I wish it could have been different."

"Me, too, but I'm glad about where we ended up."

Kai had agreed with her. "You're happy?" he'd checked just to be sure.

"Very. You?"

"Over the moon."

Kai focused on the chatter of his visitors and noticed Felicity was fully awake now, reaching out to touch the hair of a woman who was bending over to select another tidbit of sausage.

He redirected the baby's hand. "Want to try?" He pulled off a tiny chunk of sausage and put it carefully in her grip. She transferred it to her mouth, chewed with her few teeth and swallowed.

"Yummy?" he prompted.

"Mmm!" she replied heartily and reached for more.

"She's going to fit right in here, isn't she?" a man said.

"That she is."

ADDISON HURRIED UP the hillside, the skirts of her Regency gown swishing around her ankles, and entered the manor through the back door that led to the kitchen. All the women were dressed up today.

"I'm back," she told Avery, who was replenishing drinks and snacks on a tray.

"I'll just put this in the ballroom," Avery told her. "Don't worry, there have been plenty of us to head up the tours while you were gone. All the newcomers love the chance to show people around."

Avery was right; there were always women from the newer Base Camp settlements angling to get a turn at working in the manor. They were running Alice Reed ragged keeping up with requests for Regency attire, too. Addison knew Alice had begun to outsource much of the work to Caitlyn Warren at the bridal shop, who appreciated the extra income.

Today they were taking shifts, three or four at a time, to walk visitors through the manor and answer questions about vacation packages and other events held here.

"We've given out so many brochures," Avery said when she came back with another empty tray, "and so many snacks," she added with a laugh. "The hardest part is keeping people moving. By the time they make it up here they've seen the rest of Base Camp and they're tired out. They keep sitting on the furniture and lagging behind."

Addison chuckled.

"Heard from Felicity senior recently?" Avery smiled impishly at the nickname she'd given Addison's sister once baby Felicity made her way into the world.

"She's coming here for Christmas. I can't wait to see her. She and Evan are so happy in Rome."

"She's still modeling?"

"A little, but she's started her own modeling company on the side, and I think she's getting ready to transition to being behind the scenes."

"Smart. What about your mom? How is she handling Felicity staying away for so long?"

"Better than I thought." Addison worked to fill the tray Avery had brought back with her. "She's been volunteering with a group that helps low-income women with finding jobs. She works with them on their interview skills. She's a natural."

Avery laughed. "From everything you've told me, I can imagine."

"I can imagine, too." Addison copied her mother's tone. "Stand up straight. Shoulders back. Chin up! You are proud. You are strong. You are going to win!"

"I wonder if it works?"

"Mom claims it does. She's very proud of 'her new hires,' as she calls them."

"Good for her for finding an outlet for her energy. Speaking of which, I'd better get to the studio."

"Go ahead, I'll hold down the fort here."

When Avery was gone, Addison carried the tray to the ballroom but nearly dropped it when she saw how many people were clustered around the food. No wonder they kept having to restock so often. With all the offerings down in the main cluster of buildings at Base Camp, she'd wondered if serving snacks here was even necessary, but she'd long since learned to always over-deliver. Today that was paying off.

"Are you the one to speak to about booking a wedding? It looks like my daughter is going to get engaged soon, and I know she'd love to hold her reception here," a woman said.

Addison handed her a brochure and went over the various packages they offered.

"I was hoping to do a sisters' reunion here sometime this winter," an older woman said. "But I'm afraid nothing will be in our price range."

"We have options for every budget," Addison said smoothly. They'd worked hard to make sure they kept things affordable when the show made their bed-and-breakfast a hit last year. They wanted locals to feel they had access to Base Camp.

She continued answering questions and handing out brochures and cards.

"You're a natural at this," one of the newer members of Base Camp said, bringing a tour to the ballroom, where they fell on the refreshments with vigor.

"Thanks." Addison always felt she'd finally found the place where she belonged. Thank goodness for her sister and her crazy ideas.

She didn't miss New York City at all. Couldn't care less about living in a penthouse.

Wanted nothing more than to stay right here with the people she loved.

"ARE YOU SURE I couldn't persuade you to come to Houston for six months?" a tall man in a cowboy hat said. "You're just the man to give my house all the finishing touches it needs."

"Sorry," Curtis told him. "There's too much for me to do right here."

"I'd pay you plenty for your time."

"No can do," Curtis told him. "I'm sure there's someone in your neck of the woods who'd be happy for the work, though."

"I hope so," the man said disgruntledly.

As he wandered off, Curtis stepped away from the booth he'd been manning and took a long swig of water. It was hot, and the open house had been going on for hours. He was ready for a break.

"Can you handle things for a minute?" he asked Clay.

Clay waved him off. "I'm fine."

Curtis whistled for Daisy and made his way past the bunkhouse toward the pastures where he knew he'd find Hope. The man in the cowboy hat wasn't the only one who'd tried to hire him, but the truth was he had projects booked for months, on and off the ranch. Although he'd added special finishing touches to all the tiny houses he'd built for the original members of Base Camp, there were far too many being built for him to do so for all of them. Their team had expanded, and while every tiny house was finished well, if someone wanted his personal work, they had to hire him like anyone else.

He'd also taken on several commissions in town and on the surrounding ranches. He didn't want to book anything more until he'd made a dent in his current commitments.

He was proud of everything he was doing and for his skills to be so recognized. He got inquiries from all around the world now that people had seen examples of his work on the show. A gallery had gotten in touch recently, wanting to add some of his carved wooden pieces to a collection they were going to show next year. He'd never expected that, but their theme was the crossroads of art and architecture, which was definitely his niche.

As he approached the closest pasture, he caught sight of Hope standing a little to one side while Walker talked about bison herd management and the grazing patterns they were using to a group that had gathered to listen. Everyone was focused on the tall Native American man, which was unfortunate, because they were missing what Hope was surreptitiously doing: waiting until one of the bison ambled closer and closer, grazing contentedly, until it lifted its face to gaze at the crowd and Hope reached out and stroked its nose.

The bison blew out a huff of breath and ambled off again. Curtis walked up to her, shaking his head.

"You'll be sorry the day one of them bites off your hand."

"It's only Charlie I do that to. It's a game we play." She bent down and patted Daisy's head.

"Weren't you going to be a park ranger at Yellowstone? Park rangers know better than to pet bison. Besides, how do you know which one is Charlie?"

"I would have made a lousy park ranger," she admitted, straightening again. Daisy flopped down at their feet. "But I love studying bison, and for your information, every one of them looks different. Just ask Avery. Do you think I could prove they have a sense of humor?"

"Nope."

She laughed. "You're probably right, but I swear that one does."

"I thought you were studying the effects of cropping patterns on the health of the pasture."

"I am. I'm getting together with Evan Mortimer and Jake Matheson to compare notes next week and see where we are in the study. If our suppositions match the data at all."

"I'm glad you found some partners to work with." Curtis tucked a strand of her hair behind her ears. He still had to take a breath and let his jealousy settle when Hope talked about other men. He realized that some part of him might never truly get over being left at the altar, but he trusted Hope, and the jealousy passed in moments. They saw each other throughout the day, stole moments alone between their working hours, and every night with her was heaven—

Even those early days when their son was first born. Zeke Matthew Lloyd had taken several months to figure out the difference between daytime and nighttime, but Curtis treasured every moment with him. He was a serious baby, who watched everything around him with a slightly offended tilt to his eyebrows. Hope told him he'd grow out of it, but Curtis thought he understood.

"The world is a weird place," he told his baby when Hope wasn't around, "but it's not so bad. You'll see."

As one of the Contingent, Zeke was just over eight months old, pulling himself up to standing and thinking about taking his first steps…. but not taking them yet.

Hope was already talking about wanting a girl, but Curtis wasn't sure if he was ready to think about that. They had their hands full already.

"The second baby is three times as hard as the first," his mother had told him last week. "Oddly, the third one is no trouble at all."

Curtis wasn't sure what to make of that.

"Where's Zeke?"

"At Savannah's. She's watching a few of the kids for the last couple of hours so everyone can help with our visitors.

"Catch up with you at dinner?" She reached up for a kiss, and he met her halfway.

"Can't wait."

"WHAT TIME IS the first seating at the manor again?" Hope asked Riley as she approached the bunkhouse. "I want to stop and check on Zeke before I head up there." They were offering people two different types of dining experiences: a rustic picnic near the bunkhouse and a formal sit-down dinner at the manor house. She and many of the other women, dressed in their Regency gowns, would help at the manor.

"Where's your planner?" Riley joked. "Just kidding. It's in forty-five minutes, so join us as fast as you can.

I'm headed there now."

"Be there in a minute." Hope hurried to Savannah's tiny house, but Raina, her best friend and the reason she was here at Base Camp to begin with, found her first.

"There you are! I held off bothering you while you were demonstrating the bison, but I couldn't keep away any longer. I'm so excited I get to wear a gown and help tonight."

Raina was almost an honorary member of Base Camp, she and her husband, Ben, came over so often from Bozeman to visit.

"I need to see if Zeke is okay."

Raina followed her happily and made sure to get her share of cuddles from Zeke before they left for the manor.

"Curtis should be here soon to pick up Zeke," Hope told Savannah.

"As soon as he does, I'll join you all," Savannah assured them.

They met with several other female residents of Base Camp as they walked to the manor, their gowns a bouquet of colors as they clustered together to get through the back door into the kitchen.

"All right, everyone," Addison said. "We're not taking orders, just bringing dishes to the tables for people to share around, as if they were with their families. Your job is to keep those dishes replenished, refill drinks and keep everyone happy. Got it? There'll be a demonstration dance at eight."

That was to cap off the evening. Then everyone

would go home. Hope knew that dance would result in a flurry of calls tomorrow for people wanting to learn Regency dancing and spend a weekend at the bed-and-breakfast. The beauty of the Regency dances hooked everyone.

The next two hours were so busy she barely got a chance to breathe. She and the other women took turns eating a bite in the kitchen when they could, so no one fainted with hunger, then kept going. At the end of the meal, they cleared the tables.

A space was left at the center of the large room. When the men of Base Camp filed in, so did a quartet of classical musicians, who began to tune their instruments. Curtis found her.

"Where's Zeke?" she asked.

"With Leslie and Byron in the front room. Don't worry; all the children are being well cared for. Daisy's there, too."

"Good." Byron and Leslie had become fixtures in their community. Byron worked on a variety of projects, and Hope had no doubt he'd go far in the film industry. Leslie might talk a lot, but she was an organizational wizard and was helping to take their food production to great heights.

"I remember the first time we did this," he said as he led her to their positions for the first dance.

"It's romantic every time. I never dreamed I'd find a man who'd actually dance with me."

"I never dreamed I'd find a woman who'd want to keep dancing with me."

"Well, I do. And that's not going to stop."

The music started, and they executed the first few steps of the complicated dance. Hope's heart swelled as Curtis's gaze lingered on hers, and she knew he was thinking about what they'd get up to later tonight, when everyone had gone home and Zeke was asleep.

She thought about it, too, letting her desire show in her eyes.

"We could duck out right now," he said.

"No, we couldn't. Be patient." But she had to smile.

"I'll do my best."

"DON'T LOOK NOW, but I think your father is flirting with Bev Regis," Eve said to Anders as he led her through the steps of the dance.

Anders scanned the crowd as he continued in a circle. He'd done these Regency dances so many times now he could execute the steps in his sleep. There was his father near the door talking to a woman who'd joined the community just a few months ago. Bev was in her late forties, a striking woman with a sweep of dark hair, and his father... his father was actually smiling while they chatted.

Johannes looked ten years younger than he had two years ago when he'd been hassling Anders to come home and take over the family oil business. The last two years had changed a lot of things for them. It wasn't the work of a day to transition Hansen Oil to Hansen Energy. In truth, the final transition plan would take nearly a decade to fully enact. Still, Anders was optimistic that they had arranged things in a way to make that transition smooth, without letting down their employees or shareholders, and that was replicable for other companies.

He had fielded some uncomfortable questions today from people on both sides of the energy spectrum. One man who worked the oil fields in northeast Montana was downright rude, but on the whole, people seemed interested, and a number of them had asked for more information on ways to make the transition to renewables.

He and his father had found a new CEO for Hansen Energy who shared their vision, which made it possible for Johannes to step back and for Anders to work more as a consultant than full-time on-site, which he appreciated, because he loved it here and didn't want to leave his wife or daughter. Isabel Claire Hansen was the apple of his eye. The youngest of the Contingent at just seven and a half months, she seemed determined not to be left behind by the other babies. She was already standing steadier than some of the older ones, and she'd taken her first step yesterday.

"Soon she'll be running rings around us," Eve had said with a happy sigh.

He didn't want to miss a single milestone of his daughter's journey to independence, and Johannes seemed to enjoy it at Base Camp, too. Anders never thought his father would be comfortable with letting someone else oversee the day-to-day business of Hansen Energy, but Bill, the CEO, wasn't fazed by technology and video chatted, texted and called so often, Johannes might as well have been in Texas.

Only last week he and his father had gone for a ride to Chance Creek with their fishing gear and spent a couple of hours at it. The fishing was better up north, but Anders had still enjoyed his afternoon—and the new connection he was forging with Johannes.

As the dance went on, it was his wife who consumed his attention, not his father. Let Johannes flirt. He had the woman he wanted, and that made him feel everyone should have their share of love.

Eve smiled at him. "What are you thinking?"

"You know what I'm thinking." If this were a waltz, he'd pull her in tighter. He'd come to think that Regency dances were a very effective form of flirting. You came together and moved apart, never keeping your partner as close as you wanted her.

But tonight, once Isabel was asleep, he'd get to be as close to Eve as he could wish. He saw the answering interest in her eye and knew they'd have a lot of fun.

"How much longer does this shindig go on?"

"Not much longer," she promised him.

"Good."

ANDERS STILL GOT her motor racing, Eve thought happily as they completed the dance and moved smoothly into the next one. Over the last year and a half, they'd polished up a half-dozen dances they could all do at the drop of a hat. It always impressed visitors to Base Camp. Plus, she loved them.

"You never finished telling me about the movie," Anders said when a minute or two had gone by. "We got interrupted yesterday when Isabel bumped her head."

Their daughter was sporting a small bruise on her forehead, the first of many, Eve predicted. She was a tiny thing but determined and fearless, and that step she'd taken yesterday had been followed by some fast crawling after a ball Anders was rolling around on the floor. She'd gotten so excited to catch it she stopped looking where she was going.

"Your CEO is thinking up movie ideas faster than I can make them," Eve told him. "Now he wants one about the restoration of oil fields. It's going to take a lot of research."

"Which is going to make you one happy documentarian," Anders said.

"You got it." Eve didn't think she'd ever get tired of making movies. As soon as Hansen Oil had started to transition to Hansen Energy, Johannes and his new CEO began to commission movies to explain their activities. She had found a crew that did great work but had previously struggled to find funding. With Hansen Energy's deep pockets, she could let them run wild, traveling to immerse themselves in localities and collect footage that was astounding not only in its beauty or interest but also in the information it conveyed. She'd begun to get into some of the voice-over work herself, finding she had a talent for it, but it was editing footage that she loved best.

The next time the dance brought them close, Anders stole a kiss, holding her in place a moment too long, which made her stumble and nearly upset all the dancers around them. There was some laughter in the ranks, and the audience craned their necks to see what was happening.

"Behave," she told him, spotting her best friend, Melissa, on the sidelines watching the dance. She was grinning—she'd definitely seen Anders's illicit kiss.

"I will. For now. I'm not making any promises about later."

"I wouldn't have it any other way."

She waved quickly at Melissa, who turned to show her how huge her belly had gotten. Melissa was expecting her first "little cowboy," as she kept calling the baby, in a couple of months and was over the moon—as was her husband. Eve was so glad her good friend had settled close by. She'd made so many wonderful new friends since being here, but Melissa was still the tether for her kite, although Anders and Isabel were certainly doing their part these days.

A husband, a baby, a number of good friends. The job of her dreams.

She had it all.

SOMETIMES LIFE CAME full circle, Greg thought, switching his baby from one arm to the other. Ten years ago he'd stood next to Renata in Peru as she'd faced a busload of schoolgirls who didn't know they'd just lost everything. Now the two of them were waving to a busload of visitors riding back to town after the open house.

Funny how he'd known the minute he saw Renata that she was the woman he wanted to build his world around. Amazing that all these years later, his dream had come true. What if he hadn't taken the chance and come to Base Camp?

Where would he be now?

He doubted he'd be married; no one suited him like Renata did. She woke up each morning ready to get to work documenting all the troubles of the world—and all the solutions, too. She was as committed to Base Camp's purpose as he was. She valued family and community, the things most important to him.

He doubted he'd have found his place in the world, either. If he hadn't seen that Renata was going to direct the television show documenting its progress, he never would have signed up for Base Camp. After his years growing up at Greenleaf, he'd thought he wanted something different.

He'd been wrong.

He was finding that his years at the Oregon commune had given him knowledge and skills that were coming in handy now that Base Camp was expanding and transitioning from a top-down military-style establishment to a democratically run community. He'd grown up learning consensus-building techniques, knew how to listen and give feedback and knew, too, when people needed a break and a chance to think things over before coming back together to solve a problem.

He'd been elected to serve on the advisory council for Base Camp, along with a mixture of old and new members, and together they were building off Boone's initial governing document, holding meetings, making plans—and deciding how big was too big for Base Camp to grow.

Now that there were plenty of volunteers to fill out the green energy crew, he'd shifted to leadership full-time, which suited him better, he had to admit. As much as he was interested in making their carbon footprint smaller, there were other men and women here whose skills far surpassed his, and he'd taken to working part-time in the garden to keep from being fully sedentary but spent the bulk of his time keeping Base Camp running.

He liked how it meant he got to work with everyone in one capacity or another. He'd been part of the team creating orientation materials for new arrivals and ended up developing an entire weeklong program that every new Base Camp community member went through when they moved in. It got everyone on the same page, made it easy to find out where they'd best fit in the picture and sparked friendships between old and new members alike.

When Renata bent to look at Adalynne, he whispered, "She's sound asleep."

"Better get her home."

"You sure? I heard something about late-night snacks at the bunkhouse after everyone's gone."

"Let's get some and take them with us."

Greg followed her happily. Renata was a people-person in her own way, but at the end of the day she needed hours to recharge alone before she was ready for another day. He would happily curl up with her on the couch, knowing tomorrow he'd get to spend time with a dozen or more different people.

They ducked into the bunkhouse, where Kai and Addison were just putting out platters of finger foods. Jess was helping. After her fling with Brody had fizzled, she'd asked to stay on at Base Camp after the show ended. She'd soon met a man in town who shared her interest in sustainability and gotten engaged recently. They lived in one of the new tiny houses. She'd been pitching in on the documentary projects, but she seemed to have boundless energy for everything going on in the community.

After they filled their plates, they headed to their own tiny house.

When he and Renata moved in together, they'd found they had similar collections of artifacts from their separate journeys around the world, and now their home reflected that. "It's like a teeny, tiny museum," Avery had once told him, and he agreed; their collection was small but interesting.

They worked quietly together to get Adalynne settled, her button nose, rosebud mouth and tiny hands too cute for words to Greg's way of thinking. He'd secretly hoped for a son, thinking he'd know how to bond with a boy better than a girl, but as soon as she was born, she'd wrapped him around her finger. He was probably going to spoil Adalynne rotten. Good thing she had a sensible mother, who would set them both straight if need be.

Greg pulled Renata down beside him on the small but comfortable couch in the living room, and they watched the others trail up to the manor or to the bunkhouse or to any number of places depending on where they lived and what chores they needed to finish before settling down for the night. Greg loved his home's huge windows and the way they brought the outside into their little space.

They sat at opposite ends of the couch. He absently rubbed her feet with one hand, feeding himself tidbits with the other, washing it all down with a beer.

"I think I talked more today than I usually do in a month, and that's saying something." He'd been tasked with ushering folks from place to place, suggesting what parts of Base Camp they might find interesting and trying to keep it so no one place got swamped.

"You should be exhausted, but you're not."

"I'm energized," he admitted. That's how he felt all the time now because he'd found the perfect occupation in the perfect place. "What about you? How'd your day go?"

"It went well." She sighed and leaned back, offering him her other foot. "People are excited to find out I'm going to direct a feature-length movie that isn't a documentary. I wouldn't have thought anyone remembered I wanted to, seeing as I took so much time off."

"A year is hardly that much time."

"Not many people have the luxury to do that," she pointed out. "I think a lot of them wondered if I'd let my career go once Adalynne was born."

Greg shook his head. "I doubt that. You're too driven."

"I was afraid some of them would think I should just stay home."

He shook his head again. "Your love for your work is too obvious. You can't be contained for long. Even if you devoted yourself to Adalynne until she grew up, you'd go back to film then. You can't help yourself."

"I guess not."

RENATA SNUGGLED INTO the puffy cushions of the couch, closing her eyes and letting Greg's fingers work their magic. He might be energized, but she was exhausted. Adalynne still woke up to nurse most nights, and Renata had been scrambling for months to put together her feature film project. It documented the journey of a young Peruvian girl from her traditional upbringing in her mountain-top village to her rise through environmental activism to politics. Based on the life of one of the girls she helped support after the mudslides wiped out Mayahuay so many years ago, she'd built on the bare bones of the story with Philomena's permission and helped to create a movie that would grab a wide audience. Philomena had come to Base Camp two months ago to work a paid internship with her, with the hopes of transferring the skills she learned to Peru to start making films of her own. As they worked together, they hoped to create a program Renata could use to teach skills to other young women like Philomena and satisfy that part of her dream.

Tonight she just wanted to hang out with her husband and child, however. She was more relieved than she could say about the way the day had gone. What she hadn't told Greg was how worried she'd been that their visitors would blame her for her part in making it hard for the others to win Base Camp, or that they'd think she was lazy taking time off, or was a bad mother for going back to work as soon as she had, even if she was working right here, which meant she got to see Adalynne all the time.

That was succumbing to old fears. In the first months after marrying Greg, she'd struggled to really feel a part of Base Camp after so many months of hovering around the outskirts filming their activities. She'd assimilated over time, however, so it was interesting the way those old worries cropped up today. Doubtless the visitors reminded her of *Base Camp*'s audience, especially since Byron had been documenting the day for a special follow-up show Fulsom wanted to run.

Those times of being on the outskirts were long gone, though. She was as much a part of the community as anyone else, and to her surprise she was loving it. She appreciated how the other women made such an effort to include her in their get-togethers, especially. She hadn't learned to cultivate female friendships in her childhood as she moved from foster home to foster home. Sometimes she felt she was getting a second chance at being a teenager, especially when someone suggested a women's-only movie night at the manor when it wasn't booked, and they all piled together to watch something sweet and sappy, eat popcorn and stay up way too late.

She'd grown to be grateful for all the men at Base Camp, too. It wasn't just women she'd avoided when she was younger. Now she was learning that for all their rough-and-tumble ways, she could appreciate their humor, energy and dedication to getting things done—and the way the men here always stepped up to protect their homes and families.

People were… okay, she decided. She didn't need to keep them at arm's length, boss them around or always be in absolute control of the situation. She could be one of the group and let things happen the way they happened.

It was a new way to be in the world.

Adalynne uttered a little sound from her crib, and they both stilled, listened and waited until it was clear she wouldn't wake up.

Motherhood had softened her in some ways, Renata mused as Greg worked away on her tired feet, and it had made her fiercer in others. No one was going to hurt her daughter. Nothing could ever persuade her to leave Adalynne behind.

She was determined to be here to usher Adalynne through every step toward adulthood. And if something did ever happen to her and Greg, there would be a dozen people ready to care for and love their daughter for as long as she needed them.

That's what security was. Not money. Not possessions, or accolades, or career triumphs.

It was knowing there was a community of like-minded individuals ready to step in and raise your child should you ever need them.

"Ready for bed?" Greg asked softly.

"More than ready."

"MOMMY!" IRIS CRIED, toddling toward Win, a grin splitting her little face. Her red-blond hair glinted in the last rays of the setting sun. Angus's heart squeezed to see his wife bend down and scoop up their daughter, twirling her around until Win's skirts swirled, too.

At just over a year old, Iris Eliza McBride was one of the happiest creatures Angus had ever met. Her unending wonder and joy at every new sight that met her eyes kept him looking sharp for new things to show her, just to get to experience it with her.

She was a handful in the greenhouses these days, wanting to touch, tug, examine and squeeze the life out of everything she could reach, which made her dangerous around the hydroponics setup. He tended to take her to the outside gardens when he was caring for her so she could dig to her heart's content in the dirt, "plant" sticks and rocks and dig them up all over again. She was a bundle of energy until she conked out. Then she loved for them to read her stories, especially when he put his accent on thick and acted out all the characters' voices.

Iris attended Base Camp's child-care group every weekday morning, during which time he and Win scrambled to get their work done. They ate lunch together, put Iris down for her afternoon nap and got some more things done—or spent some time together, then took turns with Iris through the rest of the day. With Kai cooking most of their lunches and dinners and all the extra hands around, everything seemed to get done sooner or later.

Angus was working hard to figure out how they could grow more vegetables through the winter, which meant he was learning a lot more about hydroponics, greenhouse growing and the green energy systems in use at Base Camp than he'd previously known. He'd gotten to know many experts in the field online and video chatted with them often, reporting on his progress and brainstorming new systems to try.

His cousin, Douglas, who'd created so much havoc when he first arrived at Base Camp, had moved to California to work with Fulsom and now traveled with Fulsom the way Renata once had. It was his job to arrange the billionaire's meetings and appearances, troubleshoot problems and smooth the way so that Fulsom could simply show up and do his thing. Douglas was making contacts in every industry and level of politics and couldn't be happier. The rest of their family was happy, too. Angus had realized how much the part of his family left behind in Scotland had resented the opportunities won by those who'd made it here. Now

Douglas was flourishing, and communications among them all had ramped up.

He thought almost every living member of his extended family had visited Base Camp in the last year. His mother and stepfather, John, came to see him every few months. At first he'd been suspicious of her attempts to reconnect, but now he welcomed them. Everyone made mistakes, he realized. Everyone wanted to be loved. Being able to depend on his mother—finally—had healed something he hadn't even known was broken in him.

As for Win, she was thriving, too.

Angus reached down to kiss her when she approached, Iris laughing in her arms.

As "his girls" leaned against him, delighted in the bear hug he gave them, warmth filled his chest. At one time he'd thought he'd lost Win forever, and it had been too reminiscent of the way he'd lost his mother for comfort. Now she was here with him for good, his ring on her finger, her presence in his house a reminder every single day that she'd pledged her life to his and loved him the way he loved her.

These days he knew a peace that had always evaded him previously. He had someone he could depend on and knew that she depended on him, too. When he woke up in the morning and saw Win's sweet face beside him, he fell in love with her all over again.

As part of a large community, they'd taken care to develop their own habits and rituals. They ate breakfast together every morning at home. Every other Saturday night was date night, made possible by swapping overnight child care with Savannah and Jericho. Once a month they drove into town to spend a few hours away from Base Camp altogether. It made coming back home to all their friends that much more special.

"Little girls should be in bed," Win murmured against his cheek as he held her.

"Just a few minutes longer. Let's watch the sun go down."

"Sounds good to me." She didn't pull away, and he didn't let go. This was what he loved best about his life now. Win in his arms, his little girl in hers. A circle of family that was all his.

As THE SUN went down, Win wondered how she could ever have considered returning home to California for good. Base Camp was her true home in every sense of the word now. She didn't hear from her parents often, but she was okay with that. They were struggling to clear their names of wrongdoing. Sleeping in the bed they'd made for themselves. She didn't worry that they wouldn't be okay. They still had a fortune, after all, and could remake themselves a hundred times over until they found a new way to be happy.

She kept closer touch with Rosa and Maria and their daughters, the beginning of a new family of her heart, as she put it when she thought about it.

That family encompassed all her friends here at Base Camp, both old and new, a circle that kept growing bigger as Base Camp expanded.

In the past year, she had learned that her early interest in design wasn't a passing thing, and it surprised her how long it had taken her to realize that's where her talents lay. She had fooled around with the hand loom she bought in town until its limitations began to pinch and Curtis made her an even bigger one. It was fun to weave textiles. She classed that as a hobby, creating wall hangings and bedding for the home she'd made with Angus, but it was designing patterns that could be reproduced en masse that really brought her to life.

She was currently in negotiations with her parents to take over Manners Textiles, the original company her grandfather had founded, which had expanded wildly over the years. Her parents were more amenable than she'd expected to letting the division go, but they communicated with her through their lawyers, so the deal wasn't bringing them any closer together.

Win was all right with that.

Since marrying Angus she'd realized she didn't want any forced relationships. His love was all-encompassing, and Iris loved her with an abandon so wild it was healing all the little tears in her heart. Her husband would never allow someone to kidnap her for publicity. Iris would always adore her simply for being her. It put to shame the transactional love she'd known from her parents, and she had no desire to experience that again.

Her love of design had expanded to the gardens, too, where she was helping Leslie and Boone look at their setup in a more wholistic way. All three of them had participated in a permaculture design course the previous summer, and now they were putting a number of practices they'd learned into play. Boone had taught himself many of the principles in earlier years, but even he admitted he'd learned more than he'd thought he would from the experts who taught the class. Win liked thinking of Base Camp as a whole, linking all the different parts together, following the inputs of sunshine, labor, rain and so on as they blossomed into outputs of food, compost, friendship and more.

There was so much to think about each day. So many new things to learn.

So many people to love.

She breathed in the familiar scent of her husband. Looked down into the shining eyes of her daughter.

This had to be paradise, she thought.

And she was going to stay right here.

"HE'S ASLEEP," AVERY whispered.

Walker leaned over from where he was sitting in bed and peeked into their son's bassinet, tucked between the bed and the wall. Joe Walker Norton was breathing softly, his tiny chest going up and down, his expression serious even now.

Avery liked to tell him their three-and-a-half-month-old son was like a little man.

"He's already solving the world's problems," Walker would say.

"How about we solve those problems so he can just be a kid."

Soon enough he'd be crawling and walking and running around with the other children here at Base Camp. Walker was enjoying this quiet stage when he could snuggle his son on his chest at night and let him fall asleep to the sound of his heartbeat. During those times, he let all his problems slip away and took long, deep breaths to calm them both. It worked every time.

Joe wanted his mother most of the time, but Walker was the king of bedtime.

He lifted the covers so Avery could snuggle in beside him, amazed as usual at how natural it felt for her to be there. Probably since they'd been denied the chance to be together so long, they tended to stay close. Walker figured he touched his wife a hundred times each day. Held her hand when they walked places, touched her leg when they sat next to each other at meals, guided her through a door, stealing a kiss.

He couldn't keep his hands off her.

Luckily Avery was similarly minded and leaned into him whenever he reached for her. They cuddled their way through the days, laughing and talking. People remarked that he smiled more. He supposed that was true. He'd grown up in a household marked by loss. Now he lived in one marked by joy.

"What are you thinking?" Avery asked, running a hand over his chest.

"I'm thinking I couldn't have built a better life for myself if I tried."

"I know. I keep waiting for something bad to happen," she admitted.

"Things will happen, and we'll get through them

together.

"I guess so. I think it's going to be another hot summer."

"Are there any other kind these days?"

She shook her head. "I think it's going to be pretty hot right here in our bed in a few minutes."

"That's a prediction I can get behind."

WHEN SHE WAS done making love to her husband, Avery lay on her back, holding his hand. "We should have added a skylight up here."

"Not too late for that."

"Really? Would that work with a green roof?"

"We can ask."

"I love that about you, you know," she told him, giving his hand a squeeze. "You don't shoot down my ideas."

"It's my job to lift you up, ideas and all."

She thought about that. "You're good at it."

"I hope so." He turned over and curled around her. "That first day I saw you charging down the hill from the manor ready to tear Boone a new one, I knew you'd be the love of my life."

"So it was my righteous anger that hooked you?" she teased.

"It was everything about you. I was trying to convince you to stick around, and the whole time I couldn't stop thinking about lying in bed with you just like this."

"That first day?" She pushed up to her elbows. "Really?"

"What did you think when you first saw me?"

Walker talked a lot more these days than he had when she'd first met him, but this was the type of personal question he didn't often put into words. Avery knew it deserved a serious answer.

"I thought, there's a man I could worship."

Walker stilled. After a moment, she lifted a hand to touch his face. "You are amazing. You don't know that about yourself, but you are. I would follow you any-where, Walker Norton. I'd do whatever you told me to do. I trust you not only with my life but also with my heart. Utterly."

When he reached to pull her close, burying his face in her hair, Avery wrapped her arms around his neck and held him. And when they came together minutes later, making love all over again, she gave herself to him heart and soul.

This was what it meant to be with Walker.

This was what it meant to find her true home.

Be the first to know about Cora Seton's new releases! Sign up for her newsletter here!

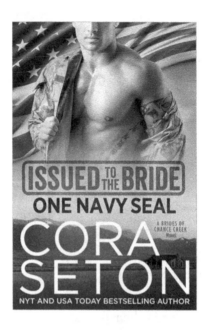

Read on for an excerpt of
Issued to the Bride One Navy SEAL.

Four months ago

O N THE FIRST of February, General Augustus Reed entered his office at USSOCOM at MacDill Air Force Base in Tampa, Florida, placed his battered leather briefcase on the floor, sat down at his wide, wooden desk and pulled a sealed envelope from a drawer. It bore the date written in his wife's beautiful script, and the General ran his thumb over the words before turning it over and opening the flap.

He pulled out a single page and began to read.

Dear Augustus,

It's time to think of our daughters' future, beginning with Cass.

The General nodded. Spot on, as usual; he'd been thinking about Cass a lot these days. Thinking about all the girls. They'd run yet another of his overseers off Two Willows, his wife's Montana ranch, several months ago, and he'd been forced to replace him with a man he didn't know. There was a long-standing feud between him and the girls over who should run the place, and the truth was, they were wearing him down. Ten overseers in eleven years; that had to be some kind of a record, and no ranch could function well under those circumstances. Still, he'd be damned if he was going to put a passel of rebellious daughters in charge, even if they were adults now. It took a man's steady hand to run such a large spread.

Unfortunately, it was beginning to come clear that Bob Finchley didn't possess that steady hand. Winter in Chance Creek was always a tricky time, but in the months since Finchley had taken the helm, they'd lost far too many cattle. The General's spies in the area reported the ranch was looking run-down, and his daughters hadn't been seen much in town. The worst were the rumors about Cass and Finchley—that they were dating. The General didn't like that at all—not if the man couldn't run the ranch competently—and he'd asked for confirmation, but so far it hadn't come. Finchley always had a rational explanation for the loss of cattle, and he never said a word about Cass, but the

General knew something wasn't right and he was already looking for the man's replacement.

Our daughter runs a tight ship, and I'm sure she's been invaluable on the ranch.

He had to admit what Amelia wrote was true. Cass was an organizational wizard. She kept her sisters, the house and the family accounts in line, and not for the first time he wondered if he should have encouraged Cass to join the Army back when she had expressed interest. She'd mentioned the possibility once or twice as a teenager, but he'd discouraged her. Not that he didn't think she'd make a good soldier; she'd have made a fine one. It was the thought of his five daughters scattered to the wind that had guided his hand. He couldn't stomach that. He needed his family in one place, and he'd done what it took to keep her home. That wasn't much: a suggestion her sisters needed her to watch over them until they were of age, a mention of tasks undone on the ranch, a hint she and the others would inherit one day and shouldn't she watch over her inheritance? It had done the trick.

Maybe he'd been wrong.

But if Cass had gone, wouldn't the rest of them have followed her?

He'd been able to stop sending guardians for the girls when Cass turned twenty-one five years ago, much to everyone's relief. His daughters had liked those about as little as they liked the overseers. He'd hoped when he dispensed of the guardians, the girls would feel they had enough independence, but that wasn't the case; they still wanted control of the ranch.

Cass is a loving soul with a heart as big as Montana, but she's cautious, too. I'll wager she's beginning to think there isn't a man alive she can trust with it.

The General sighed. His girls hadn't confided in him in years—especially about matters of the heart—something he was glad Amelia couldn't know. The truth was his daughters had spent far too much time as teenagers hatching plots to cast off guardians and overseers to have much of a social life. They'd been obsessed with being independent, and there were stretches of time when they'd managed it—and managed to run the show with no one the wiser for months. In order to pull that off, they'd kept to themselves as much as possible. He'd only recently begun to hear rumblings about men and boyfriends. Unfortunately, none of the girls were picking hardworking men who might make a future at Two Willows; they were picking flashy, fly-by-night troublemakers.

Like Bob Finchley.

He couldn't understand it. He wanted that man out of there. Now. Trouble was, when your daughters ran off so many overseers it made it hard to get a new one to sign on. He had yet to find a suitable replacement.

Without a career off the ranch, Cass won't get out much. She might not ever meet the man who's right for her. I want you to step in. Send her a man, Augustus. A good man.

A good man. Those weren't easy to come by in this

world. The right man for Cass would need to be strong to hold his own in a relationship with her. He'd need to be fair and true, or he wouldn't be worthy of her. He'd need some experience ranching.

A lot of experience ranching.

The General stopped to ponder that. He'd read something recently about a man with a lot of experience ranching. A good man who'd gotten into a spot of trouble. He remembered thinking he ought to get a second chance—with a stern warning not to screw up again. A Navy SEAL, wasn't it? He'd look up the document when he was done.

He returned to the letter.

> *Now here's the hard part, darling. You can't order him to marry Cass any more than you can order Cass to marry him. You're a cunning old codger when you want to be, and it'll take all your deviousness to pull this off. Set the stage. Introduce the players.*
>
> *Let fate do the rest.*
>
> *I love you and I always will,*
> *Amelia*

Set the stage. Introduce the players.

The General read through the letter a second time, folded it carefully, slid it back into the envelope and added it to the stack in his deep, right-hand bottom drawer. He steepled his hands and considered his options. Amelia was right; he needed to do something to make sure his daughters married well. But they'd rebelled against him for years, so he couldn't simply assign them husbands, as much as he'd like to. They'd never allow the interference.

But if he made them think they'd chosen the right men themselves…

He nodded. That was the way to go about it.

In fact…

The General chuckled. Sometime in the next six months, his daughters would stage another rebellion and evict Bob Finchley from the ranch. He could just about guarantee it, even if Cass was currently dating the man. Sooner or later he'd go too far trying to boss them around, and Cass and the others would flip their lids.

When they did, he'd be ready for them with a replacement they'd never be able to shake. One trained to combat enemy forces by good ol' Uncle Sam himself. A soldier in the Special Forces might do it. Or maybe even a Navy SEAL…

This wasn't the work of a moment, though. He'd need time to put the players in place. Cass wasn't the only one who'd need a man—a good man—to share her life.

Five daughters.

Five husbands.

Amelia would approve.

The General opened the bottom left-hand drawer of his desk, and mentally counted the remaining envelopes that sat unopened in another stack, all dated in his wife's beautiful script. Ten years ago, after Amelia passed away, Cass had forwarded him a plain brown box filled with envelopes she'd received from the family lawyer.

The stack in this drawer had dwindled compared to the opened ones in the other drawer.

What on earth would he do when there were none left?

End of Excerpt

The Cowboys of Chance Creek Series:

The Cowboy Inherits a Bride (Volume 0)
The Cowboy's E-Mail Order Bride (Volume 1)
The Cowboy Wins a Bride (Volume 2)
The Cowboy Imports a Bride (Volume 3)
The Cowgirl Ropes a Billionaire (Volume 4)
The Sheriff Catches a Bride (Volume 5)
The Cowboy Lassos a Bride (Volume 6)
The Cowboy Rescues a Bride (Volume 7)
The Cowboy Earns a Bride (Volume 8)
The Cowboy's Christmas Bride (Volume 9)

The Heroes of Chance Creek Series:

The Navy SEAL's E-Mail Order Bride (Volume 1)
The Soldier's E-Mail Order Bride (Volume 2)
The Marine's E-Mail Order Bride (Volume 3)
The Navy SEAL's Christmas Bride (Volume 4)
The Airman's E-Mail Order Bride (Volume 5)

The SEALs of Chance Creek Series:

A SEAL's Oath

A SEAL's Vow

A SEAL's Pledge

A SEAL's Consent

A SEAL's Purpose

A SEAL's Resolve

A SEAL's Devotion

A SEAL's Desire

A SEAL's Struggle

A SEAL's Triumph

The Brides of Chance Creek Series:

Issued to the Bride One Navy SEAL

Issued to the Bride One Airman

Issued to the Bride One Sniper

Issued to the Bride One Marine

Issued to the Bride One Soldier

Issued to the Bride One Sergeant for Christmas

The Turners v. Coopers Series:

The Cowboy's Secret Bride (Volume 1)

The Cowboy's Outlaw Bride (Volume 2)

The Cowboy's Hidden Bride (Volume 3)

The Cowboy's Stolen Bride (Volume 4)

The Cowboy's Forbidden Bride (Volume 5)

About the Author

With over one-and-a-half million books sold, NYT and USA Today bestselling author Cora Seton has created a world readers love in Chance Creek, Montana. She has thirty-five novels and novellas currently set in her fictional town, with many more in the works. Like her characters, Cora loves cowboys, military heroes, country life, gardening, jogging, binge-watching Jane Austen movies, keeping up with the latest technology and indulging in old-fashioned pursuits. She lives on beautiful Vancouver Island with her husband, children and two cats. Visit **www.coraseton.com** to read about new releases, contests and other cool events!

Blog:

www.coraseton.com

Facebook:

facebook.com/coraseton

Twitter:

twitter.com/coraseton

Newsletter:

www.coraseton.com/sign-up-for-my-newsletter

CPSIA information can be obtained
at www.ICGtesting.com
Printed in the USA
BVHW071144180421
605248BV00012B/831

9 781988 896380